"Hungry?" Peter asked hen. He stood there, barefoot vi's and flannel shirt, a glass

Stephanie floated acro d a sip, kissed him lightly on pt into the kitchen, enchanted by the aroma of his famous marinara sauce. "Yes." She snatched a baby carrot from the tossed salad and crunched it down. "Thank you."

He grinned, his brow crinkling in the way that made her crazy for him. "For what?"

"For being the one man—besides Matt and Monty—I haven't wished a fiery death for today."

"That bad? Well, forget about the world. You're home now."

She embraced him, molding to his frame, breathing in the spicy, leather-scented hints of his cologne. Oh, how she loved him. He was magic, and together they sparked an electrical connection.

"Go clean up," Peter encouraged. "I'll get dinner on the table."

Stephanie breezed away toward the stairs, stopping in the front hall to retrieve the mail. Sifting through the stack, she grimaced at the credit card bills, finally struck by a letter which was conspicuous because of no return address. The postmark was local. She tore open the envelope, unfolded the single page, and gasped:

SECRETS STAY SECRET ONLY SO LONG.
REMEMBER SEPTEMBER.
I DO.

* * *

Praise for Jon Salem and *Remember September:*

"Jon Salem's debut suspense novel unfolds against a vividly contemporary backdrop and bustles with colorful, sassy characters, almost all of whom have something to hide. Relationships intensify, and plenty of dirty little secrets are spilled as the novel careens at a breathless pace from the provocative prologue to the chilling climax."
—Wendy Corsi Staub, author of *All The Way Home*

"Warning: This book is unputdownable! I was hooked from the opening sentence and stayed up all night. Talk about a thriller that snaps, crackles and pops! You'll not soon forget REMEMBER SEPTEMBER. Jon Salem really hits a bulls-eyes with this hip and chilling cliffhanger."
—Judith Gould, bestselling author of
TILL THE END OF TIME and NOCTURNE

REMEMBER SEPTEMBER

Jon Salem

Pinnacle Books
Kensington Publishing Corp.

http://www.pinnaclebooks.com

ACKNOWLEDGMENTS

First and foremost, to Jim & Donna Salem, Tim, Lisa, & Noah Salem, Kenny & Betsy Nolan, and Ricky, Jennifer, Roman, & Paul Santoyo, my family . . . my best friends; to Barbara Seaman for writing the biography of Jacqueline Susann that fueled my ambition to get serious about a novel; to Linda Konner for helping me get there; to John Scognamiglio for encouragement and guidance; to Karen Winner for insight on women and divorce law in *Divorced from Justice;* to Tom Scott, III for the judicial briefing; to Charles Smith for the movie/meal breaks; to Mary Ann Downey for the lunch escapades; to Stephanie Hauck for all the best advice; to Zsa Zsa & Pookie, who were there for every word; and to Jackie Collins for *Hollywood Wives,* the hardcover I put on layaway at age fourteen, the book that got me hooked on stories to take to the beach.

Prologue

Houston, Texas, September, 1977

"I'll cut your face. I swear to God I will. Who's gonna want you then?"

Her hand trembling, Stephanie Cain lifted the arm of the turntable and clumsily dropped the needle back into the groove. The percolating beat of Andy Gibb's "I Just Want To Be Your Everything" filled the room and soothed her like a soft caress. For a moment, it muted the horror down the hall.

"You're gonna listen to me! I'm tired of the bullshit. If I say I need money, then you just hand it over. No questions!"

His voice echoed darker and more menacing than ever before. Stephanie's stomach clenched like a tight fist, and she suddenly really had to pee. There was a loud crash—the sound of breaking glass. Mother's perfume collection? He always destroyed something she treasured. Instantly, a shattered vision of the pretty, sweet-smelling bottles taunted her brain. *Leave her alone.* She wanted to scream it at the top of her lungs.

"No more! I want you out of here tonight. And don't ever come back!"

Stephanie's pulse quickened. It was her mother's voice this time.

"Oh, baby, I'm gonna teach you a lesson you'll never forget."

Stephanie experienced a rush of adrenaline. Her heart beat madly. *Mother needs my help,* she thought, rushing out of her room and down the hall.

"Mommy's crying," a voice whimpered.

Stephanie stopped and spun around. Her six-year-old brother, Montgomery, stood in the doorway of his bedroom, obviously upset and frightened. She hurried back and knelt before him. "Take Winnie the Pooh and go to your special hiding place."

"Can Mommy come, too?"

"She'll come later. Do it now. Go to your fort."

Montgomery ran to fetch Pooh and was off. Stephanie breathed a sigh of relief and dashed toward the master bedroom. Silence drummed. A chill shot through her body. She raised her arm to knock on the door, then thought better of it as her charm bracelet tinkled.

"Stephanie, are you out there?" her mother asked angrily.

She didn't answer. She didn't breathe.

"Go to your room. I mean it."

The door was flung open. There stood Jimmy Scott in tight pants, a shirt unbuttoned to his navel, and a few gold medallions glistening against his thick chest hair. He tried to look like Andy Gibb, but he didn't even come close. Andy was cute and sweet and sang about love. This man in front of her was a monster.

Her nostrils twitched. The air was pungent with perfume. Some bottles were broken and bleeding their contents onto an antique mirrored hutch; the rest were in a heap on the floor and spotting the cream-colored carpet.

"Goddammit, Stephanie, I told you to go back to your room!" her mother screamed.

Stephanie didn't understand. Why be angry at her? "Montgomery is scared and crying," she fired back in her best I'm-an-adult voice.

"Then go see about him. Leave us alone. I don't want you hearing this."

"No," Jimmy snarled. "I think she needs to hear what a bitch you are."

Her mother stared at Jimmy for one long, silent, hostile moment, as if making up her mind about something. Keeping her eyes on him, she said firmly, "Stephanie, I'm going downstairs to fix myself a drink, and I'm telling you this for the last time. Leave us alone for the night and take care of your brother."

Time passed in a dream, none of it real. Jimmy Scott was now flat on his back, his eyes closed, a strange, soft gasping sound escaping from his lips. His blood was thick and warm and pumping fast from the wound. Stephanie gripped the handle of the knife again.

Her mother appeared with another towel and splayed it out. "Drop it."

Stephanie gazed back as if in a trance.

"Put the knife on the towel," her mother whispered calmly.

Stephanie placed it down, smearing the towel red in the process. She watched her mother disappear into the bathroom, heard the clink of the metal blade hitting the porcelain sink, then listened to the sound of running water. Once it stopped, her mother returned and went straight for Jimmy's body to place her ear to his lips for several seconds before playing with his wrist. Then she picked up the phone and dialed.

"Mr. Hudson? It's Marilyn Cain. Jimmy Scott is dead, and he's in my house."

Stephanie retreated to a corner and crouched down. She stretched her T-shirt over her knees and waited. Her mother ignored her and left the room to chain-smoke on the balcony. When Mr. Hudson arrived, Stephanie was struck by his resemblance to Fred MacMurray, the actor who played the nice father on *My Three Sons*. Mr. Hudson seemed older, though just as distinguished. Closing her eyes, she said a silent prayer that he would be just as kind.

"Get over here now," Billy Hudson hissed. "Jesus, it looks like someone butchered a farm animal." He hung up and stepped out to the balcony, where Marilyn Cain was pacing like a caged panther, a burning Marlboro Light between her swollen lips, her face a mask of white-hot fear.

"Who'd you call?" The strength in her voice surprised him.

"A detective I know at the River Oaks precinct. He's on his way."

Marilyn Cain nodded, looked out into the night at the immaculate lawn, and dragged deep on the cigarette. "I started to panic . . . but . . . then it dawned on me. Fuck the police. Call Billy. He'll know what to do."

"You did the right thing," he said quietly. At sixty-two, Billy Hudson had encountered tough guys of every kind, but Marilyn Cain beat them all. When a knifed-up lover and a catatonic kid couldn't break a steely resolve, you were playing in a whole other league.

Billy stepped back into the bedroom. The poor girl hadn't moved an inch. She sat in the corner, face expressionless, body draped in an Andy Gibb T-shirt, warm blood still on her hands. Kneeling down to meet her gaze head-on, Billy whispered, "Come on, Stephanie. Let's go wash up."

The girl stared back at him blankly. "He was hurting my mother again," she finally said, her voice but half its full compass.

"I know," Billy said gently. "But he can't hurt her anymore. She's safe now. And so are you." Abruptly, Billy stood up. As a super lawyer whose record victories had earned him the nickname Magic Man, bending the truth came easy. But the last three words he'd just spoken to thirteen-year-old Stephanie Cain were nothing short of being the biggest lie ever to escape his lips.

One

"Girl power," Stephanie Hart chirped.

Nine-year-old Tuesday shuffled to the breakfast table with what looked like put-on malaise. "Not this morning," she mumbled.

"Cereal or bagel?"

Tuesday's lips formed a perfect pout. "I'm not hungry."

Stephanie stepped closer and kissed her daughter's forehead. "No fever. Upset stomach?"

Tuesday shook her head.

"Sore throat?"

"No."

"Math test today?"

Tuesday gazed up in near amazement. "Are you psychic?"

Stephanie smiled and smoothed her daughter's long, blonde tresses. "No, but I'm a mother—same difference. Just do your best, sweetheart."

"I hate math!"

"It's one of those subjects that loves to be hated. Now let's eat. You only have fifteen minutes before Mrs. Hatcher starts honking. What's it gonna be?"

Tuesday rolled her eyes. "Fruity Pebbles."

Stephanie headed for the pantry. "You got it. And I saw that."

Tuesday grinned sheepishly. "Girl power."

"You know it," Stephanie trilled, raising her fist in the air.

Tuesday giggled. "I bet you can't name all the Spice Girls," she challenged.

Stephanie didn't miss a beat before rattling off, "Baby, Sporty, Posh, Scary and Ginger Spice."

Tuesday beamed. "Jackie's mom said she'll take us to the Hanson concert when they come. Can I go?"

"Sounds like fun. We'll talk about it." Stephanie made a mental note to nominate Jackie's mom for sainthood. That she'd been saved from three hours in an arena filled with young girls doing various versions of primal screaming was reason enough for the endorsement. She reached for a glass to pour Tuesday's cranberry juice.

"Use my Sporty Spice cup!"

Stephanie cut her gaze in Tuesday's direction.

"Please," her daughter added sweetly.

Stephanie sighed. If life didn't orbit around the three goony brothers of Hanson, then it was circling around those cheeky Spice Girls. The days of Donny Osmond were gone forever. Seventies heartthrob Andy Gibb sprang to mind. Shivering slightly, she pushed away the thought. "Okay, who are you today?"

Tuesday gobbled up a spoonful of the rainbow-colored, sweetened rice cereal. "Soccer Spice," she cheered.

"I thought you were Soccer Spice yesterday."

"No, yesterday I was Ballet Spice."

"Oh," Stephanie muttered somewhat distantly, scanning the headlines of *The Houston Chronicle*. She heard Peter's heavy footsteps bounding down the stairs. "Well, I think I hear Sleepy Spice."

"Daddy!" Tuesday squealed.

"Tues!" Peter sang back, covering her ears with his hands as he kissed the top of her head.

Stephanie smiled. When she watched him at these moments, she experienced a wonderful feeling of such complete devotion. After all, Peter Hart had turned their lives around. For Stephanie, he'd thrown the lifeline to rescue her from heartbreak, and for Tuesday, he'd stepped forward to fill in the precious role that fate had robbed her of—a loving father. "Run upstairs to brush your teeth."

Tuesday exploded from her chair and dashed out, a torrent of energy.

Stephanie laughed. "More coffee?"

Peter shook his head and enveloped her in his arms. "More you."

She eased into him and playfully nipped at his earlobe, taking in his fresh-out-of-the-shower smell. "Can you play soccer dad this afternoon? I have a long day," she whispered.

He cradled her waist with his hands and grinned. "What's in it for me?"

"You get to flirt with all the soccer *moms*."

"But none of them look as good as you."

"That's why I don't mind if you flirt with them." She pulled away from him and winked.

From the driveway a horn blasted.

"Tuesday, carpool's here!" Stephanie shouted.

"My last session's at two o'clock. I'll pick up Tues and take care of dinner," Peter said.

"Have I mentioned the fact that you're not such a bad husband?"

Peter cocked his head to one side. "I'm overwhelmed."

"Thought you would be."

Two short horn blasts punctuated Mrs. Hatcher's impatience.

"Tuesday!"

Moments later she raced into the kitchen. "Where's my permission slip for the field trip?"

Stephanie's mind went blank. "What did I do with it?"

"It's right here," Peter said, snatching it from the refrigerator door.

"Hurry up," Stephanie pressed. "Mrs. Hatcher doesn't like it when you're late."

Tuesday made an ugly face. "Their car stinks. It smells like dookie."

Stephanie and Peter traded amused looks, each fighting off laughter.

"You'll be fine, sweetheart. Give me a kiss." Stephanie leaned down and Tuesday smacked her on the lips. "Have a great day. I'll see you tonight."

"Bye Mommy, bye Daddy."

Stephanie followed her out and waved to Mrs. Hatcher, whose stern expression held firm as she made a show of pointing to her watch. Once Tuesday tumbled into the backseat, Stephanie closed the door. "What a bitch," she muttered to herself.

Already dressed, Peter headed out as well, his attaché case in one hand, a banana in the other. Alone now except for the dogs hankering for their morning feeding, Stephanie closed her eyes and enjoyed a brief stay of quiet.

She thought of Kevin—her first husband, Tuesday's biological father—and most importantly, the man who opened up her heart and taught her how to love. In a dream he had come to her not long ago, and they had the kind of talk that sudden death too often precludes. He was watching from heaven, happy to see her and Tuesday loving, living, and growing. He harbored no qualms about how the short span of time from widow Stephanie to remarried Stephanie had provided her the inner peace she'd been searching for. It was just like him. Even in death, she thought of Kevin Stone as the kindest, most gentle soul, doing all he could to make her feel better.

Stephanie braced herself for the wave of hurt. This train of thought always brought it on. How wasteful it was for a man's life to be snuffed out at twenty-seven. The familiar storm of anger began to brew as Stephanie's mind shifted to the road raging drunk driver that authorities never found. That's why, whenever going after one in a civil case, she did so with a pent-up fury. In her mind, a stranger's killer could very well be Kevin's killer. Drunk drivers and domestic abusers—two cockroaches of society that Stephanie Hart worked to exterminate regularly, at least in the courtroom.

Ready to take on the day, Stephanie tended to the pets, dressed conservatively in a grey suit for the morning's court appearance, and left for the office.

The moment she locked the door of her Mercedes 190E in the underground parking deck was the moment an ear-shattering screech of tires sent a violent jolt through her body. A Ford Explorer had lurched to a stop merely ten feet away, and the feet of its driver were stomping the floor with intimidating purpose.

Walk away impervious—not frightened, Stephanie told herself, picking up the pace just enough to measure annoyance as she made a beeline for the elevator.

"Hey! Don't walk away from me!"

Stephanie sighed heavily, as if put out. "This isn't

appropriate, Mr. Dean. If you want to communicate with me, I suggest you do so through Ms. Cohen." Her tone—that of a teacher addressing a dense pupil—belied the inner anxiety, the heart hammering against her chest at breakneck speed. How crazy was this bastard? And did he have a gun?

"I fired her."

Stephanie reached the elevator control panel and pressed the button, then turned to face Rob Dean. As far as she could surmise, he was unarmed. His voice was clear, his eyes bright—no sign of the binge drinking that Josie complained about. "Does this mean you're representing yourself?" Casually, Stephanie reached into her purse and extracted a tiny pump of pepper spray, hiding it inside her palm. Just in case.

"Chuck Berg's my guy."

Stephanie swallowed that fact like a bitter pill, trying to determine the lesser of the two evils: A brute who sent his wife to the emergency room with a broken jaw and cracked ribs, or a pig who made a living representing such monsters. "Then Mr. Berg is who I need to talk to."

"Where's Josie?"

Stephanie turned away without a word. Damn this slow elevator!

"Where's Josie?" Rob repeated ominously, his voice up an octave, the menace palpable.

"I'm not at liberty to say," she replied tightly, keeping her back to him. The musical ping of the elevator was like a sweet song. Stephanie moved inside and spun quickly, relieved that Rob Dean had made no attempt to follow.

He just stood there, eyes blazing, both hands holding the handicap rail with a white-knuckled grip. "Tell me where Josie is! She's my wife!"

As the heavy steel doors began to close, Stephanie couldn't resist the Parthian parting shot: "Correction. She's your punching bag. And I have the hospital records to prove it."

Seconds later, Stephanie's heels hit the twenty-second floor of The Transco Tower. At sixty-four stories, the South Post Oak Boulevard structure was the tallest building in the world not located in a downtown area. She'd always stood in awe of the symmetrical monument and marveled at the beacon of light atop it which, from dusk to midnight, sent a beam of light for twenty miles.

Though her suite of offices was small and the lease rate per square foot enormously high, the business address communicated the right message—solid standing.

"What's up?" Matt Benedict offered as she entered the door marked Stephanie Hart, Attorney-at-Law.

"Accosted by an angry soon-to-be-ex in the parking deck." She plopped her Kate Spade carryall onto a plush reception area seat and began sifting through the tidy stack of mail Matt had organized.

"I'll take Rob Dean for five hundred," he grumbled in *Jeopardy* speak.

She stopped at the thick bank statement and leveled a serious gaze at him.

"Josie's mother called. Hurricane Rob hit her apartment about a half hour ago," Matt explained.

Stephanie experienced a flush of alarm.

"No damage done, unless you count her peace of mind."

"Did she—"

"Not a clue," Matt assured. "She thinks Rob bought the story that you were the only person who knows where Josie's hiding."

Stephanie sighed. "Call Penelope's House, anyway. Let them know what went down. Rob Dean's a hothead, but he's a calculating one—the worst kind."

Matt nodded. "Lisa called to cancel lunch—something about a client meeting. There's an e-mail from Monty waiting. You're due in Judge Gibbs's court at ten-thirty for Alexander versus Alexander, and Melissa will meet you there."

"Did Berg's office messenger over the financial records?"

Matt shook his head.

Stephanie raked her fingers through her hair. "That bastard's stalling again."

"He sought a bifurcation in a case last week, and Gibbs went along with it. Don't let them surprise you today," he said knowingly.

She now regarded Matt with intense curiosity.

He grinned, somewhat embarrassed. "I got drunk with Berg's paralegal last night. She's a talker."

"Loose lips sink ships." Stephanie smiled. "Thanks."

He shrugged diffidently. "Anything for the team. Besides, she had a certain Winona Ryder quality."

"So it was better than a root canal?"

Matt's lips curled into a secret, satisfied grin. "You could say that."

Stephanie rolled her eyes. "I don't recall sleeping with the enemy being part of your job description." She collected her mail and designer bag and headed toward her office.

"For the record, *sleeping* had nothing to do with it."

Stephanie shot him a faux warning look. Matt Benedict. Her twenty-one-year-old paralegal and office manager was straight out of MTV Casting-Central—lean, wiry frame; long sideburns; neatly trimmed goatee; dark, disheveled hair in need of a shampoo; black shirt/black jeans; a silver, chain-link style necklace. He wasn't the most obvious choice, but he'd proven to be indispensable with his uncanny photographic memory, computer savvy, and oddly resourceful skills, such as the sexual caper she'd just learned about. "What a stud."

"So they tell me. I've got another interesting development—this one for the Connie Reynolds case."

"Shoot."

"Remember the *neutral* mental health expert that Gibbs appointed?"

Stephanie nodded.

"He left Berg's office yesterday—richer than he arrived."

Stephanie felt the immediate fire of rapidly rising blood. "You got all this from one screw? Please! Marry the woman. I bet we'd get enough dirt to lock up that scum for at least ten years."

"But I'd feel so used," Matt wailed.

Stephanie laughed. "Oh, give me a break."

The telephone jangled, and Matt answered on the first ring. "Stephanie Hart's office . . . who's calling? . . . Ms. Hart doesn't appreciate surprises . . . one second," he muttered irritably, his index finger already on the hold button. "He refuses to identify himself but insists you'll welcome the surprise."

Her curiosity piqued, she reached for the receiver. "This is Stephanie Hart."

A long silence boomed.

"Hello?"

"You like keeping secrets. Don't you, bitch?" A male voice curdled.

Stephanie's brain whirled to place it. In a nanosecond she believed the man could very well be Rob Dean. "Client information is strictly confidential," she ventured primly, wanting to hear him speak again in order to be certain.

"I know your secret," he hissed.

Stephanie froze; her stomach knotted like a tight fist. The man sounded like Rob Dean, but she wasn't absolutely sure. And that's what frightened her. Suddenly the line went dead. At that moment, her heart dropped like an elevator on a fast move down. Who was that?

More important, did he really know her secret?

She braved the I-45 to make it downtown, enduring bumper-to-bumper traffic caused by a stalled truck and a minor fender bender. Preoccupied by the mysterious phone call, she almost failed to take notice of her brother's new billboard, but his unbelievably handsome face arrested her attention in the nick of time. KBLX-TV AND MONTGOMERY CAIN: NEWS YOU CAN TRUST, read the copy.

She smiled at Monty, who looked so much the anchor, striking a serious pose in his navy suit. He'd come so far . . . despite everything. Still, she worried about him. Not the default worry that every older sister harbored for a younger brother, but real concern. His mood swings bothered her, those periods of dark brooding that reminded her of that horrible night twenty years ago. Even at such young ages, Monty being only six at the time and she thirteen, the tragedy had exerted a lasting influence. The reality sent a chill up her spine.

Suddenly Matt's announcement about Monty's e-mail flashed in Stephanie's memory. Now just minutes away from the Harris County Civil Courts Building, she searched her bag as she braked to a

stop on Congress Street. Amidst a sheaf of papers,
the bold print of montyc@aol.com caught her eye.
She snatched it and smoothed the page over the
steering wheel.

DEAR STEPH,
DID YOU WATCH LAST NIGHT? LITTLE
BROTHER GAVE A FLAWLESS READING
OF THE LATEST MURDERS, DRUG
BUSTS, AND KIDNAPPINGS TO TOUCH
OUR GRAND CITY. EVERY SYLLABLE WAS
LETTER-PERFECT. NOW IF I COULD
JUST TRANSFER THAT THIRTY MINUTES
OF PERFECTION TO THE REST OF MY
LIFE, ALL WOULD BE WELL. I'VE BEEN
IN QUITE A FUNK LATELY AND NEED
TO SORT SOME THINGS OUT. ANY
CHANCE THAT DOC PETER WILL LET
ME STRETCH MY LEGS ON HIS COUCH?
I NEED A PRO HERE BUT CAN'T IMAG-
INE WALKING INTO A STRANGER'S OF-
FICE. LET ME KNOW.
LOVE & ALL THAT YUCKY STUFF, MONTY

An angry horn blasted Stephanie to attention.
She took note of the green light, responding with a
firm foot on the gas, all the while plotting the manner in which she might plead with Peter to take
Monty on as a client. Over his favorite dinner? After
making love? Whatever the approach, it wouldn't be
easy. Peter's golden rule was to refer any potential
client that he knew personally to a trusted colleague. In fact, his strictness in that regard was the
reason they were married.

Her late husband and her current one had
worked together at Texas Children's Hospital, where

Kevin was completing one of the nation's most ex-
tensive pediatric residencies and Peter was volun-
teering to counsel parents grief-stricken by their
kids' illnesses.

She'd been introduced to Peter at Kevin's wake,
at which point he passed along his business card and
encouraged her to call him. For six months she kept
it in her wallet. Dr. Peter Hart, Psychologist. Finally,
she summoned up the courage to ring him, believing
that a stint in therapy would serve her well. She'd
never dealt with the issues surrounding her mother,
Jimmy Scott, and the bloody nightmare. To not fully
confront the death of her beloved Kevin, too,
would've been foolhardy, so she'd called for help,
and Peter offered to provide it.

That first session was forever seared onto
Stephanie's memory. At first, she thought that she'd
stumbled into the wrong office. There were ladders,
sloshed drop cloths, and pots of paint everywhere.
Even now her nostrils twitched, remembering the
paint fumes. Peter had appeared, looking more
handsome than she recalled as he apologized for
the remodeling mess, and ushered her to a spacious
room in the back. Immediately, she'd been struck
by the sexual heat he gave off. It filled the room—
and triggered instant guilt. How could she have
such thoughts about another man only six months
after Kevin's death? And about her new therapist,
no less!

"I think it's important that I recommend someone else to you," Peter had said without preamble.

Stephanie had felt a blind panic. Could he read
her thoughts? Was she so obviously unstable that he
must call in a colleague who handled patients beyond his training? "Why?" she had managed, simply, fearfully.

"Because I would much rather help you with your grief by taking you to dinner and making you laugh than by working with you in a clinical setting. Let one of my equally able peers do the latter." He smiled, and for a moment she'd seen the beginning of a brand new paradise.

Six months later they were married. To date they'd lived five years of wedded bliss, and there was a lifetime to follow.

Moving her thoughts to the more pressing legal matters ahead, Stephanie parked, then navigated through the downtown underground tunnel system, a complicated business and retail maze designed to keep Texans out of the oppressive heat and rain.

Outside the Family Law Center, she saw Melissa Alexander standing alone and looking frightened, like a small child lost at an amusement park. Instantly, Stephanie noticed that she had put on at least five pounds since their last meeting.

They embraced quickly, and Stephanie drew back to assess the anxiety on Melissa's face. Something was wrong. She could read the trouble in Melissa's wide, chestnut-brown eyes like a tabloid headline. The worry was contagious; Stephanie felt her body tense. "What happened?"

Melissa shook her head helplessly. "I don't know . . . David called me before I left . . . he said all of this would be over soon . . . and then he just laughed."

Stephanie took hold of Melissa's arm in a show of female solidarity. "He's just trying to put you on edge. Ignore it."

"Ms. Hart," a male voice called.

Stephanie turned to see Chuck Berg coming toward them. David Alexander, his client, was nowhere in sight.

"A minute of your time?" he inquired.

Motioning for Melissa to go inside, Stephanie met Chuck Berg halfway, pursing her lips with implicit disapproval. He was in his early fifties, an imposing force to consider at six-foot-three with a rock-solid frame. His wavy hair was obviously a painstakingly applied rug, and his small eyes were set too close together, making him almost cross-eyed. That he dressed exceptionally well was his only obvious good point.

"How's she holding up?" Chuck asked, tracking Melissa's retreat with a steady, knowing gaze.

Sometimes Stephanie could play the game, but never with the likes of Chuck Berg, Scumbag-at-Law, so she merely stared back as if he hadn't spoken.

"It must be tough. Women her age only have a snowball's chance in hell of finding another husband. David's ready to tie the knot again."

Stephanie felt her stomach turn over. "Is she old enough to vote?"

Chuck smiled. "Yeah, but it'll be a year before she can drink legally." He placed a finger to his lips in a conspiratorial gesture to keep it hush-hush, then instantly switched to legal shark mode, a dark shadow sweeping over his face, his eyes narrowing into slits. "I suggest you take what I'm about to offer. Otherwise, that hag will end up with nothing."

The transformation made Stephanie grow cold. There was no such thing as a bluff from Chuck Berg. He always delivered on his threats.

"And remember this, darlin', David Alexander's got the cash to retain my services. Melissa's gonna be another charity case for you by next month."

Stephanie put her brain computer to work. She'd known plenty of women in Melissa's position—early fifties, no marketable skills, no assets in their own name—who'd put up a protracted legal battle only to lose out in the end. What little settlement they did win was usually eroded by attorney fees. "What's on the table?"

Chuck's gunmetal eyes gleamed triumphant. "The house, a car, and a ten thousand dollar money market account."

"Add spousal support."

He shook his head. "No way. David works for a living. So should Melissa."

"She's taken a retail job at the Galleria, Chuck, but there's no way she can maintain her standard of living with that. Come on, she busted her ass to get David through college, then worked for nothing as his secretary to get the business up and running."

"No alimony," he said tightly.

"Screw it."

Chuck Berg laughed. "You and your client are about to be."

Fighting the urge to unload her pepper spray right then and there, Stephanie turned away and broke into a quick pace toward the court entrance.

"Why do you get so bent out of shape about these things?" Chuck called out. "Are there personal demons I should know about?"

She stopped dead in her tracks, and her body froze as the memory of the mysterious phone call lanced her brain.

Chuck Berg was directly behind her now, so close she could feel his hot breath on the back of her neck. "What's your secret?" he whispered.

Her heart was on the run, but she didn't flinch. "You tell me."

"Maybe later." He stepped around to face her, winked mischievously, and moved ahead with an arrogant swagger.

Inside the courtroom, Judge Lawrence Gibbs sat perched on the bench like a squawking crow on a power line. Stephanie hated him. He was old, mean, and misogynistic, not to mention a card-carrying member of The Boys Club. Had Chuck Berg gotten to him before this court date? Such a scenario would explain David's confidence . . . and Chuck's smugness. She braced herself for a rough ride. A sixth sense told her it was going to be just that.

"Alexander versus Alexander," Gibbs screeched.

"Good morning, Your Honor." Chuck beamed. "I respectfully ask the court to consider a bifurcation in regard to the Alexanders. David Alexander has made repeated attempts to offer Melissa Alexander a reasonable settlement package, each time to no avail. My client is anxious to set a wedding date with his new love, and going forward with the divorce will allow him to do so."

Melissa's face contorted with fear, like a fawn caught in the glare of headlights. "What?" Her eyes pleaded with Stephanie, as if to save her from inevitable doom.

At once, Stephanie rose to her feet. "This is an outrage, Your Honor. Mr. Berg is only seeking to separate the divorce proceedings from the actual issues involved."

"That's what a bifurcation is, Ms. Hart. But thank you for defining it for the court," Gibbs spat.

Stephanie took a deep breath. "My point is this— *money* is the issue to be argued, not the granting of a divorce. If David Alexander obtains one before the financial matters are resolved, then he has no incentive to settle them afterwards. He could very well keep the entire estate for himself, or tie my client up in the courts indefinitely."

Judge Gibbs narrowed his gaze and leaned in to

emphasize his next point. "As I understand it, your client is holding up this court by refusing to accept a settlement offer."

"No *equitable* settlement has been offered," Stephanie replied firmly.

"What's the door prize, Mr. Berg?" Gibbs asked.

"The house, a car, and a money market account containing ten thousand dollars," Chuck announced.

Gibbs arched his eyebrows. "Sounds good, Ms. Hart. I'd take it."

"Your Honor, the Alexanders built a small contracting business into a very lucrative construction firm during the course of their marriage. My client is eligible for a share of those assets, or at least routine maintenance payments that will allow her to continue her current standard of living."

Chuck Berg shook his head.

"Mr. Berg?" Gibbs inquired with keen interest, pandering to a fellow member of The Club.

"Ms. Hart is arguing theoretical equality. In discovery, Melissa Alexander could not prove her share of the business assets. It's a complicated industry. My client has several investors, capital debt is high, and cash flow is at an all-time low. There's nothing to claim. David Alexander is being more than generous and putting himself at great financial risk to do so, I might add."

Stephanie threw up her hands in a pantomime of disgust.

"Would you like to add something, Ms. Hart?" Gibbs scolded.

"Mr. Berg's playing a shell game. Underneath the creative accounting, the assets are there."

Gibbs glared back at her. "I don't entertain conspiracy theories," he said dismissively. "Mr. Alexander, my hat goes off to you for believing in the institution of marriage enough to give it another try. It's time for this train to leave the station. Bifurcation granted." He hammered down the gavel.

Stephanie's chest rumbled in time with its loud clack. Breath got caught in the back of her throat, and her mouth went dry with despair as Judge Gibbs's words flicked the switch that was Melissa Alexander's livelihood. Off. That quick. That automatic. She chewed on her lower lip as she vibed in on the bottom-line of what had just transpired: Melissa was walking away with nothing.

"What does this mean?" Melissa wailed, the speaker fifty-two year old woman but the voice ten-year-old girl.

"It's not good news," Stephanie muttered, already playing out the scene of groveling to Chuck Berg in her mind. "Do you have any jewelry at the house? Or in a safety deposit box?"

Melissa nodded nervously.

"Secure any liquid assets you can find in a safe place. There's no protection after today. I'll call you later."

Melissa pushed back her chair and rushed out as if she were fleeing Bosnia.

Stephanie locked her gaze onto the cantankerous, incorrigible Judge Gibbs. *You old senile bastard,* she wanted to scream.

Chuck Berg slid a hip onto the table as she started to gather her things. "Don't bother asking me for the original settlement. We're not feeling generous anymore."

Stephanie stood abruptly. "This isn't a courthouse—it's a clubhouse." She threw a look to David Alexander, who lingered behind Chuck. "How can you do this after twenty-six years of marriage?"

"Nobody has to starve," Chuck put in. "That's what welfare is for." He turned to David, and in unison, they chuckled.

Stephanie's head began to throb. "How do you sleep at night?"

Chuck grinned suggestively. "Depends on who I'm in bed with."

"And how much money exchanges hands," Stephanie shot back, preparing to leave.

"Oh, just so you know," Chuck began casually, "I'm going for full custody in the Dean case."

Stephanie stared back, shocked silent. "You're not serious," she finally managed.

He challenged her with his steely gaze. "Try me."

The rest of the day passed by in a blur—a visit to Penelope's House to warn Josie of the legal nightmare ahead; a speech to Mothers Against Drunk Drivers on post-criminal legal options; a guest lecture on matrimonial law at the University of Houston Law School; depositions in a no-brainer personal injury case that would pay the month's rent.

Now, as the car clock struck seven sharp, Stephanie was turning into the driveway of her Tanglewood home, feeling spent. Liz the Pekingese and Richard the Welsh Corgi greeted her at the door, all wagging tails and flapping tongues. She dropped her carryalls into a brown leather chair and knelt down to give the dogs a proper hello.

"Hungry?" Peter asked from the foyer that weaved into the kitchen. He stood there, barefoot and movie star handsome in his faded Levi's and flannel shirt, a glass of red wine in each hand.

Stephanie floated across the room, accepted the

offering, downed a sip, kissed him lightly on the lips, and swept into the kitchen, enchanted by the aroma of his famous marinara sauce. "Yes." She snatched a baby carrot from the tossed salad and crunched it down. "Thank you."

He grinned, his brow crinkling in the way that made her crazy for him. "For what?"

"For being the one man—besides Matt and Monty—I haven't wished a fiery death to today."

"That bad?"

"I suffered through the Berg and Gibbs variety hour."

"Damn . . . well, I've got cheesecake from eatZi's."

"I see the silver lining already."

"Good. Forget about the world. You're home now."

She embraced him, molding to his frame, breathing in the spicy, leather-scented hints of his cologne. Oh, how she loved him. He was magic, and together they sparked an electrical connection. "Where's Tuesday?"

"There's an environmental conference going on at Barbie's Dream House." He smiled. "She's upstairs. By the way, she made the salad."

Stephanie kissed Peter's nose. "Yummy."

"The salad or me?"

"Both."

"Go clean up," Peter encouraged. "I'll get dinner on the table."

Stephanie breezed away toward the stairs, stopping in the front hall to retrieve the mail, Liz and Richard constantly underfoot. Sifting through the stack, she grimaced at the credit card bills, finally struck by a letter, conspicuous because of no return address. The postmark was local. She tore open the

envelope, unfolded the single page, and began to
read:

SECRETS STAY SECRET ONLY SO LONG.
REMEMBER SEPTEMBER.
I DO.

Two

Stephanie stirred herself awake to the frantic itching of Richard, who was creating a seismic tremor at the foot of the bed. In a tight little ball, Liz slept on beside him, peacefully oblivious. The digital radio alarm on the nightstand tripped over to six o'clock.

Glancing over at a still zonked Peter, Stephanie felt a storm of guilt come down as hard and relentless as hailstones. Things became so much more clear in the morning. How could she have allowed that stupid letter to derail a family evening? She'd feigned illness, sequestered herself in the bathroom for hours, then gone to bed without a word, ignoring Peter, Tuesday, and the dinner they'd prepared.

She nudged Liz awake and led the dogs down the hall and through the kitchen door to the backyard for their morning frolic. Her body—stiff from more hours awake than asleep—craved coffee. After getting a pot started, she pattered into the hall to grab the stack of mail that had sent her into a tailspin and headed back to wait out the java.

The anonymous letter stood out like neon, but Stephanie purposefully avoided it, reaching instead for a colorful postcard that caught her attention. At the sight of Denver's downtown metropolis, she smiled. Flipping it over, she read the sweet message from "Julia Turner," who reported that she'd been promoted to PR manager at the software design firm and was dating a cute architect.

Stephanie read the postcard a second time, her thoughts drifting back to Julia's days as Ginger Simon, a young woman relentlessly stalked and beaten by her estranged husband Bruce. Stephanie had seen Ginger suffer black eyes, broken limbs, and cigarette burns on her breasts and buttocks. Just when Stephanie thought the abuse had reached its limit, Bruce Simon issued a chilling threat: If Ginger ever tried to leave him again, he would track her down and kill her. Nobody believed he was bluffing.

At this point, Ginger had stopped caring about divorce and wished only to escape. Knowing it was Ginger's only chance of survival, Stephanie studied how to relocate under a new identity, determined to help the tormented woman seek out a better life.

Following Stephanie's instructions to the letter, Ginger drained the Simon checking and savings accounts, hocked her wedding ring, and sold her Lexus to a used car dealer, leaving home with nothing but the clothes on her back and a purse bulging with cold, hard cash. Then she boarded a plane for Miami and took up temporary residence at an extended-stay hotel, where she scoured the obituaries for the perfect fit, finding one in Julia Turner, a twenty-seven year-old white woman who'd just died in a tragic highway accident.

Playing the heartbroken friend from college, Ginger called a relative listed in the obit and skillfully secured the maiden name of Julia Turner's mother. Next, she applied for a birth certificate and credit card under the deceased's name and waited. Once the documents arrived, Ginger used them to apply for a duplicate Social Security card, then took off for Denver, where she obtained a Colorado license and began living her new life as Julia Turner. As far as Julia was concerned, Ginger Simon was dead. Essentially, Bruce had followed through on his threat.

Stephanie smiled at Julia's giddy phrases on the postcard—cuter than Brad Pitt, awesome career, and to-die-for apartment. Finally, as Julia Turner, Ginger Simon was able to live life on her own terms. Armed with this knowledge, Stephanie realized that, even though illegal, OPERATION SCRAM had been some of her most satisfying work as a lawyer.

The coffeemaker hissed to a stop. Stephanie grabbed two hand-painted ceramic mugs purchased on an anniversary trip to San Antonio and poured, taking hers straight up and sweetening Peter's with a splash of French Vanilla Coffeemate and several heaping spoonfuls of sugar.

Liz and Richard scratched impatiently at the door, but Stephanie decided they could wait and disappeared down the hall. She found Peter awake and propped up against the pillows, a look of concern hitting his face as she entered.

"How do you feel?" he asked, his voice rough with lazy morning thickness.

She got back in bed and handed him his coffee. "Better," she lied, knowing that she had only pushed away thoughts of the letter so as not to deal with it. "I'm sorry about last night. I was sick and stressed . . . I just had to check out, you know?"

Peter placed his hand on her knee and massaged it gently. "It's okay. I wish you'd let me in, though. I want to share everything with you."

Stephanie's body stiffened, and she knew Peter felt it. Almost instantly, the hurt transmuted onto his face. He dipped his head, looking down and cock-ing it to the right before looking back up again. The gesture pierced her heart, but she was helpless to do anything about it. Sharing everything meant sharing that horrible night when Jimmy Scott died. And that she just couldn't do.

Peter let his head fall back and shut his eyes.

Stephanie took a gulp of coffee for courage before announcing, "I need a favor . . . well, actually . . . Monty does."

Teasingly, Peter opened one eye.

"Promise you'll say yes."

He smiled. "First thing we do is kill all the lawyers."

Stephanie pulled roughly at the hair on his leg.

"Ouch!" he protested.

She giggled. "No lawyer jokes before nine. You swore to that once."

"I'll be happy to refer Monty to a colleague," Peter said, as if reading her mind.

Stephanie's mouth dropped open in mock shock. "What are you? One of Dionne's Psychic Friends or something?"

"That'll be three ninety-nine a minute."

Stephanie set her mug down on the nightstand with a loud thwack and moved to sit astride Peter, her lips pursed with fierce determination. She glanced at the clock. Tuesday wouldn't stir for at least a half-hour. "Monty won't go in cold to a complete stranger. You have to see him."

Peter downed a last sip and eased his mug down to the carpeted floor. "Monty's family. You know my rule." He threaded his fingers behind his head and smiled, an invitation for her to hit him with her best shot.

"He's your *in-law*," Stephanie argued. "Some

families consider them the lowest link on the human chain, with the exception of terrorists."

Peter laughed, cradling her waist with his hands, a sexy gleam in his jade green eyes.

Stephanie inched down a bit, grinning. Peter was hard—and getting harder by the second. In one fluid movement she pulled her cotton nightgown over her head.

His hands took immediate possession of her breasts, pressing them together and rising up to take both nipples in his mouth at the same time.

Stephanie moaned softly, anticipating what was to come, her body responding instantly to Peter's rising excitement.

"A few sessions," he quickly compromised. "If he wants something long-term, he'll have to go elsewhere."

Roughly, she grabbed two fistfuls of Peter's hair. "Deal."

Peter flipped Stephanie over and onto her back. "I like the way you negotiate," he breathed between coffee-scented kisses.

She pulled down his boxers, struggling to get them over his impressive erection. "Anything to close the sale. Now shut up and make love to me."

Peter smiled at her command and offered full compliance.

Stephanie locked her legs around him and arched her back as Peter gently rocked back and forth, his mouth feasting on hers. He felt warm and tight inside of her. Within minutes, the friction and pressure of his rhythmic rubbing had her riding the crest of a major pleasure wave. By the sound of his advancing sighs, she knew instinctively that they would crash down together. And they did.

Afterward, they lay spent, bodies interlocked,

drifting in and out of satisfied sleep. "So what does your day look like?" Stephanie murmured.

Peter's eyes fluttered. "A manic-depressive, a compulsive personality, a child with ADD. You know, the usual suspects."

Stephanie tightened her hold on him. At this moment, she felt so safe. "I love you."

He raised his head, giving her the benefit of a sideways look and a sly grin. "You're just saying that because I'm great in bed."

She punched him lightly on the arm. Suddenly the voice of the mysterious caller stabbed into Stephanie's memory. Her heartbeat accelerated a bit. "Did anyone call last night?"

"Same old crew—Monty and Lisa."

Stephanie nodded. "Anyone else?"

Peter shook his head.

"Did . . . anybody call and hang up?"

He turned over to face her, searching for the meaning in her eyes. "No. Why?"

"Nothing. I got a weird call at the office yesterday. I was just wondering. That's all."

"Weird how?"

Stephanie sat up. "It's nothing . . . really."

"Tell me," Peter insisted.

She hesitated a moment. "He said that he knew my secret . . . and then he hung up."

Peter's brow furrowed. "Did the voice sound familiar?"

"Sort of . . . I'm not really sure." She raked her fingers through her hair and threw glances around the room, avoiding Peter's gaze.

"You're scared," he said flatly.

"No . . . I'm . . . it was probably the ex-husband of a client. Something like that."

Peter shook his head. "I wish all your clients

weren't running from psychos. Can't you handle some mainstream divorces where the marriage doesn't work out, and the couple just calls it quits?"

Stephanie bit down on her lower lip. "Peter . . . don't. This isn't serious," she whispered.

"It's serious enough to have you freaked, Steph. Does Matt know what's going on?"

She nodded.

"Good." Peter sighed. "And at least you're in a secured building. That puts me at ease."

Stephanie nodded again, thankful she hadn't mentioned Rob Dean's appearance in the parking garage.

"I don't like this."

"It's nothing," Stephanie tried to assure him.

"Promise me that if you get another call you'll let me know right away."

A picture of the letter—typed in a standard Helvetica word processing font—flashed in Stephanie's mind. "I promise," she said softly. To burden Peter with this was something she couldn't do. He needed all of his concentration for his patients. Besides, the phone call and letter were likely harmless pranks from some disgruntled legal adversary. Certainly there was no real meaning behind it. As Stephanie struggled to convince herself, she faltered. Deep down, she knew it was something more sinister. And that it was only beginning.

The Transco Tower was minutes away from Stephanie and Peter's Tanglewood home. She'd been in the car only a short time when her cellular jingled. Switching off the radio, she hit the hands-free speakerphone feature. "Hello?"

"Steph, it's Monty," her brother announced, sounding more tense than usual.

"Good morning," she sang. "Listen, I talked to Peter. He agreed to a few sessions, but anything long-term is out of the question."

"That's great. Thanks," Monty said quickly, as if pushing the subject out of the way. "Where are you?"

"On San Felipe. Why?"

"Pull over."

"What?"

"Pull over," Monty repeated forcefully. "I have some bad news. I don't want you on the road when you hear it."

Stephanie's stomach turned a somersault as her imagination took flight. It couldn't be Peter or Tuesday. She'd just left them. Was it Lisa? Matt? A sick feeling came over her. Someone had died. She knew it. Suddenly the realization hit her like a rock from the sky—their mother. Preparing for the worst, she signaled, merged right, and pulled into the lot of an office complex. "What is it, Monty?" she asked evenly.

He took in a deep breath. "Ginger Simon was murdered last night."

"Oh my God." Stephanie's body jerked, her foot slipped from the brake, and the car lurched forward. She regained control and shifted the gear into park.

"She was living in Denver under the name Julia Turner—"

"I know," Stephanie cut in. "I helped set her up there. Was it Bruce?"

"He's the prime suspect. Residents identified him as being in the neighborhood yesterday, and airline records confirm that he flew to Denver."

Stephanie held her face in both hands as the un-bearable truth began to sink in. "How did he find her?"

"I don't know."

"Are they holding him in Denver?"

Monty hesitated for what seemed like an eternity. "He's on the run."

Slowly, Stephanie closed her eyes.

"Steph, we've got a Houston native as a fugitive and a Houston native living under an alias as a mur-der victim. This story is huge. The media's all over it. KJTV is at your office, and Channel Three is heading for your house."

"Jesus, Monty!"

"Currency of the business," he said matter-of-factly. "You were very outspoken about Bruce's sus-pended sentence for assault and battery. Now you're part of the story."

Like that of a woman on the run, Stephanie's gaze swept up and down San Felipe, searching for any vehicles emblazoned with a station logo. "What do you suggest?"

"Meet me at the station. I'll set up an in-depth interview at the anchor desk. That way you can take control."

"Okay." Ginger's happy, hopeful words still fresh in mind, Stephanie thought of her postcard, and a tear welled in the corner of her eye. "Monty . . . how did she die?"

"It was grisly—multiple stab wounds. I'm sorry."

"I'll see you soon," Stephanie blurted, cutting off the connection as a torrent of tears came bursting forth. Her brain swirled, a dizzying phantasmagoria of Ginger and Bruce, Josie and Rob, Nicole and O.J., and her own mother and Jimmy Scott. Would there ever be an end to domestic terror? Composing herself, she dialed the office.

"Stephanie Hart, attorney-at-law," Matt announced dutifully on the first ring.

"It's me—"

"Something's up," he broke in. "There's—"

"I know. Bruce Simon tracked down and killed Ginger. Pull the Simon files, close the office, and meet me at KBLX right away. *No comment* to the press." Stephanie hung up and called Peter. Luckily, Tuesday was already on her way to school. She urged Peter to get to his office before chaos erupted on the front lawn.

Monty was waiting for her in the front circular drive of KBLX, moodily smoking a cigarette. Stephanie pulled into a space marked VISITOR and got out. She scoped the lot for Matt's flashy candy apple-red Dodge Stealth but didn't see it. "I thought you quit!" she called to her cancer-courting brother.

"Certain moments make me vulnerable," he said, taking her in his arms for a tight, much-needed hug. "This is awful."

Stephanie drew back and held Monty's hand in hers. Montgomery Cain, as he was known to the rest of the city, looked devastatingly handsome. Here was a man ready for his close-up—clean-shaven, not a hair out of place, impeccably dressed in a smartly tailored suit, and teeth gleaming Pepsodent bright. With a final puff, he flicked the half-smoked stick to the ground, killing it with a Ferragamo heel. "Men suck."

Stephanie managed a weak smile. "Does that story lead at six and ten?"

Monty shrugged. "Hell, it should."

She regarded him for a moment. He appeared sad and distracted. "Are you thinking about it?"

Monty returned a half nod. "We should visit her this weekend."

Stephanie released his hand. "Yeah," she whispered.

The sonic boom of a thumping techno beat filled the air around them as a screaming, red hot rod peeled into view, its engine roaring. Matt Benedict waved a hand through the sunroof and squealed to a stop next to Stephanie's Mercedes. He emerged clutching a thick accordion file and wearing a white ribbed cotton tank with black jeans and top-of-the-line sneakers. "What's up?"

"A senseless murder—and high ratings," Monty answered, rolling his eyes. "Follow me." He sauntered over to a side door.

Stephanie and Matt fell into step behind him. They weaved through a maze of corridors, eventually spilling inside a busy newsroom. A throng of reporters and producers darted here and there. Television monitors hung overhead, three of them broadcasting soap operas and game shows from the major networks. The fourth screen was tuned to CNN, which had pounced on the Ginger Simon murder and was giving air time to a noted domestic violence authority. Stephanie had used her once as an expert witness, but lost faith when she learned that the woman would spin testimony for or against, depending on the size of the check.

Monty huddled briefly with a gray-haired man in spectacles, and then they both approached. "Stephanie, this is Dennis Perkins, our news director," Monty said.

"We want to go live with you at noon," Dennis blurted, obviously no fan of small talk. "Up-to-the-minute coverage, an interview at the anchor desk, and some calls from viewers."

Stephanie checked her watch. It was only ten o'clock. "I'll need an office with a telephone."

"You can use mine," Monty offered.

"Okay," she agreed.

Dennis nodded his thanks and disappeared.

Stephanie and Matt followed Monty around the corner to his office—a windowless room no bigger than a large closet.

"Dial nine for an outside line," Monty instructed.

"You should push for a corner office when you renegotiate your contract, man," Matt suggested.

Monty shot him a wan smile. "I'll look into that."

Stephanie's fist hammered down on the desk. "How did he find her? We were so careful! The only people who knew about Ginger's identity were me and her mother."

A mournful silence boomed.

"It was too good to be true. I should've insisted that she move again," Stephanie said.

"Don't be ridiculous," Matt said. "You did more for Ginger than any other lawyer would've done in the same circumstances."

"He's right," Monty agreed. "Don't do this to yourself."

For the next ninety minutes, Stephanie and Matt ran her practice from Monty's cubicle—returning calls, rearranging the day, conferring with clients and opposing counsel, and reviewing the Simon case for the imminent appearance on KBLX News.

"Hey, girl," Lisa Randall said from the doorway before bounding into the room to warmly embrace Stephanie. "Moral support has arrived."

"Thanks," Stephanie murmured, grateful to see her best friend, an award-winning copywriter for Hit The Sky Advertising and a true ally.

"What's the latest?" Lisa asked.

Just then Monty darted into view. "Bruce Simon was sighted at Houston Intercontinental. He's back."

Stephanie swallowed hard. Yesterday's phone call played inside her head. *You like keeping secrets. Don't you, bitch?* Did that voice belong to Bruce Simon? Was that his way of taunting her about Ginger's murder?

Another connection arrowed into Stephanie's brain. The letter had contained the phrase *Remember September,* and Ginger had left Houston for good about twelve months ago . . . on Labor Day. Fear turned her blood to ice water as the possibility smacked her between the eyes: Was he after her now?

"Are you okay?" Lisa inquired, breaking into her reverie.

It took a long time for Stephanie to answer, but finally she did with a calm, reflective, and unflinchingly honest, "No, I'm not."

"Count from one to ten for me, please," a technical man instructed.

As if on autopilot, Stephanie did as she was told. Godzilla could've been stomping about. She wouldn't have noticed.

"Sounds good," he snapped into his headset microphone. "Connect with camera one right here or address Tyson, whichever you prefer."

Stephanie nodded. She'd heard Monty's praise of Tyson Moore, and felt certain that this interview would be on target.

Checking her appearance on the monitor, Stephanie adjusted her collar and shook her kinky red mane to the point of fashionable unruliness. At thirty-three, she looked no older than twenty-five.

And thanks to her morning tumble with Peter—ten years her senior but still a dynamite lover—a healthy glow was tattooed to her pale as milk cheeks. She moistened her lips with her tongue and twisted her wedding ring for something to do.

"Sixty seconds!" someone hollered.

At fifty-nine and counting, Tyson Moore's clicking heels punctuated his journey across the studio and onto the set. Young, black, and beautiful, he exuded enough charisma to start a war, but underneath the pretty boy polish, the drive and ability of a serious journalist was palpable. He settled into the anchor chair and fastened his mike, giving Stephanie the benefit of his dazzling smile.

"Thirty seconds!"

"Monty's big sister, huh?" Tyson asked, adjusting his tie.

"That's me."

"I want some embarrassing Monty stories before you leave."

Stephanie laughed.

Tyson winked and scanned the teleprompter, then scowled. "I hope an intern wrote this shit. The opening reeks."

"Ten seconds!"

Stephanie took a deep breath and hoped Peter was watching.

"And five, four, three, two . . . one!"

Tyson leveled a stoic gaze into the eye of the camera. "A Houston native is dead. Her husband is a fugitive from the law. I'm Tyson Moore, and this is the KBLX noon report. Our top story today—the brutal murder of twenty-eight-year-old Ginger Simon."

As video footage hit the monitor to illustrate Tyson's overwrought and *Hard Copy* stylized delivery,

Stephanie sat transfixed. Images of O.J. and Nicole Simpson were intercut with wedding photos of Bruce and Ginger Simon. Even video of the infamous Bronco chase had been dusted off to underscore Bruce's official classification as a fugitive.

Stephanie's stomach cramped with regret. To be a part of such a sensationalized media circus was humiliating. Still, if only one woman benefited from today's broadcast and avoided a fate like Ginger's, then the slumming would be well worth it.

"With us in the studio is Stephanie Hart, the attorney who represented Ginger Simon. Thank you for joining us," Tyson said earnestly. "Tell us about Ginger."

"Unfortunately, I only knew her as a frightened and battered young woman," Stephanie began. "She was consumed by the fear that her husband would one day kill her. He made frequent threats to that effect, and the reports so far suggest that he made good on them."

"Ginger was living in Denver under an illegal alias. Why?"

"Bruce Simon received no jail time, little more than a slap on the wrist, for beating Ginger with such brutality that she suffered internal bleeding. At that point, relocating under a new identity became a matter of simple survival."

"Do you believe our system of justice failed Ginger Simon?"

"I think the facts speak for themselves. A sadistic and habitual abuser was set free to finish what he started."

"As an officer of the court, you represent that system," Tyson challenged.

"Exactly. And I know its shortcomings first hand, especially in regards to women. Every nine seconds a woman is battered by a husband or boyfriend. Domestic abuse is not a private matter. It's a crime. We should up the ante on treating it like one."

Tyson nodded, his head tilted, his lips set in a thin, serious line. "Let's go to our first caller. Kim Bradley, you're on the air."

"I think that when battered women hear about people like Nicole Simpson and Ginger Simon, they get scared into staying right where they are."

Stephanie leaned forward, straining to hear the crackled voice but able to capture every word. "I'm afraid there's some truth to what Kim says. For most women, however, that's an irrational fear. Simply put, every abuser is not a murderer. To let that kind of thinking stop you from getting out of a harmful situation is foolish."

Tyson nodded again. "Our next caller is Jimmy Scott."

As the name registered, Stephanie felt twin splotches of glowing red heat splash her cheeks. She couldn't speak.

"I have a question for Stephanie Hart." The man's voice was slick, deep, and dark.

With absolute certainty, she knew it was him. The anonymous caller. The letter writer. A terrible wrongness registered. She felt a moment's pure fear.

"Go ahead, please," Tyson prodded.

"Do you remember September?" he rasped.

Sickness welled in the pit of Stephanie's stomach. Her bones turned to ice, and she clamped her hand across her mouth to stop the scream. Ripping the microphone from her collar, she gave in to the overpowering need to get off the set, run out of the station, jump into the car . . . and drive fast.

Three

New York—September, 1997

Lunch at Le Cirque 2000 with a literary agent meant one of two things—a joyous celebration or a sweet good-bye. As Abby McQueen stalked past the mirrored columns and took note of the tycoons, philanthropists, and assorted Manhattan movers dotted along the path, a gut thing told her that today's occasion marked the latter.

Jeff Lowenstein waved from a small table along a wall painted with a French pastoral scene. He broke off a hunk of brown bread and proceeded to slather it with butter as Abby approached. "You're late."

She settled into her seat and leaned forward to capture a whiff of the lovely rose and orchid arrangement between them. "Sorry. The dry cleaner had trouble locating my suit." A nervous hand smoothed a seasons-old quilted pink shoulder. "This is the only Chanel number I have left."

Jeff shrugged. "Swallow your pride and buy knock-offs."

Abby blanched. "I'd rather go naked."

Jeff tossed a cautionary look across the table. "Now might be a good time to look into nudist colonies."

Abby attempted to laugh it off; Jeff didn't. At that

moment, she knew. The wrecking ball was about to take its last swing and demolish what little remained of her once brilliant career. She took in the elegant lunchers around her with a sweeping gaze that oozed malignant envy. The Masters of the Universe hadn't downsized from a Central Park West condo to a dingy one room walk-up in Queens. And the lacquered, bouffant-haired society matrons hadn't been forced to sell off their home furnishings and designer clothes for quick bucks.

"Olympic Books canceled the Costner contract," Jeff said.

Abby sucked in a tiny breath. "What about—"

"It's over," he said firmly. "Your brand of cele-bicide is considered publishing poison. I can't sell it."

Abby felt beads of perspiration prickle under her arms. So the deal for *Kevin Costner: Field of Dreams and Betrayals* was off. That meant the $50,000 advance was history, too. Panic swelled inside of her. "Offer them a better deal. Take . . . anything."

Jeff shook his head.

Abby's fists hit the table. The Limoges dinnerware clinked as heads turned to take note of the frustrated moment. "My books should start a bidding war!"

"Think Stallone," Jeff remarked patiently.

Abby McQueen bristled at the mention of the superstar's name. *Sylvester Stallone: Italian Stallion* had been a sensational, runaway bestseller, her first major success . . . and also her downfall. The actor's lawyers had pounced on some of the more lurid accounts of Rambo's sexual exploits, and after paying attorney fees and coughing up a brutal out of court settlement to stave off further litigation, Abby

McQueen was shoving her hand between couch cushions for loose coins.

"Face it. You're no Kitty Kelley."

Abby fought the urge to smash a water glass on the table and cut Jeff's throat with a jagged edge. She hated that bitch and her millions, and he knew it.

"I've got an idea for you, though."

Desperate curiosity tickled her brain. "I'm listening," she said tersely.

"I graduated from Brown with a guy named Francisco Juarez. He's editor of *Texas Today* now. Something big's cooking."

Unimpressed, Abby sighed heavily. "What?"

"Where were you twenty years ago this month?"

Abby gave him a quizzical look as she ransacked her memory for the answer. In September of 1977 . . . she'd been twenty-five years old, living in Houston . . . and covering the Cain family scandal. Yes! Her first cover story, the piece that had put her on the map—and on the fast track. "Jimmy Scott," Abby whispered, the gruesome images of the young womanizer at the bloody crime scene flashing like a sick slide show in her mind.

"Francisco's got a hard-on for a twenty year anniversary piece with a Where Are They Now angle," Jeff said.

Abby's spirits sank. Had it come to this? Excavating old headlines and slumming in regional mags that registered flatlines on the who gives a shit meter? She thought of her prospects, and experienced a painful moment of reality. "How much?"

"Five grand plus lodging and a sixty dollar per diem."

The higher they climb, the farther they fall, Abby thought miserably. "That's fucking minimum wage."

"Every bit of it's yours," Jeff said cheerfully. "I'm not taking my usual fifteen percent."

Abby chuckled bitterly. "A clever way of letting me know that I'm being dropped off your client list."

Jeff opened his hands as if to say, "What can I do?"

Abby tried, knowing she sounded pathetic. "I'll bounce back."

He winced. "We had a pretty good run, Abby, but the race is over. You know I don't have time for this nickel and dime crap. I did it as a favor. You're finished in this town. Go to Houston."

As Jeff Lowenstein's cruel words eroded her already critically low self-esteem, Abby recalled the copy that had graced the cover of *Texas Today* twenty years ago: LOVE AND SEX AND MURDER IN RIVER OAKS. The scandal came back to her in fragments. An ice queen mother. Her beautiful teenage daughter. Their slick lawyer. A dead stud.

Something about that incident had troubled her back then, but she'd been too young, too inexperienced, and too stupid to find the answers. Today, however, she was none of those things. And if, in fact, the truth *had* been buried, then this could very well be the stuff that dotted lines were made for. Book deals. Movie options. Forget brain-dead celebrities. They didn't corner the publishing market. True crime was big business, too.

She felt a tingle on the back of her neck. Goosebumps sprang up on her arms. For the first time in a long time, Abby McQueen smiled. "When do I start?"

Four

"Stephanie, wait!"

She heard Monty's voice behind her but kept on running, even as the crunch of his heels on the pavement loomed closer. Now she could make out his heavy breathing, then the feel of a firm hand on her arm. Tears streaming, she stopped, turned, and fell into his embrace.

"It's okay," he whispered.

Stephanie drew back to face him. "I got a phone call yesterday, a letter last night . . . and now this. He's coming after me."

Monty leveled a ray gun gaze. "The police will find him."

She regarded him for a moment, uncertain.

"Bruce Simon won't get near you."

Stephanie took in a deep breath and wiped the dampness from her cheeks. "What if it's not Simon? When that caller identified himself as Jimmy Scott, I thought it was Bruce . . . but . . . now I'm not so sure. Dredging up my past isn't Simon's style. It's too personal."

Monty shook his head. "If he's clever enough to track down Ginger, then he's clever enough to find your Achilles' heel."

Stephanie wanted so much to believe. "Maybe."

Monty admonished her with a stern look. *"Definitely.* Bruce can't elude them much longer. This will all be over soon."

Jimmy Scott. Tyson Moore's perfectly enunciated delivery still rang in her mind. "I haven't heard that name spoken aloud in years."

"He's taunting you."

"It's working." She buried her face in her hands.

"Don't go back there," Monty whispered.

There. The past. That horrible night in September, 1977. "Easier said." For a moment she saw Monty as the meek little boy clutching his Winnie the Pooh, not the confident, candy-for-the-camera news personality in front of her. "Let's go see her." It was all she needed to say.

Monty nodded. "Meet me here after the six o'clock report."

Stephanie opened her car, got in, and turned the key over. As she coasted away, she wondered if her mother would speak to her tonight. The silence had lasted twenty years, but a girl could hope.

"Roll it back," Tyson Moore ordered. The six-foot-one anchor stood, arms folded, as the booth wizard worked his magic. In seconds, the noon newscast that had just wrapped got a reprisal on the studio monitors. He watched intently, brown eyes narrowed, concentrating on himself as if the subject were hard science. His body stiffened the moment Stephanie Hart's unexpected bolt from the set played back. Luckily, the camera had been on Tyson Moore; miraculously, the anchor had played the disturbance with computer cool, not giving up so much as a flinch. "Man, what a save!" Tyson erupted, giving a high-five to a passing production assistant.

It took only a few hot seconds for Lisa Randall's fear, worry, and concern for Stephanie to meld into anger at this Stone Phillips wannabe. She stalked toward him, ready to rumble. Maybe he didn't deserve her wrath, but she needed to vent, and Narcissus here had just provided the perfect opportunity.

"My best friend freaks out and all you care about is how you look on camera? Well, let me give you some impromptu focus group results—you're not ready for prime time."

Tyson took a step backward, his eyes wide and his mouth agape.

"What's wrong, honey? Can't speak without the aid of a teleprompter?"

"You think so!" Tyson said, trying to sound mocking.

Lisa cocked her head and gave him a piercing, drill-bit stare. "I've heard nothing to prove otherwise."

"Well, check it out." He popped his shoulders and splayed out his hands. "Bitch, this is my place of work, and if I want to watch my motherfucking ass *fifty* times in a row, then that's my goddamn business!"

Lisa nearly toppled over. Bryant Gumbel had metamorphosed into Puff Daddy. Usually her first impressions were infallible. At first glance, she'd taken this guy for a coddled, upper-middle-class sellout, the kind of man who avoided conflict just to keep ripples out of the water. Wrong. Tyson Moore was a brother with street credibility, and his vulgar outburst had triggered a cruel irony: The woman who dreamed up clever phrases to make the rent was standing stock-still, at a loss for words.

"How do you like me now!" Tyson boomed.

"Better than before," Lisa said slowly, smiling in

spite of herself. "I'd apologize, but somehow I think we're even . . . or maybe you're ahead."

He smiled, too, almost bashfully, though still hyper-aware of his certain appeal. "I'm sorry about Stephanie. Really, I am. What's up with that?"

Lisa unleashed a heavy sigh. "I don't know. That's why I'm on edge." In a last ditch attempt at formality, she held out her hand. "Lisa Randall."

Tyson returned a firm shake that lasted a moment too long. "Tyson Moore. You a lawyer, too?"

Lisa shook her head. "Nothing so serious. I'm a senior copywriter for Hit The Sky Advertising."

He flashed a quick, mischievous grin. "What's your favorite ice cream?"

Lisa narrowed her gaze. Where had *that* come from? "*Ben & Jerry's* Chocolate Chip Cookie Dough. Why?"

Tyson just nodded. "Favorite singer?"

"Marvin Gaye."

"Actor?"

"Morgan Freeman."

"Fast food?"

"Wendy's burgers. McDonald's fries. Why all these questions?"

He paused as if in deep thought, then unleashed a killer smile. "Let's go out."

"What?" Lisa asked, slightly confused as to the precise meaning of the statement. She'd just attacked this man for the vanity that goes hand in hand with broadcasting, cast insulting doubt about his ability to move up in the industry and about his intelligence, then raised out of him a stream of unbridled profanity that rivaled among the worst rap music had to offer. And now he wanted a date! Saying yes would be the only hospitable thing to do, she told herself before becoming distracted by his hands. They looked big, warm, and safe, and he even had calluses. Could it be—a pretty boy with calluses? A smooth news guy who turned gangster on a dime? What delicious contradictions!

"Let's go out," he said again, as if it were the most logical of all moves.

She still couldn't quite believe the turn of events. Suspicious thoughts roared inside her head. "So you can stand me up and teach me a lesson?" Lisa asked haughtily.

He laughed. "Listen, baby, I know this much— You wouldn't go out with me just because I'm on television. If anything, you'd hold that against me. The way I figure it, this is real."

Stunned, Lisa fished into her purse and pulled out a business card. She started to hand it to him, but pulled back at the last moment. "You do realize that this is just a bad day for me, right? I mean, I'm no dominatrix. I don't want to spank you and tell you what a nasty boy you are."

Tyson reached for the card. "Good. 'Cuz I don't play that shit."

"I'm canceling the rest of your day," Matt said, his voice crackling from the car phone speaker.

Not a single cell in Stephanie's body was alive with the willingness to protest. She *needed* to play hooky. Unfortunately, her preferred partners in crime were unavailable. She knew that Peter's patient schedule was booked solid, and that Lisa would ask too many questions about the abrupt exit. Answers she would give her, just not today. What she wanted was a break from the madness.

So instead, Stephanie checked Tuesday out of school early and treated her to an afternoon at the

Galleria, where they lunched in the Neiman-Marcus café, shopped the fancy boutiques, and killed time watching iceskaters in the center rink. Stephanie stroked her daughter's wheat-gold hair as she looked on in youthful marvel, fascinated by the double axels and triple jumps of one exceptionally strong skater.

"Can I take iceskating lessons, too?"

"We'll talk about it in a few weeks, sweetheart. See how you feel about it then." Stephanie smiled. If any interest of Tuesday's passed the two week litmus test, it was usually worth indulging. This one would likely fade as soon as they tumbled back into the car for the short ride home.

"Mommy, are you sad?"

Stephanie bristled slightly. Trust Tuesday to arrow through to the heart of the matter. "I'm just preoccupied, honey. Something's on my mind."

Tuesday scooted closer and tucked her arm under Stephanie's. "Things will look better in the morning," she said earnestly, giving her mother's arm a gentle squeeze.

Stephanie gazed down at the nine-year-old source of comforting wisdom and felt a surge of love, so much that she blinked back a tear. "How did you get so smart?"

Tuesday beamed. "My mommy's a lawyer, my biological daddy was a doctor, and my new daddy's a doctor, too," she said, shrugging her shoulders. "I can't help it."

Stephanie laughed, and for the first time she allowed the tension to truly subside, but only for an instant. A terrible feeling came over her. She went rigid with fear as the ominous sensation stormed through: Someone was watching them.

Abruptly she spun one hundred eighty degrees,

anger flooding her, heart pumping with fury. She scanned the area—up, down, and all around. Her intensity magnified the sights and sounds, distorting them. People darted here and there, paying them no mind. Was she losing it? Her hands were shaking. *He could be here,* she thought. *Walking among us. Hovering in a corner. Lurking inside one of the shops.* The realization made her frantic.

"Look, Mommy!"

She jolted and turned back to the source of Tuesday's amusement.

"That girl jumped in the air and twirled around!"

Stephanie reached for Tuesday's hand and held on firmly. "It's time to go."

"But—"

"*Now,* darling," Stephanie said, more sharply than intended. She broke into a purposeful, aggressive stride down the retail stretch, into Neiman-Marcus, past the ubiquitous perfume snipers and cosmetic commandos, and out into the sun-drenched parking lot. Once they reached the car she stopped, taking in the scene with a circular gaze. Nothing suspicious. She hesitated. "Everything's okay. Let's go home."

The moment she heard the click of Tuesday's seatbelt, Stephanie shifted into reverse and hit the accelerator.

"Mommy!" Tuesday cried.

A Chevrolet Suburban was heading straight toward them on the passenger-side. Stephanie's mind froze on the nightmare unfolding, and she held up a hand to stop the unstoppable, the sound of squealing tires ricocheting inside her brain. No! She prayed the Mercedes could withstand the crash and braced herself for impact . . . but it didn't come. They were saved from collision by mere inches.

A horn blasted. "Are you crazy?" the driver screamed before screeching away.

With a trembling hand, Stephanie shifted the car into drive and moved back into the narrow parking space. Her hands gripped the wheel tightly as she let reality sink in. Crazy was right. She hadn't even looked once before pulling out. Tuesday could've been killed. *Count to ten slowly,* she told herself, fighting for calm. *One thousand one, one thousand two . . .*

"That was close," Tuesday said.

"I know, sweetheart," Stephanie whispered, "and it was all my fault. I'm so sorry."

Tuesday looked both ways. "It's safe now, Mommy."

In more ways than one, she prayed her daughter was right. Feeling ashamed and frightfully stupid, Stephanie struggled to come up with some pabulum of maternal reassurance. "I made a big mistake that put us in danger. You did the right thing just then by checking for cars in both directions. Let's make a promise to each other that we'll *always* do that."

"I promise."

"Me, too, sweetheart. Me, too."

Tuesday fiddled with the radio dial, searching for the pop music station that played her favorites. The old Paula Abdul hit "Will You Marry Me?" filled the car at a deafening volume.

Stephanie played with the rheostat, bringing it down as she turned onto Westheimer, thankful that home was minutes away.

"How come Uncle Monty isn't married?" Tuesday asked.

Stephanie smiled tightly. She'd taken great pains to always answer Tuesday's questions honestly, even if those questions raised discomfiting issues of sexuality. Better to earn trust and respect early on with straight facts, she figured, than risk losing her daughter's inquisitiveness to less thoughtful peers. But explaining Monty's lifestyle was not something she could handle right now. "He's only twenty-seven—still a young man. There's plenty of time for that," she attempted casually, hoping to thwart further interest.

"My friend Jackie says she's going to marry Uncle Monty."

Jackie had better have a Plan B, Stephanie thought. Montgomery Cain. Heartthrob news anchor adored by the city. Deeply troubled man too often hated by himself. He preferred closet living to honest living, and kept the sexuality trackers guessing by an ongoing series of mostly short-lived affairs with some of Houston's most beautiful women. The chronology never strayed from this pattern: He courted; they fell in love; he moved on. Each woman foolishly believed she could *change* him, and each broken romance left Monty in an alarming state of depression that he nursed with a less than discreet binge of booze and male hustler types who could be counted on to leave him guilt-free. Stephanie hoped that working with Peter would help Monty break this destructive cycle and move on toward happiness and self-acceptance.

"If Jackie marries Uncle Monty, then she'll be my aunt. I don't want that to happen!"

Stephanie laughed. "Don't worry, honey. It's a little soon to book the church."

"You're going tonight?" Peter asked incredulously.

"It's something Monty and I have to do."

Peter fell silent, regarded her with solemnity, and

then began studying her with a thoughtful, clinically minded expression.

"Please don't do that," Stephanie complained. He knew how much his *psychologist* look got on her nerves.

He put up his hands in quick surrender. "Apologies."

"Forgotten."

"Seeing her is hard on you, and it's already been a stressful week. I'm just looking out for you, not making judgments."

She sighed deeply. "I know."

Peter took her in his arms and rotated his hands in the small of her back with a gentle, soothing, circular motion. "Did you get one of those crank calls at the office today?"

He hadn't seen the news. "No," Stephanie murmured. Technically, her answer was true, but she felt instant guilt all the same. How could she call him to task for his psychology look when she slipped out of tricky moments like this one with semantics?

Peter's hands scaled down and slipped into the rear pockets of her Ralph Lauren jeans. "I'm sorry about Ginger. You did everything that you could."

Stephanie gave in. To the enormous wave of sadness. To the blinding anger. To the aching, hopeless despair that had been hovering over her like an ominous, gathering storm cloud. With each shuddering sob, Peter held her just a little bit tighter, his arms like bands of emotional steel. A burning sense of failure ripped through her. Ginger Simon was dead; Melissa Alexander was alone and poor; Josie Dean and her two-year-old boy were hidden away from family and friends in a shelter, facing—of all the horrifying things—a custody battle with an abusive husband and trophy-minded father.

The strength to go on fighting seemed, for the first time, elusive. Being saddled with the blame for her own mother's wrecked life had been difficult enough, but adding the additional freight of other women's nightmares was becoming too much to endure. Understanding their plight wasn't enough. Maybe they needed someone stronger, better, smarter.

"I don't know if I can do this anymore, Peter," she managed tearfully, gripping his shoulders, "I just don't know."

He rocked her gently from side to side, wrapping her up with warmth and support. "Listen to me," he began, his voice at once soothing and scolding, "you've chosen this path because it's what you're passionate about. There are no Hollywood endings here. You know that. Sometimes you lose. And sometimes the loss is so great that your heart breaks, like today." Peter leaned back and held her face in his hands, wiping away tears with the satiny smoothness of his fingertips. "You know what's so incredible about you?"

"What?" Stephanie gulped, facing the intimate heat of his gaze.

"You *feel* the losses for the people living them. And it makes you that much more formidable the next time. Cry tonight, Steph. Have your pity party and doubt your commitment and competence, if you must. But get out there and fight tomorrow. It's what you were meant to do."

Stephanie's breath sat caged in her lungs as she smiled against Peter's chest. He was her miracle worker, the one who kick-started her engines to a loud roar on those rare moments when they killed. She kissed him lightly on the lips, muttering, "My personal Tony Robbins."

* * *

They drove in companionable silence, Monty at the wheel of his vintage BMW, Stephanie beside him gazing outward. Clear Lake, the city built by Exxon and its Friendswood Development subsidiary, was just ahead. Though NASA and a satellite of other space enterprises made up the soul of the area, Clear Lake and Galveston Bay also floated a well-heeled boating culture and the tourist trappings of a seductive waterfront industry.

Stephanie rolled down the window and welcomed the attack of night air. It whipped and snapped like a wet towel. The smell of sewage and saltwater blew strong in her nostrils, and in her throat she tasted the sharp tang of the Gulf of Mexico.

Suddenly the window rose up, and she turned to see an annoyed Monty executing the control panel with manicured fingers, his once gel-slicked, perfect black hair a breeze-battered mess. "Come on!" he wailed, "I have to be back for the ten o'clock report."

She laughed. He cared more about his appearance than any *woman* she'd ever met. "Viewers will think you just had sex. It'll be good for ratings."

The smile curving onto his lips was so obviously against his will. "Shut up," he mumbled.

They drove on, sixties era Streisand on the stereo, seventies era dysfunction on the brain. What a piece of work their mother had been. Marilyn Cain—a flashy dressing, chain-smoking, profanity spewing, big living tornado—the kind of woman who's the center of attention *before* entering the room. After all, just knowing she was on her way created enough buzz.

"Fuck 'em." That was Marilyn Cain's constant refrain. To the poor family she left behind in Kentucky. To the contesting heirs she triumphed over in court when first husband—and father to her children—Oscar Cain left her the bulk of his paper products fortune. To the Houston society mavens who froze her out of their charity leagues and country club playpens. To the daughter whose only wish was to set her mother free from a cash sucking punk who talked with his fists.

Put the knife on the towel. Those were the last words Marilyn Cain had spoken to her directly. Billy Hudson had done all the talking after that fateful night. Beyond that, all contact had been controlled, delivered through a kindly nanny, housekeepers, and even Monty. No conversation of substance, just enough to get by, preferably within a group. To call Mother cold was the understatement of the century; more accurately, Mother was an arctic freeze.

That Monty had received the love and attention Stephanie was denied never made her resentful, simply because he needed it more. Even as a child Monty had been weak-willed, overly sensitive to basic cruelties, and uncertain of his place. In contrast, Stephanie was strong, resilient, and proud—much like her father, neighbors often told her.

Oscar Cain, stubbornly refusing to give up the tobacco and liquor doctors swore would kill him, succumbed to heart failure when she was just six, but Stephanie kept her small memories of him intact—the smell of cigarettes on his breath, the pleasant roughness of his beard, the comical way he called her Steffi-Muffin. How different life might have been had he lived on. Jimmy Scott never would have entered their lives. She shook away the thought.

"Penny?" Monty said, breaking into her aerial castles.

She tossed him a puzzled look.

"For your thoughts," he clarified.

"Ancient history," Stephanie said.

Monty nodded knowingly, turning past a sign that read SUSANN CENTER FOR DISABLED SENIORS and onto a long and winding drive. Parking for visitors was in bountiful supply, given the late hour. Stephanie paused before getting out. She had to muster up the strength to go inside. Leaving the dread and revulsion at the door always took some doing.

Following that horrible night and the aftermath of the investigation, Marilyn Cain had continued to toy with a series of young and useless men, each one robbing more of her money than the last. By the time Guy Fulcher came along, Marilyn's fortune was all but gone. To the bastard's credit, he married her, anyway, and they remained so for nine years, living in the same River Oaks residence where Jimmy Scott had died. But when Marilyn suffered two strokes in quick succession that left her completely paralyzed, unable to walk, talk, and, for a time, even breathe, Guy Fulcher disappeared.

Under no strain of melancholy, Stephanie and Monty sold the River Oaks house, and then—on advice from Houston's top neurologists and psychiatrists—moved their mother to the Susann Center. The phalanx of physical, occupational, speech, and recreational therapists on staff meant the finest care possible, but the severe damage to the right and left sides of her brain meant chances for even marginal recovery were slim.

The old woman they visited in that odorless, claustrophobic room was a stranger. Mute. Immobile. Ex-

pressionless. Once Stephanie had fed her yogurt.
Gently stroking her mother's throat to smooth it
down, she told stories of Tuesday to fill the silence,
hoping for a response, some outward sign of communication. It never came.

Monty reached for the batch of flowers on the
backseat. "No time like the present," he sang more
brightly than the moment called for.

Stephanie took a deep breath and followed him
inside to the front desk where a stern, horse-faced
woman, clad in a ghastly flower print frock, greeted
them. The desk plate pronounced her M'Lou. "You
have fifteen minutes," she intoned bitterly.

A short, Hispanic man carrying a bundle of crisp
white sheets, ambled toward them, breaking into a
big, warm smile as he approached. "It's the prince
and princess," he said with a laugh. "It's been a
while since you come to the castle."

Stephanie appreciated the familiar mustachioed
orderly who referred to Marilyn as "the Queen" and
promised to see to it that she lived like one.

"How is she, Luis?" Stephanie asked.

The curve of his lips flattened into a thin, hard
line. "No change. I'm sorry." He eyed Monty's flowers. "Ah, you treat the Queen right. Follow me. We
get a vase, yes?"

Monty set off after Luis.

Stephanie ventured into Marilyn's room alone. It
was as still as a tomb. A sunken figure, her mother
lay motionless in the hospital bed, looking much
older than her sixty-four years. Marilyn's face, like a
weathered tombstone carving, appeared stressed
and worn down.

"Hi there," Stephanie whispered, almost choking
out the words, suddenly hit with the full frontal assault of the tenebrous task: Sitting beside the

mother who resented her; sitting beside the stroke victim who didn't know her.

Their eyes met.

Something flickered in Marilyn's eyes. Was it recognition?

Stephanie smoothed a hand across her silver hair.

Marilyn opened her mouth to speak.

The mere possibility hastened Stephanie's pulse. Where was Monty? She wanted him to witness this, too.

They rippled through the old woman's thorax so very faintly, but the shadow breath produced the unmistakable shadow words: "He's alive."

Five

Flying coach sucked. Abby McQueen sat miserably in the middle, tightly sandwiched between a teenage mother with a squalling baby in the window seat and a fat furniture store manager on the aisle. Even a tasty new Jackie Collins novel couldn't distract her from the inhuman conditions.

"So what brings you to Houston?" Bill Booker lisped out the question as if it were a juggernaut ensuring brilliant conversation.

Abby knew the name only because the retail roach had just dumped a worthless business card on her. Jesus Christ, weren't there laws against littering, even at ten thousand feet? She iced him down with a sub-zero glare, freezing him with all the contempt she might unleash on a child molester, a noisy born-again, a card-carrying Democrat, or Jerry Springer.

"Murder," she said, wrapping her apricot painted lips around the word with such coiled venom that the air between them just hung there, thick with ominous ambiguity.

The unfortunate passenger gulped down the implicit message: If he didn't shut the fuck up and leave her alone, one of the possibilities could very well be his own murder. His puffy hands performed a thumb twiddle as he turned his attention upward to inspect the plane's ceiling.

Bus travel by air—that's what this American Airlines flight felt like. Within minutes, the automaton attendant, beleaguered by requests for extra peanuts, trash pickup, and other shameless in-flight coddling, would announce the imminent landing. Abby decided to steal away to the lavatory while she still had the chance. In one fluid movement, she rose up, slipped out, and pounced down the corridor, strutting fast, avoiding eye contact, a fiery feast of female fission that made mortals look and made mortals wonder: *Who is she? What does she do? Where is she going?* As recently as one year ago, the answers were, respectively: Someone very important; anything she wants; places others dream about.

She stepped into the vacant stall and slid the lock into place. At least she still had her looks. The light was forgiving, but even without the help she would have been pleased. At forty-five, she had most women beat. Others her age were two sleepless nights away from an AARP commercial, but Abby had skin uncannily smooth and taut, bereft of crow's-feet and laugh lines, artificially basted a succulent, honey-brown from a self-tanning cream perfected by the finest Parisian dermatologists. Her Soloflex body was thin but still powerful enough to take down Wall Street wimps in an arm wrestling contest.

Turning slightly to survey her profile, Abby smiled. The new breasts—bought with blab money from an exclusive *Hard Copy* interview—were a showstopper. Six months ago she'd booked a consultation with the best tit man in New York, thrown down a picture of Elizabeth Hurley in the famous Versace dress, and said, "Put these on me." After all, nine

out of ten men liked them big. *So does the tenth man,*
she thought with a devilish snicker, *but pleasing him
would require* another *procedure on the* other *gender.*

The hint of dark roots in her hair caused a shiver
of alarm. Who was she kidding? An evening at home
with Clairol couldn't replace professional color sessions with the swishy boys at Bergdorf Goodman.
"Shit," she spat, now sighting a chipped nail on her
forefinger. Doing her own nails didn't cut it, either.
Sure, she'd saved thirty bucks on the Manhattan
manicure, but now her hands looked no better than
a ten dollar hooker's. Fury welled up inside of her.
Sticking to a budget was for the middle class. SHE
WAS ABBY MCQUEEN, GODDAMMIT! Journalist.
Author. Media darling. *Poor girl.* Balls! There was
nothing worse.

"I will make it through this," Abby chanted. She
tried to muffle her internal screams about a life in
shambles, a career in ruin, a financial future uncertain. What a death drop—from plugging a bestseller
with Jay Leno to chasing a bargain basement story
from yesteryear. Damn them! Hate flared, and she
practiced the soothing art of visualization. Her ani-
mosity was a firestorm, an orange ball of searing
heat and marmalade flames that exploded into the
palatial homes of her enemies, engulfing them as
they slept, awakening them to the horrible pain of
flesh on fire. His lawyers, who won. Her lawyers, who
lost. Sylvester Stallone. Jeff Lowenstein. In Abby
McQueen's fantasy hell, they all died burning alive.

The plane dipped quite suddenly; she steadied
herself against the door as a voice garbled something over the intercom and the FASTEN SEAT
BELT sign lit up. Tottering back to her seat, she
recalled that Billy Graham had once described the
sprawling metropolis below as "a more wicked city

than Hollywood." Abby's lips curved into a secret smile. She had to admit, it had its moments. After all, twenty years ago, it was here in Houston that a girl got away with bloody murder.

"You must be Abby McQueen."

"Depends who's asking."

"Francisco Juarez."

She wasn't prepared for masculine overload, and the man greeting her was industrial strength testosterone personified. Dark olive skin. Thick black hair. Deep ebony eyes. Everything about him was tip-top—the dressed down, washed out Gap gear, the hard rock body that it contained, and the creamy, heavily accented voice that had already cuddled up for a nap in her memory. Too bad he was a nobody: On the food chain of publications, *Texas Today* was plankton. *What a waste,* Abby mourned. In her eyes, a mini-career could reduce even the best-looking man to windshield bug status.

"How was your flight?" he asked.

"Coach class. Need I say more?"

Francisco rotated his head from side to side—chin up, gaze level—offering up his best angle. "Many would consider that a luxury."

Something in his eyes told Abby that he had lived through two lives to her one. Fired on instinct, she would have bet all the money she no longer had that he was a refugee from Castro Cuba. "Where are you from?"

"Cuba," Francisco confirmed. "Do you have luggage?"

Abby nodded. They started for the escalator. "When did you leave?" she asked.

He paused a beat. "I swam over when I was seventeen. Six of us left together. Only two of us made it here. So I'll never view traveling *coach* as a problem."

Abby whistled. Such a battle for freedom was beyond the ken of her reality, but she had zero interest in hearing this man sing the immigrant boy blues. "Big deal," she snorted. "I was sexually abused by my grandfather."

Francisco froze and regarded her sharply. "What?"

Abby kept moving. "You heard me."

He quickened his pace to catch up. "Are you mocking me?"

Now she halted. "If you need to whine about spoiled Americans, start a Cuban boat buddies support group. In my world, coach travel is second best, and your sob story doesn't change that. Are we clear?"

The sandbagged look on his face said it all: No one had ever gone that far before. His lips tightened. "Jeff was wrong."

Abby raised her brow haughtily. "How so?"

"He said you were a bitch. I disagree. You're the Antichrist."

She laughed mirthlessly. "Jeff Lowenstein is a prick."

Francisco's chin jutted upward pugnaciously, his dark eyes flashing anger, and comeuppance. "Did you come to this conclusion before or after he dropped you from his client list?"

Abby swallowed hard. It went down like the bitter pill that it was. Jeff had told him all the gory details. Francisco would know that she'd lost everything in the Stallone lawsuit, that no publisher would offer shit for her Kevin Costner bio, that she needed the lousy sixty-dollar per diem to pay for tonight's dinner.

"This is a pity job, Ms. McQueen. Jeff supplied the pity. I supplied the job. It's really quite simple."

His words whacked into her. This man had suggested that she was market poison, a charity case to be passed down between old college pals. What a bastard! The sluice gates of anger opened. "Yes, but not in the way you think it is."

"*Texas Today* is a fine magazine," Francisco said, remarkably with a straight face. "You should be proud."

Abby didn't bother to contain her laughter. Francisco Juarez spoke the language of the delusional. The pairing of *Texas Today* and pride was a textbook example of oxymoronic thinking. Could he possibly believe his own pathetic words? Was he so far gone that he thought the editors of *The New Yorker* and *Vanity Fair* his professional equals? "Does the term *denial* mean anything to you?"

"Yes," Francisco said crisply. "It explains your bad attitude."

Abby sucked in a deep breath. The Lou Grant pretender had stepped across the line, and he deserved the lesson that only her machine gun mouth could teach him. "I may be out of money, Mr. Mambo King, but I still have my brain. You hired me because my name on the cover will move newsstand copies. Abby McQueen is *still* a marketable commodity. Have I hit a career slump? Yes! But I'll regain solid footing. Bet on it. And don't hold your breath for my grateful-to-be-here speech, because you'll pass out waiting for it. *Texas Today* smacks of amateur night, but what the fuck—I need the dough. One more thing: You're looking at a broad who's used to first-class air travel and chauffeured limousines, so don't be offended if a coach seat and a personal shuttle by way of the hack editor's Toyota doesn't cream my panties."

She extended her arm and forefinger, pointing to the baggage claim area. "Look for a Vuitton hanging bag and hard case. I'll be at the airport bar."

Six

"How could this happen? I'm fifty-two years old, and I don't even have health insurance!"

Stephanie reached out, clasped Melissa Alexander's hand, and squeezed it tightly. Chuck Berg's scorched earth tactics had claimed another victim. If only Melissa had come to her first, Stephanie lamented, remembering that the recent divorcee's first lawyer had been one of Berg's many outside business partners. Together, the two had churned motions, delayed agreements, and generally obstructed the proceedings until Melissa ran out of money. The real kicker—the sum had been an inheritance from her mother, and the only funds in her name. Even worse, by the time Stephanie took over as Melissa's attorney Berg had successfully destroyed the woman's credibility in front of Judge Gibbs. Stephanie had fought hard, but deep down she had known that they didn't stand much of a chance.

"Does that judge have any idea what he's done?" Melissa demanded, tears streaming down her cheeks in dark rivulets.

"I'm sure that he does. He did it to *his* last three wives," Stephanie said.

Melissa looked up, astonished. "But—"

Stephanie waved away the idealism before it hit the air. "Judges are not always screened for their own family histories. Lawrence Gibbs is uninformed, insensitive, and believes that domestic matters are *women's issues,* and therefore beneath him. That's why he doesn't listen impartially to both sides. He makes rulings based on his whims and his bias against women. This is the same man who gave up as little as possible through three bitter divorces of his own, so he sees a man like your ex-husband as a fellow war veteran."

"And he's still on the bench?" Melissa shrieked.

Stephanie nodded shamefully. "What can I say? Judicial ethics commissions are weak."

"Can we sue for misconduct?"

"Very difficult to prove. And the state's attorney general would represent him if a lawsuit went to trial." Stephanie sighed deeply, fixing a stern but supportive gaze on her client. "It's terribly unfair, Melissa, but the truth is, federal courts have ruled almost exclusively that family issues belong in the lower state courts. There's little recourse."

Melissa Alexander seemed to fade rapidly before Stephanie's eyes. Finally, she swallowed hard and whispered, "I'm afraid," sounding old, pathetic, and powerless. It was heartbreaking.

Moments like these confirmed to Stephanie that her decision to practice family law had been the right one. The outcomes weren't always easy to take, but at least she was helping a class of people who needed her. And more importantly, she wasn't screwing them over with bogus billings. Wasn't the system corrupt enough? Political webs. Inbred lawyers and judges. Conflicts of interest. How obscene it all was. And the Lawrence Gibbs/Chuck Berg brigade was a Central Casting example of the worst of the lot. A shiver of revulsion swept through her as the bitter song of irony played inside her head: The people who provoked her thoughts about leaving the profession were the same people who'd provoked her thoughts toward entering it.

"You'll live through this," Stephanie said. "Please believe that."

"Look at me!" Melissa exploded hotly, rising from her seat. "I'm old. Men stopped making passes at me years ago. I take a nap in the middle of the day. I need plenty of notice before taking a trip. I can't start over!"

Stephanie clapped gleefully and shot up from her chair to celebrate the breakthrough in the making. "This is great!"

Melissa returned a look of utter shock.

"You're *angry,*" Stephanie explained with almost giddy exuberance. "That's a positive emotion. What purpose does fear serve a woman? You're old. Big deal! Older is what you *get,* so move on."

Melissa's face became a portrait of affront.

Though fully aware that this was tough talk—coming from a thirty-three-year-old, no less—Stephanie pressed on. "Get mad, Melissa. Get as ferociously mad as a junkyard dog! Living well is the best revenge, so promise yourself that you'll do *whatever* it takes to live like a queen, even if it's in a one bedroom apartment. Go out and screw a younger man. Or stay at home and enjoy your own company. Just don't let that son of a bitch make you miserable for one more second!"

What began as a tentative giggle from Melissa soon rolled into a reluctant cackle, then erupted to wild bursts of whooping laughter.

Stephanie joined in. She couldn't help it, the sound alone being so infectious. For such a long time Melissa Alexander had been silent, terrified, filled with self-doubt, and desperate for reconciliation with the husband who betrayed her. Maybe a good laugh would work miracles.

Melissa made a sudden grab for the phone and dialed at super speed, her face flushed with pink and glowing with animation, her eyes alight with a sinister mischief. "David? It's Melissa. You're a lowlife cocksucker, and I've always hated your mother. She's a stupid cunt!" The receiver hit the cradle with a bang as Melissa howled.

Stephanie collapsed into side-splitting laughter.

Matt knocked once and pushed open the door, surveying the scene with puzzled amusement. "Sounds like a slumber party in here. Should I order a pizza and dig out the yearbooks?"

Melissa looked at Matt, then back at Stephanie. Her eyebrows curved suggestively. "Hey, is he free tonight?" she cracked before starting in with more uproarious laughter.

Stephanie broke up, too, begging Melissa to stop between guffaws.

Matt shrugged, rolled his eyes, and left them alone to their silliness.

Stephanie could not believe Melissa's quicksilver transformation—dispirited one moment, brimming with vitality the next. A sharp, determined look was back in her eyes.

"No more crank calls," Stephanie scolded playfully. "They'll be traced to this office."

Melissa drew several sobering breaths to calm herself. "Oh, Stephanie, that felt so *good!* I should've let myself get pissed off a long time ago. I'm not protecting him anymore!"

Stephanie stopped short of congratulations.

Melissa's odd statement gave rise to a burning question. "What do you mean?"

Melissa fished an envelope out of her purse and plopped it onto Stephanie's desk. "I found these buried in my jewelry box. I'd forgotten about them. Open at your own risk."

At first, Stephanie hesitated, but then curiosity arrowed straight through to her fingertips. She ripped open the seal and out dropped a set of Polaroids. The sight caught her off guard. "Oh, shit," she muttered.

David Alexander in a black lace teddy. David Alexander in a bra and panties set, bright red lipstick smeared across his fleshy lips. David Alexander on all fours with a cucumber rammed up his ass.

Stephanie locked eyes with Melissa. "Does he know you have these?"

"He probably forgot about them, too. This is how that pervert gets his kicks. Watching pornos. Dressing up. Penetration by vegetables. He begged me to do these things with him. I tried at first because I wanted to please him, but I just couldn't do it. I felt so creepy."

Stephanie shuddered and returned the photographs to the envelope. "I take it your ex-husband and Marv Albert are summer sisters." She leaned against her expansive marble desk. "What do you plan to do with these?"

"Make copies for every Alexander construction site in the city *and* put them on the Internet," Melissa said flatly.

Stephanie suppressed a titter. No doubt the bastard deserved the embarrassment, but these snapshots had more lucrative possibilities. "Let me keep them for a few days."

Melissa appeared crestfallen. She obviously

wanted to lash out and draw blood sooner rather than later. "Why?"

Stephanie brought a forefinger to her lips; her eyes narrowed as the plot took shape in her mind. "We didn't get a fair settlement in Judge Gibbs's court, so let's appeal that decision to a higher court of our own creation—Hell hath no fury—"

"Like a woman scorned," Melissa finished sweetly.

"Justice is on the way," Stephanie trilled.

Once Melissa left the office, Stephanie focused on the paperwork stacked atop her desk. Her body buzzed with good vibrations. Chuck Berg and David Alexander had been so smug about their victory. Typical for that stripe of worm. But now the pigs were going to get it—a hard knee to the tender groin by way of the fat wallet. Yes!

Her private line jangled. Only four people had the number—Peter, Tuesday, Monty, and Lisa. She picked up on the first ring. "Talk to me."

"Can you meet for lunch at the Empire Cafe?" Lisa asked. "I have news."

Stephanie leaned back, taking note of the oppressive paper pile. Lunch today was out of the question. Hell, so was lunch for the next month. "Rain check. I'm swamped."

"Rats," Lisa hissed.

"Give me the postcard version."

"I'm going out with Tyson Moore."

Stephanie whistled. "Ooh. What a gene pool that'll make."

"You're telling me. He's prettier than I am."

Stephanie made a mental note to quiz Monty for the scoop on Tyson. Lisa's track record with men ran parallel to her track record with all things financial—straight into the toilet. In fact, only a year ago Stephanie had ushered her through the legal minefields of personal bankruptcy. Lisa Randall was a chocolate-drop beauty who lived in the moment. *Saving* was a foreign term, and *charge it* rolled off her tongue as easily as *hello*. Deadbeat boyfriends had taken advantage of her extravagant generosity, and in some cases, helped themselves to their own indulgences—on her magnetic-striped nickel. Despite her foibles, Stephanie treasured Lisa's friendship. The sassy copywriter was fiercely loyal—a rare quality these days.

"I wanted to check on you, too. Are you okay?" Lisa was saying, passively making reference to Stephanie's on-air meltdown with Tyson Moore.

"I'm fine," Stephanie assured her. "Just busy with some complicated cases."

"If you need to talk, I'm here," Lisa said, her voice somber, almost full of disappointment. Sitting quietly on the outside of a secret wasn't the Lisa Randall way.

Stephanie took in a breath. She and Lisa had never discussed that horrible night, but Lisa was a Houston native and certainly privy to press accounts. That it happened in River Oaks and involved a mother, daughter, and shady young man about town had given the incident more caché than most Houston homicides. Even the house itself had become a part of local folklore. "You're aware that twenty years ago a man died in my mother's bedroom, right?"

"Sure, but that's ancient history."

"It should be. Anyway, his name was Jimmy Scott, and that's the same name the caller used."

"Houston's a big city, Scott's a common name, and Jimmy's not so special, either," Lisa challenged, trying to bring Stephanie out of the darkness.

"Point taken. But how many of these Jimmy Scotts would say 'Remember September,' which is the month he died? Add to that an anonymous letter sent to my home and a phone call here at the office."

"This is freaking me out!" Lisa exclaimed, her words wrapped up in horror.

"I'm praying it's just a prank, Lisa. That it'll all go away. I'm not trying to shut you out. It's just that talking about it is too frightening and brings up a lot of toxic history I'd rather not delve into."

Lisa paused a few beats before asking, "Is there any word on Bruce Simon?"

The mere mention hastened Stephanie's pulse. "Not so far."

"Do you think . . . it could be him?" Lisa ventured cautiously.

"Let me put it this way—Ginger was murdered the same day these messages started, and that's not a coincidence I'm comfortable with."

Matt burst into the room, a look of red alert plastered across his face. "You're not gonna like this," he said gravely.

Stephanie's fingers tightened around the receiver. The cease-fire of bad news must be over. Matt wasn't one to overreact. "Lisa, I'll call you back," she muttered quickly, hanging up. She stared at Matt expectantly.

"Rob Dean has petitioned for full custody."

Stephanie's body stiffened. Chuck Berg had made good on his threat. A flash of anger ignited a fire in her stomach. Rob Dean was a binge drinker and wife beater. To fight for custody of a two-year-old boy was unconscionable. "Berg told me this was coming, but I thought he was bluffing."

"It gets worse," Matt said, his voice unemotional,

level in the way that terrible news is often delivered. He swallowed hard before dropping the bombshell. "The case has been assigned to Judge Gibbs."

Stephanie could only blink in open-mouthed disbelief as a sick feeling rose up within her. Josie and Jason Dean had walked through the fires of domestic hell. They didn't deserve this. No one did. The possibility of Josie losing her son to that brute chilled Stephanie to the bone.

A frightening pattern of mothers losing custody to abusive husbands was happening all over the country. Many judges blamed women for not meeting their husbands' desires, intimating that they brought the abuse on themselves. There were judges who believed that women fabricated stories of abuse only to hurt the husband. And some judges simply accepted the testimony of the husband over the wife as an act of male solidarity.

Stephanie stood up and grabbed her purse. "I'm going to see Josie."

"What can I do to help?" Matt asked.

"Research every case you can find that awarded custody to the father. And get me everything you can on judicial gender bias. As frightening as it sounds, I want to know how that old bastard thinks."

"Consider it done."

"I'll check in later," Stephanie said on her way out the door. Visions of Josie and sweet, adorable Jason haunted her as the elevator dropped. Who knew how much emotional damage the boy had already sustained by being forced to witness such sadistic violence against his mother? She knew the consequences of Chuck Berg's strategy were potentially devastating. If Josie lost Jason . . . no! Stephanie refused to consider that outcome—even hypothetically. She would win. No matter what she had to do.

Her body traveled through the parking garage on autopilot as her mind raced through the witnesses who might be critical to the case. The housekeeper. The doctors and nurses from Josie's two emergency room visits. Extended family—Josie's mother, particularly. The clicking of her heels on the garage floor created a reverberating echo, and with each step she tried to pinpoint an advocate who would strengthen the case for Josie.

Suddenly she picked up on a sound and stopped abruptly. In the immediate quiet that followed her halt, she heard two heels clack on the ground . . . then nothing. The footsteps were heavy—a man's. Stephanie held her breath, listening. Was that a shuffle? Furtively, she circled the area, her gaze wild. A car door slammed; a European engine purred to life; she released an extended sigh of relief. The explanation was simple: Someone had been walking to their vehicle, just like her.

"Ste . . . pha . . . nie." The voice rushed forward in a sinister hush. It seemed to come from everywhere.

Deep on the opposite end, a Lexus backed out of a space and coasted toward the exit. Panic swept over her as the realization hit: Those footsteps didn't belong to that driver. No chance in hell. What she heard a moment ago had been too close to be so far away now.

"Is anybody there?" Stephanie called out defiantly.

Silence.

Where was security? Probably slumped in a booth scratching out a crossword puzzle, she thought bitterly. One thing was certain: If anything happened, rent-a-cop would never get to her in time. She was on her own. Her body trembled slightly, and then she tensed, her molars grinding, her nostrils twitching with readiness.

"Ste . . . pha . . . nie." He was closer.

She felt her face turn ashen, and her stomach convulse. Could he hear her banging heart? Did he know how scared she was? Up ahead her black Mercedes gleamed, its location precarious—a van on one side, a cement column on the other. *Eyewitness News* reports played back in her mind. Predators hid under cars to grab ankles; attackers flung open van doors to pull victims inside.

Safety was out in the open. She was no fool. To sneak up on her would be impossible. That's right. She'd see the bastard coming. Even better, she'd be ready for his ass. Stealthily, she unzipped her bag and slipped a hand inside, keeping eyes peeled in all directions as her probing fingers wrapped themselves around the pepper spray.

It wasn't enough, not for the fear cocooning her. Forget gun control—right now she wanted a piece that shot more than chemicals. After all, Mace delayed; bullets killed. And this girl needed something she could count on.

"Gotcha!"

She spun quickly, both hands up, knees slightly bent, forefinger on the pump.

Chuck Berg stood there, leaning against the stairwell door, his lips curved in a satisfied smirk.

Stephanie stared back at him with hate-filled eyes. She felt a wave of relief and a blinding anger—all at the same time. Goddamn him! "You think that's funny?" Her shout boomeranged in the cavernous place.

He shrugged and snarled, "It's like sex. I enjoyed it. What else matters?"

"You're a lucky son of a bitch. If I carried a gun, you'd have a lot in common with Larry Flynt right now, and I'm not talking about the fact that you're both disgusting."

"Guess I'm blessed." Chuck snorted laconically.

She tucked the tear gas back into her purse and started for the car. "That's one interpretation."

He fell into step beside her, the soles of his Rockports mute against her clicking Joan & David heels. "Rob wants some time alone with Jason."

Stephanie laughed humorlessly. "Pauly Shore wants a career. That doesn't mean it'll happen."

Chuck stopped.

Stephanie walked on.

"Josie fucked around. That's why he beat her—she had it coming."

She turned back on him with fury. "You're a liar!"

His tongue snaked across his lips. "Yeah, but this is civil court. Everyone lies, and everyone knows it. Besides, Judge Gibbs will eat it up."

"And the old fart will choke on it before I allow Jason to be handed over to that monster."

"That sounds kind of personal. What's wrong? Does Rob remind you of somebody?" His tone was teasing. "I saw you on TV the other day," Chuck said, walking slowly toward her, "and that second caller really did a number on you, didn't he?"

Stephanie backed away.

Chuck moved forward, menace in every step. "What was his name?" he asked rhetorically, feigning memory loss. "Oh, yeah . . . *Jimmy* . . . *Jimmy Scott!*"

She froze but kept looking at him to see what he

knew; his eyes betrayed nothing. Was Chuck Berg her tormentor? Or just another asshole? Unwilling to wait for the answer, Stephanie proceeded to her car wordlessly, and despite her own place in the profession she felt instant fondness for the phrase, KILL ALL THE LAWYERS.

Suddenly Melissa's trump card sprang into mind. "Oh," she began casually, reveling in the chance to take the offensive, "I need a meeting with you and David Alexander. *ASAP.*"

"The settlement offer was revoked. Case closed."

Stephanie slid into the front seat, turned the key over, and zipped down the window. "Consider it reopened."

"Not a problem," he said cockily.

She backed out and turned the wheels sharply, aiming straight for him.

He called her bluff until the final second, at which point his eyes went wide, his veins popped up on his forehead, and his six-foot-three frame hopped out of the way like a Mexican jumping bean. "That bitch isn't getting a dime!"

It was Stephanie's turn to laugh. "Don't count on it." She punctuated her revolt with a deafening screech of the tires and a take-off worthy of a rocket. Tracking the heartless scumbag's fading figure in her rearview mirror, she smiled. The smaller he got, the better she felt.

Then, like a bolt from the blue it dawned on her . . . Chuck Berg's shoes, his soft-soled Rockports, were quiet. The man stalking her in the garage had clunked around on hard heels!

Suddenly a large figure loomed into view, and her heart took a leap. As if in slow motion, she saw the face. Shock coursed through her. Those dark eyes.

That hard, granite-like face. From mug shots. On television. It was Bruce Simon.

911. Her right hand made a dive for the cellular. She glanced away to punch in the number, then turned back. He **was** gone.

The *Texas Today* editor offices or so forth
were as inauspicious as the magazine spell. One
look, and Abby McQueen knew the place. Space was
leased, supplies were recycled, and assistants didn't
exist, with the exception of the occasional clueless
intern. In short, nothing had changed. After twenty
years, the same movie played, only the cast was different—one more cluster of eager upstarts and
doomed-to-obscurity washouts.

Abby followed Francisco through the mini-maze
of occupied cubicles. Most staffers offered no more
than a disinterested glance, but some threw hostile
looks her way. They knew who she was. The bitch
waltzing in to get the cover byline that eluded them.
The has-been earning for one lousy article what
amounted to twenty five percent of their annual
salaries. If she were in their shoes, she would be
pissed off, too, Abby thought. But she wasn't. So
tough shit.

Francisco ushered her into his inner sanctum, a
small, windowless room tucked away in the back.
Framed *Texas Today* covers adorned the walls, along
with his diploma from Brown and a Selena poster.
Two mugs—one Garfield, the other an obvious free-
bie from Temp Staff Solutions—sat atop his desk,

_____ngly,
_____ a chair as he
_____ a seat."

_____into the vinyl cushion. Damn Jeff
_____owenstein! What kind of career guidance had that
silver-spooned Jewish brat provided? She'd gone
from glorious mountain peak to seedy gravel pit in
the time it takes a drunk fraternity boy to make love.
"I'll need a researcher and a secretary," she said
tightly, pushing her luck and crossing her legs in the
same moment.

Francisco laughed.

Abby bristled. "That wasn't an opening joke."

"Which makes it even funnier," he pointed out.
"Writers here do their own research. And the idea
of a secretary is a fantasy—right up there with winning the lottery."

"What about a car?"

He snickered. "Your Jaguar is waiting out front."

"Cut the diva crap. I'm not having a star trip
here. These things are *basic.*"

Francisco sighed wearily. "This is a bare bones
operation, Abby. You know that. We get our own
coffee, make our own copies, and type our own stories."

"Well," she scoffed, "I'm serious about a car."

Francisco gave her a diffident shrug. "So rent
one."

A feeling of powerlessness crept up on her, and
when the realization hit, it stung like a wasp. Since
leaving for college at seventeen, Abby McQueen had
never needed a goddamn thing from anyone. And
now, at forty-five, even the resources to do business
at Hertz were beyond her reach. Jesus Christ, with
no credit cards and no current driver's license, she

couldn't rent a little red wagon. "I've been in New York for such a long time," she began casually, "so I don't have a valid license."

He pulled open his top desk drawer and grabbed a set of keys hooked to a GOD BLESS TEXAS ring. "Ford Escort. Take it or leave it."

Part of her wanted to leave it.

Francisco jangled the keys.

Abby's sensible side won out, and she reached forward.

He pulled back. "Any damage comes out of your final check."

She stood up and snatched them from his hand. "Speaking of checks, where's my advance?"

"You'll have it in the morning."

Balls! How would she eat *tonight*? "What about my per diem? Jeff promised me sixty bucks a day."

"Save your receipts. We'll reimburse you."

Abby shuddered involuntarily, cursing herself for the state she was in. "I'm strapped," she murmured reluctantly. "I need cash now."

Francisco seemed to be regarding her in a whole new light as he nodded with sickening patronization and said, "I didn't know things were that bad for you. Let me see what I can do."

She blinked back a tear of humiliation. Money— everything arrowed down to that one green detail. Power. Mobility. Self-respect. Options. Love was nowhere in the mix. *Fuck romance*, Abby thought. If a genie appeared and asked her to choose between George Clooney and a one hundred dollar bill, right now she would take the cash.

"How about dinner tonight?" Francisco asked. "My treat."

Abby groaned inwardly. Pretty soon he'd be passing a tin cup around the office on her behalf. "That's not necessary."

"Come on. You have to eat. And this saves me from another night of frozen pizza." He smiled.

Against her will, Abby felt a carnal stirring. This man's face was a billboard for lust, with Little Boy Lost dark eyes, slightly sucked-in cheeks, and a wide, sensual mouth. All the antagonism had built up a sizzling charge between them. Did he feel it, too? Or was she just jet-lagged, broke, and desperate for the first available distraction? She locked onto his gaze. "It's . . . nice of you to ask." Gratitude didn't come easy.

Francisco drew in a deep breath. "Good. We'll call a truce and talk about this anniversary piece."

"Any chance you have the original issue close by? I don't have a copy."

"That's ridiculous!" he erupted in a tone far less placid. "You should have greater regard for your work."

"That was twenty years ago!" Abby protested. "You should have greater regard for progress."

Fiercely, Francisco shook his head.

Incorrigible bastard, Abby steamed. She made a mental note to fill up on appetizers tonight. Making it through dinner looked to be a long shot. "You sound like the kind of guy who keeps his old freshman composition essays," she chortled.

A slight blush splashed onto Francisco's cheeks. He tried to slope his shoulders insouciantly, but the damage was done.

Abby knew she had scored a direct hit. In fact, Francisco Juarez appeared to be so exposed that she felt certain the essays in question were somewhere in the room. She holstered the urge to take the ridicule further, and left it alone.

Was this *fondness* that she felt so suddenly? She did like his rich, chocolate cream voice, his ability to hold his own in verbal warfare, and the importance he placed upon work. But as quickly as these thoughts sprang to mind, Abby banished them. *Discipline.* That was her mantra from this moment forward. She was in Houston for one reason only: To turn this chump change gig into a million dollar opportunity—no matter what the cost.

From a wire basket on his desk, Francisco retrieved the October, 1977 issue of *Texas Today* and laid it in front of her. "Consider it yours. And take proper care of it," he cautioned.

A tearful Stephanie Cain, with a maturity belying her thirteen years, stared back from the cover. Abby had forgotten how beautiful the girl was. Now she couldn't wait to delve into the past that held the key to a more comfortable future. "Where am I staying? I'd like to shower and rest before dinner."

"We put you up at the Marriott—West Loop, in the Galleria area."

Abby pulled a face. "It's not the Ritz-Carlton, but who's complaining?"

Francisco grinned. "You are." He rose up from his chair, raised a forefinger, lifted three twenty dollar bills from a well-worn brown leather wallet, folded them in half, and pressed them into her hand.

His touch was warm, and on a deep level it seemed to reach her. *A nice man.* Did such a creature exist? Apparently so. Too bad he didn't meet the prerequisites. Too bad he couldn't do anything else for her. Too bad the money he just handed over gave her the freedom she needed to stand him up for dinner tonight.

* * *

The Ford Escort's engine could muster up all the power of a lawn mower. With a map strewn across the steering wheel, a marginally frustrated Abby managed to navigate her way to the hotel. Once there, it dawned on her how life had been reduced to one nauseatingly pedestrian acceptance after another. Grateful for a car that runs. Thankful for a safe and clean place to sleep. Relieved that she'd pocketed the cash to buy a hot meal. Still, no matter the meager circumstances, an almost breathless anticipation buoyed her spirits.

Abby's body tingled with nervous energy, a breathless anxiousness to rediscover the scandalous scribbling that had catapulted her to the bigger and the better: Stints at *The New York Post* and *People;* a contributing editor position at *Fascination*—a sub grade *Vanity Fair* but a slick, glossy monthly all the same; finally, cut-and-paste biographies of Madonna, Tom Selleck, and Don Johnson, which, admittedly, revealed nothing new, but did strategically place her on the outer edge of celebrity publishing.

Abby started a hot bath, pouring in the hotel's trial size shampoo to generate some suds. What she needed now was to conjure up the relentless determination which had been her motor of purpose on the infamous Stallone hatchet job. For that opus, digging through garbage, betraying confidences, and good, old-fashioned double-crossings had been the ho hum order of the day.

She stripped, taking great care to hang the vintage Valentino number on one of the padded hangers she'd brought along. Pushing back her shoulder-length hair with a headband, Abby eased into the scalding bath, sank down amidst the frothy bubbles, flipped open the two decades old *Texas Today,* and stepped back in time.

LOVE AND SEX AND MURDER IN RIVER OAKS
BY ABBY MCQUEEN

Until a month ago, Stephanie Cain was like most thirteen-year-old girls her age. She listened to the records of pop idol Andy Gibb, fell into dreamy sleep under a John Travolta poster, and failed to appreciate all the intense mourning over the recent death of bloated superstar Elvis Presley. Stephanie parted ways with other teenagers on September 17, when she killed her mother's lover with a kitchen knife, penetrating his liver, portal vein, and aorta in one murderous gash.

The seeds of this tragedy were planted seven years ago. Paper magnate Oscar Cain's hardworking, hard drinking, chain-smoking habits had taxed his heart and pushed him to an early grave at fifty-eight, leaving behind a wife twenty years younger, Marilyn, a six-year-old daughter, Stephanie, and a newborn son, Montgomery. Single motherhood suited the widow, who, unlike her dead husband, had a lot of living to do.

First, she promptly unloaded the family business on a conglomerate for a cool eight million. Next, she started up with a string of young admirers. It should be no surprise that an aging broad with money in the bank and no husband to worry about is lucious game for young and studly hunters. Either by choice or by folly, Marilyn Cain fell prey to many a man's sweet little lies. But these Joes, typically lacking education and hindered—or perhaps blessed—with the attention spans of toddlers, were harmless, fly-by-night gigolos, in it simply for the easy sex and free vacations, plus the token gifts of clothing and jewelry Marilyn tossed their way.

One such subject, Chip Waltman, a self-described

*model and actor (with no body of work to back up
the claim), picked erotic fruit from the Marilyn tree
only days after Oscar's funeral. "She bought me a
cashmere coat and gave me an old Rolex her husband used to wear," he remembers innocently.*

*Jimmy Scott was not so benign. Even at twenty-
three, this ex-marine wanted more than hot women,
designer duds, and a flashy watch. His pipe dream
was to become a gambling kingpin. Dark, brooding,
and slightly dangerous, he was just the type that
Marilyn went ape over. They met poolside at the
River Oaks Country Club. Marilyn is, of course, a
member. Jimmy was there as socialite Toni Raffin's
guest. With her children watching, Marilyn bonded
with him over frozen piña coladas, then boldly left
with the guy, promising the kids she would dispatch
their nanny to pick them up.*

*"It never bothered me that Marilyn stole him right
in front of my eyes," Toni Raffin recalls with no
trace of bitterness. "She actually did me a favor.
Jimmy was very domineering and always needed
money to pay off gambling debts. In all honesty, I
worried about the children. They were so young and
impressionable, and he was so disgusting."*

*Marilyn's River Oaks neighbors, aghast when
Jimmy Scott took up residence in Cain's palatial
home on Inwood Drive, considered the act a hostile
invasion to the exclusive enclave. They witnessed ex-
plosive arguments, after which Marilyn paraded
around in scarves and large sunglasses. The children's longtime nanny quit, young Montgomery
grew increasingly fearful, and Stephanie began to
assume parental duties for her brother, eschewing social outings with friends. All signs pointed to a family in crisis, but Marilyn refused pleas to let go of
her young paramour. "He's a champ in the bed-*

room," she confided to a friend, "and it's worth all the pain to have him in my arms."

Late Saturday night, September 17, he died there. The evening began like any other. Marilyn, Stephanie, and Montgomery ate dinner together, watched television, and prepared for bed. Jimmy was hours late and, as was his custom, had failed to call. When he finally showed up, intoxicated, Marilyn was already hot with anger. Minutes into their row, Jimmy threatened to cut her face.

Stephanie took the man at his word, and according to police reports, secured her brother in his favorite hiding place under the stairs before taking an eight inch knife from the kitchen and racing back to her mother's bedroom. Stephanie recalled hearing her mother's crying grow more and more hysterical as she ascended the stairs. "I thought he was killing her," she told authorities, "so I stuck him with the knife." The autopsy confirmed that death came in a matter of minutes.

The body was still on the bedroom floor when attorney Billy Hudson first mentioned "justifiable homicide." His reasoning went unchallenged through a coroner's inquest and a juvenile court hearing, at which point the judge admonished Marilyn Cain for parental negligence but nevertheless released Stephanie back into her custody.

Today, Marilyn, Stephanie, and Montgomery are battle-scarred veterans of this war within a family. It continues to rage on. The family of Jimmy Scott has filed a million dollar wrongful death lawsuit against the Cains, alleging that Scott was killed while sleeping peacefully. Lawrence Gibbs, attorney for the Scotts, maintains that Marilyn Cain "failed to exercise adequate guidance, proper control, or sufficient supervision over Stephanie."

> *Billy Hudson calls the suit "ludicrous" and "a pathetic attempt at extortion."*

Abby stopped reading and tossed the magazine onto the tiled floor. Oh, how young and stupid she had been! To trust police reports! To be swayed by a lawyer's passion for payment sell-out! She couldn't endure another word of that naive rubbish!

It was bullshit.

All of it.

Her gut told her so.

Eight

Penelope's House existed somewhat anonymously in the Shepherd area, upstaged by a busy mix of bookstores, trendy restaurants, art boutiques, and specialty shops. Inside the Martha Stewart inspired two-story home, battered women and emotionally damaged children were hard at work, attempting to put the broken pieces of their lives back together.

Stephanie arrived there as if in a whirlwind, still reeling from her encounter with Chuck Berg, still tormented by the Bruce Simon sighting. Was her mind playing tricks? The vision of him had seemed so incredibly real, then just as suddenly . . . a vanishing act. Perhaps it was her imagination in overdrive. Only last night she had heard her mother say "He's alive," and for a fleeting, insane moment, believed her to be speaking of Jimmy Scott. What was happening to her could only be expected. Too much anxiety too soon. She drew in a calming breath, praying for equilibrium. All she needed was a quiet evening at home with Peter. That would return her to form.

Toni Raffin, the shelter's principal donor and a regular volunteer, greeted Stephanie at the door. "I'm so glad you're here. Josie's a wreck," Toni whispered.

"Where is she?"

"Out back with Jason."

Toni guided her through the cozy living area, where five women shared the couch in front of a large screen television tuned to *Days of Our Lives.* They sat forward expectantly, lost in stories as tragic as their own. Across from them on an overstuffed chair, a fat calico cat stretched languorously. The pleasant scent of mulberry—from fragrance candles and bowls of potpourri—blew strong in the air. Stephanie smiled forlornly. What a crime against humanity that they couldn't find this tranquillity in their own homes.

"I just made a pot of tea. Care for a cup?" Toni was saying.

"That would be nice," Stephanie whispered, not wanting to disturb the women as she followed the socialite-turned-activist into the kitchen.

Toni poured from an antique silver service. "This is just legal posturing, right? Who could seriously entertain the idea of that man getting custody?"

Stephanie gazed out the picture window to see two-year-old Jason, his face a mask of pure joy as he chased after an energetic Alpine white puppy. Josie watched over him, smiling with sad eyes.

"His first dog," Toni remarked wistfully as she offered up a beautiful antique cup and saucer blossoming with an intricate yellow rose design. "She brought it to him yesterday, and he hasn't stopped talking about it for a minute. Sugar?"

"This is fine," Stephanie declined, taking a small sip. She preferred her coffee and tea straight, unlike Peter, who transformed his into a hot ice cream cone with mounds of sugar and milk. "Josie's face seems to be healing nicely."

Toni managed a tight, half smile. "For the most

part. There'll be some permanent scarring. His signet ring left a nasty mark on her cheek."

Stephanie cast her eyes downward and allowed a beat to pass. "I admire your work here, Toni. It's inspiring."

While her peers dedicated their considerable time and philanthropy to become high priestesses of the arts, Toni Raffin chose a decidedly less glamorous path. It seemed incongruous that this Waspy blue blood, pushing sixty with dark, flashing eyes, refined bone structure, and a Twiggy-like figure, would immerse herself in a cause so . . . ugly. When Toni entered a room, she commanded attention. The hair was always perfect, the makeup flawless, and the clothing crisp, stylish, and unquestionably appropriate.

That she had once cavorted with Jimmy Scott—however briefly—was impossible for Stephanie to fathom. But because of that union, Marilyn Cain, already filled with a malignant envy over Toni's unpurchasable substance, swore the woman an enemy for life and shunned friendship overtures before and after the murder. Stephanie recalled how she had often daydreamed for hours, imagining a happier life . . . with Toni Raffin as her mother.

"You haven't answered my question," Toni said archly. "Will the court actually consider a wife beater as a custodial parent?"

Stephanie's heavy sigh was caught somewhere between fatigue and dread. "I wish I could tell you that it's never happened. I can't. I wish I could tell you that a father has to do more than just make dinner a few nights a week and hire a killer lawyer to be looked upon favorably in a custody battle. I can't do that, either. Here's the truth of it—we're in for a fight."

Toni's eyes blazed with anger. "That boy will be ruined! He's already acting out aggressively toward other children—just like his father!"

"I hope you're willing to testify to that," Stephanie said softly.

Toni's lips fell into a firm, determined line. "Damn straight."

Stephanie smiled and set down her saucer. "Thanks for the tea." She stepped outside to join Josie and Jason.

"Dog! My dog! Dog!" the boy chirped, clutching the squirming, furry creature close to his heart.

"And who's this?" Stephanie asked lightly.

Josie struggled to pull off a faint grin. "We haven't named him yet. He's a little bichon frise—seven weeks old," she said distantly.

"How about Lucky?" Stephanie suggested.

Josie stiffened. "Is that what I need to be to keep my son?"

Stephanie's heart ached for the woman before her. Josie Dean was barely thirty-years-old, a top radio sales executive for Houston's number one country station, and a strong, forthright personality, but a slap had turned to a punch, a shove against the wall to a push down the stairs, and sudden outbursts to planned beatings. Now she lived in fear, out of a suitcase, and away from family and friends. Her once brilliant aquamarine eyes were still rheumy from the last assault, and the bruises on her neck and arms had turned to a purple hue.

Stephanie decided to give it to her straight, no chaser. "I'm concerned about the judge assigned to our case, Josie. He's unpredictable, and you being the mother doesn't necessarily mean an automatic edge."

"But Rob is unfit! He's violent, and he drinks, and—"

"He's going to accuse you of infidelity," Stephanie broke in. "Among other things, I'm sure."

"What?" Josie asked incredulously.

"I heard this a short while ago from his attorney."

Josie covered her mouth.

Stephanie was troubled by the acute look of guilt and regret in Josie's eyes. "Is it true?" she ventured cautiously.

"Yes . . . I mean . . . no . . . I . . . I spent the night out—once. With a friend—a male friend. But nothing happened. I swear. I needed to talk, and that's all we did. *Talk*." Josie burst into tears. "He should be in jail for what he did to me," she cried softly, working hard to suppress her emotion for Jason's benefit, "and suddenly I'm the one on the defensive."

"It's okay," Stephanie murmured. "But get used to it. Rob hired a snake of a lawyer, and they're going to take this all the way. Dirty tricks are to be expected."

Josie's eyes got big; she opened her mouth to speak, but words failed her.

"You have to leave Penelope's House," Stephanie said flatly. "Rob isn't a threat to you anymore—at least not physically. He plays master of terror games, and right now that's using the legal system to win custody of Jason. He'll be on his best behavior until this plays out. I guarantee it."

Josie weighed her options. "We could go to my mother's," she put in.

Stephanie nodded. "Good idea. She has a nice home in Bellaire—great school district, safe neighborhood, three generations under the same roof. That's tough to beat."

Josie brightened.

"Stay strong. We're going to win."

"Even if we don't," Josie began, her voice tremulous, a flash of fear sweeping across her face, "I won't give up my son. I don't care what the judge says. I'll run away with Jason, and they'll never find us!"

Stephanie didn't doubt the veracity of Josie's threat. "It won't come to that."

"I wish he was dead," Josie whispered, shifting uncomfortably. "Have you ever wished that on a person?"

Stephanie hesitated. "Yes." The unforgettable image of a blood-drenched Jimmy Scott gasping for his last breath flickered in her mind. "I understand those feelings, Josie. Honestly, I do . . . but be careful what you wish for."

Lisa Randall wafted her spoon through Painted Desert, an artfully delicious mix of black bean soup and corn chowder, her favorite dish at Mesa Grill, a swank eatery in the heart of River Oaks. Across the table was Tyson Moore, body on display in a form-fitting mesh T-shirt and circulation threatening jeans. Where did the fabric end and the taut muscle begin? The drool-over-this attire testified to his youth. She didn't know how old he was, but if the slab of beef before her was a day over twenty-four, she was the Sugar Plum Fairy.

Tyson took a swig from his margarita, tongue flicking briefly across the rim to capture what remained of the rock salt.

He's a *boy*, Lisa thought miserably, coming to

terms with the fact that at thirty-one, she should be asking him if he had an older brother.

"You look beautiful tonight," Tyson said.

"Thank you," Lisa whispered demurely.

Tyson smiled and leaned in for emphasis when he said, "I'm twenty-four. Does it bother you that I'm younger?"

Lisa smiled back. A *perceptive* boy. Could a man be so gorgeous and read minds, too? "How much older do you think I am?" she shot back, boldly throwing herself under the ego guillotine.

Tyson studied her for a long moment.

Lisa braced for the reply, vowing that if any number ten or higher dropped from Tyson's overripe, marvelously thick lips, the Painted Desert would be thrown onto his lap in one big, soupy glop.

He opened his mouth to speak.

She sucked in a tiny breath.

"Five years, tops."

Lisa grinned, vanity secured. "Good answer. The actual figure is seven."

He shrugged. "So does it bother you?"

"You betcha." Lisa laughed, tossing her mane of shoulder-length hair that possessed the sheen of a panther as she fixed her emerald green eyes on him in the suggestively sly manner which belonged only to her. She called it raising the stakes. Stephanie called it asking for trouble. Monty called it, simply, cock-teasing. Tonight it was an exciting hybrid of all three.

"Hey, I'm cool with the boy toy thing if you are."

Lisa blanched, her mouth dropping open. *Boy toy?* Did he think she was some horny old woman?

Tyson chuckled. "I'm kidding." He reached out and put his hand over hers. "You can close your mouth now."

Lisa could feel her own body responding, an invisible chain of nerves connecting his touch to her pulse, every one of them singing out with heat and promise.

"What's a few years?" He dismissed the thought with a macho, backhanded gesture.

Lisa turned to her left. There was a hum at the next table, a steady buzz of local celebrity recognition.

"Is that really him?" someone whispered. The party of five craned their necks for a better look at the news anchor turned club kid. A few hours ago, he had soberly recited the city's murder stats on their Sony Trinitrons, but right now he was tequila-happy and a dead ringer for one of Janet Jackson's sculpted dancers.

Tyson lapped up the attention like a stray kitten does milk. His onyx eyes brightened, and he tossed over silent greetings in response. No doubt about it—naked ambition ruled his universe.

Lisa drank deep from the cup of regret. His stock had just taken a nosedive. When men like Tyson Moore gazed into a woman's eyes, it was only to see themselves. "A year ago I was stressed about turning thirty and kicking myself for all the mistakes I made in my twenties. Meanwhile, you were probably bumming notes for some humanities requirement that you needed to graduate." She shook her head. "This wasn't such a good idea. We're worlds apart."

Tyson raised his brow. "Age ain't nothing but a number. I've packed a lot of living into twenty-four years." He motioned for the waiter to double back with another round of margaritas.

"Are you trying to get me drunk?" Lisa accused lightly.

"Whatever it takes for you to give me half a chance here."

"Don't you think that's a very *college boy* thing to do?"

Tyson cocked his head to the side and bit down on his lower lip. "Hey, so what if I'm younger? I bet you've kicked it with a lot of brothers who weren't doing shit with their lives. At least I've got a future."

Lisa suddenly regarded him in a different light. The truth was, Tyson had scored a direct hit. Usually *she* chose the men in her life, and from high school on those choices had been incredibly bad ones. But Tyson Moore had picked her out. Maybe that was the magical difference. So what if he craved attention and loved himself to the nth degree? Better that than an insecure loser any day of the week.

The waiter rushed by and swooped down on their table with the second batch of margaritas. Lisa picked one up and sipped greedily. "Tell me, Tyson. Where did you come from?"

They ate heartily, shot back a third drink, and left feeling jazzed, tickled to discover that both of them were from California—Tyson born and raised in Oakland, Lisa an army brat with roots in Los Angeles. The trek back to her Yorktown Drive apartment was frustratingly short. As they navigated the three flights of stairs to her door, their pace slowed to a crawl as they savored the moment.

"Do you have an early call tomorrow?" Lisa murmured.

Tyson checked his Gucci watch and let out a guttural groan. "This is *way* past my bedtime, baby."

She leaned against her door. "Sorry. I've kept you out too late."

Tyson moved in closer. "It's been worth it. Besides, if things go right I'll be anchoring the evening news soon. Once that happens, late nights won't be a problem." He muttered the last sentence against her mouth, his breath coming fast.

Lisa fought against her own instincts. She wanted so desperately to kiss him, but his announcement had triggered a silent alarm: If he was heading for the evening anchor desk, then Monty must be leaving it. "What . . . about Montgomery Cain?" she managed to stammer before his lips made contact.

Tyson sighed, grazed her cheek with his mouth and nipped gently at her lobe before slipping his velvet tongue into her ear.

Lisa's knees buckled as an involuntary moan escaped her. This guy was good. This guy was *very* good.

"It's complicated," Tyson hushed, and then he kissed her, not too passionate, not too deep, not too long. Just right.

How perfect, Lisa marveled as he pulled back to meet her gaze.

"I'd better go," he said softly.

She wanted more and he knew it, yet he was strong enough to let the night end where it was. Lisa nodded. "Drive carefully."

"What are you doing tomorrow night?"

"Spending it with you."

He touched a finger to her lips and walked away.

Lisa stepped inside, swaying with the tide of desire, aware of the sweet agony of sudden want. Tyson Moore was special in a way that no other man had ever been. Buoyed by sheer giddiness, she started a bath, divested her little black Donna Karan dress, and fired up the stereo to play a Diana Krall CD, singing along with the smoky-voiced jazz stylist:

Pop me a cork, french me a fry
Crack me a nut, bring a bowl full of bonbons
Chill me some wine, keep standing by
Just entertain me, champagne me
Show me you love me, kid glove me
Best way to cheer me, cashmere me
I'm getting hungry, peel me a grape

The telephone cut short the impromptu concert. She hit the PAUSE button on the remote and snatched up the cordless. "Hello?"

"I miss you already." It was Tyson.

Lisa curled her toes and smiled.

"Check it out—I noticed a suspicious looking man hanging around the bottom of the stairs. I asked him what the problem was, and he shuffled off. Call security and let them in on it. I got a bad vibe from this cat."

Lisa's heart skipped a beat. She roamed the apartment, securing the front door, windows, and balcony, thinking of Stephanie and Bruce Simon's fugitive status as she worked. "Thanks, Super Fly. And don't worry—I'm locked in, safe and sound."

"Good," Tyson said. "Cuz I don't want anything to happen to you."

To linger over a family meal with Peter and Tuesday was the most peaceful activity Stephanie could have hoped for. Peter had prepared thick, juicy steaks and a medley of squash, carrots, and zucchini on the grill. With Stephanie's secret recipe for twice-baked potatoes and Tuesday's favorite ice cream added to the menu, it made for a delicious dinner and a soothing, almost therapeutic time together.

"Daddy, you know the Backstreet Boys?" Tuesday

was saying, finishing her dessert with a satisfied smack.

Stephanie turned to Peter. The confused look on his face told her that he didn't have a clue. She smiled, coming to his rescue with, "Sure, sweetheart. They're a singing group. We bought you their CD last week."

Peter chimed in as if well-versed on the subject. "Yeah, Tues."

Stephanie's smile broke even wider. Peter Hart knew the teen heartthrobs in that bubble gum pop quartet like he knew the scientific nuances of biophysics.

"Some of us at school are gonna form our own group. We're calling ourselves Back Alley Girls," Tuesday said.

Peter had timed his spoonful of ice cream most unfortunately. It shot down the wrong pipe as he choked on Tuesday's announcement. Stephanie tittered. "Are you okay?"

"I think so," Peter coughed, massaging his throat, his eyes laughing.

"Sweetheart," Stephanie began tactfully, "I think it's great that you're starting a group with your friends, but Back Alley Girls is not . . . an appropriate name for it."

"Why not?" Tuesday challenged.

"Yeah, why not?" Peter seconded.

Stephanie shot him a vengeful glare. "Well . . . Back Alley Girls . . . has a negative ring to it. It might make people think . . . that you're not nice, or that you get into a lot of trouble. You don't want that to happen, do you?"

"No," Tuesday said morosely, visibly crestfallen.

Stephanie pondered the situation a moment.

"How about Girls Next Door? That's a good name for your group!"

Tuesday's spirits soared instantly. "That's cool! Girls Next Door!" She sprang from her chair, a bottle rocket of energy ready to blow. "Can I go call Jackie?"

Stephanie threw a triumphant glance Peter's way. "What about your homework?"

"Done."

"Okay, but take your dishes to the sink, and don't stay on too long."

Tuesday stacked the dessert bowl onto the dinner plate, gathered up her silverware, carried the set to the counter, and gleefully scampered off.

"Hey, pops, thanks for nothing," Stephanie said, perching herself onto Peter's lap and resting her hands on his shoulders.

"You're brilliant under pressure," he said, kissing her lightly on the cheek. Peter's face turned serious. "You seem relaxed tonight."

Stephanie finger-combed his thick hair. "I am," she said softly. "It helps to have the best family in the world."

"I saw Monty today."

Stephanie hesitated. It would be improper to probe Peter for any information that Monty disclosed in session. Still, Peter *had* just opened the door. . . .

"I'm not sharing my notes with you."

Stephanie grabbed a lock of his hair and gave it a sharp tug. "I would never ask you to!"

Peter winced, smiling. "I'll tell you this—don't worry so much about your brother."

"I can't help it," Stephanie whispered, though Peter's tidbit would likely ease her mind.

"You haven't mentioned the visit to your mother last night."

"Still no change. It's as if she's not there. Of course, even when she *was* there, she wasn't," Stephanie said sadly.

Peter pulled her in for an embrace. "But you're a wonderful mother, Steph. You didn't become her, and I've seen so many children of emotionally abusive parents who do. I think you're amazing."

Stephanie closed her arms around him as tightly as strength allowed, not wishing to lose any part of the wonder that was Peter Hart. But the worry in her mind was hard at work once more as a heavy feeling of dread began to pass over her. It didn't matter that Peter made her feel safe, that Monty was on the road to happiness, and that she felt confident in the fact that Chuck Berg would lose big in both the Alexander and Dean cases. Something terrible was going to happen. And there wasn't a sinew of her body, a muscle, a nerve, that didn't feel that to be true.

Nine

Where to begin? *That* was the million dollar question. Abby stalked the Marriott lobby like a jungle cat on amphetamines. First order of business: Give cutie pie Cuban the slip.

"This is for Francisco Juarez. He'll be here soon to inquire about Abby McQueen." As she passed the thanks but no thanks note to the front desk clerk, the memory hit her. Who better to provide the city-wide lowdown than reliable gossip Jack McCrary?

She sized up the impeccably groomed Hispanic clerk, who was cherubically faced, not a day past nineteen, and giving off major bitch god vibrations. Abby's gaydar could sniff out even the most secretive closet case, so spotting the young lion before her was a simpleton's game.

"Ever heard of Jack McCrary?" she launched without preamble.

A ripple of recognition shadowed across his face before he could control the response. It was a dead giveaway. Her first shot had hit the bull's-eye.

"He's an old friend," Abby went on to explain. "I'm in town for a few days and want to catch up. I know that he used to tend bar at one of those clubs in the Montrose area."

"Sweet Rewards," the clerk confirmed.

"That's it," she sang.

"He's still there. We call him Uncle Jack."

"Thanks, kid. And make sure Mr. Juarez gets that message."

Montrose Boulevard connected the museum district to the south with the lower Westheimer area to the north. Between the two extremes was Houston's gay mecca—always fashionable, sometimes dangerous—a chic spot here, a seedy hole-in-the-wall there. Trapped somewhere in the middle was Sweet Rewards, a bar/dance club/theatre with staying power.

Abby entered through a small doorway and climbed the steep staircase, dressed for night moves in white lycra top, second-skin antique jeans, black boots, and Hermes shoulder bag.

"Ten bucks," the punk at the door demanded.

Shit! In these lean times, every dollar counted. No way was she pissing that much away. As she glanced around, a poster caught her eye. SUPERSTAR JOEY DANZA LIVE! SEE THE STAR OF *HARD ENOUGH* TAKE IT OFF IN THE FLESH! Underneath the lame copy, a nerve-jangling beauty of a hunk stared back, shirtless and hairless, his Calvin Klein briefs packing an impressive bulge.

"Look, I'm not here to drool buckets over the stripper, so screw the cover charge. Is Jack McCrary around?"

"He's at the bar," the doorman replied, annoyed.

An impatient line was forming behind her, but she didn't give a damn. "Tell him Abby McQueen's here."

He stepped aside, exasperated. "Tell him yourself."

Abby pushed past him, and suddenly her senses

were assaulted by the smell of sweat, smoke, semen, and overdone cologne. Throbbing house music impaired her hearing as she eyeballed the sepulchral dump. Everything about it screamed for emergency repair: The walls painted a bargain basement green; the gold tinsel curtains on the stamp-sized runway stage. Her vision adjusted to the multicolored rain of light pouring down on the sad looking dance floor, strobes bursting on the stormy sea of dancers as they swayed to the hard rhythm of the monotonous beat.

Behind the bar, Jack McCrary served a beer and a wink to a gym rat with biceps for brains. Twenty years had taken their toll. His hair was thin, his body soft, and the baggage under his eyes the compounded interest from too many years as a perpetual adolescent. Was he still toiling anonymously in middle management at the downtown bank? If he needed this scene for regular social stimulation, then the answer was pathetically obvious.

Abby squeezed past a Brando biker hopeful and approached the bar. "Who do I have to fuck in this place to get a martini?" she shouted above the music and planted both elbows on the counter.

Jack McCrary turned fast, beaming instantly. "Sorry. No takers here, honey. We only break a sweat for dicks."

She laughed.

He rushed over and embraced her across the counter. "Abby McQueen. What the hell are you doing in Houston?"

"A girl's gotta make a living."

"Shouldn't you be digging up dirt on Tom Cruise or Sharon Stone? By the way, I read your Stallone book. Classic dish."

She blew him an air kiss. "That market's so volatile right now, and to be perfectly honest, it bores me. I'm working on a major true crime story."

Jack nodded, motioned for the other bartender to take over, and mixed up one of his famous martinis. "Let's move on down," he suggested.

Abby slid to a seat on the far end, which placed her directly under a *Valley of the Dolls* movie poster. She took a deep swallow of Jack's signature poison, knowing that on an empty stomach the buzz would strike as fast as hard liquor to a teenage brain, but she needed it. For Abby McQueen to be ingratiating, heavy duty chemical assistance was required.

"It's so great to see you!" Jack enthused.

"Same here," Abby lied.

He raked her up and down with his gaze, then admonished her with a shaming look. "Honey, I remember the rest of you, but I sure don't remember those tits!"

Abby cackled and kicked back her drink. Most men wanted to touch her new breasts; this one wanted to wear them. She thrust her chest forward, thrilling him. "Stallone bought these."

Jack howled. "Honey, you are too much!"

Abby tossed glances around the bar, making a sour face. "How long have you been schlepping beers in this dive?"

"Twenty-two years," he said proudly. "It's like home to me. Plus, you know what a busybody I am. Tending bar is like having your own personal wire service, honey. Only it's news you can *really* use!"

Abby smiled, feeling no pain. "Which is exactly why I'm here. Remember the Cain murder scandal in River Oaks from nineteen seventy-seven?"

"Oh, yes!" Jack yelped, clapping with girlish excitement. "Miss Thing sliced and diced Mommie

Dearest's young and well-hung boyfriend. That kept me talking for years."

Abby felt her own eyes shining. "Any idea where the players are now?"

Jack whistled. "I know that the little boy is all grown up."

Abby thought back to her bathtub reading. Stephanie's younger brother. He was only six at the time of the murder. "Montgomery Cain," she said firmly.

Jack's head bobbed up and down. "He's a big news anchor for Channel Eleven. Billboards all over the city—the whole bit. And talk about a good-looking man. Honey, it's up periscope every time the news comes on!"

She leaned in, her body language talking conspiracy. "So tell me about his big sister."

Jack flicked his hand, dismissing the subject. "Oh, she's just some boring attorney. Hangs her own shingle. Champion for the battered woman. It's like a bad TV movie come to life. The brother is the one to write about. Hey, you might even catch him tonight. His boyfriend puts on a show about an hour from now."

Abby made a grab for Jack's sleeve, almost tearing it. "You don't mean the stripper?" she demanded, not believing her brilliant luck.

Jack smirked. "He prefers dancer."

She let go, rolling her eyes. "Oh, and I suppose *Hard Enough* is really a character study."

"Joey would like to think so," Jack snorted.

Fuzzy with martini oblivion, Abby's head swam for a moment, then cleared. The fact that opportunity was knocking triggered instant sobriety. "Is he a Texas boy?"

"No way. Joey's from the Mississippi Delta. He's

on a Houston Dallas San Antonio dance tour that won't quit. You know how it is. Bottoms need all the work they can get," Jack said derisively.

Abby's razor sharp mind went to work. Back in 1993 she had written an in-depth *Fascination* piece on the West Hollywood all male adult video scene. "Bottoms" were passive performers in anal sex, active ones in oral, and treated like stepchildren by the industry power brokers. The real stars were the "tops," those macho types who pumped asses for profit and commanded lesser mortals to their knees for cock worship. After all, work in films paid out pocket change, but sidelines like rubber dildos—actual castings of the actors' true talent—earned megabucks. That kind of product marketing eluded the second class bottoms, who relied on strip shows and hustling to shake the money tree.

"What's his story?" Abby asked, certain Jack McCrary would know it. His mission in life was learning anything and everything about sexy young men.

"Here are three sad facts—sexually molested by a Little League coach. Left home at sixteen. Never lived up to father's expectations." Jack's lips formed an exaggerated pout.

"Stop in the name of textbook cases," Abby trilled, holding up a hand Supremes style. "Paging Montel Williams!"

Jack scratched the air between them. "Meow!"

"Honestly, Jack, is Montgomery serious about this loser?"

The banker bartender predator shrugged. "Serious enough to play house." His brow bounced upward. "Joey just moved in."

Abby gave Joey Danza some super-powered thought. She was already certain of two things—the first, porn stars are suckers for fame; the second, a runaway's natural instinct in relationships is to cut out before caring too much. She quickly surmised that both character flaws could be used to her advantage. "I'd love to meet him."

Jack grinned. "I think that could be arranged. By the way, how long will you be in town? We should get together. You know, party!"

Abby speed-searched her brain for an easy out. She didn't have time for this tired old queen. Once Jack McCrary made the necessary introduction to Joey, his usefulness would expire. "Work comes first. *After* my deadline; we'll have a blast. I promise."

"I'll hold you to that. Follow me."

She trailed him—out of the bar area, across the dance floor, down the steps, into the theatre, and around to the back. What appeared to be a dressing room beckoned. "Will the *star* see us before the show?" she whispered.

"If he wants to collect his fee," Jack grunted under his breath, knocking once and turning the knob.

Joey Danza stood in front of a full-length mirror, admiring his reflection, naked save for a leather G-string.

Abby clicked to attention, checking out his steel sheet abdominals.

"What's the crowd like?" Joey asked, looking past her to coolly connect with Jack. Tension thickened the tiny space.

"Average. But it's still early," Jack said tersely.

"The publicity here sucks!" The exotic and erotic dancer's words sprayed about like spit.

"Joey already thinks he's *Mrs. Montgomery Cain,*" Jack hissed into Abby's ear.

She snickered at the remark.

"We did no less for you than we did for Gino Ramm, and he packed the house," Jack said impatiently.

"Just make sure my music's right," Joey grumbled. "Last night the asshole played the wrong tape. It messed up my choreography."

"I'll pass that concern along," Jack muttered. "Listen, this is Abby McQueen. She's a famous writer and wants to meet you. Don't ask me why."

Abby smiled, staying put as Jack ambled off wordlessly. She noted the duffel bag and cigarette carton on the bench, the Nestle Crunch wrappers littered around the room, and the sudden rapt attention Joey devoted to her once the words *famous writer* entered the dingy atmosphere. If ever there were a man desperate to make up for years' worth of deferred hopes and denied dreams, then that man was Joey Danza. Manipulating him would be a no-brainer. "I see there's no love lost between you and *Jack.*"

Joey's delicious looking mouth curled into a snarl. "He thinks I'm some free slut just because I did some pornos. Let him pay for it like all the other old-timers."

"Does Montgomery Cain pay for it?"

Joey shifted uncomfortably. "That's different." He reached for a white terrycloth robe and slipped it on. "You want to write about me?" It came out half question, half plea.

"Not exactly," Abby replied, softening the blow with a gentle tone. This guy was a tough case of intellectual poverty, a man who had learned much too early that sex could bring solace—and a source of income. He displayed all the obvious signs of major league dysfunction, everything but a stamp on his forehead that read MADE IN A FUCKED UP CHILDHOOD.

"Why'd you want to meet me?"

"I saw you in *Hard Enough.*" Abby lied.

"Yeah?"

"You were great—a major screen presence." She almost gagged on the bullshit.

"Thanks."

Abby paused a beat for dramatic effect. "How would you like to star in a *mainstream* movie? And by that I mean one that doesn't require you to stay on your knees or on all fours."

Joey's eyes got big. "You offering me a part?"

"Eventually."

He hesitated. "What do I have to do?"

Abby read between the lines. The *what* had nothing to do with auditions, test screenings, and casting issues. While interviewing subjects for her *Fascination* article "This Boy For Hire," she discovered that trading sex for vague promises of legitimate acting roles was apple pie normal in the demimonde of gay porn. Big shock. "All you have to do is a little detective work."

Joey stared back quizzically.

Abby lowered herself into a chair and dropped her purse at her feet. "When Montgomery was six years old, his thirteen-year-old sister stabbed their mother's lover to death—according to the *official* story. But I think there's more to it, and that's where you come in."

Joey's face was a portrait of affront. "You mean, like a spy?"

Abby scoffed at the description. "Spy is such a pejorative term . . . think of yourself as an indiscreet lover, nothing more."

"I couldn't do that . . . I love Monty."

Abby's laugh tinkled from her throat. "That's sweet, Joey, but hardly practical."

He shook his head stubbornly. "Count me out."

"How long have you and *Monty* been together?"

"About a month."

"You boys sure do fall in love quick. Jesus, it's the relationship equivalent of dog years."

Joey ran both hands through his wavy chestnut hair. "I've got a show to get ready for," he announced pompously.

Abby stood abruptly, rigid with hostility. Stupid *and* love-struck! The combination was frightening. "It won't last."

"Says you," he shot back.

Abby snatched her purse and slung it over her shoulder with a huff. "I've written about the world you come from, Joey, and it's not the same one where the rest of us live. Get this straight: There's a morals clause in Montgomery Cain's contract. Somehow I think shacking up with a hard core porn faggot pretty much violates it."

Joey Danza looked like an impaled animal.

Abby's hopes were going up, up, and away. A nerve had been hit. She pressed on. "When the suits in management ask him to make a choice—and believe me, they will ask him—the career will come first. Does he take you out to dinner? Have you been introduced to his family? Do you know his friends?"

Joey merely stood there, silent.

It was the answer Abby wanted to hear. Time for the hard sell. "My agent is waiting for this story. So is a Hollywood producer. And in the movie, *you* will play *Montgomery.*" She stepped closer, releasing a heavy sigh. "He's going to dump you, Joey. It's only a matter of time."

Before her eyes, Joey the lover did a quick change

into Joey the survivor, and he was ready to abandon rather than risk being abandoned. "Where can I reach you?"

Abby McQueen smiled the smile of a winner. Her work was done here.

Ten

"He'll be with you shortly," the receptionist said curtly.

Hospitality was not the order of the day at the firm of Berg, Chinn, Glickman, & Maxey. *Something to drink would be nice,* Stephanie thought, but such a polite offer was nowhere on the horizon. She searched her purse for a breath mint, striking it rich with the familiar rattle of a Tic-Tac container. Popping two, she glanced up, aghast.

The fashion tragedy at the front desk had a tanning salon pallor, frosted blonde do, swelling breasts, and inch-long, fire engine red nails. She looked like a *Baywatch* dreamer who had missed the last bus to the bimbo beach. No doubt one of Chuck Berg's personal hires frequently asked to *work late.*

Time dragged on. Stephanie checked her watch. The bastard had kept her waiting for fifteen minutes. Suddenly, a realization brought a smile to her lips, and patience to the rest of her. The truth was, Chuck Berg could stall until Charlie Sheen had a hit movie—the pictures of David Alexander playing dress up were in her possession. She picked up the glossy monthly *Texas Today* and began flipping through it.

Minutes later, the telephone chirped out three

short beeps, an obvious internal ring. The Pamela Anderson Lee look-alike picked up, whispered, "She's still here," giggled, and replaced the receiver. "He'll see you now," she announced coldly. "Down the hall, take a right, last door to the left."

Stephanie closed the magazine and returned it to the coffee table. As she rose, a wide grin stretched across her face. This *negotiation* was going to be very satisfying. She walked toward Chuck Berg's office slowly, savoring the moment in the making. Once she passed through that door, justice would be hers, and more importantly—Melissa Alexander's.

The expansive office was nothing more than a corporate phallic symbol. Big views. Big furnishings. Big art showpieces. In short, size mattered. Chuck and David were seated side by side, copping smug attitude behind a marble conference table, laughter in their eyes. Stephanie had seen that look before on a fraternity brother accused of spiking a freshman girl's punch and then raping her. She'd wiped the fuck-you-I'm-invincible scowl from his face with a seven figure civil judgment that raided his trust fund; she'd do the same here.

"Ms. Hart," Chuck said tightly.

David Alexander just sat there, as if nothing could be more boring than this meeting. He was straight off the construction site, a He-Man dead ringer in scuffed boots, jeans, and a denim shirt rolled up at the sleeves to reveal Popeye forearms. Who would ever think that this Wrangler man had a predilection for the delicate undergarments of Victoria's Secret?

"Gentlemen," Stephanie began, confidently taking a seat across from them, "and I only use that term as a figure of speech. Please don't take it personally." She smiled.

David Alexander glowered.

Chuck Berg leaned back and gave her an intense stare. "What's this all about?"

"A fair settlement for Melissa," Stephanie said flatly. The tone of her voice held no request. It was an announcement. Plain, simple, and forceful.

David shot a look to Chuck. "I thought this was over."

Chuck never took his eyes off Stephanie. *"It is."*

"Guess what, fellas? It's just getting started."

Chuck narrowed his gaze.

David turned to him. "She's no longer my wife, so she doesn't have any rights! That's what you told me!"

Chuck raised a hand to calm David. "You're wasting your time, Ms. Hart. Melissa will never see a dime of David's money. And we're prepared to tie this up in court until dogs piss ginger ale to make sure that happens."

Stephanie drew in a deep breath, fighting to stay on a cool course, to hold back the storm of hatred threatening to derail her. She pursed her lips into a small, stubborn smile and shook her head. "Not good enough."

"They're both crazy!" David erupted. "Melissa called me yesterday cussing like a street whore, and now this chick can't understand English!"

Chuck Berg's relentless gaze never faltered. Why was she playing this ballsy game? What bombshell was she ready to detonate? The questions were all over his face.

Stephanie turned to David. "It's in your best interest to offer Melissa a fair settlement. Her respect for certain . . . *private matters* . . . depends on your generosity."

"I got nothing to hide!" David blurted.

Chuck swallowed hard. Worry lines creased his brow. He knew that he was about to learn the expensive way that flowers could shatter stones.

"We all have *something* to hide," Stephanie remarked ominously.

David's eyes got smaller. Perspiration beaded his upper lip.

Chuck threw a disapproving glance his way, then zeroed in on Stephanie. "Go on. Show your hand."

"Happy to oblige." She pulled three Polaroids from her jacket pocket, dropped them onto the table with a loud thwack, and watched the perverted images pummel the intended targets.

David Alexander jerked backward, head rolling on his shoulders, face knocked clean of expression. In his great American pecking order, holding onto money was swiftly losing first place to avoiding public humiliation.

Chuck Berg winced, refusing eye contact with David, focusing instead on the Post Oak Lane view nine floors down. He rubbed his chin, his temples pulsating. Defeat was not an outcome he accepted easily, but the final scores here had been tallied the moment the photos scorched the tabletop. Melissa's settlement was a done deal. It only needed to be drafted and signed.

David was the first to speak. "How much?"

Stephanie retrieved a thick agreement from her bag, pushing it in Chuck's direction. "The house, a car, monthly payments for the rest of your life, and a lump sum due within thirty days of signing."

Silence boomed among them.

"Don't act so sad," she told David, going heavy on the patronization. "You walk away with your pride *and* a lucrative business. There are worse scenarios. Believe me, we considered them."

"That bitch!" David whined. "I thought I had all the pictures!" His fist crashed down on the table.

Chuck, never one to exhibit blatant signs of weakness, silenced David with a cold glare before leaning back to assess Stephanie. He shrugged ambivalently. "We'll consider this and get back to you."

She stood up. "Don't take too long. One of those could turn up as Melissa's Christmas card."

"You're playing dirty," Chuck said, his voice sandwiched somewhere between annoyance and admiration.

Stephanie's eyebrows went skyward. "What can I say? You inspire me."

Chuck's voice cut in like an icicle. "I fight hard for my clients, but I've never killed a man."

She took one short, fast step backward.

"Can you say the same?"

Stephanie felt warm patches of heat splotch her cheeks as an immediate anxiety clutched her insides like steel fingers. "You have forty-eight hours."

"That wasn't my question."

"I think we're through here." She turned, starting for the door, hearing Chuck advance behind her but charging forward anyway, refusing to look back.

Midway down the corridor, he grabbed her upper arm and squeezed tight. "Not so fast," he snapped.

The pain was fast and swift, like a snakebite, and before Stephanie could open her mouth to protest Chuck had pushed her into a small room and shut the door behind them. The airless space was a supply closet. "Let go of me!" she cried, jerking her arm free.

There was a tiny and momentary hardening of Chuck Berg's eyes, then a sinister smile. "No problem, Stephanie."

Her throat tightened. She continued to hold his

gaze and wait. What did he want? "Is this the way you learned to negotiate in law school?"

Chuck pulled a Swiss Army knife from his pocket, extracted the three-inch blade, and held the weapon out for her taking. "Come on," he taunted in a hushed voice. "Don't you want to stab me? Just like you did Jimmy Scott?"

Sickness welled in the pit of Stephanie's stomach as that horrible night came flooding back in fragments.

The red, pulpy liquid gushing from Jimmy Scott's wound.

The smell of iron.

Her mother's ferocious anger.

The unspeakable shame that paralyzed her.

No! Stephanie broke free of the nightmare images, grabbing the offensive tool and throwing it down to the floor. "You're sick!"

"I'm a sore loser." Chuck's voice darkened. "This win is going to cost you."

His words chilled her. "Is that a threat?"

"No. It's a fact of life. Tell Josie to update Jason's photo albums. She'll learn to appreciate those memories when he's living with his father."

Stephanie's heart thumped, her face turned to fire, and the words sputtered out of her mouth at breakneck speed. "I show you up in an unrelated case, and you want to punish a two-year-old boy? Rob Dean is violent! He's a binge drinker!"

Chuck didn't flinch. "But he can afford to pay my hourly rate, and misery travels downhill."

"Move," she demanded angrily. "Or risk walking doubled over for the rest of the day."

He gave her a cold smile and stepped aside.

Stephanie flung open the door and rushed out. *This win is going to cost you.* Her mind hummed with

Chuck's dark, painted threat. A terrible sense of foreboding came over her.

She phoned Peter on the way back to the office, needing to hear his voice, but his answering service picked up. Disappointed, she signed off. Right now, only Peter or Tuesday could soothe her tethered nerves. Monty seemed terribly preoccupied of late, as if he were hiding something, and Lisa was caught up in the early throes of pulse-pounding attraction to Tyson Moore, a state which rendered her unable to talk of anything else.

When Stephanie arrived, Matt was handling several things at once—a client on his headset mike, incoming faxes, and the results of the on-line research he'd compiled for the Dean case.

Sitting in the reception area was a professorial looking man in his early forties, campus casual in a tweed sportcoat, khakis, and white button-down. Stephanie acknowledged him with a nod and made a beeline for her private sanctuary.

Matt wrapped up his call and followed her inside. "How'd it go?"

"What?"

"The showdown with Berg!"

Stephanie closed her eyes for a moment. "Our team won," she said distantly, unable to ease her troubled mind. Why was Chuck Berg so vicious in his attempts to rattle her cage? Was it simply a power play . . . or something else?

"Do you feel okay? You look pale," Matt observed.

Stephanie waved away the concern. "I didn't eat lunch . . . I'll be fine. The day's almost over."

"Not quite. There's a walk-in waiting."

"Who is he?"

Matt smiled tightly. "Wish I could tell you. He

wouldn't fill out the client information form or give me any background on his legal situation. All I got was a name—Dwight Duckworth."

"Send him back," she said, at once curious and thankful for the diversion.

The average looking, baby-faced man sauntered toward her, carrying a brown parcel about the size of a shoe box. He extended a pleasant smile, a firm handshake, and sincere appreciation for being seen without an appointment. Stephanie noted his wedding band, rimless glasses, and self-assured stance. She knew the type—a man vain enough to wage a twenty pound weight loss war, but not vain enough to win it. And his bonhomie—even after the brief hellos, how are yous, and I've heard great things about you—came off poorly disguised. This much she knew: Dwight Duckworth struck her as a man on the make—the kind of husband who needed a leash and an electric fence.

Stephanie deep-sixed the chit chat. "Matt tells me you were reluctant to share the background of your legal situation."

"I . . . I wanted to explain it once . . . to you," Dwight stammered.

She held out her hands, indicating that he had her full attention. "Fire away."

Dwight shifted in his seat, grinning with obvious discomfort. "I don't come off very sympathetic in this story."

She stared back humorlessly, sensing something amiss. "That's not a prerequisite."

"That's good news!" He laughed, too hard. When she didn't join in, he turned pink-cheeked and straightened up.

Stephanie reached into a drawer to retrieve a yellow legal pad. "Don't let my note taking distract you."

"I'm on the English faculty at Rice University," Dwight began. "A few months ago I got involved in a brief relationship . . . with a student. It was wrong . . . I know that . . . I've never done this type of thing before . . . I—"

"Mr. Duckworth," she cut in, "I'm not a priest, so drop the Boy Scout routine and just give me a truthful account of what happened and the reason why you're here."

Dwight stared at his hands, then took a deep breath and started in. "I had an affair with a student, Tina Fox. When I broke it off, she didn't take it well. My wife and I have received all kinds of hate mail, mostly pictures of corpses and dismembered animals." He placed the parcel in the center of her desk. "And this was left on our doorstep."

Stephanie winced. The plastic baby doll was obscenely disfigured—neck slashed, iodine smeared all over to simulate blood, white makeup caked onto the face, eyes pierced out to leave gaping holes. "This is horrible!" she exclaimed. "Have you filed a police report?"

"No."

Stephanie regarded him curiously. "This is a matter for the police, Mr. Duckworth. As for the harassing mail, that needs to be reported to the Federal Bureau of Investigation."

Dwight shook his head. "I don't want to . . . I *can't* bring any attention to this situation. Tina was my student. I was her professor."

"So what do you think I can do?"

"As my attorney, I want you to go see Tina and tell her that I'll file a civil suit for harassment if she doesn't stop this nonsense. If you talk tough enough, she'll back off. I'm sure of it."

"Number one, I don't represent you."

"I'll retain you," Dwight put in quickly.

Stephanie paused a beat. "That's expensive."

He lifted his checkbook from the inside pocket of his sportcoat. "Name your price."

Stephanie noticed his watch, a very expensive Jaeger-LeCoultre piece in stainless steel and gold with a black crocodile band. A tingle slithered up her spine. Something didn't smell right here, but a paying client was a paying client, and she needed the revenue. "Five thousand."

Wordlessly, he scratched out the check and anchored it under her Tiffany paperweight. "Never thought I'd have my own fatal attraction." Dwight chuckled, making it sound more like a fantasy than a nightmare. He cleared his throat. "This has been very frightening, especially for my wife, Shelly."

"You have no doubt that Tina Fox is the woman responsible for these acts?" Stephanie asked gravely.

"None whatsoever."

Stephanie formed a pyramid with her hands, resting her chin on the tips of her fingers. "I'll have a conversation with Tina and explain the legal options open to you and your wife. Where can I find her?"

"Tina recently moved, so I don't have an address. But she dances at That Touch Of Pink off the Southwest Freeway."

She dropped both hands onto the desk.

"To help pay tuition," Dwight explained. "Tina's very smart."

"Oh, so it was an intellectual thing?"

Stephanie took a few more notes before sending the horny professor on his way. By then it was six o'clock. If she hurried, she would make it home in time to help Peter and Tuesday with dinner. Grabbing her purse and attaché case, she bounded into Matt's domain, imploring him to take off as well.

"I'm right behind you," Matt promised. "Got a fax coming through."

Stephanie listened to the laborious beeps and paper churnings for one quick second and decided it could wait until morning. "Have a good night," she called, starting for the door.

"Stephanie!" Matt shouted. "I think you should see this."

She stopped and turned, alarmed by the tension in Matt's face. "What is it?" She stepped closer. Printed in large type in the center of the fax was a very simple, very terrifying message: REMEMBER SEPTEMBER.

Lisa Randall felt as if the look of instant love was plastered across her face. What an incredible night! Tyson had surprised her with tickets to a Toni Braxton concert. The show had been sold out for weeks, and Lisa had surrendered her coveted pair to one of Hit The Sky's biggest clients as a peace offering for a major copy error. So when anchor babe held up the two front row center seats, she had smothered him with sloppy kisses of unrestrained delight.

How special it had been! To hold his hand while Toni belted out "You Mean The World To Me" and "Breathe Again." To snake her hand down his diamond-hard thigh as Toni delivered a sexy, slow-burning "You're Makin' Me High." *Romance.* Lisa had all but given up on the concept, leaving it to Harlequin readers, soap opera fans, and foolish optimists. But Tyson Moore had turned her into one of the believers.

And the night got better and better. After the concert, they ducked into Birraporetti's on West Gray for an Italian feast—hot crusty bread, Caesar salad, tomato basil pizza from a woodburning oven, and sinful white chocolate mousse. They scarfed down every bite, along with too much wine, too much laughter, and easy conversation. A weekend date for a trip to the movies, shopping, and more decadent eating had already been set.

Now they were taking the private party upstairs to Artuzzi, the new hyper-sophisticated night spot where edgy artists commingled with Rat Pack pretenders. Lisa and Tyson's arrival onto the hip scene triggered a mini stir, rubbernecking all around. Her body tingled in response. They were running on the super-leaded fuel of physical self-respect. Lisa Randall and Tyson Moore—two wild, crazy, beautiful people, already in lust, falling in love, and meant to be together.

Tyson laced his hand through hers possessively, piloting them to a cozy corner sofa. She took in the lofted ceilings, exposed brick, and art house decor. A DJ pumped an ethereal Sarah McLachlan number through the killer sound system. They sipped Manhattans, holding hands, stealing kisses, wishing the night would never end. And then Tyson stole a glance at his watch, bit down on his lower lip, and shut his eyes regretfully.

Lisa's heart felt light as she realized that at this moment, she didn't give a damn about anything but Tyson Moore. She gazed into his jeweled eyes, her look intense. "This night . . . was very special."

"I'm not ready to end it," Tyson said.

"Duty calls."

"I don't want to answer it."

Lisa smiled. "Come on," she said, standing. "I

want my man to be bite-your-knuckles fine when he delivers the news, and that means at least a few hours of sleep." She pulled him up.

"You mean, you don't want no bag under the eyes, saggy faced, slow-talkin' brother?"

She giggled. "You didn't know?"

Tyson admired her for a moment, then drew her in for a clenched embrace, nuzzling his cheek against hers. His goatee grazed her skin, and a soft, involuntary sigh escaped her lips.

"You smell so good," she whispered, deep inhaling his manly scent, tightening her hold, feeling him respond.

Tyson groaned and pulled back. "Don't get a man started. I'll never fall asleep."

"Save that thought for another night."

"You didn't know?"

They laughed, locked arms, and started out. It occurred to Lisa that she had yet to ask Tyson about Monty's position as lead anchor, the very one he was hoping to fill. Perhaps Monty was getting a promotion or transferring to another market. No, she decided, remembering Tyson's odd choice of words. *It's complicated.* That didn't sound like a move up. Once they reached his fully loaded Honda CRV sports utility vehicle, she buckled herself in and raised the subject. "Any word on the evening anchor slot?"

Tyson turned the key over, smiling as he backed out. "What's wrong? A morning guy's not good enough for you?"

"Maybe, maybe not," Lisa teased.

"It's a done deal. Just a matter of time."

She hesitated, stuck between wanting to congratulate him and wanting to know how the change would impact Monty. "Where does that leave Montgomery Cain?"

Now it was Tyson's turn to hesitate. "Nothing's official yet. I really shouldn't be discussing it. You know what I'm saying?"

"Off the record," Lisa pushed. "Don't get me wrong. I'm . . . happy for you, but . . . Monty's a friend. I *need* to know."

Tyson groaned his acquiescence. "Okay, check it out," he began, forcing the answer past reluctant lips, "Monty's gay—"

"Bisexual," Lisa corrected.

"Whatever. The dude likes boys. He's got some star of fag flicks on his jock pretty heavy, and the suits are tripping out. He was even seen kissing this guy in the station parking lot."

Lisa experienced a flash of anger. "What Monty chooses to do in his personal life isn't anyone's business but his own. And don't use that word in my presence. It's offensive." She shifted positions and gazed out the window.

Tension thickened the dark cabin.

Tyson cut off the stereo, drowning out Mariah Carey. "Don't pull that politically correct shit on me. Have you seen the motherfucker that Monty's hooked up with? Dude's all over the Net. One of the assistant producers looked him up. This cat's a *porn star,* baby. Shit!"

The car turned onto Yorktown Drive; Lisa's apartment was about sixty seconds away—not a moment too soon. "It's a private matter," she said quietly as she went about digesting the disturbing news, wondering if Stephanie knew.

Tyson shook his head. "An anchor's job is to *read* the news, not *be* the motherfucking news. Baby, this ain't *Ellen!*"

"But—"

"But nothing," Tyson cut in. "Listen, I ain't got a problem with Monty's way of life. That's his bedroom, that's his dick, that's his business. But the dude's got a very public job, and he can't flaunt that shit and not expect some consequences. The world just ain't that accepting yet. It's fucked up, but that's the way it is."

Lisa regarded him sharply. "Oh, can I quote you on that? Brilliant speech. *It's fucked up,*" she mocked.

Tyson's eyes flashed fire. "Yeah? Well, baby, I must be making a whole lot of sense if all you can talk about is my vocabulary. Besides, I'm just the messenger."

"More like beneficiary."

Tyson parked and killed the engine. "Someone always is." He sighed. "Are you telling me that you never benefited from another copywriter's mistake at the ad agency?"

Lisa fell silent as guilt kicked in. What a hypocrite! Was it not Sherry Myers' addiction to pain pills that had paved the way for her own ascension to senior copywriter? Had she fought against the pink slip and protested the unfairness of it all? No way. She had responded in the manner any other ambitious person would have: Wished the bitch good luck in rehab and stepped right up for the salary increase and A-list assignments. "I was out of line," Lisa whispered.

Tyson reached for her hand. "I'm not gloating, but at the same time it's a big career move for me. I've got a right to be happy."

Lisa squeezed tight in reply. "I know." She felt so helpless, wanting to protect Monty but realizing that protecting himself seemed nowhere on his own list of things to do.

She sat with Tyson in the dark, saying nothing, holding his hand. Had the evening crashed and burned? Lisa pondered the thought and decided the answer was no. In a strange way, she felt even more drawn to him. What they shared was cosmic, once in a lifetime . . . a soul connection. "Our first fight," she said softly, with an embarrassed smile.

"Actually, it's our second," Tyson replied. "But who's counting?"

They took the stairs slowly, walking as one until they stopped in front of her door. Lisa slid her key into the lock, then turned to face Tyson. "Thank you," she said earnestly.

He returned a perplexed look. "For what?"

"For making me feel special. I've forgotten what that's like."

"I want to come inside," he began thickly.

Lisa felt surrounded by sounds . . . a car horn below, muffled rock music from the apartment next door, the creamy cadence of Tyson's voice. . . .

"But I want our first time to be a romantic adventure, and I have to be at the studio in a few hours," he finished.

Lisa's heart beat quickly, as if she'd already taken that first step. Suddenly she could feel his warm breath and lips on her cheek, his fingers on the back of her neck. Tyson pressed his mouth to hers hungrily. The heat and wetness of his tongue melted into hers, and they kissed as if they could devour each other.

"Goodnight, baby," he finally said. Then he walked away.

What a magical evening! Love songs, Italian food, nightcaps in a cozy bar, and kisses at the door. It was a *real* courtship. She kicked off her shoes and slipped out of her lightweight pink cashmere short-sleeved cardigan, dancing around in her French-blue slip dress with lace trim. Getting to know him first. Now there was a novel concept!

A soft knock rapped the door.

Lisa felt a thump of adrenaline, an immediate drying of the mouth. It was Tyson. He couldn't go home. And she didn't want him to. Racing to the door, she flung it open, not bothering to check the peephole.

Staring back was a man in a black ski mask.

Her heart lurched.

The first stunning blow knocked her to the floor, split her lip, and splattered her blood across the room in a fine mist.

Noise rang inside her head.

She steeled herself, preparing to scream, but it died in her throat as another blow sent her reeling. Her left eye was closing. The tearing noise was the silk charmeuse as he ripped it from her body.

Pain.

Horror.

Darkness.

Eleven

Francisco Juarez didn't give her so much as a cross look the morning after she stood him up for dinner, and his business as usual bit toyed with her mind. A man rebuked by Abby McQueen was not supposed to react this way! Where were the passive-aggressive curt replies, the angry glances, the hurt feelings, and last but not least, the pleas for a second chance?

Upon her arrival he had been cordial, professional, even solicitous. At first sight, he handed over a *Texas Today* envelope containing three twenty dollar bills and a check for two thousand five hundred dollars, her per diem plus half her take for the article. When she asked for a computer with Internet access, he provided her with his own, insisting that she set up camp in his domain.

"I'm going after a second cup of coffee. Can I get you some?" Francisco asked.

Abby spun to face him and smiled. "Sorry about last night," she ventured, poised to take his mood temperature on the subject.

"Don't apologize," he said easily. "I ended up with Chinese take-out and a new episode of *NYPD Blue*. No complaints." He clapped his hands. "What about that coffee?"

Pour a scalding cup in your ass, she wanted to scream, instead turning away with a tight, "No thanks."

"Suit yourself."

She pushed Francisco from her thoughts and concentrated on the task at hand. *Texas Today* was plugged into a host of subscriber based on-line news services, which saved several trips to the public library and hours of research time. The laser printer was spitting out the data at a fast clip. In 1992 alone, Stephanie Cain had lost one husband and snagged another. "Busy year for the former teenage murderess," Abby chortled to herself. She noted Stephanie's career path, made for a news magazine profile—lots of high coverage cases championing the cause of battered women and once rich, now poor divorcees bilked out of their rightful shares.

As she moved on, two reports troubled her, the first being Marilyn Cain's health status. After two major strokes, the old hag probably couldn't remember what she ate for breakfast, much less the lurid details of an incident twenty years old. No matter, Abby planned a trip to the Susann Center to see the indigent witch up close and personal. The second blow was the news that Billy Hudson had croaked six years ago. She scanned the laudatory obituary:

An often cunning but always highly respected leader in the legal community . . . affectionately referred to as the Magic Man for his uncanny ability to emerge victorious from the most difficult trials . . . survived by his only daughter, Anna Belle Hudson.

Abby exited the document and called up *Yahoo's People Finder,* hitting pay dirt with a Pasadena address and phone number for the dead man's closest relative and only living offspring. A visit to the spinster just might be worth it. Granted, she had high hopes for Joey Danza's pillow talk discovery, but she wasn't leaving anything to chance. After all, digging up truths buried twenty years deep was serious anthropology.

She jockeyed back to the Billy Hudson obit, clicked twice on an Internet link option, and drew in a deep breath as a cyber shrine to the legal eagle downloaded to life on the nineteen-inch screen. The image's impact sliced out at her like a sharp wind. Billy Hudson ate up the screen with what looked like old Hollywood DNA: Baby blues like Paul Newman; drop dead handsome looks like Rock Hudson; impeccable style sense like Gary Cooper. Billy Hudson had it all. "You cagey bastard," Abby whispered. Her heart began to race, and her cheeks to flush, as she remembered being put under The Magic Man's spell. . . .

"Oh, God, Billy! Oh, God!"

It had become her standard battle cry not long after the Jimmy Scott murder. Billy Hudson liked her naked, propped up on a bed of pillows, and her wrists tied to the headboard with velvet rope. How much she had wanted to run her fingers through his thick silver hair as he buried his face between her legs, never failing to bring her to hot, quivering, voluptuous climaxes whenever they stole away together. But touching him had been strictly forbidden . . . until it was *his* turn to be a prisoner of passion.

She had just turned twenty-five. The moment she caught wind of the River Oaks murder she knew it would be a career juggernaut. An interview with The Magic Man had been just one of the monster gets of the day, and she'd pursued it with youthful vigor—letters, phone calls, stakeouts on the courthouse steps, sit-ins at his law firm. Finally, the old fox had caved in to her gutsy campaign and agreed to a lunch meeting.

It had taken place at the Original Ninfa's on Navigation, a rundown Mexican cantina famous for Mama Ninfa's cheap but delicious platters and oh so potent margaritas. Immediately, Abby responded to Billy Hudson in a way she never had to another man. Even at sixty-two, he possessed an impossibly seductive aura. He was virile, authoritative, intelligent, and adventurous. Next to him, other men in her peer group became little boys who didn't know shit about life—or women. They became secret lovers that afternoon.

The legal legend had been old enough to be her grandfather, but the age difference never bothered her. Sure, there were Freudian quacks who would've taken a bullet for the chance to analyze the coupling, but she already knew the predicating factor. Her own father was an emotional iceberg, a monosyllabic plumber who believed little girls should grow up to be wives and mothers, not intrepid reporters.

And then there was Billy Hudson—older, kinder, a fascinating man filled with heart, brains, and a lot of information. He was amused by her turbocharged ambition. In fact, he embraced it, and one night, after a marathon sex session and a heated debate about President Jimmy Carter, he paid her the ultimate compliment: "Abby, you're a real broad—a whore in the bedroom and one of the boys everywhere else." At that moment, she knew she loved him . . . but never dreamed of telling him so.

His hints along the way, offered surreptitiously, had helped shape her story for *Texas Today:* What details to scrutinize in the police report. Who to interview at The River Oaks Country Club. Why Stephanie Cain's actions were justifiable homicide. At the time, she'd thought the personal coaching was an act of affection, a clever method of nudging her in the right direction while maintaining his attorney-client privilege. Not once had she stopped to question his motives, so blinded was she by admiration, lust, and paternal longing. Billy Hudson knew how to stir her stew. He'd zapped a lover-mentor-daddy hex on her that rocked her world, all the while spoon-feeding her the version of the truth he wanted unleashed to the media.

After the issue had hit the stands the press had tapered off, and her usefulness as his personal voice box had run its course. Then the offer from *The New York Post* arrived out of nowhere.

"Take it, doll," Billy had encouraged her as they put themselves back together following a tryst at The Remington Hotel. "This town isn't big enough for a barracuda like you."

"Maybe I don't want to leave," she had shot back, stopping herself from whining the more needy, more pathetic, "What about us?"

Billy, half-dressed in an unbuttoned, hand-tailored, monogrammed shirt of the finest Sea Island cotton, had strode across the room and pulled her roughly to her feet. "Listen to me. If you go to New York, we're history. You know it, and I know it. But even if you stick around here, we're still history.

Lovesick girls don't do it for me. The reason you're so goddamn exciting is because when you want, you want big. The moment you settle is the moment you become just another dumb chick. Now go after it!"

So she left and never looked back—not to the father who resented her for rejecting his June Cleaver expectations, not to the mother who resented her for living dreams instead of burying them, and not even to Billy Hudson. She thought she'd never get over him. But she saw him for what he really was when stacked against what New York had to offer—a worn-out old coot with a cock that wouldn't quit. Still, she'd loved him.

Abby felt the regret rise through her toes and arrow straight up to her brain. She'd believed that she was so fucking smart, leaving behind the sand-bagged local losers to join the real winners on the national success track. Reflection. It was a humbling exercise, indeed. Billy Hudson hadn't coached her; he'd manipulated her. And the *Texas Today* piece hadn't been tenacious, right-place-at-the-right-time reporting; it'd been a scheme for him to practically ghostwrite his own propaganda.

Abby McQueen at twenty-five—stupid girl.

Abby McQueen at forty-five—smart woman.

In 1977, they'd played her for the fool that she was. But it was 1997 now, and time to show them just how much life had taught her. She drew in a calming breath. When the going gets tough, the screwed get even. Billy Hudson was in the grave, so mucking up his spit-polished reputation was her only shot at retribution. But Stephanie Hart was still walking the streets, playing Harriet Tubman to weak-willed women who should drop the crybaby act and fight back or move out.

She still had Jimmy Scott's blood on her hands.

Justifiable homicide, my ass, Abby thought. What happened that night was anything but self-defense. Proving it would put Abby McQueen back on top . . . right where she belonged.

Twelve

The telephone blasted her awake. Groggily, she struggled to make out the time—quarter past three. Her heart lurched. It could only be the wrong number . . . or very bad news. "Hello?"

"Stephanie Hart please." The man's voice was vaguely familiar.

"Speaking."

"I apologize for waking you. This is Kirk Mulroney."

Captain Kirk Mulroney, Houston Police Department. Stephanie sat up, her senses already hyperalert.

Peter began to stir.

She reached out to touch him, for the strength her instincts told her she would need any moment now. "What is it?"

Kirk paused. His silence seemed to linger for an eternity. "Lisa Randall was raped."

Fifteen minutes later she stood in the trauma center of Hermann Hospital, facing Dr. Hitomi Tokunaga, a severe Japanese woman of stern countenance. "No questions about the attack. The police have already put her through it. I'll give you two minutes. She needs rest."

Stephanie braced herself and crept into the cold

room. A wave of faintness welled up inside her as the sight of her dear friend swam in and out of focus.

Lisa was sleeping under heavy sedation, her left eye bandaged, her cheek badly bruised, and her lips split and swollen.

Moving closer, Stephanie gripped the bed's safety rail. "Oh, Lisa," she gasped.

Lisa's exposed eye fluttered. There was a glimmer of recognition, and her hand fell open.

Stephanie clasped it gently, wincing at the sight of caked blood on Lisa's teeth. "I'm here, honey. I'm here," she whispered. A big tear rolled down her cheek.

Lisa faded back into sleep.

Stephanie remained there stoically. Everything had changed for her friend. Victims of rape didn't get over it; they simply lived around it. This free spirit would never be the same again.

"Ms. Hart," Dr. Tokunaga called firmly.

Stephanie nodded, kissed Lisa's hand, and followed the doctor out. Once in the corridor, she fetched her cellular from her purse and dialed home.

Peter answered on the first ring. "How is she?"

"Oh, Peter," she cried softly. "What she must have gone through!"

"It's okay, Steph," he murmured. "Have you talked to the doctor?"

"No . . . I'm about to."

"What happened?"

"I don't . . . know yet. Did Tuesday wake up?"

"She's sound asleep."

"I'm going to stick around for a few hours and get all the information I can."

"Okay. Don't worry. I'll see her off to school. We'll even make waffles."

Stephanie smiled wanly. "Fry some bacon, too."

"We will."

She hugged herself, wishing his arms were holding her tight. "I love you. Kiss Tuesday for me."

"Lisa will get through this," he whispered.

Stephanie clicked the END button. Just hearing Peter's voice filled her up with a quiet strength. Now she felt ready to face the daunting task ahead—learning exactly what Lisa had endured. She stepped over to join the police captain's huddle with Dr. Tokunaga.

Kirk Mulroney was all big white teeth and Olympic hopeful body—a matinee idol with a badge. His dark brown eyes were kind and intelligent, revealing a depth of character not always present in men who looked so divine. She'd called on him regularly to testify as the chief investigator on several spousal abuse cases—including Ginger Simon's and now Josie Dean's—and his performance in court was always unimpeachable. Kirk Mulroney was a great cop and a sensitive man—a rare combination.

"I'm sorry, Stephanie. I know the two of you are very good friends," he said.

"The best."

"The son of a bitch really worked her over."

She drew in a deep breath. "What are the chances of finding him?"

Another pregnant pause. "Not promising," he began. "This wasn't a break-in. Lisa opened the door for him, expecting someone else. She didn't stand a chance."

"Did she give you a description?"

Kirk shook his head regretfully. "The lowlife wore

a ski mask, gloves, and dark clothing. White male. That's all she can tell us."

"What about DNA evidence?"

"He used a condom, then threw Lisa in the shower with the cold water running. There's not a trace of him in that apartment—or on her."

Stephanie grimaced, turning to Dr. Tokunaga.

The stone-faced woman offered a curt nod of agreement. "I performed a full rape exam—vaginal swab, pubic hair combing. No evidence of semen. My colposcopic exam did reveal tears and abrasions on the vulva. That's to be expected. The attack was brutal, but physically she'll recover nicely. Apart from her lips, there were no breaks in the skin."

"Less than fifteen percent of rapes are by strangers," Kirk put in. "Is there an old boyfriend—or maybe a new one—that you think we should talk to?"

Stephanie wracked her brain, running her fingers through her wild mass of red hair. "I've only known her to date black guys. She just started seeing Tyson Moore. They went out last night."

"The news anchor?"

"Yes."

"I'll talk to him," Kirk said, jotting down the note on a small pad.

Stephanie addressed Dr. Tokunaga. "When will she be released?"

"I'll be administering a penicillin shot and morning after pill shortly. I'd say mid-morning. If you'll excuse me, I have other patients."

Kirk shot up an eyebrow as Dr. Tokunaga disappeared into an exam room. "So much for bedside manner."

"As long as she's a good doctor," Stephanie muttered distantly, her heart almost numb with a dull hurt for Lisa. "Oh, God," she sighed miserably.

"Why don't we sit for a few minutes?"

"I'd like that," she whispered. There was something so comforting about Kirk Mulroney. Despite his soft voice and docile demeanor, he emanated dependability and strength. They settled onto a couch in the waiting area with two coffees from the vending machine.

"Lisa's blood alcohol level exceeded the legal limit," Kirk announced gently.

Stephanie bristled. "Is that significant?"

He sipped slow on the steaming java. "It explains the fact that she can't remember many details. And if she does eventually identify someone, it tarnishes her credibility."

"Oh, I forgot," Stephanie remarked. "Defense Strategy 101: A woman who has a few drinks deserves to be raped."

Kirk shrugged. "Hey, I don't make the rules. It sure makes me crazy to think that only two percent of rapists actually get imprisoned."

Stephanie held the hot Styrofoam cup against her cheek. "Is this reality check for my benefit?"

He gazed down at the tiled floor. "I don't hold much hope that Lisa will remember anything to help us. Memories don't get better with time. We surveyed all of her neighbors. They didn't see—or hear—anything. And nothing about this attack resembles any of the serial rape cases that are ongoing."

His point was sledgehammer subtle: The man who raped Lisa Randall would not be captured. "I appreciate your candor, Kirk."

* * *

The snakes surrounded her. Hideous, evil creatures. They wrapped themselves around her body, slashed into her skin with their razor-sharp fangs, and pumped deadly venom into her bloodstream. Lisa tried to scream, but could make no sound. She was mute. Lisa tried to move, but had no muscle control. She was paralyzed.

Slowly, she came up from the deep to the place of no mercy. Bit by bit, agony squeezed her with its icy grip. A film of sweat slicked her body as a merciless wave of nausea came over her. Associations of thought began to develop. Tyson Moore . . . a romantic evening . . . Monty . . . the kiss . . . a knock on the door . . . no!

Lisa brought a trembling hand to her face, touching the gauze over her eye, brushing her dry, cracked lips. Terror smacked her to attention. She moved to sit up, but a wall of pain pounded into her like a hammer. Her head began a sharp throbbing. In the fog of her brain a voice played . . . a man's voice . . . it repeated in her head over and over and over again, like a needle stuck on an old phonograph.

"You've got bad taste in friends, bitch. You deserve this."

Stephanie and Peter were cleaning up from an early dinner while Tuesday watched *Saved By The Bell* reruns in the living room.

"I know an excellent therapist," he whispered. "She's treated a number of rape victims. I think Lisa would respond well to her."

She nodded absently, her mind racing as she wiped down the counter-tops. Stephanie had wanted Lisa to stay with them for a few days, but she had refused, not wanting Tuesday to see her in such a state. Too frightened to return to her own apartment, she had insisted on staying with Tyson Moore.

Monty was also a source of worry. She'd attempted to reach him several times throughout the day to tell him about Lisa. It was odd for him to be so unavailable, even more so for him not to return calls. When she tried him at the station, the receptionist informed her that he was out sick. Something was amiss with her brother, and she was determined to find out what.

Matt had checked in for instructions on how to handle a very persistent Abby McQueen, who was calling to request an interview. The name rang familiar. She was the tabloid dweller who'd been caught in a libel trap by Sylvester Stallone's legal posse after the release of her scathing unauthorized biography of the international movie star. *A toast to Rambo*, thought Stephanie, no fan of the muckrakers. What could a celebrity basher possibly want with her?

"What did I just say?" Peter quizzed.

Stephanie stopped and met his gaze, her face betraying her guilt. "I have absolutely no idea." She smiled, almost laughing.

He smiled back, enveloping her in his arms. "I'm worried about you. There's the Josie Dean case, the Bruce Simon issue, and now . . . Lisa's attack. Steph, something's got to give."

She pulled back. "Peter, I didn't create any of this."

"I realize that, but it will take its toll just the same. *My* concern is *you*."

"Calm down. I'll be fine."

"How many hours of sleep did you get last night?"

"Between your patient emergency and Kirk's call . . . about three hours."

"It shows."

"Just what a girl wants to hear."

He laced both of his hands through hers. "You know what I mean. And you need to make up those lost hours. Your mind will function better."

She bent back his fingers. "Yes, doctor."

He regarded her seriously and drew her in closer. "This is your husband talking."

"Yes, Mr. Hart."

He kissed her forehead. "That's more like it."

"I have to take care of something for a new client, and I'll probably stop by Monty's while I'm out." She assumed a soldier's stance, saluting him. "But I promise to be home in time for an early bed check."

Peter shook his head, grinning. "Foreplay begins promptly at twenty-one hundred hours."

Minutes later, Stephanie left Peter and Tuesday in a Super Nintendo fight to the finish and headed out, hoping that one visit to Tina Fox would be the only measure necessary to stop her Glenn Close style antics against Dwight Duckworth. To have an unseemly case like that get complicated was the last thing she needed right now.

She located That Touch Of Pink with no trouble. Located just off the southwest freeway, the club's neon lights screamed illicit goings on as she exited Hillcroft. HOUSTON'S HOTTEST GIRLS, praised one marquee. OUR DANCERS AIM TO PLEASE, promised another.

Inside the smoky den, Stephanie sipped on the cocktail glass of Coke that had zapped ten bucks from her wallet—seven-fifty for the soda and two-fifty for the waitress in trashy lingerie. She surveyed the darkened dump. A few banker/stockbroker

types peppered the scene, and a gaggle of white
prepsters on a drunken binge whooped it up in the
corner. The rest of the bodies were bikers, conven-
tioneers, and regular working stiffs.

As the third rock song thrashed from the speakers, Stephanie hoped she wouldn't need Miracle Ear
the next morning. Tina Fox gyrated buck naked,
pumping her hips with grinding gusto. She'd started
the first number in a silk robe, then doffed it at the
second chorus to reveal a strapless bra and G-string.
The next song revealed her firm breasts and quarter
sized nipples. And when she finally flashed her velvet triangle, the crowd roared like a cage of hungry
lions confronted with fresh meat.

Strobe lights flashed, lasers scanned, and mirrors
amplified as Tina danced around the lone prop—a
pole. She twirled, hugged the steel, and straddled it
upside down, then slid backwards. The gawkers hollered as she writhed on the stage floor, giving the
front row a gynecologist's eye view. She splayed her
legs wide apart, and beads of sweat smeared a wet
trail as her bottom eased across the floor. With a
flourish, she raised up and lifted her backside to the
crowd.

A sauced frat boy rushed the stage to make a grab
for her. Stephanie watched stripper transform into
killer. Fuck *me* became fuck *you,* and the impression
lingered that she would prefer cutting off dicks a la
Lorena Bobbitt to rubbing up against them. As
Stephanie studied Tina's face, she was struck by the
fact that, although obviously young, this girl was
completely without a trace of youth. Her beauty had
been held as if by torque, in a tension that some
cataclysmic event had come along and snapped. She
was a hard, tough-looking woman.

The set ended. Tina slipped her robe back on and

paraded around, shaking down a fistful of fives and tens from the tongue-lolling men.

Stephanie held a crisp twenty firmly between her fingers until the dirty dancer made eye contact. "Can I buy you a cup of coffee?" she asked.

"If that twenty's for me I can buy my own coffee."

She let go of the bill, expecting Tina to bolt, but the girl stood her ground. Stephanie admired her beautiful feet. The bubble gum-pink polish on her toenails shimmered. A sweet citrus perfume was strong in the air.

"A lap dance will cost you another twenty," Tina said, standing ramrod straight, a sassy hand on an impossibly thin hip.

"I just want to talk."

"Wrong place, wrong girl for conversation, honey. Try one of the lipstick lesbian bars on Montrose."

"My name's Stephanie Hart. I'm an attorney. I represent Dwight Duckworth, and I need five minutes of your time." She offered a business card to drive the point home.

Tina accepted it and smoothed her fingertip over the raised surface of the embossed logo. "Ooh, I'm impressed." Suddenly her eyes flashed with anger, and her pouty, thickly-glossed lips tightened into a firm line. "Fuck Dwight Duckworth."

"Apparently that's where the problem began."

Fearlessly, Tina stared her down.

"Come on, Tina. I gave you twenty dollars. Give me five minutes."

"Didn't you know? Gratitude isn't a stripper's long suit. I'm on to the next twenty, and I'm not up for any bullshit."

Stephanie could see the brittle strength in Tina's eyes. It stood out like neon. Did this girl know a man who hadn't used her, abused her, or simply let her down? "Dwight's a jerk," Stephanie said in her best girlfriend to girlfriend voice. "Major league asshole. My representing him is strictly business, just like your lap dance will be for the fat guy with the SIZE MATTERS T-shirt over there."

A faint smile played around Tina's lips, giving Stephanie the hope that a real conversation might be on the horizon.

Now another dancer, taking off a schoolgirl's uniform to the beat of Def Leppard, had the place in a frenzy. Stephanie shook her head. Bad eighties rock. Cigarette smoke curled up to the ceiling. Horny losers all around. So this was safe sex in the age of AIDS. Pathetic. Whoever said stripping was easy money had watched *Showgirls* one too many times.

She followed Tina to the back. There were five individual stalls arranged into mini stages. Two steps went up into each. Wall-to-wall, floor-to-ceiling mirrors gave the place a funhouse feeling. Tina reached into her robe pocket and pulled out a pack of Kool Lights. She tipped one out, flicked on her lighter, burned the cig into action, and dragged deep.

"You know, secondhand smoke can kill," Stephanie said lightly.

Tina blew out a cloud, slowly and deliberately. "Oh, yeah? Well, too bad Dwight's not around."

A tall, skinny, greasy man with an unkempt moustache slapdashed into the room. "Hey, Tina, when your little tea party's over, I've got some guys out here who want some action. By the way, Kim was fired tonight because I caught her with a beeper. Don't let the same happen to you." He leered at Stephanie and stomped out.

Tina laughed. "That's Malcolm. He owns the

place and handles all the public relations. Can't you tell?"

Stephanie couldn't bring herself to even crack a smile. "What are you doing here?"

"Making five hundred a night. It beats retail."

"Is it worth the money?"

Tina stifled a yawn, fluttered her Nordic blue eyes, and combed her fingers through her golden blond hair. "That depends on the day."

"How often is the answer yes?"

"Whenever I go to the bank."

So young and so cynical. Stephanie regarded her with sadness.

Tina's face went dark with a shadow of annoyance. "Spare me the social work routine."

Stephanie backed off, holding up a hand. "Only curious."

"You want my sob story? Here goes. My mom's an alcoholic and my dad's a deadbeat, so saving for my college education didn't exactly top their list of priorities. I'm not like the rest of these girls. What doesn't pay for my tuition gets crammed into a safety deposit box. The rest of these sluts need to strip to afford coke, and they need a hit of coke for the nerve to strip. Not me. I have a plan."

A nervous college boy stumbled into the room.

Tina snatched the folded cash in his hands and pointed to a chair. "Sit on your hands. Feels aren't part of the deal."

Out went the cigarette. Off went the robe. Cold, machine-driven techno music blasted into the small space. She pressed her entire weight into his chest, holding her shoulders very still as she rubbed her lower half, slithering like a serpent, grazing his crotch, at times grinding into it.

A liquid tide of hormones moved within him. It

was all over the fraternity boy's face as his brain sampled the offering and sent it back down to the erection straining against his Polo khakis. He shut his eyes for a moment, no doubt praying for sexual control. The brothers would laugh at him if he left the room with a mess in his pants.

Tina tossed back her head. She swung it forward. Her hair flew and whipped. She wrapped her hands around his neck as she bucked and heaved with a vengeance, ignoring his moans about how beautiful she was.

The music stopped.

So did Tina Fox.

"That was great!" he shouted.

"Yeah, I didn't want it to stop. Oh, baby."

The sarcasm painted his face red, and he bolted from the room.

"Dork," Tina spat. She connected with Stephanie and threw her gaze to the door. "Get to the point, Marcia Clark. I have a living to make and a political science paper to finish."

"Tell me about your relationship with Dwight."

Tina sighed, as if bored by the subject. "He pretended to be impressed with my mind. I stuck around to talk to him after class, he took me out for drinks, and all we ever discussed was literature. Then I let him get into my pants. Surprise, surprise—his interest in my intellect died. Suddenly all he had time for were quickies in his office and the occasional bang at my apartment. He's one of higher education's finest."

Stephanie hesitated a moment. If Tina Fox was obsessed with Dwight Duckworth, then she deserved Best Actress accolades. Here was a girl whose only focus was Number One. "How did it end?"

"His wife confronted me, and I told her I didn't

want her creepy husband. I stopped it cold after that. Besides, he was a lousy and neurotic lay. Sex dehydrated him. He'd drink a six-pack of bottled water afterward. Really weird."

"Dwight maintains that you delivered a mutilated doll to his doorstep and that you send hate mail to his house. I'll be honest with you, Tina. He's considering a civil suit. If these allegations are true, it could mean serious legal trouble."

A primal rage flashed in Tina's eyes, and she unleashed a bitter laugh. "This . . . is . . . unbelievable," she muttered.

"He'll take no action if the harassment stops today," Stephanie went on. "You're—"

"She's doing it!" Tina screamed.

Stephanie stared back, puzzled. "Who?"

"His wife! She told me I'd pay for tempting her husband. The woman is *psycho.* Shit, her whole family's psycho. Her brother is Bruce Simon, that guy on the lam who just murdered his wife O.J. style."

Thirteen

Monty's BMW was in the driveway of his rented home in an old, tree-lined neighborhood inside the West University area. Parked behind him was a Mitsubishi Eclipse with a California tag.

She rang the doorbell twice and knocked several times before her brother, clad in a black silk robe, opened the door. He was not thrilled to see her.

"You should've called," Monty said, pointedly not inviting her inside.

"I did," Stephanie replied sharply. *"Several* times."

"I've been busy."

"The station thinks you're *sick.*"

"Yeah, sick of the suits," he said bitterly, employing his derisive nickname for KBLX management.

"May I come in?"

He stole a backward glance. "I have company."

Stephanie pushed her way past him. "It's a big house. Tell California friend to wait in another room. Your sister's here, and she doesn't like to be ignored."

Monty sighed and proceeded down the hall, disappearing into one of the bedrooms.

She noticed that her once neat freak brother had either kicked the habit or been otherwise occupied.

Dirty dishes were stacked on the coffee table in front of the television, and beer cans, newspapers, and magazines were scattered about. Bass-heavy house music hummed at a low volume, throbbing like a pulse. A colorful video box atop the VCR captured Stephanie's eye. Taking a step closer, she blanched at the sight: *Hard Enough.* An all male porno movie starring some tattooed mannequin named Joey Danza.

"Oh, Monty," she groaned, wishing her brother could find his way out of the sexual labyrinth that taxed his happiness, self-esteem, and—God forbid— one day his health.

"Do you want a drink?" Monty asked, returning to the living room, now in gray sweatpants and a white Dolce & Gabbana ribbed cotton tank.

"I'm fine."

"What's so urgent?"

"Lisa was raped last night."

"Jesus." He sank down onto the edge of the couch.

Stephanie joined him, relaying all the facts as she knew them.

Monty was speechless.

"She's staying with Tyson Moore. She didn't want Tuesday to see her so beaten up. It's probably for the best."

"I'll drop by and see her in the morning," Monty said.

And then a long, uncomfortable silence hung between them.

Finally, Stephanie could ignore the pink elephant no longer. "Who's back in the bedroom?"

"His . . . it's . . . just a friend."

Stephanie watched Monty's eyes as his last sentence petered out. It was as if the pressure he felt

to open up had numbed to better instincts. He
looked desperate—full of all the anxiety, grief, pain,
and torture that desperation brings. "Why can't you
talk to me about this? After all that we've been
through. I can handle it. Trust me."

Monty stood up. "Leave me alone, Stephanie. I
mean it."

Her heart sank. Was he in trouble? Was he sick?
The questions moved around in her mind like a
twister. A tear formed in her eye, but Stephanie
turned and started out before he could see it. She
left without saying good-bye.

Monty peeled off his clothes and slipped under
the covers.

Immediately, Joey molded to his frame, reaching
around to pinch his nipple as he slipped a warm
tongue into his ear.

"Not tonight," Monty said, his rebuke certain but
gentle.

"Do you want me to go?" Joey asked in a small
voice full of hurt.

"Of course not. Just hold me."

Joey responded in kind, interlocking his body
with Monty's. "It must be hard."

"What's that?"

"Keeping so many secrets," Joey said softly.

Monty couldn't remember living life any other
way.

His memory of that horrible night in September
twenty years ago.

His feelings for men.

His ambivalence toward women.

His career in quicksand.

His passionate relationship with a XXX adult video star.

It all added up to one big fucking secret.

Joey nuzzled his chin on Monty's shoulder. "I want to know everything about you."

Monty squeezed his shoulder blades in reply.

"I'm serious," Joey implored.

"Go to sleep," Monty said sweetly.

Within minutes, Joey was in dreamland, but Monty was still wide awake, his mind active with Lisa's unspeakable terror . . . and Joey's tender plea for intimacy. The truth of it—both frightened the hell out of him.

He shut his eyes, praying for Lisa. She now shared something that he and Stephanie knew only too well: A defining tragedy that would draw an unerasable chalk line through her life. Before the rape. After the rape. From this moment forward, all events would be classified that way. Knowing this, his heart ached for her.

Monty brought his own breathing to pace with Joey's. It was crazy, but they were so very much alike. Both had sought ways to feed their hunger for attention. What most people found through interpersonal relationships, Monty and Joey garnered via fame—one by the respectable local worship of a trusted TV news reader, the other by the subculture devotion to an *actor* in an underground industry. Different paths to the same destination—loneliness and emptiness.

Did he love him? Monty pondered the question. As long as Joey was around, nothing else seemed to matter. KBLX, his hobbies, his family—all of it took second billing to Joey Danza, a man with serious street appeal. Sometimes he possessed the simmering hostility of 1950's Marlon Brando, and other times he played like James Dean, a wounded bird impossible to comfort, yet strong enough to fly away. No matter, they'd spent enormous amounts of time together without ever disagreeing. Somewhere along the way, Monty had wandered off and looked back to discover that Joey had become the most important person in his world.

"I want a life with you," Monty whispered, holding his breath to let the profound moment steal over him.

Stephanie had Peter.

Lisa had Tyson.

He had Joey.

Monty liked knowing that his capacity to love existed. No one else had ever brought out these feelings. The heady danger gave him a rush of pleasure. It was official. His heart had been stolen. Now he wanted to warm himself around the concept, do something that he'd never done before. Yes, Monty decided, he was willing to take such a risk with Joey.

Soon.

Very soon.

He would seal their love in the crucible of dark demons shared.

"No more secrets," Monty whispered into the night.

Lisa Randall took a hot shower, followed by a hot bath, another hot shower, and yet another hot bath. No matter what, she couldn't get clean. His smell, his touch, his semen, continued to contaminate her body.

It was strange, but she felt oddly euphoric, knowing that he could have killed her last night. How absurd it was to be grateful to him—the sick bastard who had kicked the world out from under her.

Tyson's one-bedroom apartment made her feel safe. Only seven hundred square feet, the compact surroundings became her private cocoon. He had sweetly insisted upon her taking the full bed, while he settled into the chaise lounge beside it. With him nearby she slept peacefully, and she wondered if she would ever be able to live by herself again.

It pained her to see Tyson react to the attack with such agony and confusion. He blamed himself for not being there, for not protecting her, and Lisa sensed that he also felt as if someone had robbed him of something. Even now, just days after the rape, she saw in his eyes the guilty desire to make love to her. Why? Lisa contemplated the situation. Was it to make certain she was normal, that her interest in sex and the touch of a man were not permanently damaged? Of course, it was much too soon to determine that. However, one thing was certain: Right now, the very thought of sexual intimacy with Tyson filled her with an unspeakable dread.

The rapist had forced himself onto her in the missionary position, pinioning her hands over head in the classic power stance as he pummeled into her, watching her fearful, tearful eyes. To have a man on top of her . . . the mere thought triggered repulsion, and it was a reaction that would never go away. Of that, Lisa was sure. How patient would Tyson be, she wondered. Granted, they barely knew each other, but the special connection was there, and Lisa already had grown dependent on him.

Under normal circumstances, staying cooped up in a small apartment would have driven her mad, but circumstances were normal no more. She could not fathom the thought of going to work . . . or anywhere, for that matter. Everything she needed was at Tyson's—him, all her favorite foods, and a big screen television to numb her senses. Within a few days, she grew to think of the warm, chatty images of Regis and Kathie Lee, Rosie, and Oprah as family. Also soothing was Cosby, Tyson's solid black, animal shelter cat, who renounced his master in favor of her upon her arrival. When Cosby wasn't crunching Meow Mix or scratching litter, he was curled up beside her, lulling her with his hypnotic purr.

She had just poured her cranberry juice and toasted a Pop Tart when the doorbell chimed. Her heart raced, her knees buckled, and her mind flashed with images of the masked attacker. Why had she opened the door without peering through the peephole? Lisa would never make that same mistake again. Slowly, she moved toward the door, comforted by the knowledge that Tyson had installed an extra, state-of-the-art deadbolt to make her feel more safe. Rising up on her toes, she managed to peek with her one open eye.

It was Monty, carrying a thatch of flowers and an enormous box of Godiva chocolates. The sight of him brought a smile to her face. The moment he entered, Lisa went to work securing the apartment. Knob lock. Old deadbolt. New deadbolt. Chain.

Monty pretended not to notice her compulsiveness about safety; he pretended not to notice her busted lips, bruised cheek, and swollen eye. Instead, he simply wrapped his arms around her for a very long time.

Lisa cried softly.

Monty cried, too.

Finally, she pulled out of his gentle embrace, wiping her tears and regarding his flowers and candy offering. "This isn't the prom, Monty," she teased playfully, attempting to lighten the mood as she relieved him of the gifts.

He grinned, embarrassed. "Are you up for a visit?"

"Let's watch *Judge Judy,*" Lisa suggested excitedly, opening the gold box to pop a Caramel Shield into her mouth.

Monty groaned, reaching for a candy as well. "Isn't *The Young And The Restless* on?"

They nestled onto the couch, holding hands and laughing as the cantankerous Judge Judy berated the hapless clods in her court of idiocy.

Lisa looked over at Monty, feeling a surge of warmth. He had so kindly avoided any mention of the attack, obviously trying not to upset her. She had always been struck by how sensitive Monty was. In fact, he sometimes appeared to be a shock absorber for all the insensitivity around him.

She fired the MUTE button on the remote control. "Is there a question in your head that can't make it past your lips?" Lisa inquired gently.

"How are you?" Monty asked. And he meant it, even if the answer took an hour to complete. The earnestness in his eyes told her that he really wanted to know.

She pulled a pillow to her chest and hugged it. "I'm a different person."

Monty averted her gaze, staring down at Cosby, stroking him. "It's still so soon—"

"No," Lisa interjected, "I will never be the same again. I know that."

"You should see someone, a professional. I'm sure Peter—"

"That's not my style."

Monty hesitated. "That wasn't your style *before.*"

She parted her lips in protest, then thought better of it. "I'll think about it."

"Good."

"Are you working today?"

"I called in sick."

Lisa gave him a knowing look. "Do you realize what you might be giving up?"

Monty shrugged. "It's just a job."

"It's more than that to you."

"If the station forces me to make a choice, it sure as hell won't be them."

"But is it the principle at stake here, or is this guy the better choice?"

"He's the better choice." His voice rang with certainty.

Lisa sighed and slapped his knee. "Come on, Monty! Gay or straight, or in your case, undecided, when a man pulls down the zipper his brains fall out. How much do you know about this guy?"

"Enough to know that I don't want to give him up, even if it means losing my position at the station." His lips curved into a cynical smile. "It'll do wonders for Tyson's career."

Lisa merely stared, convinced that Monty was making a terrible mistake. "In Tyson's defense, he's not thrilled about the circumstances, but he'll take the gig. Somebody has to anchor the news."

"I'm sorry. I didn't mean that. Tyson's cool."

It hurt to smile, but Lisa endured the pain. "Yes, he is." A thought shot into her mind, and she experienced a stirring of panic. "Did I latch the chain?" she asked, her voice full of alarm.

"Yes," Monty assured her. "And both deadbolts."

"Okay." She glanced around nervously.

"Do you need anything from your place? I could drive you there and bring you back."

"No," Lisa replied quickly. "I don't want to leave. I might miss Tyson's call." She tried to imagine venturing outside, but the prospect gave rise to anxiety, coupled with minor palpitations and visions of the attack.

His eyes. Flashing hate . . . and recognition.

His voice. *You've got bad taste in friends, bitch. You deserve this.*

Monty touched her arm.

Lisa flinched and began to cry. "I knew him, Monty," she managed through the torrent of tears. "I knew him, and he knew me, but I just can't place him!"

Monty retrieved a handkerchief from his pocket and offered it to her. "I'm here to listen."

"He hated me so much . . . but . . . it was like he was punishing me . . . for something . . . someone else did to him."

When Stephanie marched into her Transco Tower office Matt was already there, waiting with a stack of mail, telephone messages in order of importance, and a prioritized list of things to do.

"I want a meeting with Dwight Duckworth *and* his wife, today. Rearrange whatever you have to."

"What's up?"

"Mrs. Duckworth is Bruce Simon's sister."

"Small world."

Stephanie smiled tightly. "If we lived in the land of Disney, I might accept that." She picked up the mail and messages and proceeded to her office.

Matt trailed her, referring to a thick plastic folder. "There's an expert at the University of New Hampshire's Family Research Laboratory we should consider for the Dean case. He calls child witnesses of domestic violence an unrecognized victim population. Toni Raffin's observations of Jason's behavior at Penelope's House are right in line with this center's findings."

Stephanie nodded, liking what she was hearing. She hoped Matt would consider law school one day. He had too much potential to stay a paralegal forever. "Get him here," she said firmly, knowing Matt would handle all the details. "Any insight on Gibbs?"

A weary look swept across Matt's face. "Peter might be better suited for this job. Didn't he study deviant behavior in medical school?"

"That bad?"

"As if we didn't know," Matt answered, rolling his eyes. "Gibbs ordered a woman who sued her boyfriend for beating her to marry the guy! In another case, he played like Siskel and Ebert and weighed in on key testimony with the thumbs up or thumbs down sign. But then again, there are a number of other cases where he's rendered very solid rulings. The old fart's hard to peg."

Stephanie massaged her temples. Lisa and Monty raced through her mind, but she pushed them from her thoughts, trying to focus. "Is that it?"

"He always rules orally from the bench just after testimony concludes."

"So much for thoughtful deliberation."

Matt played with the tiny gold loop in his ear. "And he relies heavily on his personal observations of the warring parents."

"Any patterns on his views toward working women?"

Matt wrinkled his nose and sifted through the folder, pulling a spreadsheet and placing it in front of Stephanie. "I created a legal scoreboard on his rulings over the last eighteen months. There's no negative pattern on working women in general."

Stephanie caught an ominous tone in Matt's voice. She scanned the data and looked up. "But?"

Matt smoothed his goatee. "Working women more successful than their husbands don't fare well with Judge Gibbs."

Stephanie leaned back in her chair. "Shit," she muttered.

Matt dropped the full report onto her desk. "My first thought as well."

Rob Dean came from rich stock, but he'd never made a mark on his own. He hopscotched from job to job. For him to stay in one place for a year was heavy duty commitment. Conversely, Josie was full of fiery ambition, going from clerical temp to top ad seller for the city's highest-rated country station within two years. The quantum career leap had only exacerbated Rob's abuse. Stephanie hoped Judge Gibbs wouldn't hold Josie's success against her. Unfortunately, Matt's research didn't paint an optimistic picture.

"Set up the Duckworth meeting," she instructed, "and I'll give this a closer look."

"Okay," Matt said, starting out.

"Matt," Stephanie called before he hit the door.

"Yeah?"

"Thanks for the great work. You're indispensable."

He grinned cockily. "I know."

A few hours later, shortly before noon, Matt ushered Dwight and Shelly Duckworth into Stephanie's office. Dwight appeared as pleased with himself as before, and this time Stephanie caught him casting a rakish glance up and down her body. Shelly struck her as a cauldron of simmering hostility with her Peter Pan hairstyle, extra thirty pounds of girth,

Softer Side of Sears attire, and fingernails bitten to the quick.

Once the perfunctory introductions were history, Stephanie launched into the real business. "I'll make this brief because enough of my time has already been wasted. Last night I met with Tina Fox, and to be perfectly frank I find her story more credible than yours."

"What did that slut tell you?" Shelly asked evenly. "Wait! Don't bother answering. I've got the proof right here." She reached inside the free-with-purchase Estee Lauder totebag she carried and pulled out a wad of pictures, spreading them atop Stephanie's desk.

Stephanie shook her head and proceeded to stack up the gruesome images, trying not to capture any sight of the tortured and mutilated animals for more than a second. She shoved them back into Shelly's hand. "That's not proof."

"But—" Dwight began.

"Here's a refund on your retainer, Mr. Duckworth, minus my hourly rate for last night and travel expenses. Seek counsel elsewhere." Stephanie pushed a check to the end of the desk.

"I don't understand," Dwight said.

Shelly Duckworth simply stared back with small, venomous eyes.

"Tina seems more inclined to move on than the two of you. Good therapy is what's needed here, not legal posturing." Stephanie stood up, her body language talking immediate dismissal. "I believe we're through here."

Shelly rose slowly from her seat. "Dwight, I'll meet you outside," she said sharply.

He looked at his wife, a surprised expression on his face, then sauntered out, shaking his head.

"I know who you are," Stephanie announced.

"Oh, really? And who might that be?"

"Bruce Simon's sister."

Shelly smiled primly. "In the flesh."

"Tina didn't send those awful pictures and deliver that doll to your doorstep. *You* did."

Shelly slipped the totebag over her shoulder and shrugged. "I don't appreciate Dwight screwing around. I wanted to torture the cheat."

Stephanie stepped around her desk and moved toward the door, ceremoniously opening it. "That's very interesting, but take your sideshow someplace else. I have work to do."

"You helped her disappear. Ginger was too stupid to think all that up on her own," Shelly said.

A chill slithered up Stephanie's spine. She closed the door.

"Bruce doesn't like people getting the best of him. That's why he tracked her down. That's why he killed her. You drove him to it."

Stephanie took in a deep breath. "A woman who sends herself photos of dead animals would believe that."

"Maybe he'll get you, too," Shelly said.

Stephanie froze.

"Or maybe he'll make something *you* love disappear." Shelly reached for the framed portrait of Tuesday on Stephanie's desk. "Such a pretty little girl."

Fourteen

"She's in a meeting."

"She's *always* in a meeting."

"Her schedule is tight."

"What's your name?"

"Matt."

"Well, *Matt*, this little game is growing tiresome. I'm trying to get Stephanie Hart on the phone, not the Queen of England," Abby snarled.

"Perhaps I can accelerate things. What's the nature of your interview request?"

Abby paused. "I'll discuss those details with Ms. Hart."

"Fax me your interview questions. She'll look them over and get back to you."

Abby dug her nails into her palm. This little shit was driving her crazy. The trouble was, her name carried baggage galore, and the only people who wanted to talk to her were those with axes to grind. Frustrated, she slammed down the receiver.

Francisco appeared in the doorway. He looked scrumptious in a formfitting black T-shirt, black jeans, and scuffed boots. "Ready for lunch?"

The sight and sound of him sent good vibrations to all the right places. Francisco Juarez was very fuckable indeed, and Abby vowed that before she left Houston, she would sample this Cuban delight.

They hit Mark's on Westheimer, the hot new eatery owned by Mark Cox, a longtime chef for restaurant king Tony Vallone. The place was warm, modest in size, and possessed the casual glow of a Pottery Barn showroom. It had once been a red brick church.

Francisco took in the surroundings, obviously pleased with his selection. "This spot just opened a few months ago. There's been a crush to get in."

Abby watched a beautiful older woman approach their table. She was certain their paths had crossed somewhere before.

"Francisco!" the woman exclaimed. "Darling, I've missed you so."

He stood up to embrace her, kissing her cheek. "Toni," he cooed. "How good to see you."

"I've really been enjoying the magazine. Every month it gets better and better," Toni gushed.

Francisco beamed. "Thank you." Suddenly it dawned on him that Abby was sitting there. "Forgive my poor manners. Toni Raffin, this is Abby McQueen."

Toni cocked her head curiously and extended her hand. "I believe—"

"We've met," Abby cut in, shaking firmly, having retrieved the memory while gagging on the lovefest. "Twenty years ago, to be exact. I covered the Jimmy Scott murder for *Texas Today*. We talked poolside at the River Oaks Country Club."

"Of course," Toni replied archly.

"I'm working on a twentieth anniversary piece, and I'd love to sit down with you," Abby said.

Toni turned to Francisco and laughed. "I don't

think anyone would be interested in that old story. You sound a little desperate for topics, dear."

Wrinkled bitch! Abby came very close to dousing the Christian Dior-clad fossil with iced tea, but she kept her cool, assessing the situation. Besides, it was Francisco's place to defend her editorial honor.

He touched the senior socialite's elbow. "We're not digging up skeletons, Toni. There are great stories to tell about those people *today.* Like your work at Penelope's House, Stephanie's legal career, and Montgomery's popularity as a news anchor."

Abby smiled, nodding with eager affirmation. Right now the look on Toni Raffin's face indicated she thought this story would be the best thing to hit the market since Depends. Francisco Juarez was serving Abby the old bag's cooperation on a silver salver.

"That would be great PR for Penelope's House. We would be so honored," Toni trilled, putting limp wrist onto heart in a gesture of mechanical humility.

"Wonderful. I'll have Abby get in touch," Francisco said, grinning.

Toni cut an ambivalent gaze. "Please do."

Francisco sat down and whistled relief.

"Great save," Abby praised, laughing lightly. "But just so we understand each other, if Toni Raffin wants a puff of pretty smoke blown up her ass she'll need to publish her own newsletter, because I'm going after the truth—the uglier the better."

As Francisco opened his mouth to protest, Toni swooped by once more, her eyes alight with excitement. "I just had the most fabulous idea," she launched. "Forget about that ancient *incident.* There's nothing enlightening in rehashing that. How about a story on the legal abuse of women and children by divorce lawyers and judges?"

Francisco turned to Abby and arched his brow. "I like it."

Let Oprah dedicate an hour to it, Abby thought. There's no Big Deal potential with a crybaby story like that. "Me, too," she lied. "I'm sure one of the staff writers would be happy to take it on."

"As a matter of fact," Toni continued, "Stephanie Hart is involved in a major case right now. A wife beater is suing for custody of his two-year-old son. What's even more frightening is that he actually stands a chance, especially with Chuck Berg as his counsel and Lawrence Gibbs on the bench."

Abby moved fast to edit the surprise on her face. *Lawrence Gibbs.* No doubt the same ambulance chaser who led the charge in a wrongful death suit against the Cains twenty years ago. "This *is* a very strong idea. Francisco, don't bother with a staff writer just yet. I'd love to do the initial leg work."

Francisco opened his hands to the heavens and smiled broadly. "Then I guess we're all set."

Toni clasped his hand in hers. "You're the best." And she was off.

He leaned across the table toward Abby to whisper, "There's no extra money in it for you. Our budget for this issue is stretched to the limit."

Abby gave him a diffident shrug as she studied the menu. "I don't give a shit about the story, but I can use the angle to get access to Stephanie Hart."

"Listen," Francisco began seriously, "Toni's a friend."

Abby looked up from the menu. "What kind of friend?"

"Last year the magazine did a feature on her home in Puerto Vallarta."

"You fucked her," Abby accused.

Francisco threw glances at the surrounding tables,

hoping they hadn't heard. "Why do you have to be so vulgar?"

"You *did* fuck her. I was only guessing." She laughed.

He tried ignoring her, turning to his menu, but his desire to respond soon overwhelmed him. "You make it sound so dirty, when it wasn't. Yes, we were lovers, briefly, . . . but we parted as friends, and both of us have fond memories of our time together. Is there something wrong with that?"

"I bet she bought you presents," Abby sang.

He nodded, reluctantly. "A few." His tone was defensive.

"A Rolex?"

Francisco looked surprised, then quietly replied, "I wouldn't accept it."

"Of course not—too extravagant. But the new suit wasn't a problem, right?"

He shifted in his seat, darting glances around the trendy restaurant. "Toni's a generous person."

"Oh, I'm sure you reciprocated to the best of your ability."

"It wasn't like that," Francisco said tightly.

"Oh, come on! Older woman. Younger man. Gifts from her. Sex from you. Where I come from the name for it is gigolo."

"Very funny."

"Jimmy Scott had a similar arrangement with Toni before he moved on to Marilyn Cain. Wouldn't you consider him a gigolo?"

Francisco beamed back a glare and signaled for the waiter. "I'd consider him a two-bit hood."

Abby leaned forward, and in a teasing hush she said, "What do I have to do to get a little attention?"

"Act like a human being."

* * *

Shortly after her New American lunch Abby McQueen was sitting in Chuck Berg's office, looking to scratch out a mutually beneficial arrangement. "I covered the Jimmy Scott murder for *Texas Today* in 1977, and I've been wooed back to write a twentieth anniversary piece."

Chuck Berg leaned back and smirked. "Not the follow-up you'd expect to a bestseller on Stallone."

Abby stewed on the insult. Who did this schmuck with the bad toupee think he was? "Get this straight— I didn't seek you out for career counseling."

Chuck Berg leered suggestively. "So what can I do for you?"

Abby's stomach turned over. *Not that.* She had jumped into bed with men far worse than him to get ahead on a project, but at this point it was too early in the game to torture herself. "I've heard some interesting talk about a custody case that puts you and Stephanie Hart at legal odds."

Chuck nodded, betraying nothing.

"I'm looking for a professional colleague of Stephanie's to draw inferences about her troubled childhood and her chosen career path. Someone who can paint a picture of gross impartiality, perhaps even raise the possibility that *innocent* men have been victimized by her legal efforts."

Chuck's eyes widened and then narrowed as he calculated Abby's motives with a steely glare. "Not a bad idea. Do I get a picture in the spread?" He reached into one of his desk drawers and presented a five-by-seven color portrait, retouched Hollywood style.

Abby threw down a polite glance. Robert Shapiro had nothing to worry about. "That depends."

"On what?"

"How *significant* your views are." She retrieved a voice-activated microcassette recorder from her purse and placed it at the end of his desk.

"Let me tell you something," Chuck began to thunder.

The red light blinked on and off.

"Stephanie Hart marches with all those women's groups that cry foul whenever an ex-wife doesn't get the whole enchilada or a father gets the chance to raise his kid. Her office is like an animal shelter for *victims* who claim they've gotten the shaft by divorce lawyers. *Bullshit.* These women don't listen. They don't hear. They don't ask the right questions. Stephanie Hart is blind to the obvious. She's so shell-shocked from killing Jimmy Scott that she believes every soon-to-be-ex is as dangerous as *he* was. Not true. And in the case of Rob Dean, when judgment day comes he'll walk out of the courtroom as sole custodial parent. I'll make sure of that."

Abby tapped her foot to the music of Chuck Berg's outburst. It had a nice beat; she could sensationalize to it. "Before we go deeper, can you point me in the direction of any other sources?"

Chuck's fleshy lips curled into a devilish grin. "Hart's guy Friday got some trade secrets out of my paralegal when he boffed her not long ago. A looker like you could give him a taste of his own medicine." He winked.

Abby feigned indignation. "I resent the implication."

Chuck snorted. "Yeah, I bet. His name's Matt Benedict. Looks like the twin of Bob Dylan's son, the kid in that new rock group that's all over MTV."

"Jakob Dylan of the Wallflowers," Abby confirmed.

"That's it. Anyway, he's a fixture at The Blue Iguana on Richmond Avenue."

Abby jotted it down. One way or another, this story was going to put her back in business.

Fifteen

Shelly Duckworth was only a few steps past the door when Stephanie reached for the phone to call Kirk Mulroney. Luckily, the police captain was at his desk.

"Nothing new on Lisa Randall's case, Stephanie," he began as soon as she identified herself. "I'm sorry."

"I'm calling about another matter, Kirk. Who's handling the Bruce Simon case?"

"We're working on it, but essentially it's in the hands of the F.B.I. What's up?"

Stephanie relayed the whole sordid tale—Dwight's initial visit, her encounter with Tina Fox, and Shelly's thinly veiled threats just moments ago. She hung up feeling more at ease. Kirk had promised her that Shelly Duckworth would feel the full weight of both the HPD team and the Feds. But could he promise that Tuesday was safe from harm? No. And the nightmarish possibilities swarmed inside her head like killer bees. It would only take a moment—that fast—and her beloved daughter could disappear from sight.

"Find the bastard," she whispered aloud, more certain than ever that Bruce Simon was behind the cryptic notes and the stalking. Perhaps Shelly was helping him as well. It certainly fit in line with her character, considering her scheme against her own husband for carrying on with Tina Fox.

Matt burst into the room, his expression full of alarm. "Gibbs's clerk just called. Josie's court date has been moved up. It starts tomorrow."

Stephanie experienced a jolt. "What?"

Matt's eyes were wide with disbelief. "I had the same reaction. Something came up that forced him to rearrange his calendar."

"More like *someone,*" Stephanie hissed.

"You think Berg is behind this?"

"They're either hunting buddies, golfing buddies, or lovers. I can't decide which."

Matt chuckled.

"Dammit. I haven't even made a dent in that research you compiled."

With a flourish, Matt produced a cassette. "Here's the abridged audio version. No time like the present to test its efficiency."

Stephanie was momentarily speechless. "Brilliant. I'll listen in the car." She gathered her things and hit the elevator, her mind whirling with anxiousness for Josie . . . and despair for Lisa.

Matt's deep, DJ quality voice filled the cabin with sobering evidence that Josie's fight was a frightening one indeed. Most men don't challenge their wives for custody, but those who do prevail more than seventy percent of the time. Some seek custody for financial relief only, the old cheaper to keep 'em excuse. Because noncustodial parents are expected to hand over twenty percent of their earnings in child support, many cases show men filing for custody simply to maintain a better standard of living from their higher earning wives. Rob Dean fit squarely into that mold. While he stumbled from job to job, Josie pulled in one hundred grand a year.

Stephanie tightened her grip on the wheel as she tried to predict Chuck Berg's strategy. Taking the she's a slut offensive would only be part of his arsenal. No doubt he had teased her with that tidbit just to piss her off. Suddenly a sinking sensation came over her. Chuck Berg had something big on Josie Dean. The proverbial smoking gun. A piece of evidence, or a witness who would discredit her beyond repair in the eyes of Judge Gibbs. Despite the awesome power of her feeling, Stephanie prayed she was wrong . . . and that Josie Dean had told her everything.

Lisa worried about her reaction to Monty's request that they leave Tyson's apartment to pick up some things at her own place. A quickly beating heart, sweating hands, a churning stomach—she had suffered all of that, and more. The mere thought of stepping outside of her safe haven, even for a moment, was more than she could fathom. In her mind, Lisa had written a narrative of what would happen if she ventured beyond these comforting walls.

He would be waiting to rape her again—only this time to kill her.

The image was so vivid, and the only placating thought was the knowledge that serenity was in the space around her. As long as she stayed within these surroundings, she would remain free from danger. Her vision of the consequences not only described her fear but locked her into it. For a moment, she mourned the determined young woman, the sassy sister with the will of iron, that she had once been.

Stephanie's arrival triggered more anxiety. Each time she opened the door she caught a glimpse of the world that now terrified her. But hearing the click of fastening locks massaged her raw nerves. Until Stephanie prepared to leave, she would be fine. They embraced warmly and settled at the small dining room table for tea.

"Tyson's place is so *small*, Lisa," Stephanie observed. "Are you sure you don't want to stay with us for a few days?"

"No," Lisa replied quickly, the notion eliciting a pang of panic. "I like it here."

Stephanie regarded her curiously. "Okay. I suppose it doesn't matter. Before long, you'll be back at your place."

"I'm never going back there."

"Of course," Stephanie muttered quickly. "Well, I'd love to help you shop for a new place. There's—"

Lisa set down her KBLX mug with a bang. "Can we talk about something else please?" Her tone was shrill.

Stephanie was taken aback. "Sure."

Lisa sighed. "I'm sorry."

"Don't apologize."

"Have you talked to Monty?" Lisa inquired.

Stephanie sipped slowly on her tea. "I've seen him. We didn't do much talking. He's . . . involved with someone."

"Joey Danza," Lisa confirmed with remorse.

Stephanie's hand went to her forehead as her eyes closed. "No," she groaned.

"I'm afraid so," Lisa whispered. "He probably didn't tell you the station knows about it and has asked him to make a choice. Apparently there's a morals clause in his contract that gives them an out." She hesitated before announcing, "They're grooming Tyson for Monty's slot."

Stephanie sat immobile, frozen with shock.

"There's no getting through to him," Lisa muttered, exasperated. "He thinks he loves this guy."

"I don't understand," Stephanie wailed. "This is career suicide."

"Monty says it's just a job."

"In a market the size of Houston, you don't lose an anchor job over a porn star and then end up on CNN."

"The heart's a stubborn thing. It does what it wants and can't be commanded to do otherwise," Lisa murmured philosophically.

Stephanie shot her a cross look. "I don't think his *heart* has anything to do with it."

Lisa laughed in spite of herself. "That's *exactly* what I told him."

Stephanie managed a weak smile.

"What are you going to do?"

"I'm not sure. I just know that I don't approve . . . and that I have some tough decisions to make."

Lisa, noticing that Stephanie looked tired and stressed to the maximum, felt a little guilty about calling her here to ask for her help. Who else could she turn to? Last night she had broached the subject with Tyson, who issued a strong, emphatic, "Hell no, baby!" Hopefully, Stephanie would be more open-minded.

"Enough about Monty," Stephanie began. "You said you needed a favor. Name it, and it's yours."

"I want a gun," Lisa said flatly.

Stephanie swallowed hard. "Okay . . . I'll talk to Kirk Mulroney. I think the police department has a good training class."

"I don't have time for all of that," Lisa said quickly. "I need it now."

"For peace of mind?"

Lisa nodded. "And to protect myself."

"Well, regardless, these things take time. You have to think long and hard about it, do some research, and then be properly trained."

Lisa became visibly agitated. For Christ's sake, it wasn't rocket science.

Load.

Aim.

Pull the trigger.

Bang bang.

The bastard's dead.

If Stephanie didn't act quickly on her behalf—and judging from the hesitant look on her face, chances were slim that she would—then Lisa was determined to fall back on Plan C. The safety of Tyson's arms and Tyson's apartment was almost all the security she needed, but *almost* didn't cut it. Lisa Randall wanted tangible assurance that the motherfucker who raped her would die trying the next time.

The next six days were swift and merciless. Chuck Berg pulled every dirty trick in the book, and most of them worked. To ignore Judge Gibbs's implicit disapproval of Josie Dean was to ignore a three ring circus in the courtroom.

"If one missed the extreme anger and hostility you have demonstrated to this court, one would have to be blind as a bat," he had screeched on day five.

Stephanie struggled to convince Josie to maintain

her composure, but the battery of injustices eventually caused the embattled mother to come undone.

The Dean's housekeeper testified that Rob never yelled, or worse yet, that he never so much as got impatient. Even more damning, she relayed the time Josie called Rob a "shit-for-brains son of a bitch" within earshot of Jason.

Some members of Rob's immediate family and one former friend of Josie's put forth false claims of her sexual promiscuity, mental illness, and bitter vendetta against Rob. They helped build Judge Gibbs's negative attitude toward Josie to a crescendo, but it was Berg's final witness who sealed the tragic fate.

A former resident of Penelope's House testified that Josie had threatened to kidnap Jason and go into hiding if she lost the custody hearing. Stephanie knew that to be true. After all, Josie had uttered the same to her. Ironically, the one seed of truth Chuck Berg planted helped fertilize all the lies.

Nothing Stephanie presented turned the tide— not the doctors and nurses on duty during Josie's two emergency room visits, not her mother, not Toni Raffin, and not even the expert from New Hampshire who provided empirical evidence to show that children in domestic abuse situations exhibit some of the same traumatic symptoms as prisoners of war.

"There's no standout quality in either parent here that particularly strikes me," Judge Gibbs began on the sixth and final day of the hearing, "so the better choice is not because of one single indiscretion. Quite honestly, there were many of those on both sides. When all is said and done, it's a matter of totality." He shot a glare Josie's way.

Stephanie braced herself for the worst. It was going to happen. The unthinkable. This senile old goat was seconds away from separating a mother from her child. Under the table, she gripped Josie's hand. In her peripheral vision, she caught the tears streaming down Josie's face.

"And it all comes down to my gut feeling, doesn't it?" He slipped a hint of a smile to the Berg-Dean table, another scowl to the Hart-Dean contingent. "I used to subscribe to the tender years doctrine, wherein mothers had presumptive rights to their young children. I don't anymore. This boy belongs in the more ordered environment and with the less volatile parent. Taking into account everything I've seen and heard this week, that parent is the father, Rob Dean."

Josie cried out, collapsing into gut-wrenching sobs. Stephanie went through the motions, but she was inconsolable.

Chuck and Rob stood quickly, stealing a quick, backslapping bear hug.

"Furthermore, I feel inclined to suspend the mother's visitation rights until such time as a court-appointed psychologist can determine that there is no longer a reasonable threat of child abduction and flight." He hammered down the gavel.

Disbelief flooded into Stephanie's heart as she sat there speechless, impaled by the spear of the judge's ruling.

"What d-does that mean?" Josie whispered.

"We'll appeal," Stephanie whispered back confidently, knowing that Josie fully comprehended Judge Gibbs's final words, but in a drastic measure of self-preservation was simply refusing to acknowledge them. "We'll get him back. I swear it." Anger welled up inside her.

Josie began to shrink before her eyes, shell-shocked and forlorn. "You promised me this wouldn't happen!" She stood quickly, shouting, "No! I want my son! I want my son!"

Stephanie moved fast to calm her. "Not here, Josie. Not now. I know you're upset, but any outburst will only come back to haunt you. Trust me."

"Ms. Hart, please restrain your client," Judge Gibbs blasted venomously.

It took every bit of Stephanie's strength not to blow her top. Justice didn't live here anymore. Wife beater Rob Dean had won custody of two-year-old Jason. Josie Dean had lost it. But it didn't have to stay that way for long. The words that kept spinning round and round in her mind were *don't give up*.

Stephanie went through the rest of the day like an automaton. Luckily, Tuesday was engrossed in a major school project. She carried most of the dinner chatter, cleared the table, and disappeared to her room to complete her assignment as she always did—alone. Tuesday asked for help only when she absolutely needed it, for she was possessed by a fiery independence.

"Are you up for a movie?" Peter asked.

Stephanie didn't answer.

"I'll make a video run for some mindless action flick."

Finally, she shook her head. "Not tonight." Wordlessly, she stepped outside onto the deck, greeted the excited dogs, and settled into a wrought iron chaise. Liz insisted on curling up at her feet; Richard was content to park beside her.

Stephanie gazed up at the night sky, going over the horrors of the last few weeks.

Ginger Simon's murder.

The REMEMBER SEPTEMBER messages.

Lisa's rape.

Monty's life crisis.

Josie Dean's loss in court.

The sum of it all was taking its toll. She didn't want to cry because she was afraid she might never stop.

From the outdoor speakers, the supper club jazz sounds of Sade came wafting out at low volume. A moment later, Peter joined her with two glasses of red wine. He sat quietly, and together they languished in the cool night air, sipping greedily as the breeze pushed the wind chimes into song.

She turned to him, realizing that for the last six days she had been waiting for a moment such as this to ask him the questions burning in her heart about Monty. "Have you seen my brother this week?"

Peter reached down to pet Richard, who responded by rolling onto his back. "A few days ago."

"You told me not to worry." There was an edge to Stephanie's voice that hit the air against her better judgment.

Peter regarded her curiously; the undercurrent of hostility was not lost on him. "That's right. I'd tell you the same today."

Stephanie averted her eyes to the backyard. "He's living with a porn star, Peter. And he's about to lose his position at Channel Eleven. If this is the kind of therapy you practice, I'd say it's time for a referral." She bolted from the lounge to the edge of the deck and downed the last of her wine. *What a bitch you are,* she scolded herself, regretting every word.

"This is why I was reluctant to take Monty on, Steph. His problems are becoming our problems," Peter said evenly. Then he went back inside.

Stephanie wanted to go after him, but it just wasn't in her tonight. She decided to apologize later. He was right. She had bulldozed him into seeing Monty as a patient, and now she was blaming him for less than miraculous results.

Peter returned with what remained of the wine, refilling her glass as well as his own. "Monty's a twenty-seven-year-old man, Steph. He's in love for the first time, and he's not sure that he wants to stay in a job that invades his privacy and forces him to keep a very important part of his world a secret. Would I make the same choices? Would you? No. But Monty's thinking through all the angles and trying to decide if what he's getting is worth what he'll be giving up. It's his life."

"And he's ruining it."

Peter's brow furrowed, and he took a large sip of wine. "It's his to ruin.

Sixteen

Abby barged into Blue Iguana and scoped the scene, feeling as ridiculous as a teenager at a Barney concert. A punk rock band called Sugar Shack played their ear poison at blistering speed. They were loud, rude, and obviously still angry at their parents. The people graffiti of fans pumped fists in the air, slammed bodies, and more or less agreed with Sugar Shack's fuck the world attitude set to music.

She had discovered Jakob Dylan's clone at the bar, nursing a beer. Unlike the rest of the crazies, he looked as if he could drum up a serious thought without causing permanent brain damage.

The band came to a thrashing halt, shouting their need for a booze break. As the lights flooded the floor, so did The Rolling Stones. "Start Me Up" kicked ass as the crowd parted like a wave.

Abby moved fast to claim the empty barstool next to Matt Benedict before some punker could plant his pierced and tattooed body on it. She ordered up a beer and waited. Sure, at forty-five she was old enough to have breast-fed the boy, but he was at least old enough to drink. Senators and congressmen didn't make such distinctions. By comparison, she was a woman with conservative family values.

"You don't look like a Sugar Shack girl," Matt said, giving her a lop-sided grin.

Abby smiled back. "What kind of girl do I look like?"

"The Neil Diamond type."

"Fuck you," she said lightly.

He laughed. "I'm Matt."

"I know. I've asked around. I'm Abby McQueen. We've argued on the phone."

Matt leaned back, surprised, and already a little drunk. "You hung up on me!" His words were slightly slurred.

"You shouldn't feel singled out. It's a big club."

He gestured to the bartender for another drink. "I wasn't up for this Sugar Shack shit tonight, but what the hell—there's beer."

Abby threw back a tequila shot like a gunslinger in a hot saloon. "Tough day?"

"Lost a big case."

"Ah, the custody battle," she said knowingly. "I take it Chuck Berg prevailed."

Matt returned a guarded look.

"I interviewed him. He gave me his version of events."

"Well, as long as you're not interested in the truth, you should be in good shape."

"Hit me again," Abby commanded the bartender.

Matt gave her a sideways glance. "Slow down . . . or I'll have to drive you home."

She turned to face him. "Could you do that without a note from your mother?"

He laughed, then guzzled half his beer. "You're funny."

Abby knocked back her second round and stood up. "Cartoons are funny, kid. I'm horny. Do you want to follow me back to my hotel, or sit here trading one-liners all night?"

He lost his balance momentarily and almost toppled to the floor. "Are you serious?"

"Just call me Mrs. Robinson."

"Who?"

"Didn't you ever see *The Graduate*?"

A blank look clouded Matt's face.

Abby drew in a deep breath. "I'll probably regret asking this, but here goes—what's your favorite movie?"

"That's easy. *Jurassic Park*."

She groaned. He might as well have said *Dumbo*, as young as it made him seem. Regardless, one look at his heat-stoked gaze and she knew he could become adult where it mattered—between the sheets.

Sugar Shack cranked back up at deafening volume. Reading lips wasn't Abby's thing, so she grabbed Matt's hand, leading him out to the parking lot, where the noise relief was so great it felt like going under water.

"Where's your car?" She had to know his make and model before fessing up to the fact that she had arrived in a borrowed Escort.

He pointed to his spit-polished Dodge Stealth parked a stone's throw away. "It's fast, but not as fast as you."

"I'd let you take me for a ride, but you're drunk."

"Hey, I drive better when I'm drunk."

Abby cackled. "Spoken like a true high school senior." She leaned against his driver's side door.

Matt regarded her suspiciously. Unfortunately, he wasn't drunk enough. "Just what do you want with me?"

"Let's pick up a twelve-pack and go back to my hotel. I'll show you."

His mouth found hers, and the stubble of his goatee was so deliciously rough against her smooth skin. He twisted and pulled her hair as he forced their lips together with such indelicate hunger, teeth clashing, tongues at war. And then he pulled back from the cruel merger of lust and asked once more, "What do you want?"

"Everything I can get."

He drove like Speed Racer to the mini mart and dashed in to load up on Michelob Light and condoms. Abby hollered out the window to add Altoids to the list. She chewed four on the elevator ride up, then went to work giving Matt a blow job the second they hit the room.

"Shit! I've never held on this long before," he exclaimed several minutes later, applying pressure behind her head with his hands, commanding her to keep on, challenging her to test his stamina.

Abby moaned, opened wider, and took in all that she could without choking.

"This is fucking awesome!" Matt cried, thrusting his hips. "Oh, God!"

Oh, please, Abby thought. The peppermint oil in the candy was taking effect, stimulating the skin of his penis, rushing the blood there, prolonging his erection, and making him feel like the biggest stud in the world. With a little more of this and a lot more beer, Matt Benedict would sing like a canary and not remember the song the next morning.

What she hadn't counted on was the fact that he possessed the endurance of a triathlete. He could produce a hard-on as easily and often as most men could a belch. Abby rose to the occasion, thankful for the release after a long sentence in the prison of celibacy. He wasn't a creative lover, but he was a quick study, and she taught him things that would turn his next one-night stand into a got-to-have-him obsessive. Matt was the best time she had had in the sack since a three-way with a daytime soap hunk and a Bloomingdale's fragrance model.

In between passionate trips, he mumbled freely. Spurred on by her gentle prodding, he went on and on about the Dean custody case, boring her to no end. She was certain Stephanie Hart knew nothing of Lawrence Gibbs's connection to her past, recalling Billy Hudson's stories of Marilyn Cain's exaggerated lengths to keep media coverage far away from her daughter. Unless the murderess had delved into the archives of her own crime, she would likely never put the two facts together.

Of more interest was learning about the Bruce Simon scare, and even better, about the sicko sending Stephanie Hart messages to REMEMBER SEPTEMBER. Was it just a coincidence that the anonymous note referred to the same month as the Jimmy Scott murder? On that thought, she drifted off to sleep.

A few hours later the sun blazed, fighting through the heavy curtains of the Marriott Hotel. Abby stretched lazily and smiled. The space beside her was empty, but it was still warm. Matt Benedict. Last night he'd taken her on a trip to the moon.

He emerged from the bathroom, nude, wearing his nakedness with the smug confidence that only youth allowed as he jerked the curtains open. In poured the blinding orange ball.

Abby shielded her eyes and looked out at the sprawling metropolis. Granted, Houston wasn't New York, but the city had its appeal. She liked the knee-slapping contradictions. Cuddled up near weed-infested parking lots and call-the-wrecking-ball-please buildings were high-priced shopping palaces for big-haired big spenders.

"After I take you back to your car I have to go home and change, then get to work," Matt announced, beginning the scavenger hunt for his brooder's night out costume of black this and black that.

"Call in sick," Abby purred, punctuating her suggestion with a filthy smile.

Matt shook his head. "I'd never do that to Stephanie. Not after the day she had yesterday. That custody case took a lot out of her."

Abby frowned. She had pleasured this man-child until dawn, and all he cared about was playing kiss-ass games with some Gloria Allred wannabe.

"Like I said, I'll talk to Stephanie and plead your case. Maybe she'll come around. You know, agree to the interview."

Abby stopped herself from leaping out of bed and slapping the shit out of this sex-crazed slacker. He was talking to her as if she were some groupie who had just fucked a roadie for a slim chance at meeting Jon Bon Jovi. "Oh, do you think she might?"

Matt nodded vigorously, deaf to the facetious tone.

"What about the fax? I want to see that Remember September business."

Matt stepped into his tattered boxers. "That's up to her."

"Just make me a copy."

"No way." He grabbed his jeans.

"Come on," Abby cooed, "there's no harm in that." She reached out to stroke him where it counted. Too much blood was pumping to this kid's brain. She needed it to start moving south.

"I've gotta go," Matt said. He didn't move an inch, but his cock grew several.

Abby let the sheet fall, exposing all of her as she continued stroking him, amazement steaming over her. Matt Benedict was hot, hard, huge, and ready. Mortal men would be comatose after the last eight hours.

A melodic moan escaped his lips as he freed himself through the slit in his boxers.

"Won't you do me that one little favor?"

His answer was a firm hand on the back of her head, pushing her down to the straining, throbbing part of him. "I'll bring it to you tonight."

"Good boy," she breathed with an air of rapt and sensuous finality, as she opened her mouth to take him in, sucking hard, wanting to get it over with. While she worked, Abby prayed for something sinister. In fact, she closed her eyes and wished for a psychopath. A spin like that would surely keep her off the bread line.

Seventeen

It was one of the hardest calls Stephanie would ever make, but she was determined to hold true to her conviction, painful though it might be. Taking a deep breath, she dialed Monty's number, and he answered on the third ring.

Stephanie's heart sank. Part of her—more accurately, all of her—wanted the answering machine to pick up. "Feeling better?"

"I won't be on the air tonight, if that's what you mean."

"Another sick day?"

"Something like that," he muttered dismissively. "How's Lisa?"

"She wants a gun."

"I'd want one, too."

"That's not a decision to make out of fear."

"Well, I don't think her fear will be going anywhere for a long time."

"Yeah," Stephanie agreed somberly, "you're probably right. So how are you?"

"Fine. I'm looking forward to Tuesday's sleepover tonight. We're going to make pizza."

Stephanie bristled. Did she have the heart to go through with it? She twisted a lock of hair tightly around her finger. "That's one of the reasons why

I called, Monty. It's . . . not a good time. Tuesday won't be able to make it."

"What's wrong? Is she sick?" he asked, his voice equal parts concern and disappointment.

"No . . . it's . . . there's just . . . a lot going on around here."

Monty fell silent.

Stephanie closed her eyes. What a terrible liar she was. But how could she possibly tell him the real reason without crushing his spirit? The truth was, she no longer trusted his judgment, and allowing Tuesday open contact with a bonafide porn star wasn't something she could sit by and let happen.

"It's me, isn't it?" His voice went up an octave. Anger crackled through the receiver. "It's because I'm living with a man."

"No, Monty, it's because you're living with *that* man."

"You don't know Joey."

"And I don't want to. I was over there. Your place was a mess. One of Joey's porn *movies* was in plain sight. How did you get mixed up with him?"

Monty brooded, refusing to answer right away. "I met him at a bar."

"What was he doing there?"

Monty failed to answer.

"What was he doing?" Stephanie challenged, even though she already knew the answer. At her request, Matt had surfed the Net for everything on the object of her brother's affection. Joey Danza was twenty-five, a veteran of more than one hundred all male adult movies, an exotic dancer, and a professional escort. Those willing to pay thirty-nine ninety-five with a Visa or Mastercard could download exclusive photographs of Joey pleasuring himself.

"Dancing," Monty said, finally.

"Fred Astaire *danced*. Joey Danza *strips*. There's a difference."

"So what? He does a half-hour show, he takes off his clothes, and he gives people a thrill. It's legal. No one's getting hurt."

"How can you respect him? He's . . . he doesn't have any morals! Monty, you're intelligent. People . . . people look up to you in this community. You're in a position to go to a major network in the future. How can you throw all that away?"

"You haven't met him."

"True. But I've seen his Web site. For a couple hundred, I could do whatever I want with him."

"You're a bitch," Monty spat.

Stephanie holstered her words, not wanting the situation to digress any farther than it already had. For long seconds, she gripped the receiver, alarmed at how heavy it felt. A terrible sense of fatigue came over her. She was losing him. The man on the other end of the line was almost a stranger. "Where do you expect this to go, Monty?" she asked softly. "You're giving up so much."

"I don't think so."

"So the career you've worked so hard for means nothing?"

"Channel Eleven can kiss my ass. Who I sleep with is none of their goddamn business!"

"What about Tuesday?"

Monty laughed mirthlessly. "What? Are you, like, holding her for ransom? This is emotional blackmail?"

Stephanie steadied herself. "You can visit her at the house—*alone*. But my daughter won't be anywhere near a man like Joey Danza." Her voice dropped several degrees. "Is that clear?"

"As a bell." Then he hung up.

Stephanie shut her eyes to block the tears . . . and then gave in, crying with quiet and pained restraint.

Lisa Randall knew people who knew people. First, she called a friend from Hit The Sky, who happily came over to run a banking errand. Next, she contacted Hype Washington, a hip-hop music producer she was acquainted with. Initially, he'd thrown her heavy shade, but after learning what had happened to her he quickly promised to send one of his boys from the Fifth Ward over—no questions asked.

"T-Ball will take care of you," Hype had assured her.

The kid was in front of her now, younger than Tyson, outfitted head to toe in Tommy Hilfiger, and packing a portable Guns R Us shop for her benefit. "Hype says you need a little something. T-Ball got you covered."

Lisa smiled faintly, amused by the third person reference, amazed at the turn her life had taken. The thought of setting foot outside the apartment terrified her. Physically, she couldn't leave. In fact, she couldn't even *imagine* herself venturing out.

Stephanie had refused to buy her a gun unless she got commando training, and Tyson wanted no part of guns at all. "You can miss me with that shit," he had told her. "I'll get a Great Dane first."

Now here she stood, facing an illegal arms dealer from the hood, shopping for a hot piece. It was the only way. Lisa couldn't go to the gun, so the gun had to come to Lisa. She needed it to feel safe.

T-Ball had retrieved half a dozen hunks of metal from his backpack and spread them onto a towel on the dining room table. "Try 'em on for size. See what feels right. They're not loaded." He loped around for a moment, then settled on the couch, entertained by Cosby.

Lisa picked up a Lorcin L thirty-eight. Initially, it felt loathsome, but then she began to feel the potential of its power. Extending her arm to take deadly aim, she closed her eyes and imagined the man in the ski mask. Next time, she would be ready.

"Hey, you're holding history there," T-Ball called out.

"What do you mean?"

"That's a piece a gangbanger looted from a pawn shop during the L.A. riots. I love that gun. It's got a story behind it. You know what I'm saying?"

"Yeah," Lisa replied softly. "I do." She recalled a special series Monty had done on stolen handguns during one of Channel Eleven's ratings periods. It was a big racket—half a million robbed each year. Eighty percent of hot weapons came from private homes, the rest from cars, firearms makers, stores, even military bases. And a hefty majority of violent crimes were committed with guns from that lot.

If someone had whispered in her ear while she watched Monty's segment that she would one day be a customer of a street dealer like T-Ball, she would've laughed and called them crazy.

"Try 'em all," T-Ball encouraged. "It's like a glove. It's gotta fit right."

Lisa reached for a big black monster of a gun. "What's this?"

"Shiiiiiit," T-Ball exclaimed. "That's a Glock—guaranteed to fuck a nigga up! The Austrian Army uses it. That right there don't play."

Lisa was surprised by its light weight. "It's not as heavy as it looks."

"It's got polymers in the frame—you know, plastic."

She pointed it at the window and smiled, feeling invincible.

"Now that's some heavy duty protection. Pull the trigger and the motherfucker's dead!" T-Ball shouted.

"I want this one."

"Sold."

"How much?"

"You're a friend of Hype's . . . four hundred."

"Show me how to shoot and I'll pay you five."

"Deal. I know a place out—"

"No," Lisa cut in. "I can't leave. Show me right here."

"But—"

"Save it, T-Ball. Just give me the basics. I'll only need to use it once."

"I had a few drinks with her. She's not so bad," Matt was saying.

Stephanie cocked her head, barely paying attention. "You need to raise your standards."

"Chuck Berg granted her a full interview. Don't you want the chance to tell your side of the story?"

Matt was the second person in as many days to lobby on behalf of Abby McQueen. The first had been Toni Raffin. Though she, too, had been skeptical of Abby's motives, she assured that with Francisco Juarez as editor-in-chief of *Texas Today*, Stephanie could count on evenhanded reporting. Maybe the idea did have merit. Stephanie began to waver, almost caving in. Perhaps a media war was the best way for Josie to win back custody of Jason. "I'll think about it."

Matt punched the air victoriously. "Cool!"

"That must have been some drink," Stephanie said.

He grinned like some lucky geek after prom night.

She threw some papers into her attaché case and gathered up the rest of her things. "I've got one word for you."

"What's that?"

"Latex."

Matt smiled the smile of the guilty. "It's not what you think."

Stephanie held up a hand lightheartedly. "Good. Because I don't even want to think about it." She started for the door. "I have a husband and daughter who arrive home every day by four o'clock. For once, I want to meet them there."

"Have fun."

She winked at him. "You, too." On her way down, Stephanie thought about her painful conversation with Monty. Was she being unfair? No, she decided, determined not to let the discomfort sway the true feelings in her heart. She had a nine-year-old daughter to consider. Joey Danza made his living in a sleazy, exploitative industry. Depravities paid his rent, and it would not surprise her if she learned that he was into the drug scene as well.

Stephanie wished things were back to the way they were before they got so bad. She preferred Monty having boys pass in the night to having one porn star stay indefinitely. But what she really preferred, of course, were more options—for instance, a nice woman for her brother. Hell, a nice *man* would do at this point.

As she approached the car she caught sight of a note affixed to the windshield. She tossed her bags into the front seat and tugged at the paper to release it from underneath the wiper. There was a sharp intake of breath when she read the two words. REMEMBER SEPTEMBER.

Stephanie shivered. Her heart took a leap at the sound of a car door opening and closing. She looked around, saw nothing peculiar, and then got into her vehicle and locked the doors swiftly. Within minutes, she was home, rushing inside, frantically calling for Tuesday. But the house was as still as a tomb.

There were two messages on the machine. She played them back. The first was from Peter, citing a crisis with a patient and the hope that he would wrap it up in time for dinner. The second was from Mrs. Hatcher, curtly informing Stephanie to notify her in the future whenever Tuesday wouldn't be riding home with the carpool. Stephanie brought a finger to her lips and played it again as her limbs went leaden with fear.

Such a pretty little girl. Shelly Duckworth's words curdled her brain.

Stephanie flung open a kitchen drawer, rifling through coupons, old grocery slips, and receipts to locate Mrs. Hatcher's number. Dammit! She'd written it down on something in this drawer. On her second pass she found it.

Please, God, let there be a simple explanation, she prayed as the telephone rang and rang. An answering machine picked up. She slammed down the receiver and called Peter. His machine clicked on, as well. "Shit!" she screamed, banging it down again, in desperate need of reassurance.

And then it dawned on her. Monty. Had he defied her wishes and collected Tuesday at school's end? Deep down, she hoped that he had. She hit the speed dial button earmarked for him and waited, drumming her fingers, thinking speed dial was more like snail dial. Monty had barely gotten hello out of his mouth when she demanded, "Is Tuesday with you?"

"No. What—"

"She didn't ride home with carpool. I don't know where she is!"

"Calm—"

"I'll call you back." She set the receiver down once more with a crash, her mind in hyper-drive, wondering who to call, what to do, where Tuesday could be. In a fury she yanked out a volume of the telephone directory and looked up Tuesday's school. An administrator answered, and after an excruciating wait, Mrs. Nelligan came to the phone. Luckily, she was still there.

"Ally Kerner's mother took Tuesday and several other girls to the Hanson concert at The Summit," Mrs. Nelligan explained in a shrill tone, more put off by Stephanie's distress than concerned by it.

Stephanie put her hand over her heart and threw her head back.

"How could you forget?" the teacher wondered. "It's all they've talked about for weeks. I could barely contain them today."

"I feel so silly," Stephanie said.

"I should say so!"

Stephanie was flooded with relief . . . and shame. So much had happened over the past week. Her mind had been in a million places, and Tuesday's special night had gone forgotten. *Never again,* she vowed, feeling foolish. Things were going to change.

She took a moment to savor the sweet discovery. Tuesday was having a great time with her friends. Peter was helping a patient through a tough time. Her family was safe. Yes. Everything was okay.

* * *

Matt Benedict couldn't wait to get to Abby McQueen's hotel room. She would be happy to get the cryptic fax, and even more happy to hear that the prospect for an interview with Stephanie was better than hopeful; it was almost a sure thing.

He'd thought about Abby several times during the day, and the arousal it triggered had been frustrating and inconvenient. Discipline. Major discipline. That's what it had taken not to sneak into the bathroom and jerk off. Besides, he wanted to save it all for his lusciously erotic, deliciously vulgar new lover. She couldn't get enough. And he had it to give.

Matt was almost out the door when a call came through. It was Linda, an off-again on-again girlfriend who wanted to meet up for drinks. He shrugged her off. Compared to Abby, Linda was a block of ice in bed. Plus, she refused to give head, and Abby treated the act like a trip to Zanzibar.

He locked up, whistled his way down the elevator, and drove a few minutes out his way to a gas station in a questionable area where the beer was always on special. Grabbing a twelve-pack, he realized that he had to piss and asked the clerk for the restroom key. With the open sesame in hand, he sauntered around to the rear of the building.

Against the wall. With his pants at his ankles and her skirt rucked up to her waist. That's how he would take her first, Matt decided, ruminating hard on the subject, imagining how open and juicy Abby's body would feel. He turned the key and pushed open the door. As he stepped forward, someone crashed into him from behind, shoving him inside the tiny room.

In a few seconds it was over.

The cold steel at his temple.

The voice hissing, "This is what you deserve for working with that bitch."

The hollow sound of the advancing chamber.

The blackout.

Eighteen

Abby stewed in her hotel room. As the hours ticked by, the obvious became clear: Matt Benedict was not showing up. What else could she expect from a punk kid with a two-year degree? He'd gotten his kicks, so now it was time for him to shuffle on to the next conquest.

She experienced a tight fight-or-flight feeling in her chest. This story was going nowhere, which meant so was her life.

Joey Danza crept into mind. She hadn't heard shit from the dancing porn queen. Lit with anger, she dialed Jack McCrary at Sweet Rewards, deflected his pleas to get together, and hung up with Montgomery Cain's unlisted home number.

"You shouldn't call me here," Joey hissed when he came to the phone.

"Maybe I'm a club owner who wants to hire you to do a show. Once in a while, you should let the blood flow to your head, asshole. By the way, I'm talking about the head on top of your shoulders."

"Hang on," he said in a hush.

Abby flopped herself onto the bed and hummed impatiently until Joey came back on the line.

"Okay, I'm outside now."

"What do you have for me?"

"Nothing yet, but I'm getting close. He's almost ready to confide in me about something big. I can feel it."

"Do what you can to speed it up. I have a deadline."

"Maybe you can use this—he's on the outs with his sister. She won't let him see his niece because of me."

Abby jotted the nugget down on the yellow legal pad she always kept at her bedside table. She drew a circle around the note. "That's good. I can use it. What else?"

"That's it."

Being on the telephone put her at a disadvantage. She couldn't tell if this creep was lying his ass off or speaking the truth. There was only one way to find out. "Meet me at the Galleria la Madeleine in one hour."

"I can't," Joey said immediately.

"If you want that role in the movie, I'm sure you'll find a way."

She got there early, ordered a bowl of tomato-basil soup with a small salad, and sat outside. Pangs of loneliness played over her. There wasn't a single message on her machine in New York, and she'd been gone for several days. No one had called to have dinner, to see a show, or even to say hello. She knew why. Somewhere along the way, she always managed to trade on a friendship for a boost on a story or a book. If not that, she inevitably crossed an ethical line that others couldn't get over. Subsequently, they always cast her out of their loop.

When she was on top, all the fuck you bravado had a nice ring to it, but Abby McQueen was no longer at the peak of success mountain. To be true, she'd hit rock bottom. Suddenly the independent routine was hard to do with a straight face.

Her parents were still alive, but they were such simpletons, living on a fixed income, oblivious to the larger media world where their daughter had scratched out a life. Communicating with them was such a chore, so she had scaled back to those do or die moments—holidays, birthdays, and anniversaries—which arrived frequently enough to create the illusion of a relationship. As for men, she only went after the ones who could do something for her. Once she collected, she cut out fast.

Her thoughts drifted to Francisco Juarez. He was so damned attractive, and such a righteous bastard, an overgrown Boy Scout type who prided himself on doing the right thing—stopping to help people in an accident, and eschewing the stress and notoriety of the big leagues for the peace and dignity of small work. That she and Francisco both walked on two legs was their only commonality. Still, there was something between them . . . a little spark. Maybe this time was for real. After all, she already had the *Texas Today* gig; he was in no position to prop up her career. *An unfaked romance.* She liked the sound of it.

Joey Danza finally arrived, looking very go-go boy in a spandex shirt, too short denim cutoffs, and worker boots. "This better be good."

She zeroed in on him with laser concentration. "Look me in the eye and tell me we still have a deal."

"We've got a deal!" Joey assured her. "The pressure's on. His sister's trying to control his life, and the station's going to fire him any day now. I just hope I get what you want before he says something like, 'I need my space.' He's been real moody lately."

Abby waved off the concern. "Don't worry. That's good psychological food. It's only pushing him to love you more. Of course, eventually he'll realize that you're not worth it, but my money's on him spilling his guts before that epiphany."

"Thanks a lot," Joey mumbled.

"Anytime. Just remember this—you're trying to land a movie, not a husband."

Joey's face brightened. "Have you told the producer about me?"

"I sent him a tape of *Hard Enough*. He's dying to work with you. In fact, he was so impressed that he's not even going to make you do a screen test."

Joey nodded dramatically, vibing in on every word. "When can I read the script?"

Abby grinned, leaning in. "There's already a writer attached to the project. As soon as he gets my story, he'll need maybe four weeks to knock out the screenplay." She drew back and crossed her legs. "So you see, Joey, you're the hold up."

She drove back to the hotel, ordered a glass of wine from room service, and watched *Politically Incorrect*, longing for the days when she had been hot enough to appear on the late-nite gabfest and mix it up with bimbo actresses, dorky politicians, and dumb rock stars. By the time the final credits began to scroll, she stopped fighting off sleep and simply gave in.

The next morning, she woke up feeling lucky. Perhaps that meant the day's travels would yield a smoking gun. She'd planned jaunts to Pasadena for a visit with the late Billy Hudson's daughter, Anna Belle, and to Clear Lake for a drop in with Marilyn Cain.

Abby nearly buckled and sank to the ground when Anna Belle Hudson opened the front door. Did she live in a giant litter box? It certainly smelled that way. She stepped inside and saw two open containers chockablock full of kitty waste in the front corridor. What looked like an entire pride pounced this way and that.

"I hope you're not allergic," Anna Belle sang. She was rotund, carrying enough extra pounds to feed Chile, and swathed in an emerald green tent dress.

"Not at all," Abby lied sweetly. "I love cats." The truth was, she loved one cat, two at the most.

"I have some tea and Danish for us," Anna Belle announced, leading her into a sitting room.

Abby navigated through the clutter and tasteless decor. A tea service and platter of sweet rolls sat in the center of a coffee table. Also there were two silver-haired felines licking off icing with sandpaper tongues. "Just tea for me. I had a big breakfast."

"They say it's the most important meal of the day."

"Who's they?" Abby inquired, playing with the eccentric hag. Anna Belle looked puzzled. "The experts."

Abby smiled. "Of course." They *also say fat old women who live with twenty cats are insane,* she wanted to shout.

"I'm so glad you called. I'll take any opportunity I can get to talk about Daddy." Anna Belle poured Abby's tea and passed her the cup and saucer.

Abby wondered if she should down a hairball remedy before indulging. "He was a special man."

"Were you one of his students?"

"In a manner of speaking. He took a personal interest in my career as a journalist."

"That's Daddy!"

"Yes," Abby began, shifting gears with her tone. It was clear that if this spinster heard the truth about her fuck around fox of a father, her world would come crashing down. "I'm working on a twentieth anniversary piece that concerns one of his most infamous cases—the Jimmy Scott murder at Marilyn Cain's home in River Oaks."

"Oh, my goodness," Anna Belle exclaimed, fanning herself. "That was quite a time."

Abby's heart took off. "So you remember?"

"Indeed."

"Tell me, what stands out in your mind?"

"Daddy was so concerned for the girl—"

"Stephanie."

"Yes, I believe that was her name . . . Stephanie." The telephone jangled.

Shit! Abby fought the urge to yank the cord from the jack.

Anna Belle brought a fat finger to equally fat lips. "I wonder who that could be," she said, struggling out of her seat to shuffle across the room.

Abby waited for long, impatient minutes as Anna Belle rambled on about one of her cat's psychological problems to someone who was obviously her veterinarian. Finally, she terminated the conversation.

"I'm so sorry about that! Dr. Lobrano is worried sick about Cracker Jacks. Lately he's been—"

"Listen," Abby cut in sharply, stopping just short of belting her in the mouth, "I don't have time for cat tales. Maybe on another visit."

"Oh . . . uh . . . of course," Anna Belle stammered, the sting of the rebuke all over her face.

"You were talking about your father's concern for Stephanie Cain," Abby went on.

Anna Belle contemplated the thought. "Yes," she

said, quite firmly. "I remember how afraid he was that she would kill again."

Abby experienced a tiny jolt; the tea cup scraped across the saucer, but she managed a save at the last moment. "What?"

The woman's eyes went wide, and she whispered conspiratorially, "I overheard him say once that murder was in Stephanie's heart. He thought she enjoyed it, that she planned it." Anna Belle shrugged. "But Daddy's job was to get her acquitted."

"And that's exactly what he did," Abby murmured softly to herself, thunderstruck by the revelation.

The ride to Clear Lake was fraught with anxiety. If what Anna Belle said was true, Abby knew her story could explode as sure as a terrorist's bomb. Maybe Joey Danza would provide the confirmation.

Just ahead was the Susann Center for Disabled Seniors. Abby groaned and turned into the facility. She hated hospitals. She hated geriatric asylums more. Once inside, the effluvia of imminent death hit her like a hammer to the head. She tried to close her nose to it, to stave off the nausea, so she breathed through her mouth.

The receptionist was easily duped. Abby hoodwinked the twit into believing that Marilyn Cain's east coast-based niece had come for an impromptu visit. She followed a chatty orderly named Luis through a maze of corridors crammed with cell-like rooms side to side. The general miasma of the place threw her mind into morbid fast-forward—to life as a helpless old woman. *Memo to self,* she silently mock recorded, *jump in front of a bus before it gets to this point.*

Luis chuckled to himself. "I call Ms. Cain the Queen, and joke to her kids that they're the Prince and Princess."

"How clever," Abby snarled.

The sarcasm passed right by him. "She's had quite a few regular visitors lately. That's nice to see."

Abby stifled an exasperated groan. In her great American pecking order, conversation with an idiot orderly fell below cockroach collecting.

"The kids are great. Stephanie and Monty always stop to chat, and they remember me on holidays." Luis smiled. "The man who's been visiting is different. He's cordial, but he's very guarded."

Finally, they reached Marilyn Cain's room.

"Don't expect much," Luis said mournfully. "She's been very tense lately, less responsive than usual."

Abby nodded soberly.

"You have about fifteen minutes before she eats lunch. Would you like to feed her?"

The disgust hit Abby's face before she could put the brakes on it. "I'm here for quality time, *Luis.* Meals and bedpans are your job. But thanks for the offer." She left him standing there, his mouth agape, and proceeded inside.

The sight of Marilyn Cain left her momentarily stunned. Pictures of the big-living, larger than life woman were still fresh in Abby's mind from studying the 1977 issue of *Texas Today*. But the woman before her was an age-ravaged shell; the strokes had taken their toll, worn her down to almost nothing.

Tentatively, Abby approached the bed. The stench of old age made her weak.

Marilyn Cain, her face suddenly urgent, gestured

for Abby to come closer, and the words she spoke were not empty ones.

"He's alive," Marilyn creaked.

Nineteen

"Stop," Peter commanded Stephanie, blocking her path to the kitchen. "Do you know where Tuesday is?"

She made a face and inclined her head. "Upstairs brushing her teeth."

He bowed extravagantly. "Good answer."

"You're making fun of me."

His eyes crinkled. "Yeah, I am."

Stephanie smiled faintly and moved around him to finish packing Tuesday's lunch. "Well . . . please don't."

"On one condition."

"What's that?"

"We go away. The three of us. Even if it's just for the weekend. How about San Antonio?"

"When Josie Dean's case is settled. I can't leave her right now." She gave him her best pleading look. "But it sounds like a dream. We'll do it. I promise."

Tuesday raced into the room bedecked in a Hanson T-shirt. "All the girls are wearing their shirts today." She giggled and put a hand on her hip, copping a Rizzo attitude from *Grease*. "We're going to *rule* the *school*."

The telephone rang.

Peter laughed, shaking his head, and picked up. "You have the Harts," he bellowed into the receiver with good humor.

Stephanie messed with Tuesday's hair for a moment, pushing it away from her eyes.

"Steph," Peter said solemnly. "It's Nick Benedict, Matt's father."

She stared at him. Something terrible had happened. She touched her heart. Her pupils dilated.

Silently, Peter passed her the phone.

Stephanie shut her eyes and answered the call.

Matt Benedict.

A bright young man with everything to live for.

Dead at twenty-one.

She clutched the counter with a clawlike grip, feeling herself spin down into the dark depths of grief.

Peter ushered Tuesday from the room.

"I'm so sorry, Mr. Benedict," Stephanie cried. "I'm . . . so . . . sorry."

From the driveway, Mrs. Hatcher blasted the horn. Stephanie jerked as though stuck by a pin. There was nothing more to say. A senseless act of violence. The wrong place at the wrong time. She ended the conversation and saw Tuesday to the door, fighting off tears as she checked all of her things and kissed her good-bye.

The moment the door closed, Stephanie's eyelids fluttered, the room swam all around her, and her limbs went limp.

Peter caught her just in time and held her tight.

"Somebody killed him, Peter," she wailed. "Somebody killed Matt."

"I know, Steph," he whispered soothingly. "I know."

Her abdomen convulsed, and the sobs ripped

through her, as if in seizure. She could hear and feel her heart pounding out a percussive beat. "He was so young. He would have been a brilliant lawyer."

Peter rocked her back and forth.

Stephanie felt dead inside. This was one kick in the teeth too many. The seemingly endless succession of cataclysmic upheavals had pummeled her to nothing.

A shock coursed through her, and she stepped away from Peter, lost in her own thoughts, trying to make sense of the conundrum but just as quickly swamped by panic as the reality took shape in her mind.

Ginger Simon was murdered after the REMEMBER SEPTEMBER letter.

Lisa Randall was raped after the REMEMBER SEPTEMBER fax.

Matt Benedict was killed after the REMEMBER SEPTEMBER flyer.

"Steph, what is it?" Peter asked.

A sharp pain shot through her heart. *It's my fault!* she wanted to scream. *It's all my fault!* Instead, she took in a deep breath and attempted to compose herself. Stephanie knew what she had to do.

Nobody was going to tell Montgomery Cain how to live his life, least of all a phalanx of hypocritical management types who allowed trends, ratings, share points, and demographics to rule the world. How could they look him in the eye and lecture him about the appropriate lifestyle? What a fucking joke. The general manager had just left his wife and kids for a travel agent young enough to be his daughter, and the news director was a known bigot.

I could sue for discrimination and damages, Monty

thought, certain there was a pit bull of an attorney out there hungry for a case like this. As he considered the move, his enthusiasm for it cooled. Shit, the opportunity cost would be his whole life. Court TV would be all over it. Ditto for *Dateline, 20/20,* and Larry King. He imagined the headlines. GAY ANCHOR FIGHTS TO KEEP PORN STAR BOYFRIEND. Good-bye, privacy. Hello, general public weighing in with opinions. The mere thought churned his stomach. No way was he stepping into that minefield.

Tyson Moore had kindly helped assemble a videotape of Monty's finest Channel Eleven work, even jumping through the production hoops of having it edited and duplicated. Now Monty was armed with a crate of copies, systematically dispatching them to larger markets for feedback. New York. Los Angeles. CNN. If they called, he would go running. So far no one had called, and any day now he would be forced to decide how he was going to make a living.

It was one o'clock, and the sun was bright, the sky periwinkle blue. Joey slept on, exhausted from a late night of dancing for dollars at Sweet Rewards. He had boasted about his take in tips—two hundred bucks. Monty considered Joey's age—mid twenties, rounding the bend toward thirty. What would he do when the club offers dried up? Already there was younger, fresher talent nipping at his heels—guys who hadn't been seen in every gay club across the country, guys who hadn't overexposed themselves by starring in one hundred plus movies. Time would definitely cast a pall over his future.

Monty heard a rustle in the kitchen. It was Joey, finally up, guzzling orange juice straight from the carton.

"Good *afternoon,*" Monty said. He wrapped his

arms around Joey from behind, causing him to spill
a trail of juice down his bare chest.

"Clean me up," Joey ordered.

Monty snatched a towel from the counter.

"No," Joey protested, twisting it from his grasp
and tossing it across the room. "*You* clean me up."

Monty grinned. For a man who paid the rent with
sex, Joey Danza's carnal appetite was superhumanly
ferocious. A soft sigh escaped Monty as he stepped
around and lapped up the mess, bathing Joey's
sculpted, hairless body with concentrated feathery
flicks and whorls of his tongue. And then he stood
up to face him, staring intently, his eyes hoping,
studying, deciding.

"What's wrong?" Joey wondered, obviously unnerved by the intensity.

Monty brushed a hair from Joey's eye. "If I left
Houston, would you come with me?" He held his
breath for the answer.

Joey hesitated. "Are you serious?"

"Yes," Monty said, swallowing hard, his eyes suddenly wet with tears that would not roll down. "I
love you, Joey. It's crazy . . . we don't have much in
common . . . but . . . I love you."

"Me, too," Joey laughed. His eyes were glistening,
a strange mixture of relief and sadness.

"I want to escape, you know? I want to leave here
and start over someplace new. It's something I
should've done a long time ago."

Joey drew back a little, and Monty could almost
hear the portals of his lover's heart slam shut.

"I want to go with you," Joey whispered thickly,
"but sometimes I feel like I don't even know you.
There are too many secrets between us." He took
Monty's hand in his. "I'm playing for keeps here."

Monty didn't trust himself to speak. Suddenly the

planets shifted and he knew. Joey Danza was the
one. The catalyst for a new life. The trap door to
new surroundings. Monty never should've returned
to Houston after college. But Stephanie had lost her
first husband, Tuesday was here, and their mother's
health had taken another downward turn. He
couldn't stay for them anymore. There were too
many memories here. Too many horrible memories.

"Get dressed," Monty blurted.

"Huh?"

"I want to take you somewhere." Monty clapped
his hands. It was time to close the deal.

The sunroof was open, the windows down, and
the stereo at full volume. Wind whipped and buf-
feted, slapping Monty's hair into a Don King do, but
he did not care. Stealing a glance at the man beside
him, he squeezed Joey's knee and pressed down on
the accelerator, weaving through lanes to lose the
slow movers.

He turned past the pink, stucco-faced piers that
marked the entrance to River Oaks, the planned
residential community built by two brothers and
their investor friend in 1923. Now coasting along
Lazy Lane, he watched with amusement as Joey's jaw
dropped in awe of the palaces designed by John F.
Staub. American Federal. English Regency. Louisi-
ana Creole. All that architecture and more lined the
richly manicured, painstakingly landscaped neighborhood.

Joey pointed to a Texas-sized plantation home.
"I'm going to have a house like that one day."

Monty took the curve onto Inwood and stopped
in front of an expansive neo-Georgian estate. Massive oaks decorated the lawn. Cast aluminum balco-

nies faced the upstairs windows. It took such effort to face the house without looking away. He turned off the radio. "I used to live there."

"Man!" Joey exclaimed. "*Rich* kid. You were lucky."

"No," Monty chuckled ruefully. "That's one thing my family's never been."

Joey sat quietly for a moment and then whispered, "You can trust me, Monty. You can tell me anything." He put a hand over his heart. "I'll keep it right here."

Monty tightened his grip on the steering wheel until his knuckles turned white. He decided to just hold his nose and jump. That was the brave way into the deep end, and that's exactly where his relationship with Joey was heading.

"I was only six when it happened. . . ."

"It's time. Watch my lips, baby. It's time."

Lisa threw her gaze around the room wildly, like a cornered animal calculating a way out.

"It'll do you serious good," Tyson said. "How long has it been since you've been out of this apartment?"

She shrugged indifferently. But she knew the answer. Down to the day, the hour, and the minute. Her heart picked up steam and so did her breathing, and perspiration suddenly prickled her scalp, the crease of her elbows, and behind her knees.

Leaving the safety zone wasn't an option. Lisa Randall could deal only in this controlled environment.

Where she trusted Tyson Moore.

Where she depended on monster locks bolting the door.

Where she banked on the loaded Glock stuffed inside her purse.

Everything else was a gamble, and Lisa was not about to roll the dice. The Pope would sing in Reno first. As the tears built up, sadness weighed in as well . . . for the woman she was before, a fearless explorer of new clubs, new restaurants, and every summer a new part of the globe—India, Africa, Ireland, Australia. Now, traveling beyond the door of an apartment was even too far a journey.

"I can't . . . I don't want to go . . . I . . . I made lasagna."

"Freeze it," Tyson said, nipping at the heels of her excuses. "We're going out."

Lisa began to tremble. "I'm not ready."

Tyson took her hand in his and led the way into the bathroom. Standing behind her, he met her gaze in the large mirror. "I see a girl who's healing nicely," he said.

Lisa's mouth betrayed a small smile. He was right about the healing—at least on the outside. Her eye was open now, the bruise on her cheek all but gone, and her lips returned to form. With shrewdly applied makeup, she would draw only stares of admiration.

Tyson wrapped his arms around her. "You're beautiful, baby."

She placed her hands over his and closed her eyes, allowing the strength and smell of him to steal over her. There was only one way to combat his insistence that they go out. She wasn't ready, it was too soon, but it would buy her some time. "Make love to me."

"Are you sure?" Tyson asked, unable to mask his relief.

Lisa could read his face as easily as a child's big

letter storybook. He wanted possession of her body, to take back what should've been his that night, to put to rest the fear that she was sexually damaged goods. She unbuttoned the crisp white dress shirt, his dress shirt, and slipped it over her shoulders, then took his hands and placed them over her bare breasts. "I'm sure," she whispered.

Tyson made a concerted effort to ease her into the moment. He played romantic music, he treated her as gently as he might a fragile porcelain heirloom, and he murmured the sweetest things into her ear. Yet her body continued to shudder, not from ecstasy of spirit but from fear. She was limp, passive, and silent.

He piloted her into the bedroom, drew the covers back, and placed her down on the mother-of-pearl colored sheets, and slowly removed the rest of her clothes.

Lisa was naked now, watching him, feeling only dread but stroking her own body just the same, hoping to elicit some erotic response. *It has to happen,* she told herself. *Please let it happen.*

Tyson's pants were crumpled into a pile on the floor, and he steadied himself with one knee on the bed as his fingers danced over the buttons of his shirt. And then he stood there, looking down at her for what seemed like a very long time.

Lisa expelled a little sigh as her mind whirled and beat. He was aroused, his hard penis pressing against the soft fabric of his boxers. She fixed her eyes on it, watching it pulse and twitch, allowing her gaze to travel up and down his body, admiring the impossibly flat terrain of his abdomen, his long muscular thighs, and the sinewy strength of his chest and arms. She could muster up no desire. The old Lisa would've been hypnotized by this black Adonis.

The new Lisa was merely numb. This union of bodies seemed so wrong . . . so unnecessary.

He was beside her now, intensely overprotective, gentle to the point of being awkward, covering her face and hair with shy kisses as his warm hands explored the gentle curves of her body, like a blind man.

She forced out a soft moan, if only to make him believe that she was still alive. The contrast of their dark skin against the pale sheets captured her eye. It was an art director's dream. She thought of work. So far she'd managed to get by using Tyson's computer, cooking up lame copy and sending it out via e-mail. But there were staff conferences and client meetings to consider. Hit The Sky deserved better than what she could offer. There was no other way around it. She would quit.

Tyson's hands parted her thighs.

Lisa's body jerked. Oh, God! She'd almost forgotten he was there. How could she be so unresponsive? Unless she was dead from the neck down.

He didn't thrust. There was just one smooth movement, a rhythmic adjustment of the hips, and he was inside her.

She arched back in agony, feeling impaled.

He slipped his fingers around the curve of her throat.

Fear raced through her. Was he going to choke her?

He rocked back and forth, ever so slightly.

An arc of pain knocked the breath from her body. It was like a knife through a nerve.

His breathing advanced.

Her mind swooped toward unconsciousness. Finally, she mustered up the courage to meet his gaze head on, and the sight of him left her paralyzed. All she saw was her attacker, the rapist in the ski mask.

You've got bad taste in friends, bitch. You deserve this.

The sick words reverberated, and her heart lurched. He'd forced himself on her in this position. He'd wrapped his gloved hands around her neck. All of it was so horrifyingly familiar. Unable to endure another moment, she cried out, "No! Not this way. He was on top when he raped me."

Instantly, Tyson's face became a masterpiece of torment. His eyes were shining with failure and regret. "I'm sorry," he breathed, though it was clear by his tone, by the faraway look accompanying his words, that he didn't know what he was apologizing for. He slipped out of her body.

Her fear dissipated. "Oh, Tyson," Lisa whispered sadly, hating herself for putting him through this. She reached for his hand and pressed it against her lips.

He cast his gaze downward. "I don't want to hurt you."

She blinked back a tear. "You're the best person I've ever known."

"I don't . . . I don't know how to help you."

Her heart thumped. His midnight message was crystal clear: Nor would he continue trying to. There wasn't enough history between them to weather this storm, Lisa realized. In fact, she was lucky he'd stuck with her for as long as he had. Most men were pretty non-negotiable. Tyson Moore bucked that trend, but even he had his limits. As his spicy body burned beside her, she already started to miss him, wondering how she would cope without his strength of presence.

And then it dawned on her—breaking up meant moving out. Compared to what it would put her through to leave his apartment, sex too soon was child's play.

Tyson fell back onto the bed and pulled the sheet up past his waist. He glanced at the clock scornfully. It was still early. Other women were out there. Women thirsting to drink up the city's night life with a rising media star. Women hungry for a night of passion with a young, clean-living, and incredibly good-looking man. Lisa could almost feel those thoughts radiating from him.

He looked at the ceiling for a long time, his face conflicted, his body still. Then he said, very deliberately, "I think we need to—"

Lisa knew the script and cleaved into it before the dialogue hit the air. "Let me be on top," she blurted. "Or we'll do it side by side. You can take me any way you want. Anything but the missionary position."

A glimmer of hope came back into his eyes, although the uncertainty remained. "If you're not ready . . ."

Lisa moved quickly to sit astride his hard-as-granite thighs and flattened herself against him, slowly moving from neck to navel with soft, velvet kisses, her tongue flickering. She stroked him in a certain place, in a certain way, until he was big and hard again.

He breathed in a long sigh, almost groaning. "Oh, Lisa," he murmured, his hands moving up and closing over her breasts.

Lisa's head felt muzzy, shadowy imaginings spinning and whirling. Her mouth went slack, wet with saliva. Pleasure shot through her like a flame. Somehow it felt wrong to enjoy it, so instead she concentrated on the fear, calculating its precise nature.

You've got bad taste in friends, bitch. You deserve this.

There'd been something familiar about his eyes. Everything went black and hot as the steam cleared in her mind, as the phantom horror materialized. She'd simply been a receptacle for his rage. He was really punishing someone else.

Tyson held her tightly, gripping her upper arms firmly as he began to lose control. He shuddered, crying out, coming in spasm after spasm, spurting life inside of her.

But Lisa Randall felt like she was dead.

Twenty

Stephanie sat across from Captain Kirk Mulroney, shifting uncomfortably in a straight back chair, sipping bad coffee from a Styrofoam cup, imploring him to heed her warning. The messages were splayed out on his metal desk—the original letter, the fax, and the more recent flyer.

"You're taking quite a leap, Stephanie. There's no threat in this correspondence, not even an implicit one," Kirk said.

"But there's a meaning behind it. Ginger left Bruce on Labor Day, and he blames me for it. His sister told me so in no uncertain terms. The day I received the first letter, Ginger Simon was murdered. The day I received the fax, Lisa Randall was raped. And the day I discovered that flyer on my windshield, Matt Benedict was killed. This is a *pattern*, not paranoia." She waited for Kirk's answer, her chin jutting out defiantly.

"And you believe Bruce Simon is responsible for all of this."

Stephanie went hot with anger and impatience. "Well, Columbo, he was in Denver the day Ginger was stabbed over twenty times, he was sighted here twenty-four hours later, and he has yet to be apprehended by Houston's finest."

Kirk lobbed a look over the desk that translated loud and clear. *Don't talk to me like I'm an idiot.*

She shook her head, feeling ashamed. "I'm sorry."

"Forget about it."

"You think I'm crazy."

Kirk held up his hand. "Hey, I'm a cop. I've got dibs on crazy. You're a lawyer, so we can stop right there with you."

Stephanie laughed in spite of herself, then turned gravely serious. "Tell me what you think, Kirk. I want your gut feeling."

He paused, his expression turning from one of pleasance to one of stone. "Ginger's death was a crime of passion, an emotional rage killing. It wasn't the work of a smart man. Bruce used his own name to book his flight to Denver, and he allowed several of Ginger's neighbors to see him in broad daylight. What you're suggesting is diabolical and psychopathic. It just doesn't fit. Beyond the coincidental timing of these anonymous notes, I don't see a link between the attacks. You know all of them. I understand why you feel so troubled, but that doesn't mean there's a conspiracy here."

Stephanie clicked her tongue and drooped her shoulders in a show of petulance. "How do you explain the notes?"

Kirk shrugged. "A prank. Maybe an admirer. Could be the work of Shelly Duckworth. She's not wrapped too tight, but she's no killer."

"So you paid her a visit."

He nodded. "There's nothing to indicate that she's harboring Bruce. Plus we canvased the neighborhood. No one's seen him around."

Stephanie wasn't right in her mind and body. She felt a fear that subsumed the world. There would be another message. There would be another tragedy. "I expected more from you, Kirk," she said sadly.

He shot up his eyebrows and tilted his head. "There's not enough here to pursue."

Stephanie stood abruptly, sending the desk into a shimmy. Her coffee sloshed back and forth but didn't spill. "When a member of my family is hurt, you'll be the first person I call."

Kirk winced.

She put a hand over her mouth, her eyes wide and apologetic, not believing the venom of her words. "That wasn't fair. I didn't mean it."

Kirk rose and slipped his hands into his pockets, jingling keys and coins. He sighed heavily. "Give me a few days. I'll look at all three case files with a razor's edge, and if you get another message call me right away. You've got my direct line and home number."

Stephanie experienced a shudder of relief. He was still a friend. "Thank you, Kirk." She embraced him tightly.

He patted her hair and kissed her on the forehead, chastely. "Take some time off. You look tired."

"Yes, Captain," she whispered, noticing the absence of a ring and wondering why Kirk was unmarried. He would be so perfect for Josie Dean, Stephanie thought, ever the matchmaker. "How's your love life?" she inquired.

Kirk regarded her with humorous caution. "Let me put it to you this way—they'll never make a late night movie about it for Cinemax."

"I'd like to fix you up with someone."

He quickly shook his head. "I don't deal in blind dates."

"Ah, but this isn't a blind one. You've seen her.

You've met her. You've even testified for her. Josie Dean."

Kirk merely stared, a plastic smile on his face. Then he shook his head again. "Too much baggage."

Stephanie rolled her eyes. "Oh, please. How old are you?"

"Thirty-four."

"Baggage is part of modern society now. Everyone is allowed at least two carryons."

Kirk chuckled, but firmly stated, "Thanks, but no thanks."

"Just dinner," she persisted, almost jumping up and down.

He smiled the smile of the exasperated. "Do I need to call a guard to escort you out?"

Stephanie pursed her lips into a foiled again pout. "No, Captain. That won't be necessary."

She left the police station and factored distance and traffic as she approached the car. There were few minutes to spare. Today was a pivotal day for Josie Dean. Stephanie had lobbied tirelessly to get the visitation suspension order lifted, ultimately arguing successfully that Josie's impressive position in the corporate sector, her stable living situation with her mother, and her lifelong unblemished record as a Houstonian all spoke loudly against the possibility of her being a kidnapping and flight risk. Her statements to the contrary were made under extreme duress, Stephanie had maintained.

More than a week had gone by since Josie Dean had seen two-year-old Jason in the flesh, and the torture had nearly wrecked her life completely. It wasn't just sheer, unbearable agony, Josie had confided in Stephanie on the third day of separation from her son. It was a trip to hell that killed off everything that made her a functioning human being. Stephanie had digested the chilling description quietly, for she'd been there—twice. The first time was on that horrible night twenty years ago, and the second when Kevin died. Once was definitely enough.

She turned into Pascal's Playhouse, a pricey preschool where Rob had deposited Jason to spend his mornings and afternoons. Josie was already waiting in the parking lot. Stephanie wondered how long she'd been sitting there.

"I've only been here a few minutes," Josie announced. "But I've been parked down the block for several hours."

Stephanie took hold of her hand. "We won this battle. We'll win the war."

Josie nodded. "Let's go."

They proceeded inside and were shown into the director's office, offered something to drink, which they both declined, and asked to wait. Minutes ticked by. The bulletin boards entertained them— collage after collage of little ones at play, in costume, and in various holiday jubilees.

Josie grew more impatient by the second, wringing her hands. "What's going on?"

"It's very quiet," Stephanie observed. "Maybe they're all taking a nap."

Through the panes on the door she caught a glimpse of Mary, the woman who'd ushered them into the office. Her worried eyes cut back to Stephanie and Josie more than once as she addressed another woman.

Sensing something amiss, Stephanie sprang from her seat. "Wait here." She joined the two women in the corridor, to their obvious displeasure. "I don't believe we've met," she cut in. "I'm Stephanie Hart. I represent Josie Dean. Is there a problem?"

"Eleanor King, director of Pascal's Playhouse," the thick brunette said stiffly.

"Where's Jason?" Stephanie demanded.

Eleanor looked at Mary.

Mary looked at Eleanor.

"He's not here," Eleanor finally said.

"Not here today, or no longer enrolled?"

Eleanor threw back her head haughtily. "I'm not at liberty to say."

Stephanie felt something like a wolf rush up within her. She retrieved a legal document from her purse and held it in front of Eleanor's face as if it were a KICK ME sign she'd just snatched off the clueless bitch's back. "The visitation suspension order expired. This confirmation was faxed to your office this morning, and *Mary* here confirmed receipt of it."

Mary's pasty white cheeks flushed pink.

Eleanor was visibly agitated, as well. "Don't put us in the middle of this custody battle."

"That's easily avoided, Eleanor. Don't take sides. Just follow the law."

Josie flung open the office door, unable to contain herself another moment. "Where's Jason?"

Stephanie gauged Eleanor with a steely glare. "This is Jason's mother. She wants to know where her son is."

"Mr. Dean picked him up a few minutes ago," Eleanor said quietly.

Josie cried out, "No!" Tears burst forth and swam down her cheeks, and then she turned on Eleanor and Mary accusingly. "You knew! That's why you had us waiting in that office! So you could slip Jason out the back door!"

The guilt was so thick it could have been scraped off the walls.

"We only know what Mr. Dean's lawyer instructed us to do," Eleanor said weakly.

Josie's tears were stanched, her face reddened and hard. "When I get my son back, and I *will* get him back, the first order of business is taking him out of here."

"That's entirely your prerogative," Eleanor replied.

Mary started to speak, but Eleanor gestured for her to keep quiet.

"We'll try this again tomorrow. I strongly suggest you review the content of that fax," Stephanie said.

They left the preschool for a nearby Starbucks. Stephanie wanted to make certain that Josie had her equilibrium back, that she wouldn't storm Rob's house and demand possession of Jason.

"It's a dirty trick," she told her, "and not the last one, either. This is how Chuck Berg operates."

"I just want to—"

Stephanie halted her. "Don't even say it. They want you to react emotionally, so they can use it against you. The way you handled yourself back there with Eleanor and Mary was beautiful. You were upset but in total control. Stay on that track," she said fiercely.

Josie cleared her throat and fished two white pills from her purse, downing them with the last of her cappuccino. "These will knock me out until tomorrow. I'm going home now." And then she left.

Stephanie didn't really drive back to her office at the Transco Tower in Post Oak. She simply placed her hands on the steering wheel and somehow the car did the rest. Thoughts ran deeper than a river, particularly the dreadful task ahead—assembling

Matt's things and delivering them to his parents. And worse yet, having to start the process of replacing him. She stopped herself. There was no replacing him. Matt Benedict had been a technical, legal, and administrative dynamo. One of a kind.

The moment Stephanie stepped off the elevator, she noticed a tart-looking blonde pacing the area outside the office. "May I help you?" she offered as she inserted her key to unlock the heavy glass door.

"Stephanie Cain Stone Hart, I presume," the woman said, extending her hand. "Abby McQueen."

She gave the outstretched hand a curt shake and pushed open the door. "You've wasted a trip, Ms. McQueen," she said wearily. "I'm not granting any interviews at present."

Abby followed her inside. "Just know that it's a standing request." Her tone was unfazed. "You clamming up isn't a kill shot to my story. Plenty of others are talking."

Stephanie felt her abdomen contract and turned to face the queen of yellow journalism. "Well, I'm not. What else can I do for you?"

"Actually," Abby began, peeking around the empty reception desk, "I came here to see Matt Benedict."

"He's not . . ." Stephanie stopped herself. She had started to utter the words, "He's not in right now." Sadness weighed her down like bags of wet sand. "You haven't heard," she said softly.

"Heard what?"

"Matt was killed last night."

The news knocked the insolence off Abby's face.

"He was robbed at a gas station. They shot him."

"Shit!" Abby hissed, more out of inconvenience than mourning. "He was a neat kid."

"Yes, he was."

"What a kick in the ass." She regarded Stephanie with morbid curiosity. "You're no rabbit's foot, honey. Knowing you is bad luck," Abby said.

It required every bit of Stephanie's strength to deep-six a reaction. "If you'll excuse—"

"Let me get this straight," Abby cut in. "A client you put into hiding ends up Nicole Simpsoned, your best friend is raped, and your paralegal is murdered."

Stephanie felt instant heat warm her cheeks. "You'll have to—"

Abby took a menacing step closer, invading her personal space. "I know about the REMEMBER SEPTEMBER messages. How many have you gotten?"

Stephanie's hands tingled. "I'm asking you to leave."

"We can help each other."

"I'm not interested in your kind of help."

"The story about you killing Jimmy Scott in self defense is a pack of lies. What really happened that night?"

"Get out of here!"

"Is there a psycho after you?"

Stephanie's body was icy, trembling, itching. Before, these fears were only thoughts smoking in her head, crazy theories she'd failed to convince Kirk Mulroney with. Now someone else was putting the puzzle together in a very similar way. It brought the reality outside of herself, and the effect was mortifying.

"Tell me!" Abby screamed.

The she-devil was feeding off anxiety. Abby McQueen was playing psychological parlor games and winning. Stephanie concentrated on softening her pulse, bringing her breathing down a notch. It was time to take control of the situation. "I'm not telling you anything."

Abby took a step backward, a smirk snaked across her puffed-up lips. "It's so sad about Josie Dean losing custody of her baby. That Judge Gibbs is a nasty man."

Stephanie waited for the other high heel to drop.

"I've got information on Gibbs. Information that could force Josie's case out of his courtroom. No other judge would dare grant custody to that son of a bitch Rob Dean. I'm offering an even trade. Your soul laid bare for a reunion of battered mother and child."

Stephanie just looked at her, oddly fascinated by the dealing in evil, the brokering of lives for headlines. She closed her eyes, wishing the choice would simply go away. Telling the truth would send shock waves through her life, Monty's life, Marilyn's, and by association, Peter's and Tuesday's. It could only get worse. "Go to hell."

Abby flicked a card from the outer pocket of her handbag and dropped it on the desk. A glacial smile spread across your face. "In the event you change your mind."

Stephanie stood in her office alone, unable to move, burning red in the middle, white at the edges, and shaking with frustration's fury. Whatever there was on Judge Lawrence Gibbs, she would find it herself. She would never sit at the bargaining table with a rodent like Abby McQueen.

Plenty of others are talking. The words played back in Stephanie's mind, kicking like a drum. She wondered who they were. She wondered what they were saying. Clearly Matt had broken the sanctity of office confidence. How else would Abby have learned about the anonymous messages? But Stephanie felt fairly certain that he'd revealed little else. Matt was a trusted team player, though unfortunately too young and inexperienced to withstand the full frontal manipulations of an operator like Abby McQueen.

Plenty of others are talking. Her thoughts shifted to Monty. Abby preyed on the vulnerable, and if ever there was a wounded bird it was Montgomery Cain. A disturbing feeling washed over her about Joey Danza. Men like him put a price tag on everything. She hoped Monty had been judicious about spilling his guts. What worried her was that the more she pushed Monty to stay away from Joey, the closer he pulled Joey in. She prayed that his caution was prevailing.

Stephanie grabbed an empty file box from the storage closet and stepped over to Matt's desk to pack up his belongings. There were wild pictures from his trips to Mexico with friends, a dog-eared Scott Turow novel, the latest *Details* magazine, scratch and win game cards from what appeared to be every fast food joint in town, and a Swiss Army watch stalled by a dead battery. Her next discovery brought tears to her eyes—application and study materials for the LSAT, the exam to qualify for law school.

"Oh, Matt," Stephanie cried softly.

She tossed the papers into the box and began closing down the office. Tomorrow she would call for a temp. Sometime next week she would begin the search for a new paralegal. She stood there in the dark, thinking about it. The mere notion felt so wrong, but to go on was the only way.

A knock on the glass door startled her. She turned to see a man looking in, his figure and face illuminated by the light in the wide corridor. This

wasn't a trick of the mind at work. The worst case
scenario was staring back. Panic possessed her.

Bruce Simon smiled.

Twenty-one

Abby left Stephanie Hart's office feeling as if she were standing at the lip of a landslide. Right now she had nothing, but a sixth sense told her that this story was much bigger than she ever anticipated. Francisco Juarez would get the watered down version for *Texas Today;* the hot stuff would be exclusively earmarked for *the book.*

There were many angles to consider. The RE-MEMBER SEPTEMBER messages. The run of bad luck befalling people in Stephanie Hart's personal orbit. And Marilyn Cain's eery, raspy words: "He's alive." At first, Abby had dismissed her as some mindless hag teetering on the edge of death. What could that crazy talk mean?

Jimmy Scott.

The name crept into Abby's brain like a fox in the forest. It was the one part of the puzzle that she'd given short shrift to. Starting tomorrow, she would research his background, go after it with the same vigor that she had Stephanie's and Monty's. She concentrated on the memory of Jimmy Scott, determined to shake something down. When it hurtled to a hit, the impact almost knocked her down.

Yes! You stupid bitch, she berated herself, *how could you have missed it?* She slammed the door of the Escort and sat there in the parking garage, feeling like a local hack. The family of Jimmy Scott had filed a million dollar wrongful death suit against the Cains. Lawrence Gibbs had represented them to no avail. Back then, she'd given the development all she thought it deserved—three sentences.

"The Scotts are trash," Billy had told her one night in bed. "Those losers are looking for a payday, darlin'. Their scum relative deserved what he got."

Maybe, maybe not, Abby thought. But she was certain of one thing—the Scott family would get her undivided attention now. She wondered who had been behind the lawsuit. More importantly, she wondered where they were today.

Abby stirred in the vinyl seat of the cheap American car. As the possibilities piled on top of each other, she grew more and more excited. This kind of thing gave her a sexual thrill. Too bad Matt Benedict was six feet under. The kid would have done in a pinch. She pushed shagging out of her mind and started the engine. It was time to play rape crisis counselor.

Joey Danza had scored Lisa Randall's whereabouts—rising news star Tyson Moore's humble one-bedroom digs. A little cyber sleuthing had secured Abby the address. She rapped the heavy brass knocker three times and waited. Soon there was movement on the other side of the door. It opened a few inches, limited by the chain latch. Fearful eyes stared through the crack.

"Lisa Randall?" Abby inquired gently.

"Who's asking?"

"Abby McQueen. I'm a writer."

Lisa offered a quick smile and a nod of recognition. "There are some who'd debate you on that."

Abby performed her best who gives a shit shrug. "At least I'm in the Library of Congress. Critics are lucky if their work gets spread on the floor to block puppy piss from the carpet."

Lisa laughed and unhooked the chain.

Abby stepped inside and observed the beautiful black woman as she fastened several deadbolts—all with her left hand. In her right one she held a whopper of a gun, the kind of weapon suitable for a member of Iraq's Republican Guard.

"That's some gun," Abby remarked.

"A girl's gotta do . . ." Lisa said, disappearing into the bedroom, then returning, sans firearm. "So what brings you here?"

Abby knew she had to connect with Lisa to get what she wanted, and there was no better method than clasping hands in fabricated female solidarity. Sisters of the same crime united. There would be a little white lie, or more accurately, a sick, opportunistic, no-morals-here breach of humanity. Par for the course in her line of work.

"I know what happened to you," she said softly.

The temperature in the room shot down several degrees as Lisa Randall's gaze dipped to Antarctic levels. "Where did you get that information?"

Abby said firmly, but gently, "Getting information is what I do." She allowed a beat to pass, holding Lisa's eye contact, and finally announced, "It happened to me, too."

The belief in Lisa's eyes was instant; the rest of her thawed just as quickly. She picked up a black cat lounging on the back of the sofa and snuggled him close to her heart, stroking his head. The only sound was a steady purr.

"Are you in a support group?" Abby asked. She prayed the answer was no, for it would make her task much easier.

Lisa shook her head and held the cat closer, like a little girl. "I'm not a group kind of person."

"It's important to talk about what happened . . . I know it was for me."

Lisa's eyes welled up with tears, and she sank into the nearest overstuffed chair. "I don't want to talk about it because I can't bear to relive it, but all I do is relive it inside my head."

Abby reached over the bar to grab a tissue from the kitchen counter and handed it to Lisa. "I'd been in New York for about five or six years when I was raped," Abby began, recalling a recent *Cosmopolitan* article on the subject. She changed and enhanced the gory details as she went along, and by the end of the story Lisa was an emotional barnacle, clinging to Abby, having found a longed-for kindred spirit.

As Lisa half talked, half sobbed through her ordeal, Abby stirred internally with a fiery impatience. Certainly there was something to Lisa's attack that could be linked to some larger conspiracy, but if there was, she hadn't heard it. Shit, so far Lisa Randall had relayed nothing that Abby couldn't have ripped off from a lame movie of the week.

"Did he say anything, anything at all?" she pressed, nearing desperation.

Lisa shut her eyes a moment, as if to block out a thought. Her voice quivered. "Yes. He said, 'You've got bad taste in friends, bitch. You deserve this."

Abby McQueen pinched herself to prove she wasn't dreaming. Dialogue like that was priceless. She could actually feel her own eyes shining and then stopped herself, putting extra effort into looking appropriately shocked and disgusted. "What do you think he meant by that?"

"I don't know," Lisa murmured.

Abby paused dramatically. "I think you do know," she whispered.

"Sometimes I think I've gone crazy."

"I know that Stephanie Hart is a dear friend of yours . . ." Abby ventured carefully.

Lisa stiffened, going from a slouch to ramrod straight.

"She's dear to me, too," Abby gushed. "I don't know her very well, of course, but I admire her so much. I'm sure that the last thing Stephanie would ever want to believe is that something she'd done was the reason for harm being suffered by the people she loves."

Lisa rose quickly and began to pace. "None of this makes any sense."

"It's hard to imagine someone sick enough to go to such lengths, but stranger things have happened."

Lisa froze and looked genuinely puzzled. "I don't understand."

"Stephanie's been receiving these odd, anonymous messages that say REMEMBER SEPTEMBER. I believe they're linked to Ginger Simon's murder, your rape, and Matt's death."

"Matt's death?" Lisa shrieked.

Abby nodded. "Matt Benedict. He was robbed and killed last night at a gas station."

"That's awful," Lisa whispered, her eyes glazing over. "He was so young."

"Lisa," Abby began softly, dropping her classic, trustworthy tone, "I need your help. Understandably, Stephanie is reluctant to talk about her past, but I think the answer lies there. It's only a matter of time before someone else gets hurt . . . or worse."

Lisa stood stock-still, trembling with obvious fear. "At one point she was worried about Bruce Simon. The police still haven't found him."

Abby managed a wintry smile as she considered the suggestion. To be truthful, she had to admit that it held possibilities, though not the ones she longed for. She took in a deep breath. "Has Stephanie ever mentioned the death of Jimmy Scott to you?"

Lisa shook her head blankly. "All I know is what I've read from a few news accounts."

Abby couldn't listen to her another second. This paranoid bitch could offer her nothing more than wasted time. In a way, it was tragic, thought Abby. Before the rape, she imagined Lisa Randall must have been a gutsy, take-charge woman of substance. Now she was a housebound mouse, spooked by every shadow and sound, packing heat like a gang-banger.

"May I use your phone?" Abby blurted. Her hand was on the cordless before Lisa could answer. She dialed the hotel in hopes that a message from Joey Danza was waiting.

"He's here in the lobby," the front desk clerk reported, "and he's very anxious."

The tingle started in her toes and shot up to her scalp. "Tell him to wait." She hung up and addressed Lisa clearly and concisely, in a tone one might use to dictate a business letter. "You've been very helpful, but I'm afraid I must go."

Lisa gazed back pleadingly. "Maybe we could talk again. It . . . felt good to confide in someone. My boyfriend tries so hard, but I—"

Abby gave a bored gesture of the hand to cut her off. "Sure, honey. And don't forget the rape crisis line.

It's in the yellow pages." She rushed out, pushing Lisa Randall's post-trauma frailties from her mind.

More important things awaited her. There was a porn star ready to shoot his load.

Twenty-two

Transco Tower security was on the way.

Stephanie's fingertips danced nervously over the number pad as Kirk Mulroney's business card wavered in her trembling hand.

She was convinced that it was the slowest connection in telecommunications history. Her teeth grinded; her feet stomped. Finally, it began to ring. Once. Twice. Three times. And just when she was about to give up—

"Mulroney here."

The tonnage was lifted. "He's here, Kirk!" she gasped.

"Where?"

"In my office. He was watching me from the corridor. I ran into my private suite and locked the door, but a strong shoulder could knock it down."

"I'm sending a car right now. Stay on the line with me."

"I called building security. He should be here any minute."

"Smart girl."

The rich cadence of Kirk's deep voice soothed her spirit. Suddenly she realized that she hadn't identified the man, yet Kirk seemed to know exactly whom she was referring to, as if he'd somehow expected the call.

A knock on the door jolted her. She moved her lips in silent prayer.

"Ms. Hart? Are you in there?" It was Darryl, the lumbering security guard.

A shudder of relief swept through her. She blocked the receiver with her palm, crying out, "Yes!"

There was the sound of jingling keys and then the sight of Darryl as he pushed open the door.

"Security's here, Kirk."

"Stay with him. I'm on my way."

"What's wrong, Ms. Hart?" Darryl asked.

"There's a fugitive in the building. White male, six-foot-one, dark hair. He's wanted for murder."

Darryl swallowed hard. There were reasons why he chose the information desk beat. A tripped car alarm in the parking garage was within his comfort zone; an escaped killer was not. Clumsily, he groped for his sidearm.

A throng of uniformed cops barreled through, followed by some sharply dressed guys Stephanie figured for F.B.I. They raided the phones and buzzed back and forth on bulky, handheld radios. She quickly learned that the building was already sealed, that the search would take hours. If Bruce Simon was still in Transco Tower, they would find him.

Kirk Mulroney arrived with his customary cold water cool intact, though his eyes betrayed a hint of panic, perhaps a tinge of regret. He asked Stephanie for a few minutes alone, and she led him into her office, closing the door.

"Tina Fox is dead," he said in a quiet, level voice. "She was found this morning in a dumpster behind That Touch Of Pink . . . strangled."

She fell silent, remembering the fiercely intelligent, hard-bitten young woman who would still be alive today had she not gotten involved with that jerky guy, Dwight Duckworth. Stephanie looked back at Kirk, her gaze intent. "There's more," she concluded from his expression.

Kirk nodded. "I studied Lisa's case file again. She remembered her attacker saying, 'You've got bad taste in friends, bitch. You deserve this.' "

Stephanie felt weak. Once this brand of insanity began, where could it ever stop?

Kirk continued on. "That didn't resonate at the hospital. It was just some sick bastard talking shit. They all do it. But now I read it in a whole new context. So I think you're right, Stephanie. Bruce Simon is on a rampage."

She saw the sympathy and the fear in his eyes as he told her. Oddly, she felt in control. Before, she'd been alone with her crazy thoughts. At least now there were people on the same side of lunacy. Peter arrowed into her mind. She would have to tell him now, burden him with her living nightmare. He was going to be so frightened . . . and so furious that she'd kept it from him all this time.

"A few of the strip club regulars identified Simon from a photograph. He was there last night and didn't leave until Tina performed her last show."

Stephanie thought of the cryptic flyer affixed to her windshield just twenty-four hours earlier. Could Bruce Simon have killed Matt Benedict and Tina Fox in the same night? It didn't seem possible. She interrupted him. "What about Matt?"

Kirk gazed back at her with kind eyes. "Simon's a misogynist. He takes out all his rage on women— Ginger, Lisa, Tina . . . you. I'm afraid Matt was simply in the wrong place at the wrong time. I don't see a connection."

Stephanie bent her head and began to cry a little, then wiped her eyes clear and straightened up. "I'm so afraid for my daughter, Kirk."

He stepped closer, gripping her shoulders with hands like steel. "Listen to me. I'm going to find this motherfucker and lock him away forever. Do you understand me?"

She nodded, her belief in him total.

"And until he's apprehended," Kirk went on, "I'm stationing an officer at your residence."

Stephanie offered no protest. Until they captured him she would do whatever Kirk Mulroney advised.

Kirk's radio hissed and crackled. What came through was cop talk, but translating it was elementary. The search was officially over. Bruce Simon had left the building.

Peter stared into the silence for a while, then turned to his wife. "This isn't why we got married, Steph . . . to keep secrets from each other. I want to see those anonymous notes. Right now."

She gazed at him wordlessly, moving her wineglass forward and back again. Anger would've been easier to take, certainly more than disappointment. "I haven't been fair," she said in a stiff way. "I realize that. I'm sorry." And then she gave him a sad smile.

He looked at her closely, frowning. "Show me the notes."

Stephanie went upstairs to retrieve the copies from her home office. Kirk Mulroney had the originals. Passing by her daughter's doorway, she stopped. Tuesday's television was on, her boom box was thumping, and she was riveted to the computer screen, engrossed in an encyclopedia CD-ROM.

"How about turning off the TV and stereo so you can concentrate?" Stephanie suggested.

Tuesday's eyes did not leave the jungle cat stalking the monitor. "I don't mind. It helps."

"Quiet helps more," Stephanie replied firmly.

Tuesday grumbled, but did as she was told.

When Stephanie got back downstairs, Peter was gone. She stood in the center of the living room, holding the messages, waiting for him. He appeared moments later with a fresh glass of red wine. She realized that he'd opened a second bottle, which was unlike him. Normally, Peter was a two-glass man. As she looked at him, she thought about how wrong she was to have partitioned off part of her life, for what she'd tried to quarantine had now spread, tainting and corrupting one of the few things she cherished, their marriage.

Peter crossed the room without a word, gently taking possession of the pages in her hand and proceeding to the lamp by the window. He turned the beam up on the halogen and began to read.

Stephanie watched him wince. Then she turned away, unable to bear speculating on his thoughts. Stars splashed the night sky. The crescent moon looked almost silver. Everything around her was crashing and burning, but the family under this roof was intact. She would do whatever it took to keep it that way.

Peter placed his wine and the notes on an end table, took her hand in his, drew her closer, and cradled her head against his chest.

First she allowed the warmth of his body to pass through hers, basking in the incredible rightness of how perfect they were together. Finally, she gazed up at him with a pleading expression—*Forgive me*. Words were not necessary; the message was right there in her eyes.

Somberly, Peter rested his lips against hers.

Stephanie counted the seconds until he opened his mouth. And then she did the same, tasting the wine on his tongue, feeling an opium calm. As long as they were okay, all else could be in chaos.

He peered into her face and traced the lines of her brows and mouth with his fingertips. "You don't have to be so tough all the time. If you're scared, you can tell me. I won't think less of you."

Mutely, she stared back.

"Tell me that you're scared, Steph. I want you to need me."

Tears watered her eyes. She felt strengthened . . . and shamed. How could he possibly doubt that she needed him? A long moment passed before she pushed the words past her lips, faintly but clearly. "I'm scared, Peter."

A thousand perplexing sensations overwhelmed her. She'd been so tired, but now she was burning with fire, energized by a great gust of passion. With dreamy intimacy, Peter locked his gaze onto hers, holding her face in his warm hands. He was rediscovering her; she was rediscovering him.

Their breath came in deep drafts. Peter moved slowly, sweetly, and Stephanie's body pleaded for urgency, hips pushing forward in a gesture of total surrender, head nodding permission already granted. Their hands were linked, their arms outstretched, and their bodies as one, soaring in the plane of desire until the peak of ecstasy sent them off course. Somewhere in the sky they flew.

There was no waiting. There was no savoring. The

supreme beauty of the moment was instant. It was so precise, Stephanie thought as the silken folds of pleasure slowly abated. His scent, touch, and tenderness had triggered a multitude of tiny memories, all of them the reasons why she loved him.

Stephanie smiled with an intense joy. Peter was still inside her, and his head rested lazily on her breasts. She pushed a lock of damp hair off his forehead, inhaling the moment, experiencing a bewildering quietude. They had fallen a great distance, but tonight they had climbed back up to the top.

"You can't stay there forever," Stephanie murmured.

Peter peered up. "Am I being evicted?"

She laughed softly, raking her fingers though his thick hair. "Never."

"Good." He moaned, resting his eyes unwaveringly on her face, appearing simultaneously relaxed and anxious.

Stephanie felt something pulse through her mind, and in the same instant, saw it reflect in Peter's eyes: Their love for each other was stronger than before.

His hands skated down to the jut of her hips, and then he rolled over onto his back, sighing the sigh of sexual aftershock.

She sighed, too, allowing the residual tremors of delight to play over her.

Liz and Richard whined impatiently and scratched at the door.

"Go lie down," Stephanie called out to the spoiled canines. "I'll take you out in a few minutes."

Peter was watching her intently.

She turned onto her side. "What's wrong?"

"I think we should take Tuesday to school and pick her up until this situation is resolved."

She met his eyes steadily. "I think you're right. I'll call Mrs. Hatcher in the morning."

Peter gave her a sharp, questioning look but said nothing.

"What is it?" Stephanie pressed.

"Nothing," he began in an agitated way. "We're past that."

She tried to match her tone to his. "Are you sure?"

It took him a long time to answer. "Yes," he whispered, at last.

Peter was just drifting off to sleep when she spoke. "I'm worried about Lisa."

"It's too soon," he answered groggily. "Give her time."

"Peter, she won't leave Tyson's apartment. The simple *idea* of leaving makes her tremble."

He perked up, his invisible shrink hat firmly atop head as he stared at the ceiling, deep in thought. "What about work?"

"She's set up a virtual office in Tyson's bedroom. Hit The Sky sends her everything by fax and e-mail."

"How long can that last?" Peter wondered aloud.

"And I already told you about her wanting me to buy her a gun."

He nodded, still thinking. "You're certain that she hasn't ventured beyond the apartment?"

Stephanie sat up. "I'm almost positive."

Peter placed his hands on his bare chest. His fingers formed a perfect arch. "Lisa's developing agoraphobia," he said matter-of-factly.

She searched his face for the gravity of his words but couldn't get a reading. Fear for her friend rose up within her. "How serious is this?" she asked tentatively, not certain she wanted the answer.

"It can be quite serious, but to Lisa's advantage

she hasn't been ill for very long. The confidence to seek help should be there."

Stephanie shook her head in disbelief. "How could this happen, to Lisa of all people. She's a thrill-seeker, for Christ's sakes!"

Peter yawned. "A traumatic incident can bring this on. She feels safe at Tyson's apartment. Nothing else matters." His eyelids fluttered.

Stephanie nudged him to alertness. "What can we do?"

"Have Tyson call me at the office tomorrow. He needs to understand what's going on, because trying to force Lisa out will only mount tension on top of tension. There are some recovery steps he can walk her through that might prove helpful. Let's start there and see what happens." His eyes were closed now, his mouth slightly open. Peter Hart was exhausted.

Stephanie brought the covers up past his waist and kissed him on the cheek. "Go to sleep now, doctor," she whispered. Remembering the dogs, who were waiting right outside the door, she slipped on a terrycloth robe and accompanied them downstairs to let them into the backyard. They took care of business and dashed back inside.

Before heading upstairs, she parted the living room blinds a few inches and gazed outside. The patrol car was still there, directly in front of the house. There was comfort in the sight, and the knowledge, of its presence.

Knowing she felt too wired to attempt sleep, Stephanie tiptoed into her office to call Tyson Moore. He was still at the station, and she wanted to talk to him when Lisa wasn't around. Although his frustration was evident, he seemed genuinely appreciative of Peter's interest and promised to call him the next day.

Still keyed up, Stephanie switched on her computer. It had been days since she'd checked her e-mail. Surprisingly, she launched onto AOL on the first try.

"You've got mail," the computer voice chirped.

There were several junk messages that were days old, plus a new one transmitted today from an address she didn't recognize. She clicked the mouse to open it. Almost instantly, the two horrifyingly familiar words pulsated on the screen. REMEMBER SEPTEMBER.

Her stomach clenched. She commanded the computer to print and waited with agony for the laborious ink jet to spit out the page, all the while wishing she could place everyone she loved behind a force field or some shatterproof place. When it finished, she snatched the paper from the tray and rushed into the master bedroom. Peter had to know. They were in this together now.

"This is going to be the best fucking year of my life!" Joey Danza shouted. "Whoa!" He punched the air with his fist and lewdly gyrated his hips, a trademark move from his late night dance show.

Monty sat back in amazement, wondering if something other than a damn good mood was getting Joey all jazzed up.

"Let's go party!"

Monty laughed. He'd never seen Joey so animated, so incredibly alive. "What's up with you? Did you win the state lottery or something?"

"Even better," Joey shot back, sealing his lips and tossing an imaginary key over his shoulder.

Monty felt the heat of instant alarm. "Our rule is no secrets," he snapped.

"Hey, be cool. I'll tell you . . . eventually." Then he winked.

Monty produced a tense grin. He didn't like to be teased.

"So, are you coming with me or not?"

Monty nodded his acquiescence. Hitting the gay bars tonight was the last thing on his wish list, but letting Joey cruise them unescorted was out of the question. "Do I have a choice?" he grumbled.

After a quick shower together, they dressed in club kid gear and were off, speeding toward Montrose, pumping Gloria Estefan at mega volume. Monty pretended to be into the groove and psyched for the good times ahead. The truth was, he hated to go clubbing—all the monotonous music and the come-ons and the here-to-be-seen attitude. Who needed it?

An idea sprang to mind and Monty yanked the steering wheel, zipping onto North Boulevard between Graustark and Mandell Streets. He parked under a light and killed the engine, then lit a cigarette.

"What the hell are you doing?" Joey asked.

"Stalling."

"No shit."

"I'm not up for crowds just yet."

"I'm not up for quiet time."

Monty cut his eyes. "Let's take a walk." He got out of the car and stood on the sidewalk.

Joey waited a few seconds to make his point, then followed right behind.

Monty brooded. The two of them were about the same age, but sometimes he felt ten years older than Joey, at least emotionally. He looked around. The extended branches of the massive oaks stretched out over the street like a canopy, throwing shadows into the road. This area was usually a favorite spot for jogging. Tonight, however, it seemed as if they had it all to themselves. Monty clasped Joey's hand in his and started to walk. He tried to savor the moment. It was a beautiful night. They were alone, in public, and, amazingly, the beneficiaries of discreet enough surroundings to feel comfortable holding hands, in the way most lovers take for granted.

"This is nice," Joey said quietly. There was a distinct note of sadness in his voice.

Monty didn't understand. Was he melancholy because too much of the world frowned upon such a simple moment . . . or was it something else? "Do you miss California?" Monty asked, taking a shot in the dark.

Joey hesitated. "Sort of."

Monty laughed derisively. "The station's made their position pretty damn clear. You could say I have some time on my hands. We could go for a visit."

"Uh . . . yeah," Joey stammered. "I've been meaning to talk to you about that. There's some business stuff I gotta take care of. It'd be better if I went alone this trip."

Monty stopped suddenly and faced him. Realization grew. In that moment, in that single heartbeat, he knew. Joey Danza wasn't coming back. Why? It was a question that Monty let pass through his mind unsaid. Instead, he leaned in to kiss him, wanting to be certain, to erase all doubt.

Joey's lips were immobile and unyielding. Even worse, they tasted of guilt. Whatever had moved him to such excitement earlier had nothing to do with the two of them. Who was next in line?

Monty drew in a slow, sad breath, shaking away the prospect of begging Joey for answers, of imploring him to stay, of laying on thick all the parts of his life he'd given up to stake a claim for them as a couple—the career crash, the family fallout. None of it mattered. Here, in the darkness, under the giant oaks, after all the sacrifice, he saw Joey Danza for what he was, a flake.

There was the very real possibility he could lose more, Monty realized, thinking of the dangerous sex they'd engaged in. He'd vetoed common sense, if only as a symbol to Joey of how much he was willing to risk. *When you go, don't leave me anything to remember you by,* Monty thought in the midst of the watershed moment. He tried to block out the three scary letters looming overhead. And to think he'd once wanted to have this guy's baby.

Shards of glass scattered around them. Monty jolted. A bottle had come out of nowhere, shattering on the sidewalk.

"God hates faggots."

Monty's blood turned to ice water.

"Dick sucking queers."

Three teenagers, not one a day over eighteen, came at them from all sides. They wore big black boots, Hitler T-shirts, and camouflage pants. The stubble on their scalps indicated, at the most, three days of hair growth. One had a swastika branded onto his upper arm.

Joey swallowed hard. His eyes made a hypothetical run for the car.

"Go on, sissy boy. Try to make it. See what happens." It was the tallest one talking, as he smacked the business end of a bat into the palm of his free hand.

Monty couldn't stop trembling. He lost control of his bladder, and urine ran down his leg. Desperately, he tried to find something human in the skinheads' eyes, but their gazes sent nothing out and took nothing back, all in the name of Lord Jesus, feeling so righteous they hadn't bothered to conceal their identities. The monsters were cornering to kill.

"Look," the one holding the .357 magnum snickered, "this fag's so scared he's taking a piss." He pointed to the puddle at Monty's feet and laughed.

"You girls want to kiss one more time before you die?" the bat carrier taunted.

If only I could set the clock back five minutes, Monty wished. He wouldn't stop the car. He would drive on to the Boulevard Bistro, request a table for two, and chow down on Monica Pope's awesome cuisine. Leaving reality for a moment, he imagined himself there, in the funky eatery, being served by the same surly waiter with the two-tone dyed ponytail who never refilled his water.

And then there was movement. The gun toter, screwing his face into an expression of distaste, took a menacing step toward him. "You know what? I bust my ass in a fucking chicken joint fifty hours a week while fags like you get all the good jobs. I should wear the nice clothes. I should drive the fancy car."

Monty's voice slipped away to a whisper. "You can have the car . . . you can have anything you want . . . you—"

In one lightning fast movement, the skinhead bitch-slapped Monty with the .357 magnum. The steel crashed into his mouth, blood sprayed, excruciating pain hit, and everything blurred.

"We're gonna play a little game. It's called queer hunt. If you get away, you live."

Monty had never felt so helpless. Prayer was futile. Boys like this relished the torture they could bring. Producing fear was orgasmic, and killing carried no consequence, no remorse. It was the natural order of the day.

The one with the baseball bat jutted it roughly into Joey's stomach.

Monty's ex-boyfriend by a minute doubled over, gagging. And then a brutal-blow to the back flattened him onto the concrete.

The leader stuffed the .357 into Monty's mouth. He felt the bile rise to his throat. Any second now he would be throwing up. His bowels contracted, and he stared into the face of the tormentor, seeing only wide-eyed anticipation.

"We got paid for this," the trigger boy snarled. "It's nice work if you can get it, but I would've done it for free."

There was a chorus of sinister laughter.

Monty blinked away his tears in an attempt to track their gazes.

The three skinheads were eye-fucking him. They clocked every fearful motion. They relished every cruel second. It was a game.

Suddenly the gun was yanked from his mouth, leaving a bitter metal aftertaste. He puked immediately. There were some final thoughts he wanted to clarify. Words ricocheted in his mind, seeking syntax and deep meaning.

Joey was still knotted with pain, gasping on the ground.

"Run faggot. Maybe you'll get away. Maybe you won't." The ringleader raised the gun into the air. "We'll count to ten."

Monty plunged into the night. He'd always been a fast runner. His adrenaline spigots kicked open, filling his lungs with hope for life.

There was an explosion and a flash of light.

Twenty-three

Abby parked illegally and dashed into the Marriott. Her face was flushed. She paused for a count of ten, not wanting to appear too desperate. Total control. Computer cool. Killer confidence to walk away from bullshit. Those were the tools essential to deal with bombshell sources of dubious character.

She scanned the lobby with a calm she didn't possess. The ten-cents-a-dance porn star was nowhere in sight. A wave of annoyance zoomed through her. *Wait.* That had been the explicit instruction. Did the idiot have a problem understanding simple orders?

Abby approached the front desk, cutting in front of a business dweeb sporting a stain on his cheap tie. She flashed her key card. "I'm Abby McQueen. There was a visitor waiting for me in the lobby. A young man, mid-twenties."

The clerk nodded knowingly, a glint of appreciation in his eyes.

One thing about Joey Danza, Abby thought, when he entered a room, people noticed.

"He left a short while ago, but he did leave a note." The clerk produced a Marriott envelope with Abby's name scrawled in blue ink.

"Son of a bitch!" she spat, snatching it from the clerk's nimble fingers. Abby stepped away and tore

open the letter. The same mentally challenged pen-
manship appeared on the single tri-folded hotel sta-
tionery page inside.

> *YOU WON'T BELIEVE WHAT I'VE GOT TO TELL.*
> *IT'S AWESOME. I STILL CAN'T GET*
> *OVER THE SHIT.*
> *GOT TIRED OF WAITING. TONIGHT I'M*
> *PARTYING MY ASS OFF.*
> *I'LL CALL YOU TOMORROW.*
> *JOEY D.*

Balls! She crumpled the note into her fist and
threw it down, not bothering with the wastepaper
basket nearby. Tomorrow seemed as far away as next
year. Waiting would drive her insane.

"I'll find that cheap hustler if it takes me all
night," she hissed aloud.

"Abby!" a familiar voice called.

She turned to see Francisco approaching, his face
a masterpiece of eager warmth. "I've been trying to
reach you all day. How about dinner?"

Abby experienced a tingle. He'd actually sought
her out. It felt good to be wanted, but now wasn't
the time to feast on the Cuban. She kissed him
lightly on the lips, allowing their eyes to linger one
moment too long. "Rain check," Abby whispered.
And then she left, hoping she could call in the
marker soon.

She knew of only one place to begin—Sweet Re-
wards. If Joey Danza was not there, then Jack
McCrary would certainly know where to find him.
That old queen had to be good for something.

For the last time in her life, she hoped, Abby
climbed the creaky stairs of the hole-in-the-wall

erotic theatre/lounge, blew past the brainless bouncer, and hit the bar with a vengeance.

Jack was behind it, talking up a two-bit drag queen who'd seen better days. He saw Abby coming his way and beamed electric. "Honey, what brings you to these parts?"

Abby dressed the rock bottom RuPaul up and down. "Not the clientele. That's for sure."

The he-bitch glowered.

Jack suppressed a giggle, bringing a bejeweled hand to mouth.

Abby's stomach did a somersault. She hated men who wore pinkie rings. "I'm looking for Joey Danza. It's important."

"Haven't seen him, girl. Don't expect to, either. His dance card's expired here. There's fresh meat in town," Jack trilled.

She eyed the Corona bottle on the bar, imagining how great it would feel to smash it over his head. "Any ideas where he might be?"

Jack's lips curled knowingly. "A few."

"Then you're coming with me," she stated firmly.

"What?" Jack was genuinely apoplectic. "Sweetheart, I can't leave the bar!"

"I'm sure Tootsie here can step in."

The dolled up boy muttered curses under his breath.

"Come on, it'll be fun," Abby encouraged, appealing to the spur-of-the-moment teenager trapped inside the over-the-hill man. She half-smiled, then took the smile all the way.

Jack grabbed the phone at the bar and punched in four numbers. "I've got an emergency. It shouldn't take more than a few hours," he said, hanging up, leaving no room for questions or refusals. He pursed his lips triumphantly. The temporary pass was all his.

"Nice car, honey," Jack teased as they reached the Escort. "What's wrong? Is the Rolls Royce in the shop?"

"It's a rental," Abby said tightly. Irritation bubbled beneath the surface, but she maintained her composure. She needed Jack only until Joey was found. Until then, she would have to holster her guns. Right now she wanted a drink. Mercifully, they arrived at their first stop within minutes, the gay party palace known as Wet. Jack led the way inside.

A fetid odor hit her like a blast from a burning oven. The thumping dance music was so loud as she squeezed past the loudspeakers that her chest walls actually convulsed. Abby wrinkled up her nose and plowed through the sweaty dancers, staying close behind Jack, who was sniffing out Joey Danza as swift and sure as a police dog. So far, no arrest.

The visuals were super real, a crowded floor of gym-obsessed, beautiful young men. She could smell the insolence; she could smell the liquor. A hot Latino swaying dreamily to the disco slaughter caught her eye. He was a dead ringer for Francisco Juarez—ten years ago.

Finally they reached the crowded bar, where cash was being spent like Monopoly money. Jack pumped the regulars for Joey sightings. Abby left him alone to play Matlock while she bum-rushed the bartender for a tequila, elbowing a pretty boy model type out of the way.

The bull-necked drink maid frowned at her guerrilla tactics but served her, anyway. "Six bucks," he snapped.

Luckily, Jack's fat ass was within reach. Abby

pulled his wallet out of his back pocket, lifted a ten dollar bill, and slapped it on the counter.

He spun around, half-alarmed, half-excited. "It's you! I thought maybe I'd gotten lucky."

Abby gulped the poison down like water. "That'll never happen here. Not unless one of these boys has a serious daddy complex." She handed the wallet over with a smirk. "Thanks for the drink. You're too kind. What's the story?"

Jack shook his head. "No luck."

The tequila was working hard, but Abby was still running on a short temper. "Then let's get the fuck out!" She set her empty glass down with a crash and ran the gauntlet toward the exit.

Outside she opened her mouth to eat the fresh air. Music drifted behind them. "Think!" she commanded with all the manners of a drill instructor.

Jack turned on her sharply. "What's this all about, anyway?"

"In a perfect world, I'd tell you."

He rubbed his eyes wearily. "Let's try Studs. It's close by." Getting into the car, he was flagged down by a distinguished bald gentleman coasting by in a convertible.

"Jack!" the man called in a richly cultured voice, grinning proudly and gesturing at the surly young Asian boy preening in the passenger seat. Pavarotti boomed from the surround sound speakers. The Hugo Boss-suited geezer braked and twisted down the volume.

Abby slammed the door and fired up the engine. No way were these lechers going to trade boy toy tales on her time. But then something in their voices stopped her cold. She listened intently but managed to capture only snippets.

"Be careful . . ."

"How bad . . ."

"Police . . ."

"Skinheads . . ."

"Montgomery Cain . . ."

"Gay bashing . . ."

Abby's pulse was off and running. She kicked the door open and ambushed Jack and the opera lover, leaning her manufactured body into their conversation as if she were throwing javelins in the Goodwill Games. "What happened?" she interjected.

Jack shook his head regretfully. "There were two men attacked by skinheads not far from here. Montgomery Cain was one of them." He gave Abby a sobering look. "I assume Joey Danza was the other."

Her mind was racing and her blood was pounding and her prayers were shooting fast and furious to the Almighty Creator. *Please don't let this delay my interview,* she chanted silently. *He can be beaten, but let him be lucid.*

Jack navigated her to North Boulevard, where Abby parked amidst the chaos. There were flashing blue lights, flashing red lights, and gawking emergency scene compulsives watching the incident as if it were a goddamn cable channel. Boldly, she stepped toward the street cop, coughing up crocodile tears, claiming to be Montgomery Cain's sister.

"No one has been identified," the policeman said rigidly.

"I know that's him!" she wailed, channeling Bette Davis.

He blocked her path all the same. "Let the paramedics do their job, ma'am. Go on to Hermann Hospital. Wait for him there. There's nothing you can do here."

Abby pushed against the human cinder block of

black muscle, straining to gain a few extra feet on the scene happening several hundred feet away. A bloody body was being lifted onto a stretcher and into the ambulance. Shit! She was still too far away to determine who.

Another red-soaked male body remained on the ground. There was much effort on his behalf. Just as suddenly there was none. Heads shook mournfully. And then a dark blanket covered him from head to toe.

Montgomery Cain and Joey Danza. One man was barely alive; one man was dead.

Abby asked the cop for directions to the hospital and raced back to the car.

"Abby!" Jack yelled. "Wait for me! Wait!"

She ignored him. He would only slow her down. Jack carried change in his pocket. He could call a cab. Hell, for all she cared, he could walk and risk being skinhead bait.

The ambulance roared ahead.

Abby McQueen floored the accelerator to catch up, crossing her fingers that her guy was the one who survived.

Twenty-four

Stephanie was wide awake when Kirk Mulroney phoned. At first, the sound of his voice didn't alarm her. Having left a message at the station, she was expecting the call. But as she launched into her announcement about the e-mail message, an ominous vibe distracted her. She halted soon after. The intro had fallen flat. In the Mulroney silence, battle fatigue rang. Her body was ahead of her mind in figuring out the obvious: Kirk had bad news to deliver.

"Something's already happened." She gripped the receiver with all of her strength.

"It's your brother, Stephanie. You'd better get to Hermann Hospital right away."

"Tell me, Kirk." Her voice cracked.

A few minutes later, as she threw on jeans and a DKNY sweatshirt, her head throbbed with the facts at hand. Monty was in serious condition, and Joey Danza was dead. The assailants were skinheads. A resident in the area had witnessed part of the attack, then fled to call 911. Gay bashing was the apparent motivation, the giveaway being the DIE FAGS message in shoe polish defacing Monty's BMW.

Peter insisted on accompanying her. They secured Tuesday at the Fishers next door and asked the patrol car to set up surveillance there until they returned. Peter refused to let Stephanie drive. She sat catatonic in the front seat of his Infinity, unable to speak. Her last real conversation with Monty had been an argument, and over the telephone, no less. It was all she could think about. At the edge of her awareness, a dark foreboding was lapping, but she pushed it away.

Stephanie held Peter's hand tightly as they approached the emergency room information kiosk. Glancing around, she saw no sign of Kirk Mulroney. She made eye contact with a heavyset nurse whose warm brown eyes exuded kindness, then moved in to approach. "I'm Montgomery Cain's sister," she announced.

The woman's face registered surprise. "Your older sister is already in the waiting area. The doctor will see you both shortly."

"Older sister?" Stephanie wondered if she'd heard the nurse correctly. "We don't have an older sister."

Now the nurse looked confused. "She . . . was very upset—"

Stephanie broke away and stalked toward the waiting room like a missile locked onto an enemy aircraft. Abby McQueen was sitting on the sofa, sipping coffee, looking impatient, desperate, put out, annoyed—anything but sincerely worried about Monty's welfare.

"Get the hell out of here!" Stephanie screamed. Her entire body was hot. She knew her face was as red as her hair. She knew the flush was spreading fast on her neck.

Abby stood up quickly, playing the affronted, acting the innocent. "I have every right to be here. Joey Danza's a friend."

Stephanie's heart banged against her ribs as if

wanting to break out. Hatred flowed that she never knew existed. It felt frighteningly dangerous, like napalm. A media cretin like Abby McQueen wouldn't recognize a friend if one showed up for dinner with a good bottle of wine. They only dealt in sources and contacts. Stephanie did the algebra: Abby had been using Joey; Joey had been using Monty.

Peter took cautious hold of her elbow. "Come on, Steph. Let's sit over here and wait for the doctor." He gave Abby a disapproving glance, as if an enemy of Stephanie's were automatically an enemy of his.

Stephanie shook her arm free and lunged toward Abby, unable to bottle the hostility. "You bottled blonde bitch!" It was quick and dirty. She tore roughly at the made-in-Paris blouse, and to the melodic score of the pearl buttons popping on the linoleum she got in a vicious hair pull and a loud slap across the face.

"Stephanie!" Peter admonished, pulling her back with both hands, his force determined.

Abby held her blouse together with one hand and smoothed the pulsing redness on her cheek with the other. A devilish smile curled up on her shocked face. "Apparently that murderous little girl hasn't gone away."

Peter tightened his hold. "Steph, we're here for Monty. We don't even know how bad it is yet. Let's go."

Abby's smile faded faster than a pricked balloon. Monty's survival was news to her.

Stephanie picked up on it. "Joey Danza is dead." She was proud to say it, not because she wanted it to be, but because it was so obvious that Abby McQueen wanted it the other way.

Abby seemed to shrink at least three inches, her body language talking heavy duty disappointment.

"My offer still stands," she announced, though her heart was not in it. "Don't forget there's a little boy who needs his mother."

Stephanie hoped Peter was taking mental notes. The woman before them was a case study in bankrupt morality. "You don't give a damn about Josie and Jason Dean," Stephanie shot back.

"No need to state the obvious. I'm not here to play social worker. The story's what I'm after."

Peter pulled Stephanie back a few steps and moved in between them, turning to face her. "Go have a seat and calm down. I'll see this woman to the door."

Stephanie nodded blankly and walked away, thoughts of Abby McQueen fading with each step. Monty's condition was still unknown. Where was the doctor? Where was Kirk? She wanted answers! Visions of the incident haunted her brain as she imagined the horrors. By breed, skinheads were unrepentant, affectless, riding on the fuel of ignorance and hate. The cruelty and violence they were capable of was unfathomable.

"Please let him be okay." Her simple plea came out tiny, poignant, and childlike.

Within moments, a thirty-something doctor in scrubs and a weary Kirk Mulroney approached. Peter fell in step right behind them. As Stephanie rose her knees buckled slightly, but she managed to steady herself.

There were introductions all around, Dr. Nolan to Stephanie and Peter, Kirk and Peter to each other. She couldn't stand another second of not knowing. "Is he going to make it?"

"Yes," Dr. Nolan said confidently, almost on top of her own words.

She liked him immediately. He was lean, tan, and

forthright, and made solid contact with alert, intelligent eyes.

"Your brother's very lucky. He suffered a fractured skull, some facial contusions, a bruised kidney, and a laceration on his shoulder where a bullet grazed it. He's in and out of consciousness, but he's lucid. He knows his name, age, Social Security number . . . everything that happened."

Stephanie began to cry tears of joy and despair.

Peter pulled her into an embrace. "He's going to be okay, Steph," he murmured soothingly.

She wiped her eyes and drew back to face Dr. Nolan. "When can I see him?"

The doctor held up a halting hand. "I know you're anxious, but Captain Mulroney here just took Monty through some questioning that really wore him out. He needs to rest now. If it makes you feel better, he knows that you're here."

She nodded gratefully. "Thank you."

Dr. Nolan pressed his hand into hers. "He's in good care. I'll check in with you later." His once tranquil face now vehement, he turned to Kirk. "I hope you catch those sickos."

"Count on it," Kirk said.

Dr. Nolan placed a supportive hand on Kirk's shoulder and shuffled on.

"It could just have easily been Monty who died," Stephanie said to no one in particular.

"Any leads on the guys who did this?" Peter asked.

Kirk gave a troubled look. "It was dark. The descriptions I got from Monty and the eyewitness don't give me much. Shake up a bag of skinheads, and they all come out looking the same. But there's a marking on one of them that should help considerably—a swastika branded on his upper right arm."

"They'll boast about the bashing to their friends. Word will travel. Keep your ear to the street," Peter suggested.

Kirk nodded. "You're right. These guys think that what they do is justified. They're raised to believe that homosexuality is a crime against America, like communism."

Stephanie clasped both hands over her ears. She was on the threshold of pain just hearing about these scumbags. Besides, Peter and Kirk were not saying anything that she didn't already know. She'd once represented a local actor who sued the family of a teenager guilty of accosting him outside a bar and leaving him for dead. Like that hate-monger, the creeps who hurt Monty probably had police records, a tenth grade education at best, and loser jobs at restaurants that paid minimum wage. It wasn't unusual for these types to harbor homosexual feelings of their own, and beating an innocent queer was their way of beating the queer out of themselves.

Was she generalizing? Stephanie thought hard.

No.

Maybe.

Yes.

Goddammit! Her brother was almost killed tonight. If she wanted to, she had the right. But she knew the problems didn't begin and end with the skinheads and shit-kicking rednecks. Statistics on crimes like these weren't overwhelmingly reliable. First, there was the reluctance of those assaulted to report incidents and risk being identified as gay. And the police force wasn't exactly lining up to seek justice. Many cops had simply ignored homophobic violence as a problem for as long as they could get away with.

Realizing she'd been lost in her reverie for quite a spell, Stephanie shook herself free.

"Ignorance about the HIV/AIDS epidemic has exacerbated the attacks," Kirk was saying.

Peter started to reply, then suddenly went for the pager hooked to the waistband of his jeans. Frowning, he checked the number on the screen and said, "Excuse me. I need to make a call." Shortly thereafter, he returned with talk of a patient who needed counseling that couldn't wait until tomorrow.

Kirk Mulroney's face clouded with uneasiness.

Stephanie stiffened. "Is there something you haven't told us?"

"It's too soon to be certain," Kirk began tentatively, "but Monty distinctly remembers one of the skinheads boasting that they were paid to do what they did."

Peter slid a possessive hand around Stephanie and pulled her in close. "So you think this is more of Bruce Simon's work?"

Stephanie put a trembling hand to her face. The painful realization hit her straight between the eyes, sharp and burning, dull and aching.

"There's no proof yet—"

Peter cut off Kirk, who was convincing no one. "Will you escort Stephanie home? I can't put this patient off. It's an emergency."

"Of course," Kirk said.

Peter gripped Stephanie's arms and squeezed tight. "Check in on Monty and then let Kirk drive you home. I want you to rest. We'll come back first thing in the morning. There's nothing you can do here tonight but wear yourself down."

Stephanie nodded weakly. She didn't want to think. She didn't want to make decisions. Peter's plan sounded sensible enough, so she kissed him good-bye and promised to see it through.

Defying Dr. Nolan's wishes, she slipped into Monty's room. She was unprepared for the sight. Lying stock-still in the hospital bed, he looked two breaths away from death. His eyes had virtually disappeared, and the wounds on his face were just pulp and masses of blood. Stephanie steadied herself on the bed's guardrail as a powerful wave of nausea crested and receded.

Then she noticed he had black grime underneath his fingernails, like a mechanic or custodian. She focused in on it. Never before had she seen a speck of dirt under Monty's nails. He was so fastidious that way, always meticulously groomed, a slave to the cleaner, gentleman sports of tennis and golf. His hands must have been clawing the ground, she surmised, imagining the violence that took place.

"I'm . . . so . . . sorry," she whispered. Inside of her, self-loathing danced wildly. Monty was here because a psychopath had a vendetta against her. Lisa was too shell-shocked to leave her home for the same reason. And despite Kirk Mulroney's protestations to the contrary, deep down she knew Matt was dead because of it, too. Her pulse increased as the damage report formed in her mind.

The artificial light and gleaming tiles unnerved her. She experienced a tightness in her throat. She hated emergency room air. Then a shock, a vision, a foretelling, flashed like lightning. It was of her mother, calling out the same odd words she'd uttered on the last visit: "He's alive."

Why had this thought lanced into her brain at this particular moment? Stephanie searched for the meaning, feeling absurd. There was none.

Bracing to leave, she embraced Monty with a loving, mournful look. Kirk was waiting. Peter wanted her at home. She vowed to come back the moment Tuesday stepped inside the safety of her school's doors. Monty hadn't so much as fluttered his eyes. Did he really know she was here?

Stephanie closed her eyes, praying that no more harm came to anyone she loved. The people around her had suffered enough. If she could transmit a telepathic message to that son of a bitch, she knew what it would be, for the game had taken its toll. Her spirit was broken, her moxie to fight back gone.

She wondered just how far Bruce Simon would go.

Lisa never missed Channel Eleven's ten o'clock news report. She realized that there was the anchor man Tyson Moore and the b-boy Tyson Moore. More important, she realized that she was in love with both of them.

The anchor was on-screen now, no doubt melting male egos as he gave the phrase "You wear it well" a whole new standard in his Armani suit and tie. His eyes were warm, intelligent, and trustworthy, and his delivery clear, confident, and modulated.

The b-boy would be home later, eager to divest the camera-ready clothes, happy to slip on his Hilfiger gear, anxious to spin the latest hip-hop hits on the CD changer . . . and ready to make love.

Lisa had forced herself to become comfortable with the sexual aspect of their relationship. That Tyson was fantastic in bed made it easier. Plus, keeping him satisfied physically meant keeping a lid on his frustration regarding her refusal to leave the apartment.

Tyson stumbled over a line of copy.

Lisa fixated her eyes on the big screen. She'd never heard him make a mistake.

His long, slim fingers flipped up to his hidden ear mike, as if testing it. And then his expression crashed. There was genuine devastation on his face. "This is just in . . . I'm . . . afraid we have some disturbing news about a former member of the Channel Eleven team, Montgomery Cain. He's listed in serious condition at Hermann Hospital after being assaulted earlier this evening. That's all the information we have at this time. KBLX will keep you informed as this story develops. Our prayers are with the Cain family."

A recent publicity photograph of Monty flashed on the screen before a commercial cut in. Lisa began pacing the floor, sidelined by nervous energy. Part of her wanted to jump into the car and race to Hermann Hospital. She imagined herself collecting her keys, opening the door, and stepping outside. Suddenly her face burned, her throat felt as if it were closing, and her lips went dry. She headed for the front door—to double check the locks.

What a joke. To think she could ever leave the home prison fear had sentenced her to. She had to face reality. No matter what was happening in the outside world, her life was limited to this apartment.

"It makes you realize how insignificant things are," Stephanie said.

They were in Kirk's Crown Victoria, coasting toward her Tanglewood home. It was late. No doubt the Fosters had Tuesday sound asleep in their cozy guest room by now. She debated whether or not to wake her. If she did, Tuesday would ask a battery of questions about her Uncle Monty, and Stephanie wasn't certain she had the emotional strength to answer them without histrionics. Remembering that Janet Foster took her dogs for a brisk walk at the crack of dawn, Stephanie decided to rise early and collect Tuesday then.

"Are you and Monty close?" Kirk asked.

Stephanie zipped down the window and allowed the cool night wind to whip into the cabin. "We always have been . . . but our last conversation was an argument. A big one. But everything I fought against seems so small now. All that really matters is health and safety, right?"

Kirk reached out and patted her on the knee. "I wish more people in the world operated from that perspective . . . of course, I wouldn't have much of a job if they did," he remarked ruefully.

She studied Kirk Mulroney for a moment. He possessed such intense good looks, exuded such kindness and feelings of protectiveness. Why was he alone? Again she thought of Josie Dean, and how perfect he would be for her. "You know, you would really like Josie," she said.

His gaze remained locked straight ahead, but a smile did creep onto his lips. "I'm sure she's a very nice woman."

The innocuous reply made Stephanie smile, too. She was stumped. This man was a tough one to figure out.

He gave a male jogger on the neighborhood sidewalk a quick double take. "Kind of late for a run, don't you think?"

Stephanie stifled a yawn. "Not really. He's probably one of the doctors around here with a schedule from hell. Sometimes Peter squeezes in a midnight run, especially on nights like this when emergency cases throw him out of whack."

Kirk nodded.

"We're the next house on the left," she said.

He turned into the driveway and killed the engine, then contacted the patrolman next door, instructing him to position himself between both houses and to stay on red alert.

When Kirk insisted on accompanying Stephanie inside to check out the house, she didn't protest. He conducted a thorough search—garage, backyard, every room upstairs, every room downstairs, until he was satisfied that she could be left alone.

"Thank you for everything. You've been wonderful," Stephanie said, as Kirk prepared to leave.

"I'll see you at the hospital in the morning. I want to talk to Monty again. It's a long shot, but another important detail might come back to him."

She walked Kirk to the front door and noticed the late night jogger again. Now he was pounding down her street. It'd been too long since she had last exercised. A workout would do her some good, she thought. Promising to find time for it in the next few days, she fixed a cup of tea and decided to wait up for Peter. Attempting sleep would be futile, anyway.

Crossing the kitchen toward the living room, she heard a loud thump outside, the sound of something heavy being dragged. She stopped and listened.

Absolute silence.

A slight whisper and creak of branches.

Liz and Richard scampered into the kitchen to bark with unbridled aggression at the door which opened into the backyard.

Stephanie cut off the lights.

The room was beyond black. She could see nothing at all. Her heart began to beat very fast. She made herself do it—moving closer to the door, she reached out, pushed back the curtain, and peered out.

Something was wrong.

A strange feeling inched its way forward in her mind. Liz and Richard were still barking and clawing to get out. Stephanie had never seen them so ferocious.

She sucked in a breath and unlocked the door, swinging it open to set the dogs free. The hinges squeaked noisily. Making a mental note to tell Peter to oil them, she shut the door and locked it fast.

Liz and Richard went wild around the corner at the part of the fence that looked out onto the front lawn. There they remained, creating enough of a stir to wake the neighbors.

Three heavy knocks rapped the front door.

Stephanie's skin felt shivery. She rushed to the front window and looked out. The patrol car was still there, lights on, driver's door open. Gazing sideways, she saw the officer on the front step, head cast down, waiting. Had he seen or heard something suspicious? She moved to let him inside.

She didn't know what she saw first, the pale slice of moonlight or Bruce Simon in a policeman's uniform. As quickly as she clamped her hand across her mouth, he pushed himself inside and slammed the door.

"It's your turn, bitch."

Twenty-five

"That police captain is coming back any minute," Stephanie said.

Bruce laughed quietly. "No, he's not."

She thought of Peter and Tuesday. She imagined their beautiful faces, their sweet voices. The sense of closeness gave her a burst of courage as she wondered if she would ever see them again. Taking a blind step backward, she stumbled.

Bruce came after Stephanie and took her by the arms, shaking her violently. "Don't lie to me."

She let herself go limp, fighting insane panic, trying to remain rational. "I'm telling the truth." Her voice was barely a whisper.

Bruce drew her close. His grip was iron; his face was looming large over hers, his eyes full of expectation. "All women are liars. You cunts don't know how to tell the truth." He pressed his body against her.

Stephanie swallowed hard. The bastard had an erection. In his hand she saw the gleam of a knife. Ginger had been stabbed over and over again. Is that what would happen to her?

"It's . . . n-not a lie," she stammered hoarsely, feeling disoriented. Tears stung her eyes. Thank God she had left Tuesday to sleep on at the Fosters.

But where was Peter? Any moment now he could walk through the door. She had to think fast.

Bruce held the cold blade against her cheek. "If he does come back, it'll be too late."

"Don't do this, Bruce! You're not a killer. Those things people are saying about you aren't true."

He appeared taken aback.

Stephanie paused, tracking his gaze, the widening of his eyes. She had his attention. She had to keep it. "They call you a murderer, but I know that's not who you are." Uttering the words almost gagged her.

Bruce clenched his jaw. He looked like a man in trouble. Suddenly his eyes flashed rage. "You don't know me!"

She trembled, riding on the tide of paranoia. Smoke moved in her mind, clearing a sight path for the inevitable. She was going to die . . . like Ginger Simon . . . like Matt Benedict . . . like Tina Fox. His grip twisted her arm tighter than ever, and she grimaced at the pain.

"Don't pretend to know me! You don't fucking know me!"

Stephanie vibed in on the choked emotion in his voice. Hope sprang eternal in her heart. She had touched a nerve. It was a good sign. Maybe she could distract him. If she could just buy herself some time . . .

"I know that you loved her!"

Bruce froze.

"You loved Ginger. You loved her more than anyone else. That's what people don't understand."

Bruce closed his eyes tightly and shook his head vigorously.

Stephanie dressed him up and down. One of his grungy sneakers was untied, its dirty shoelace splayed out precariously. The policeman's uniform was at least one size too big, and the utility belt hung haphazardly on his hips, but the gun remained cozily locked in the holster. Was the officer still alive, or had Bruce Simon added cop killer to his resumé?

He opened his eyes and slapped her hard across the face. "You took her away from me!"

The blow sent her to the floor. She brought her hand to the cheek of impact. It pulsated with throbbing pain. As she struggled for association of thought, her breathing came in loud, deep drafts. The strategy she'd dreamed up was revolting, but it just might save her life.

"I was wrong!" Stephanie cried. "I didn't realize how much you loved her . . . not until you killed her."

Standing poised for another beating, Bruce cocked his head with bewilderment. And then he leaned down and wrapped his hand tightly around her throat, roughly fingering her lips with his thumb.

Stephanie took in a breath and held it. Her heart was a jackhammer. Her bones were ice dust. She had pushed him to right to the edge. Now she had to give him one more shove.

"It was an act of love, Bruce. I understand that now. In a way, it was beautiful. You wanted her to be yours, and no one else's. That's how much you adored her. People only see one side of this, but I see your side now. You're a victim, too."

His grip loosened. The thumb moving across her lips softened.

As liquid revulsion pumped through her veins, she parted her lips.

The rage on Bruce's face transmuted into anguish. His eyes welled up with hard tears. He pushed his thumb inside Stephanie's mouth.

She sucked on it softly, calling up every cell in her body to fight against the rising bile. "I know how much you loved her."

As Bruce nodded, the tears started down. "She made me do it," he said sharply.

"I know," Stephanie half whispered, forcing the disgusting words past stubborn lips.

"She told that boyfriend of her to call and tell me they were getting married. He said her message to me was that she'd finally found a real man. That bitch!"

Stephanie's mind whirled. Nothing Bruce was saying added up. Ginger knew how high the stakes of secrecy were. She'd given up all ties to her previous existence the moment she began living as Julia Turner. Her postcard hadn't mentioned an engagement, and even so, she would never have contacted Bruce, nor instructed a lover to do so in such a provocative manner.

Bruce stomped over to the entrance table and smashed a vase just for the hell of it. The broken glass skated across the hard wood floor. "If that boyfriend had been around, I would've killed him, too!"

Stephanie cursed silently. The softer side of Bruce was fading fast. It was the side she needed to stay alive. "But that wasn't Ginger's doing," she said passionately. "Don't you see? That was her boyfriend's game. He was jealous of you!"

"Jealous?" Bruce answered back, stunned.

"Yes! Jealous, intimidated, you name it. I assume he told you where Ginger was living."

"Yeah, he did."

"He wanted you to come there and force Ginger to make a choice."

Bruce stepped toward her, a blind man's stare on his face. "I know what you're doing. You're trying to put it on her. You're trying to put it on him. But you're the slut who helped her disappear." His tone was emotionless, calm . . . chilling.

"My husband's a psychologist," she blurted, now in sheer desperation mode. "These are crimes of passion. He—"

He laughed at her. "The stripper wasn't a crime of passion. That was a favor to my sister."

As Stephanie inched her way to a standing position, a shard of the broken vase impaled the inside of her ring finger. Blood began to trickle. She made a fist to lock the wound, wincing at the pain. Any moment now she would have to make a run for it, lock herself into a room with a phone.

"What about Lisa, Matt, and Monty?" she heard herself ask angrily. The voice was high-pitched. It didn't sound like her own.

"What the fuck are you talking about?" Bruce spat. He gave her an annoyed, quizzical look. The confusion on his face seemed genuine.

Stephanie's pulse pounded in her throat. Bruce Simon was certifiable. He'd even forgotten his victims from the last few days. He was unpredictable as hell. When he spoke of Ginger, there was a faraway look in his eyes. She had to get him talking about her again.

"You said that Ginger made you do it. What does that mean, Bruce?" Stephanie asked.

His mouth tightened. "She made me do it," he whined, as if that explained everything. "I told her that she could never leave me, that she could never be with another man. And look what she did! She left me, and she made plans to marry some guy she barely knew! I've loved her since junior high school. It was always me, you know?"

"I know," Stephanie murmured.

His eyes took on a wild quality. "Ginger knew I'd find her one day. She wasn't that surprised when I showed up. There was just this look on her face, like she was sure the day was coming. I mean, she didn't even try to get away."

Stephanie's gaze dropped to Bruce's hands. He'd dug a hole into his palm with the knife as he talked. A pool of blood had formed at his feet. It continued to drip down from the gaping cut. He didn't seem to notice.

"Her eyes were open the whole time," Bruce continued. "She was scared, but she was calm, too."

Stephanie was exhausted. She wondered if what she planned to do next was survival instinct or extreme stupidity. "Ginger died at your hands, but she still knew how much you loved her."

Bruce looked back at her, and his gaze became intent. "Do you really think so?"

Stephanie nodded resolutely. "I know so," she whispered. And then, nerves jangling, heart banging, prayers flying, she walked straight to him, stopping centimeters from his body. He smelled of blood and sweat.

Once more, Bruce wrapped a hand around her throat and brushed his thumb across her mouth. He pressed down hard, mashing her lips against her teeth. Blood gushed from his wound, blazing a warm and sticky trail down her neck.

She pressed against him. He was aroused. There was a strange gleam in his eyes. The million dollar question had to be answered. Was life worth what

she was about to put herself through? Peter and
Tuesday flashed in her mind. *Forgive me, darlings.*

His thumb was inside her mouth again, and she
sucked it, eyes half-closed, as if floating on a cloud
of erotic abandon. Her hand ventured down to his
crotch. She found the shaft of his penis beneath the
cop fabric and stroked it, nice and rough.

Bruce moaned, his breath shuddering in his
throat. He licked his lips.

Stephanie had him. Almost. The window of opportunity was so near. But the unknown gnawed at
her stomach, because her next move was do or die.

"Close your eyes. Pretend I'm Ginger. I'm here to
love you," she said, her voice barely audible, her
fingers playing with his belt buckle. A tear rolled
down her cheek. She felt dirty.

"Go on, Ginger," Bruce grunted. "Who's your
daddy?"

A wave of sickness ripped through her body. She
almost fainted. "You are," she whispered, sinking
onto her knees. With trembling hands, she unfas-
tened his belt and trousers and let them fall to his
feet. The gun hit the floor with a thud. It was close
enough to reach. Her heart took a leap as she fumbled for the hunk of metal.

She stroked him with one hand, trying to unhook
the gun with the other, keeping her gaze locked
onto him. His eyes were hooded with lust, his neck
thrown back on his shoulders.

Yes! It was almost there, the gun halfway out of
the holster. Her mouth was dry with fear, her skin
crawling. Just one more tug—

Bruce threw his head forward. His eyes zeroed in
on her. A shadow of dark rage played across his
granite face.

Stephanie froze.

The back of his hand came down fast and hard, and she fell back with the force of the blow. He lunged, the knife clenched in his fist, swinging it like a pendulum.

She screamed, her throat raw, and flattened her body. The blade missed her by inches.

"No!" Stephanie pulled her leg in and kicked it out with all the force she could muster. The rubber sole of her Keds made solid contact with Bruce Simon's balls.

He cried out in agony, doubling over. Stumbling over the pants at his feet, he stepped on the loose shoelace and toppled to the floor.

Stephanie struggled to get up. She could taste salty blood. It was her own.

The gun was tangled in the heap that was Bruce Simon's body.

For a man just disabled, he seemed to be moving very fast.

She turned to head for the kitchen.

"Don't fucking move!" Kirk Mulroney stood in the doorway. His weapon was pointed at Bruce's heart. His finger was on the trigger.

The sight of Kirk brought such intense relief that she began sobbing immediately.

"Get behind me, Stephanie." Kirk's eyes met hers for one split second.

It was the only second Bruce Simon needed. The gun was in his hand. He took deadly aim at Stephanie before she could take so much as a step. "I'll kill the bitch."

Stephanie brought hand to mouth to stop the scream. In her mind, she prayed for life. In her heart, she said good-bye to Peter and Tuesday. Instinctively, she knew it was over.

One bullet tore loose with a sonic boom.

Twenty-six

Abby didn't want to be alone, so she called Francisco upon returning to the hotel. He came over right away. One glass of wine led to another, and another . . . and another.

They made love the first time with their clothes on, two drunk, lonely people. Francisco was opposite her in temperament—kind, thoughtful, and quiet. Was that why she felt so drawn to him?

Even in the haze of inebriation, he fulfilled all her desires. Unlike Matt, who had required direction for the amateur that he was, Francisco knew the secrets of a woman's body. He was uniquely confident, and the wine overdose had no effect on his performance.

Strangely, he made her feel at ease afterwards. Usually, Abby shrank from her partners' attempts at postcoital intimacy. What was the point? Relationships were for the needy. They meant change, compromise, and sharing—three things that sent Abby McQueen packing and running.

Somehow Francisco Juarez was different. Here was a man who didn't try too hard. His air of macho pride and dignity ran deep; it was in his blood, not just laced in his attitude.

She liked him. More important, she wanted him

to like her. All evidence seemed to prove that he did. Considering his on-his-sleeve moral standards, she wondered why.

They stripped, made love again, and then ordered a feast from room service, including more wine. When the bellboy brought it up, Francisco answered the door with a pillow covering his privates.

From the bed, Abby giggled. "Give our friend a big tip."

The bellboy managed a crooked, embarrassed grin.

Francisco backed up, scouring the floor for his pants. It was a tricky balancing act, but he retrieved them and produced a ten dollar bill without flashing the wide-eyed kid.

Abby made a face as she tasted the filet mignon. "This steak is like rubber. Why'd you put me up in this dump?"

He smiled. His teeth were magazine cover perfect, alpine white against his dark olive skin. "Hey, anything tastes great to me. I just got laid!"

Abby laughed and pushed her steak aside, filling up on a loaded baked potato, asparagus, bread, and a thick slice of decadent chocolate cheesecake.

"I like a woman who's not afraid to eat," Francisco said, stuffing the last bite of tough meat into his mouth.

"Well, I'm not afraid of anything," Abby said.

"Nothing?" he challenged. "What about getting older?"

She shrugged. "That's what plastic surgery's for."

He pushed the cart away and stretched out on the bed, pulling her into his arms. "Okay, you can write a check to protect your vanity. But what about being alone?"

Abby played with the thick, black hairs on his chest. "There are worse things."

"Like what?"

"Like being in bad company."

Francisco chuckled and squeezed her shoulder. "You have an answer for everything." He sighed deeply and closed his eyes. Sleep came within moments.

Abby extricated herself from his embrace and opened the third bottle of wine for the night. She was severely unsettled. This felt too good. They were so natural together, as if it were meant to be. Naked, she filled up her glass and crossed over to the window overlooking the city.

Finding a great guy hadn't been part of the plan. She was here to get the story, toss a few crumbs to *Texas Today*, and head back to New York to start a bidding war with a knockout book proposal. With a little bit of yearning in her heart, she wondered how long this would last if she allowed it to go any further than this night.

She watched him sleep, concentrating on the rise and fall of his chest, feeling a surge of warmth. The white sheet started coverage just a few inches down from his belly button, where the hairs began to gather thickness. In her mind, she played back the steamy memory of their trip to heaven, and it filled her heart to overflowing.

She normally hit the skins with men who could be used up and thrown away, but Francisco Juarez was an anomaly. He couldn't do a damn thing for her—except make her feel special.

"Goddamn you," she whispered to the sleeping Cuban, who was lit by moonlight, who was quite possibly the best thing that had happened to her since her life had skidded into a downward spiral. In another time, another place, maybe they would have worked. Right now, they were doomed to fail. She knew that.

All the wine had taken its toll. Her head was fuzzy. She climbed into bed and wrapped herself around Francisco's warm body, falling asleep instantly. As she drifted off, her last thought was how good it felt to have a man in her bed whom she actually wanted to still be there the next morning.

Daylight came, and they woke up within seconds of each other, both of them freezing.

"It feels like a meat locker in here," Abby said groggily, pulling up the sheet and blanket.

Francisco stretched out, fumbling for his watch on the bedside table. He glanced at it and left it there, groaning as he moved back into place.

"What time is it?" Abby asked.

"Ten after nine."

"Shit."

"Ditto. I missed a nine o'clock staff meeting that I scheduled."

"Tell them you were with me. That should go over well."

She moaned. Someone was beating a drum inside her head. At least it felt that way. Why had she done this to herself? The Abby McQueen she knew and loved would already be on the way to Galveston by now, ready to check out Jimmy Scott's family background. Yet here this new version was, hung over, sleeping away precious hours, and doing nothing to improve the situation, as if things couldn't get any better.

"I have to go," Francisco announced.

"Me, too," Abby said.

Neither one of them moved, until he turned over on his side to face her. His lips were dry. She licked them sensuously, coating them with moisture. And then he brought up his hands to hold her cheeks as he probed her mouth with a tongue hot for discovery.

The world went away. So did the fever of ambition that propelled her forward. There was only Francisco's luxurious kiss.

Reality thundered back. Abby pulled away from the passionate onslaught. Ambivalence vibrated in her mind, like an arrow in the center of a target.

"I'll shower first. You order breakfast," she said. Her command hit the air like a suggestion. She was talented that way.

His black eyes were candid. "Do you regret what happened last night?"

She looked away and finger-combed the tangled mess that was her hair. "I regret opening that third bottle of wine."

He smiled. "So you waited until I was asleep and then had another party?"

Abby grinned and started to get up. "I couldn't get to sleep. It was sitting there. I figured you wouldn't mind."

Francisco reached out and took her hand, and Abby held it until she moved beyond its grasp. As the hot water blasted onto her skin, she drew up a mental ledger of everything she thought she wanted.

Money to live right.

Fame to let everyone know it.

Steam rose up. She closed her eyes and opened her mouth. One sure shot at the big leagues would get her both. She couldn't go soft now. No fucking way. Abby McQueen needed that hard edge. The truth was, love messed up her system. Case in point—Billy Hudson. She'd been in love with the old bastard, and as a result, she'd fallen for the con game of Jimmy Scott's accidental death.

Abby hated to admit it, but in many ways she was just like other women. Her biological clock ticked. Her ovaries twitched. The emotional succor of a man too often loomed as the magical solution. Francisco Juarez tugged at these deeply buried fantasies. Even though she was pulling the other way, a secret part of her wanted him to be the victor.

She stayed in the bathroom to apply her makeup and style her hair, because her motive was to dress quickly when she stepped back into the room and get the hell out. After all, the more time she spent with him, the more desire she felt to cling like a baby koala bear.

Francisco was still lounging naked. "I wasn't sure what you liked, so I ordered everything," he said, waving a hand over an impressive room service cart.

"Go ahead. I'm not hungry." She managed a quick smile as she made a beeline for the closet to pick out her clothes.

"No breakfast in bed?"

"I thought you had to go."

"I did, but I called and rearranged my morning."

She shrugged helplessly. "I have got a long drive ahead of me. There's no rearranging that."

"I could go with you."

She regarded him sharply. "Don't make those kind of noises. You sound like a bored husband."

Francisco's brow shot up. His mouth was firm. "You've obviously had a conversation with yourself that changes things. Care to let me in on it?"

Abby sighed. "All that wine did a real number on me last night. It helped me forget what happened. I'm not so lucky this morning. Daylight's a bitch."

He looked into her eyes.

She became aware of how rarely someone really looks at a person.

"You're talking about Montgomery Cain and Joey Danza," he whispered, more to himself than to her.

She slipped on a powder blue cashmere twin set. "If that idiot had just waited for me in the lobby, I'd have that information for the story right now."

There was an odd expression in his eyes, as if he were seeing her for the very first time. "That's all you care about?"

She met his gaze defiantly. "Yes. Joey knew what went down the night Jimmy Scott was murdered. That secret's what I'm mourning. It's a priest's job to worry about the rest."

Francisco showed no reaction.

"What did you expect from me?" she asked.

"I don't know . . . maybe a little humanity," he said coldly.

"I'm fresh out when it comes to porn stars. Anyway, I don't have time to argue these finer points. Today I'm heading to Galveston for a crash course in Jimmy Scott. Wish me luck. Maybe Stephanie Hart will have reconsidered my offer by then." She sprayed her neck and wrists with Chanel Number Nineteen.

"What offer?"

As she switched one knock-off handbag for another, she explained the Josie and Rob Dean custody battle, the unconscionable ruling in the husband's favor, and Judge Lawrence Gibbs' involvement in a wrongful death suit against the Cains twenty years ago.

By the time she finished, Francisco's face was twisted into a look of complete astonishment. "There's a child at risk here!" he yelled.

Abby checked her watch. It was ten o'clock. "I need to get on the road. Forget I said anything."

He picked up his boxers and stepped into them, shaking his head in disbelief. "*Texas Today* doesn't blackmail sources into cooperating. I'll talk to Stephanie myself. I'm not going to allow you to use that little boy as a crowbar. It's sick!"

Abby gave the untouched food cart her total concentration.

"I don't want to be associated with those kind of gestapo tactics. I run a reputable publication," he continued.

Christ! She would surely throw up if she had to suffer through Francisco's chapter and verse on journalistic integrity. Both hands flipped to her hips. She thrust out her breasts haughtily. "You knew exactly what you were getting when you hired me."

Francisco's neck turned fire engine red as he paced the room. He was not a man to be laughed at, even half-naked. In fact, the body perfection made him that much more impressive.

"*Texas Today* hired the name Abby McQueen, not the bottom-feeding values that go with it. Jeff Lowenstein twisted my arm to take you on. Any one of my staff writers could've handled this anniversary piece."

Abby gasped. He'd just placed her on the same level as some regional nobody. It was the ultimate abuse. Somewhere inside her she'd worried about the future pangs of regret that might erupt from choosing the career she craved over the man who could have been. But right now she declared such concerns legally dead.

"You son of a bitch! No one at that rag could do anything more than rehash old press clippings. I'm on to something big that'll put me back on the scene. And when it happens, your friend Jeff Lowenstein will give up his sling at that leather bar for a piece of the action."

His face was split screen, part cold clarity, part shock. She'd blasted his overworked, underpaid writers as incompetents; she'd rudely outed his buddy from Brown. The anger in his eyes stepped aside for a moment, making room for sadness. "What happened to the woman I was with last night?"

Abby considered the question, and the man asking it. *She is three-quarters in love with you,* she wanted to say. It had been true last night. It was true right now, even in the crossfire of sticks and stones. That was why she couldn't leave here with even a glimmer of hope for something to come back to. Nothing weakened a woman more than maybe-he-still-cares thoughts over some man. Her finger hit the imaginary DESTRUCT button. "That girl was smashed. I'm clean and sober."

His laugh was bitter, self-mocking. "And to think I was going to ask you to stick around."

She didn't look at him when she left the room, and by the time she reached the elevator the tears had ruined her eye makeup. Abby McQueen had never cried over a man in her life. Until now, no lover had been worth the Kleenex. The old cliché was true. There *was* a first time for everything.

Twenty-seven

The horrible scene played like the Zapruder film. A shot rang out. There was screaming. Dark red mist in the air. Running in grainy slow motion. Confusion all around. Stephanie cried out, but the event was already over.

On the floor, Bruce Simon trembled spasmodically, the muscles in his face twitching violently. A gaping hole had been blasted into his chest. He coughed up a long spurt of blood, then suddenly stopped moving.

Someone's gentle hands were inspecting her face and the deep gash on her finger. "You're safe now, Stephanie. It's over."

She glanced up. It was Kirk Mulroney. Her lips wouldn't move.

"I want this puncture wound checked!" he shouted to the gaggle of emergency medical technicians and police officers crashing through the front door. Some F.B.I. men from the Transco Tower search were part of the body rush.

And then she saw him, grappling furiously to push through the uniformed cluster, terror all over his face . . . Peter. Instantly, she felt calm, though she realized it was illusory. Havoc was everywhere.

He called her name. His eyes welled up with tears.

And then he reached her, scooping her into his arms, almost crushing her in his tight hold. "I should've been here . . . I'm so sorry . . . Jesus, Stephanie, you must've been so scared . . . it's all over now."

She felt ill and fragile, and didn't dare move. The prison of Peter's arms was a welcome one, and his constant purring into her ear soothed her spirit. Yes, it was finally over. Stephanie closed her eyes and let the moment wash over her.

Peter leaned back, wincing at the sight of her cheek.

"I'm okay," she assured him.

He reached out to softly trace the outline of the swelling with his fingertips.

Kirk appeared and slapped a hand on Peter's shoulder. "This wife of yours is one tough lady."

Peter kept his eyes locked onto Stephanie. "You're telling me."

"Stephanie," Kirk began gently, "They're going to dress that injury out front, and I'll need to get an official statement from you." He turned to Peter. "Then she's all yours."

She nodded blankly, following Kirk outside. The street was filled with gawking neighbors, and it sounded as if every dog on the block were barking in chorus. As they crossed the yard toward the emergency medical unit, she noticed the Fosters on their front lawn, clutching their robes.

Alarmed, she gazed up to the second story window of the guest room, the place where Tuesday was sleeping. Stephanie's stomach dropped. The light was on, the curtains pulled back. Her daughter stared down at the nightmare scene.

* * *

Lisa had called Hermann Hospital at least a dozen times to inquire about Monty's condition. Once Tyson walked through the door she pounced on him for the latest word, as well. He had little to add, except for the fact that skinheads on a gay bashing expedition were reportedly the cause of the tragedy.

She almost retched on hearing the news.

"Someone was watching over him," Tyson said.

Lisa looked at him coldly. "How do you figure that?"

"Because the other guy is dead."

Feeling instantly sick, she moved to the sofa and sat down. The wooziness passed. *Other guy.* "Joey Danza?" It came out faint, far less than a whisper.

The expression on Tyson's face was as certain as a death certificate.

"Oh, poor Monty," Lisa wailed. She could imagine the horror he'd gone through only too well. On top of that, there was the agony of loss.

"We'll go by the hospital in the morning," he said.

Lisa looked suspiciously into the eyes of Tyson Moore. He was measuring her reaction. The suggestion had been part of some trickery, a scheme to get her out of the apartment. "No," she said firmly, feeling the onset of intense agitation.

"I thought he was your friend."

"He is," Lisa shot back defensively. "I'll send flowers. I'll call."

Tyson gave her a disappointed look. "That's what distant relatives do."

She clenched her hands and started to pace, experiencing a painful ringing in her head. "It's too soon," she whispered.

"Lisa, you need to get help. Tomorrow I'm—"

"No!" She clung to him, tearing at his shirt, hungry for his skin. "I just need you." The buttons of his shirt were tight. She worked hard to wrench them free. Then there was his V-neck undershirt to contend with. Frustrated, she rucked it up past his chest and put her mouth on his nipple. "I'm still scared, Tyson, but I feel safe with you . . . close to you."

"Come on, Lisa," he started irritably, attempting to pry her off him.

She held firm, as if she were suctioned there. "Make love to me, Tyson."

"Baby, please!" He pushed her away, hard, almost knocking her down. "You can't just give me some sex and expect all our problems to go away. *You need help.* I'm not going to live like this anymore."

Lisa fought the choking panic with white-hot anger. *"You're not going to live like this anymore?* I was raped! I was beaten! In my own fucking home! Try living with that, you heartless bastard!"

Lisa felt the tears rolling down her cheeks, but she was still too mad to break down completely. She watched Cosby cower under the coffee table, then flit away with his fur standing on end.

Tyson didn't say a word. He just stood there wearily, his face buried in his hands.

Some of her anger dissolved. At least he was trying to help. Most men would've cut out long ago. Her eyes full of apology, she ventured toward him. "Let's not—"

"Don't touch me." He held up both hands to keep her at bay.

His response shocked her. The hurt came down as swift and sudden as a hail storm. "I'm not diseased." She started to cry again.

He stared at her for a long time. "But you're sick, and you're not doing anything to get better."

On Tyson Moore's face was the look of a man at the very end of the line. He was guarded, sullen, and harboring a great deal of concealed emotion. The ocean of things unsaid left her breathless. She didn't want to lose him.

"Give me some time," she pleaded. "Things will get better. I promise."

Tyson shook his head and grabbed his keys. "You're making me crazy. I've gotta get out of here for a while." He flipped the locks back with silent rage.

A sense of panic overcame her. "Don't leave me like this. I've been alone all night! I need company."

Her words had no impact. The same hard look was plastered across his face. "I'll make this as simple as possible, baby. If you don't agree to get some help, you and I are finished." Then he walked out, not bothering to look back.

Lisa raced to the door, sobbing as she secured the locks. Too much time alone brought on unbelievable tension. The inward thinking always upset her. What if Tyson forced her to move out? What if the masked attacker raped her again? Apprehension built up and up until she thought she might explode.

Bad times were far from over. Something terrible was going to happen. She could feel it so very strongly.

Stephanie returned to the land of the living. After treating her cut and giving her statement to Kirk Mulroney, she'd collected Tuesday from the Fosters and relayed a version of events suitable for a nine-year-old while Peter had worked to clean up what remained of the chaos.

Seeing Tuesday look down from the Fosters' window had been a shocking assault on Stephanie's nerves and awareness. How lucky her daughter was to have been spared as a witness to, as a participant in the night of unspeakable violence. Stephanie and Monty hadn't been so lucky twenty years ago. The realization made her feel like singing. Every inch of herself, every cell, every sense, was alive and thriving with the knowledge that her little girl was still innocent.

Remarkably, the next morning started out like any other. Stephanie, Peter, and Tuesday ate breakfast together and waited for the perpetually crabby Mrs. Hatcher to pull into the driveway and blast her horn impatiently. True to form, the carpool queen lived up to her own legend.

Peter left for the office, and Stephanie promised to call him with news about Monty. After tending to the dogs, she headed for Hermann Hospital. Once there, she was surprised to find Kirk Mulroney in her brother's room.

Monty was conscious, sitting up and sipping juice from a straw.

"Now *this* is more like it," Stephanie said with upbeat cheer. She couldn't recognize his face, and fought hard to veto any semblance of surprise or discomfort.

Monty managed a faint smile, an obvious Herculean effort. "Hey, I'm still here," he said.

She kissed his forehead. "Yes, you are."

A heavy nurse bounded into the room with a take charge attitude. "Dr. Nolan says it's time to dress those facial wounds and make you look pretty," she announced in a booming voice.

"I think my pretty days are over," Monty said morosely.

"Sugar, it's amazing you'll need practically no plastic surgery. So don't worry. The girls will be lining up just like always."

Monty threw his eyes toward Kirk. "Or the boys."

The nurse let out a guttural cackle. "Whatever you want, sugar. Girls, boys. They'll be lining up. I'm sure of it." She glanced rudely at Stephanie and Kirk. "Tell your friends here to beat it. You and me got work to do, and this ain't no picture show."

Stephanie kept looking at Kirk.

"Let's get out of her way," Kirk said easily, shuffling to the door.

Stephanie waited until they hit the corridor to say, "Florence Nightingale's charming."

Kirk laughed. "Ethel's a great nurse. Patients love her. But visitors are never quite as enamored." He paused a beat. "How are you?"

"Shell-shocked . . . relieved . . . grateful . . . even a little guilty for surviving."

"Don't think that way."

She shrugged. "I'm ashamed, Kirk. I don't know the name of the officer who was killed while working to protect us."

Kirk bowed his head. "Tom Novick. He was a good man."

Stephanie shut her eyes to block out the vision, but the image burned through her lids. Bruce Simon had been the late night jogger. He'd surprised Officer Novick, slashed his throat, and dragged him to the side of the house, where he stripped him of his uniform. Kirk Mulroney had discovered the body when he'd returned with coffee and pastries to help Novick through the night. The sweet rolls had made instant friends of Liz and Richard, allowing Kirk to jimmy the kitchen door lock and slip inside.

"What about his family?" Stephanie asked. "I'd like to do something."

"He was divorced. But there's a daughter, about Tuesday's age, I think."

"I want to help her, in his honor. Maybe assist with the college fund."

Kirk looked tired, the whites of his eyes all red. "I'll look into it for you and find out what's needed." He rubbed his temples. "Let's sit down for a minute."

They settled into two straight-back chairs near the center of everything. Doctors and nurses buzzed around, all starched efficiency. A major morning traffic accident had all of them in code red mode.

"Did you get any sleep?" Stephanie asked.

Kirk shook his head. Fatigue sagged his still impossibly handsome face. "I went back to the station, then came here to wait for Monty to wake up."

Stephanie sensed a secret connection between Kirk and Monty, and wondered what it was.

He seemed to vibe in on her curiosity. Clearing his throat, he came out with it. "Monty and I have met once before . . . at a bar."

She looked at him, surprised, the last three words dropping in her mind like a heavy suitcase. Suddenly it all made perfect sense—the reluctance to consider a date with Josie, the on-his-sleeve sensitivity. One of Lisa Randall's pre-Tyson refrains echoed in her head: "All the good ones are either married or gay."

Kirk looked down, elbows propped on knees.

Stephanie felt a surge of affection. He'd just confided in her, and his secret, for a man in his job, was something delicate, to be hidden away. She placed a comforting hand on his back, saying nothing.

"We've got a lead on one of the skinheads," he

said quietly. "His name's John Wilson—an eighteen-year-old demon seed who's been hauled in for everything from beating up his girlfriend to starting a fire in his parents' attic."

Stephanie remained quiet as a bitter anger flew through her body, quickening her pulse with its velocity. She looked at Kirk, wanting to hear more.

"There's a swastika branded onto his upper arm, and Monty's description confirmed Wilson's blue eyes and narrow lips. He's hiding out, but we'll find him. And the others, too."

"Have you contacted Joey Danza's family?"

Kirk shook his head. "That was only his stage name, I guess. He was born Edward Sykes. Left home at seventeen. We're still looking."

"Do you still believe Bruce Simon paid them to do it?"

"I don't know, but I'm damn sure going to find out."

"Stephanie Hart?"

She glanced up to greet the voice, which belonged to a hot, casually dressed Latin man. He smiled at her, conveying kindness and sympathy with unfaked sincerity. She liked him right away. "Yes?"

"I understand this is a painful time," he began earnestly, "but may I speak to you for a moment in private?"

Kirk took off, citing business on the John Wilson search, and Stephanie offered the stranger the newly vacant seat. When she discovered the man was Francisco Juarez, editor-in-chief of *Texas Today,* she nearly bolted, then launched into a tirade. "I've made my position explicitly clear to—"

"Abby McQueen," Francisco interjected, his tone dripping disapproval. "Let me say emphatically that Ms. McQueen's actions in no way represent the edi-

torial and ethical standards of *Texas Today.*" The
man had grit and drive, with no hint of easy humor.

Stephanie thawed fast. "That's good to know, but
I'm still not agreeing to an interview," she said
firmly but with no trace of venom.

Francisco waved away the refusal. "I'm not here
for that."

She regarded him curiously. "Then what can I do
for you?"

His look beamed triumphant. "It's what we can
do for Jason Dean. The information I have should
help return him to Josie's custody." He produced
the October, 1977 issue of *Texas Today*.

Poring over the article was surreal. Who were
these people? It certainly didn't seem possible that
they were her family, that she'd lived through such
an incident. All the buried emotions came cannon-
ing forward, like a fast-moving train.

Fear.

Helplessness.

Shame.

Regret.

Heartbreak.

A wide, sinking feeling came over Stephanie as
she read on. There was a reason why Marilyn had
forbidden her to read, listen to, or watch media accounts of that night. Perhaps that was her final, loving act of mothering before all the silence and
resentment.

Most parents protect their children from truth, not lies,
Stephanie thought. The twisted irony made her
dizzy. And then she closed off the memories. Marilyn Cain had stopped playing mother tigress twenty
years ago. Since then, it'd been up to Stephanie to
make her own deals to protect herself. The major
component of that was simple: Lock away the past.

When she got to the paragraph Francisco Juarez had highlighted, she stopped. Sucking back surprise, she read it. Then she read it again. As the harsh lights of her newly discovered knowledge burned down, the reasons behind Judge Lawrence Gibbs's bitterness and prejudicial actions melted before her.

"This will disqualify him," Stephanie said, recalling the sacred judicial canon of performing duties of office impartially. "But I'll afford him the dignity of stepping down."

"There's a story here," Francisco said, making his pitch in the heat of the moment.

Stephanie grinned knowingly. "So this was not a selfless act."

"Does such a thing exist anymore?" he asked ruefully.

"Everyone wants a payday," she told him. "But what the hell? You've earned it. The story's yours. *After* Jason is safe in his mother's arms."

Stephanie felt herself striding forward, all energy concentrated. Everything was clear now. The good guys. The bad guys.

She experienced a rush of optimism. Only good times were up ahead.

Twenty-eight

Abby was speeding south on Interstate 45, away from Houston and Francisco Juarez . . . and toward her future, God willing. So far, most of her leads had amounted to nothing. She felt like Geraldo must have in the empty moments that followed the opening of Al Capone's vault. Windows down, radio blasting, she reviewed the starts and stops.

Matt Benedict had pulled a die young/stay pretty before handing over a copy of one of the REMEMBER SEPTEMBER messages.

Stephanie Hart had refused to cooperate, and was likely instructing everyone in her personal orbit to do the same.

Toni Raffin had only been interested in venting her spleen as an advocate for abused women and children.

Lisa Randall had been just another spooked rape victim, providing nothing substantial.

The true loss was Joey Danza, who'd been ready to spill the toxic Cain family secrets as told by Montgomery. Now his seedy life was fodder for obits in the back pages of gay skin mags. Maybe Pat Robertson would use him as an object lesson on *The 700 Club*.

Anna Belle Hudson careened into Abby's thoughts.

The quirky, cat-loving spinster had made some far-fetched statements about Stephanie that were worth looking into.

I remember how afraid he was that she would kill again.

I overheard him say once that murder was in Stephanie's heart. He thought she enjoyed it, that she planned it.

Abby's shades were no match for the bright sun. She reached up for the visor and pushed it down as the possibilities lingered in her mind. Was there any truth to Anna Belle's words? Could the lonely eccentric actually be taken seriously? Or was it just the clucking of a mad hen?

She raced on, going seventy miles per hour, comforted by the signs announcing Galveston Island. Her hands tightened around the steering wheel, which vibrated violently when the car hit high speed.

There was also Marilyn Cain to consider. She had creaked out the cryptic, "He's alive," in her raspy voice. What did that mean, if anything?

All the jagged pieces of the puzzle made her head hurt. For a moment, she felt queasy. *It's the hangover,* Abby thought, still cursing herself for popping the cork on that third bottle.

Traffic slowed on the main drag of Texas's most celebrated resort destination, a tourist haven with thirty-two miles of Gulf Coast beaches. The area swelled with historical landmarks, galleries, shops, and restaurants. Billy Hudson had brought her here for a weekend getaway. She remembered him boasting that Galveston was home to at least sixty Texas firsts.

First post office.

First hospital.

First public library.

Abby breathed in the saltwater air. For her, it was

home to something altogether different . . . *a last chance.*

Melody Scott's shabby duplex was located in an area that the Galveston Island Convention and Visitors Bureau didn't feature in their glossy guidebooks. Jimmy Scott's mother answered the door in a huff, lips parted, revealing discolored teeth.

"What is it this time?" she spat.

In a nanosecond, Abby sized up the cheaply dressed, greasy-haired wretch. There stood a woman who worked hard, smelled like it, and never knew a day without a major problem. It was obvious that life had dealt her a crappy hand, and those unfortunate enough to cross her path wouldn't have an easy time because of it.

Abby introduced herself, refreshing Melody's memory on their recent conversation.

"I thought you were coming tomorrow."

"We agreed on today."

"Hell, I can't remember shit these days. Come on in."

Abby stepped into the front room. Her nostrils twitched at the dank odor. The furnishings were secondhand, one notch below poor college student. A fleabag mutt, too miserable to sniff out a stranger, itched furiously in the corner. Several frequent player cards from casinos were littered across a chipped desk. Atop it was a rotary telephone, its receiver off the cradle and dangling near the floor. Melody went straight for it.

"You pay your rent, I'll get your hot water fixed . . . Ooh, I'm scared . . . tell me this, if you ain't got the money for your rent, how you gonna afford some fancy lawyer? . . . pay up or I padlock the dump . . . I swear to God I'll do it . . . and make it money order or cash . . . because your check ain't worth a candy wrapper." Bang! She slammed it down.

Abby raised an eyebrow. "Tenant troubles?"

"It's always something," Melody snarled. "I charge a lousy two-fifty a month, and they expect Buckingham Palace. I say if no rats are biting and the roof don't leak, it's a sweet deal."

"Do you own this place?" Abby asked, surprised.

Melody chewed on a nail. "I own half the block."

I'd go for squatting in a condemned building before signing a lease here, Abby thought. Part of the beauty in being a slum lord was not living near one's suffering subjects. She wondered where this woman socked away her earnings.

"You play blackjack?" Melody asked.

Abby shook her head. Mystery solved. The cheap housing diva had it bad for high rolling.

"I'm down fifty grand this week. Last week I was up twenty."

"Sounds dangerous."

Melody tightened her lips. Red patches stained her ruddy cheeks. "I ain't got no problem." Her voice squealed. "I can stop anytime. I win big, I lose big. It all evens out in the end. Shit, at least I ain't hooked on drugs."

Chemical addiction would be the more logical choice, Abby thought. "Ms. Scott, putting your denial aside for a moment, can we talk about your late son, Jimmy?"

Melody sighed wistfully. "You ain't looking at no June Cleaver here. I gave birth to three, two boys and a girl. One of my sons got murdered—that was Jimmy. My other boy disappeared. Packed up one day, and haven't heard nothing from him since. My daughter married into some highfalutin' family and moved east. She's ashamed of her own mother. Don't even call or write no more."

Abby tried on her best *I feel your pain* look. For Christ's sakes, the guy who disappeared had the right idea. "Let's try to focus in on Jimmy, shall we?"

Melody plopped down onto the sofa. "Jimmy always had a way with the ladies. I kept telling him that one day he was going to get hurt, only I thought it'd be a dame's husband or a jealous boyfriend, not some crazy ass kid."

"You tried to sue—" Abby ventured, attempting to draw her out further.

"Oh, no!" she erupted, a distasteful expression on her face. "That was some of Tony's doing, my other boy. He gave all our money to some bullshit lawyer who said he was gonna make us all millionaires. Yeah, right." She rubbed her eyes. "Hey, wanna see some pictures?"

Abby nodded cautiously, worried that Mrs. White Trash would pull out the baby book. With relief, she watched Melody squeeze a card file box from a bookshelf stocked tight with series romance novels.

"I really should organize these, but who has the time? Between going to the boat, chasing down rent money, and taking care of property complaints, I ain't got time to sleep."

Abby blocked out the nerve-grating prattle and sifted through the photographs, flipping past the younger years. Her fingers slowed once she reached the stack dedicated to high school days. There were candid shots from proms and football games. One snapshot was taken on the beach. It featured two shirtless, carefree boys, eyes lit—with too much beer, no doubt—toes digging into wet brown sand.

"That's Jimmy," Abby said, pointing to the young

man on the left. Both guys were devastatingly handsome with solid athletic bodies as taut as the strings
of a bow. The one on the right tickled her memory.
There was something familiar about him, but she
couldn't place it.

"And that's Tony," Melody confirmed sadly.
"They were fraternal twins, seven minutes apart.
Ain't that something? I loved my beautiful boys. Talk
about troublemakers. Those two would—"

"Oh, my God!" Abby exclaimed. She'd moved on
to the next stack, the post high school years, when
another casual, brothers on the beach pose stopped
her cold.

"What is it?" Melody wondered in a tiny voice.

Abby didn't respond. The voice seemed to come
from so far away. She stared at the image with such
intensity that she felt the picture grow hot in her
hand. Somewhere in the room a clock ticked. Her
breathing had stopped. Hungry for air, she began
restorative measures, unable to tear her eyes away
from the Kodak proof between her fingers.

This was big.

This was bigger than anything she'd ever dreamed
of.

Abby's mind was in overdrive. She saw the future
with the clarity of supervision. Jeff Lowenstein
would clean a public john with his tongue for a
chance at the deal, and publishers would come in
their pants for a shot at the paperback rights.

This wasn't fantasy; this was inevitable reality. Her
play style would be hard ball. Part of the deal terms
would be a contract and a check with lots of zeros
behind it for the canceled Kevin Costner bio. Anyone who'd treated her like shit on her way down
would have to eat it with a fork and a smile on her
meteoric rise back up.

"I'm keeping this," Abby said.

"That don't go out the door!" Melody cried.

Abby ignored the slumlord who'd given birth to a serial killer. She left the duplex, her heart banging, her mind churning. The drive back to Houston stretched on forever. Her next move was risky . . . but essential.

Just minutes from her destination, she stopped to make a call. It rang four times until a recorded greeting came on. Abby hesitated, then left a message, if only to speak the unbelievable truth aloud for the first time. Just saying it sent an ugly chill up her spine.

And a smile across her face.

Abby McQueen parked the car and got out. There was excitement about the future in every step. She had to talk to him. She had to lock his eyes into her memory. This would make a great scene for the book, a fascinating anecdote for *Larry King Live*.

She knocked.

The door opened. Tony Scott stood before her. He didn't look like the maniac he was.

Twenty-nine

No way was Stephanie going to see Lawrence Gibbs alone. Any attempt at ex parte communication would weaken her position, so she corralled Gibbs and Chuck Berg in the same room—the judge's office.

"You have five minutes to state your purpose, Ms. Hart," Gibbs snapped. "I have a standing happy hour that I don't intend to miss."

Stephanie smiled. His orneriness tipped off his curiosity.

Chuck Berg attempted to act very smug, but he was no De Niro. The pig had a rash to find out what was up.

"You have the undivided attention of all concerned, Ms. Hart. Let's get on with it," Gibbs said.

"What's my maiden name, Your Honor?" She almost gagged on the last two words.

Gibbs simply glared, his eyes like slits.

"It's my understanding that you make it your business to know the background of counselors in your court. Given your obvious displeasure with all of my appearances, I'm assuming that I didn't escape your professional scrutiny."

"Don't fish, Ms. Hart. Get to the point," Gibbs

said, sitting there as immobile as a statue in the park.

"You're avoiding the question. What's my maiden name?"

"Your Honor, this is highly—"

"Shut up, Berg," Stephanie said harshly, not taking her drill-bit stare from Judge Gibbs.

The room was silent, the tension thickening.

"Remembering your maiden name is at the bottom of the list of things I attach importance to," Gibbs said in a controlled, chilling voice.

Stephanie matched his tone when she said, "I don't believe you."

The man in the robe shrugged diffidently. "If there's nothing else—"

She stood up. "There is, Judge. You represented the Scotts in a wrongful death suit against my family twenty years ago. I was a minor at the time. Back then my mother shielded me from press accounts, and I never had the courage to research my own painful past. I lived through it. For me, that was enough. You've known all along."

"I've been involved in a lot of cases, Ms. Hart," Gibbs said dismissively.

Chuck Berg snorted.

"It was your duty to reassign the Dean case, or any case for that matter, when I appeared before you as active counsel."

Judge Gibbs screwed up his face. He was red from the neck up. "You're out of line, Ms. Hart!"

"You're out of your *mind*, Judge, if you believe that this passionate history will be ignored. There's a reasonable question of personal bias here, enough to get you disqualified."

Chuck Berg tapped his foot nervously. He turned to Gibbs. "She's talking in circles."

"The editor of *Texas Today* brought me this information personally." Stephanie paused for effect. "The media machine will be on both your asses full-time over this. Josie and Jason Dean are primping now for the photographer, and the Polaroids of her bruises and burns are already in the magazine's possession. Fellas, you have a PR disaster in the making."

Judge Gibbs showed no reaction. "What do you suggest, Ms. Hart?" he asked quietly.

"That you transfer the Dean case to Judge Wattleton's court. She's impervious to politics and personal bias. I can't promise you exoneration in the media, of course. It's too late for that. But I'll choose my words to the press carefully."

Stephanie's eyes flashed triumph. She had Gibbs and Berg by the balls, and was squeezing until they both turned blue. It even beat a day at the spa.

Tyson stayed out all night and well into the next day. He finally showed up late afternoon, announcing, "We need to talk."

Lisa listened for the air of finality, waited for the ax to fall. Her eyes were swollen from nonstop crying. She hated being so weak. Would it make a difference to him if he knew that she'd contemplated taking her own life last night?

"I had a meeting with Peter Hart this morning," Tyson said.

She watched him pace the apartment. He was in the same clothes, all wrinkled now, and had barely looked at her. Where had he slept? She wanted to know but didn't dare ask. His mind was focused on whatever psychobabble Peter had fed him.

There was the shrill interruption of the telephone.

"Don't answer it," Tyson said.

"But—"

"Let Memory Call pick up."

They stared at each other for the four rings it took to switch over.

"That could've been about Monty." Her voice was scolding.

He ignored it. "I shouldn't have run out on you last night. For that, I apologize. But I meant what I said. If you don't agree to get professional help, you and I . . . we're over. I know you feel safe here, so I'll move out. I found a place this morning. It's ready. I just need to take a deposit by."

Tears were brimming in her eyes. How could she blame him? Tyson was only twenty-four, and this was his first real world relationship. What a burden it must be. They hardly talked. They never went out. The sex was passionless now. It'd turned into a chore, something to do to fill the time. Her vitality and high spirits had all but disappeared. That's what had attracted him to her in the first place. Now all the excitement was gone. She was scared all the time, and a girl filled with fear was just a drag.

He became very still. "It's up to you."

Lisa felt so tired, too weak to stand. She couldn't lose Tyson. She wanted things to be fun and wonderful again. She wanted to go back to Hit The Sky Advertising. Her body felt like a shell, depleted of energy, though. A spasm of fright roared in the pit of her stomach, mounting there. She wondered if it was, in fact, fear, or simply depression. The two were getting hard to differentiate. The next feeling, a flash of utter despair, pushed her over the edge. She sank down to the floor, shaking her head, sobbing.

Tyson crossed the room and pulled her roughly to her feet. "Fight it!" he yelled. His frustration was palpable. He was ready to call it quits.

Lisa ached for his touch—she wanted him to hold her—but he pushed her away. Nothing existed but the stirring possibility that he might walk out at any moment . . . for good. "I'll get help." She felt the words breeze past her lips.

Tyson looked as if all the nines had turned over. He was actually smiling. It dawned on her how long it had been since she'd seen him smile. His hand pressed against her chest. "Move against the pressure."

Lisa strained forward. There was incredible tension, the same feeling that came over her when she got close to the door or thought of venturing out.

"Push harder." His arm was locked at the elbow.

She was no match for his strength. Blood siphoned to dependent parts of her body, depriving her brain. A strong feeling of faintness registered.

"Stretch out your arms," Tyson commanded. "Move as if you're swimming in deep water!"

Lisa moved them out and in again, as if doing the breaststroke. Relaxation came immediately. She looked at Tyson, wide-eyed, amazed.

"Take a deep breath and let it out slowly," he said.

She continued to motion through the stroke. It gave her something positive to do at the moment of fear, besides withdrawing in defeat. She'd faced the panic. She'd turned it around. It was a breakthrough. There was a long way to go, of course, but it was a start. A sense of strength filled her up. And then she was laughing and crying, holding Tyson tightly.

Making up was easy to do. They made love like

wanton beasts. Then he jumped into the shower and took off for the station.

Lisa picked up the phone to call the hospital about Monty's condition. The stutter dial tone reminded her of the phone call from hours ago. Punching in the code, she listened as the computer announced one new message.

Abby McQueen's breathless voice rang in her ear. She froze, losing all sense of time and place. It was awful. How could it be? Jimmy Scott . . . fraternal twin . . . Tony Scott . . . psychopath . . . Stephanie . . . danger . . . true identity.

Lisa raced into the bathroom to vomit.

You've got bad taste in friends, bitch. You deserve this.

That scene played inside her head over and over again. The fog cleared. Why his voice had been so eerily familiar. Why his eyes had reflected a ripple of recognition. It all made sense now. She stopped breathing.

No one would believe her. The story was too farfetched.

Frantically, she searched the apartment for her purse. Minutes ticked by until she discovered it in its usual place—on the bottom shelf of the nightstand. Her heart banged. She jammed her fingers around the Glock. Payback would be a motherfucker.

Her mind shot into overdrive. The truth was so fantastic that a sliver of doubt still remained. She had to look into his eyes. She had to be absolutely certain.

Tension burrowed in between her shoulder blades. Tyson's lessons weren't forgotten. She imagined his hand pressing against her chest. She pretended to swim powerful strokes in deep water. The fear was total, the effort exhausting. And she'd only unlocked the front door . . .

Stephanie hadn't planned to visit Marilyn Cain, but something clicked in her mind and she found herself driving toward Clear Lake. It'd be a while before Monty was strong enough to visit. She decided to tell her mother that he was away on business and not to expect him. Whether Marilyn comprehended the news didn't matter to Stephanie. At least she would've made the effort.

There was no sign of Luis, the sunshine-natured orderly. She noted this with disappointment, realizing that his easy banter was often the only bright spot in her usually bleak visits.

Marilyn lay awake, staring at the ceiling, her eyes wide and clear.

Stephanie approached the bed slowly and gently took her mother's hand. "Hi, there. How are you feeling?"

She hadn't noticed the expression on Marilyn's face when she first entered the room. Seeing it now, she was mesmerized. It was a look of heart-stopping fear, frozen there as if trapped in ice. Thinking the worst, Stephanie pressed two fingers against her mother's neck. The pulse was strong.

"He's alive," Marilyn rasped.

Stephanie gazed into her frightened, pleading eyes. "Mother, what do you mean?" she asked softly, knowing full well there would be no answer forthcoming.

Marilyn's flannel gown was haphazardly buttoned, the top one missed altogether.

Annoyed, Stephanie shook her head. "Who dressed you this evening, Mother?" She set out to remedy the situation. "Because they sure didn't do a decent job—"

The words died in her throat.

There was a slash of red on Marilyn's chest.

Stephanie undid the next button. The marks on the old woman's pale skin continued on. She touched just below the clavicle. It was moist. Her first thought was blood. Panic overwhelmed her. She ripped the gown from neck to navel.

Scrawled on Marilyn's bare chest in shocking red lipstick were the words REMEMBER SEPTEMBER.

Stephanie clutched her heart. The scream came from deep within her.

"He's alive," Marilyn creaked.

A nurse's aide charged into the room. "Wha—"

"Who was here before me?" Stephanie demanded.

"I don't know. I just came on shift."

She started for the door. "Give her a bath! Get that filth off my mother! And no more visitors! I don't care who it is!"

The clatter of her heels echoed throughout the corridor. She ran faster, yelling for anyone who'd seen Marilyn Cain's last visitor. They all looked back in open-mouthed silence, as if she were a madwoman spouting gibberish.

In the parking lot she stopped to fetch her cellular. Peter had to be warned. For his sake. For Tuesday's. The battery was dead. "Goddammit!" She smashed it on the pavement and vaulted into the car.

Rush hour was over. She reached the house in remarkable time. The garage door wouldn't open. Fear clamped around her heart. Was she too late? Stephanie burst through the front door.

Peter shot up from the sofa immediately. His eyes took on a look of concern.

"It wasn't Bruce!" Stephanie cried. "The messages weren't from Bruce!" She glanced around frantically. "Where's Tuesday?"

He held her firm, watching her intently. "She's at Jackie's. Now tell me what happened."

Somehow she got through the story without breaking down. It looped, reshaped, and closed in all around her. Nothing was what it seemed. If it wasn't Bruce, then who was it?

Peter's face paled. The anxiety was right there in his eyes.

Stephanie shivered. Why was she so cold all of a sudden? She huddled against her husband.

"Kirk has to know," Peter said.

She fought to regain control. "I'll call him."

He rubbed her hands and arms. "You're freezing, Steph."

"I can't help it." Her nerves felt as if they'd been shattered into a million glistening bits.

"I want you to take a hot bath. Then we'll call Kirk together, and collect Tuesday after that. I'm thinking we should get out of town," Peter said.

Stephanie did so. The water warmed her icy skin, but to relax was impossible. From the shadowy recesses of her torment, Chuck Berg kept emerging. He seemed to enjoy haunting her, and after today's showdown in Judge Gibbs's office he had good reason to up the ante. She passed her hand wearily across her brow. Peter was right. Leaving Houston temporarily was a good idea, but she couldn't leave Monty now. There was no way.

She stepped out of the tub and wrapped herself up in a thick bathsheet, feeling a little better. Under normal circumstances, she would've lingered to lather up with body lotion and dust with perfumed powder. Not tonight. She was too anxious for Kirk to know what happened, and for Tuesday to be right by her side.

Stephanie prided herself on not weeping. She was hanging tough this time, determined to beat the faceless bastard who was making it his business to wreck her peace of mind. She puttered down the hall to the master bedroom and discovered a garment spread across the bed.

Her eyes focused; her face went ashen. It was the Andy Gibb T-shirt she'd worn the night Jimmy Scott was murdered—bloodstains and all. The horror in her gut flared ulcerously.

Through the gilt-framed antique mirror she saw him, his lips twisted in a cold rictus.

Stephanie's hands started to shake. Her body knew the truth before her mind did.

"Remember September," Peter Hart said.

Thirty

"Stop it, Peter! This isn't funny at all. Where did you get that T-shirt?" She had to fight back tears. It hurt so much to know that he could be so cruel.

"Try it on. See if it fits, you murdering bitch." His voice was hard. The sound . . . the words . . . it wasn't the Peter she knew.

"Stop it!" Stephanie cried. "Stop it now! You're scaring me!"

"I don't want to scare you." He brandished a kitchen knife. The blade was easily eight inches long. "I want to kill you."

"Peter!" She couldn't hold back another moment. Tears gushed from her eyes. Instinctively, she stepped back, moving away from him.

He sneered at her with the most hateful, contemptuous expression she'd ever seen. *"Peter!"* His voice mocked her.

"It's not funny!" Stephanie wailed. She'd seen *The Shining*. She'd watched Jack Nicholson try to kill Shelly Duvall. She'd suffered the obligatory nightmares for weeks afterward. Nothing had prepared her for this.

"It's not supposed to be funny." He took one step toward her.

Stephanie quivered.

"I'm going to finish you off . . . just like you finished Jimmy off." He punched the air with the knife. "It was one quick jab, right? Didn't you gut him like a pig?"

Her mind exploded into a thousand infinities. She couldn't speak, move, or breathe.

"You got lucky with that one stab. Maybe I will, too." He inched closer.

A frenzy of rage detonated inside her, and she slapped him hard across the face.

His head swiveled, his cheek steadily reddened, and his eyes blazed with extreme wildness.

She wanted to wake up. Certainly it was all just a terrible dream. "Enough!" The shriek scratched her throat raw.

"My thoughts, exactly," Peter said slowly, his tone passionless, yet so chilling. "All these years I've pretended to love you—"

"Don't say that!" Her eyes were burning. Her heart was breaking.

"It's true," he continued calmly, taking the last few steps.

The telephone rang four times and stopped.

She stood there, paralyzed, trapped in a trance, feeling as if someone else were living this moment. He was on her now, so close that she could taste his sweet breath. The sensation played over her. She fought the urge to embrace him.

"You know what the hardest part was?"

Stephanie shook her head, not wanting the answer.

"Making love to you," Peter said coldly. "It made me sick."

She died inside.

He raised the knife. It was sudden. It was unearthly. "I've waited too long to just cut you once." Peter hesitated, smiling into her eyes.

Stephanie sprang backward, whimpering, panting. She was unable—or unwilling—to believe that what was happening could be real, but still she ran.

The closet was right there. It locked from the inside. She beat him by seconds. On the other side, she could hear his laughter. The first kick buckled the door and knocked the breath from her body. She fumbled for the light. Brightness flooded the small space. Their life was everywhere.

Her clothes.

His clothes.

Family pictures.

Stephanie refused to believe that it was all a lie. Peter was sick. Yes! That was it! He was hallucinating, and she had to help him.

The next kick loosened the hinges and splintered the wood.

Reality hurtled back. She looked around frantically, feeling helpless. Her body was still dripping wet from the bath. A wire hanger captured her attention. What if she twisted it out and used it to stick him in the eye? It might buy her some time.

Suddenly the Fendi bag on the top shelf called out like a siren. She reached for it, yanked the zipper open, shook the contents onto the floor, and dove down after them, heart hammering a triple beat. She changed purses often, keeping a set of basics in each one so she only had to switch out her wallet and keys. There it had dropped, next to her Nike running shoes, Her fingers clamped tightly around the pepper spray just as the door gave in.

He was grunting, his face twisted with a crazed intensity. "The choice is yours. I can kill you fast, or I can kill you slow."

Her finger pumped the trigger button, and the chemicals shot out in a violent mist.

As Peter screamed in agony, his arms flailed in a vicious windmill motion. The tip of the blade caught her upper arm, slicing it open. And then he dropped the dagger, covering his swelling eyes with both hands.

Running for her life, she ignored the sharp pain and the dripping blood. Her eyes searched desperately for the purse that contained her keys. She had just enough time to get away. But it was nowhere to be found.

The garage.

Her heart soared with relief. A spare set hung on the hook under the utility rack. As she raced through the house toward her destination, the towel slipped, exposing her breasts. She stopped to cover her body, to catch her bearings, but the sound of Peter's footsteps pounding down the hall put her back on the move.

She flung open the door and slapped the wall until her trembling fingers hit the switch. After three attempts, contact was made. A super light swamped over the garage. A bone-chilling image swamped her mind: Abby McQueen's limp body hung from the rafters, her neck in a noose.

Stephanie stared at the dead woman for what seemed like forever. The room dipped and swayed, leaving her disoriented. Still, she managed to stagger over to the utility rack.

The hook was bare.

Behind her, she sensed movement. Turning fast, she stumbled.

He stood in the doorway with a blistered face.

There was no way out. "Peter, please!" Stephanie cried.

"Don't call me Peter. My name's Tony Scott."

* * *

Lisa gasped for air. The thump in her heart was disconcerting, like the jerk of a sudden descent on an amusement park ride. Only the feeling didn't start and stop. It went on and on.

She recoiled, wanting to turn back.

Tyson's encouraging words rang in her mind. "One hundred percent is the answer, baby, not ninety-nine percent."

Lisa plowed through the terror. It was imagined. She knew that now.

For the first time in weeks, she realized how trapped inside her own thoughts she'd been.

A world apart.

That's what the rest of society had seemed like.

As Lisa drove, she took in the surroundings. There were other people. They had other lives. During her weeks of obsessive self-examination, she'd forgotten that. Seeing others was like watching television with the sound turned off. It wasn't quite real.

She stopped in front of Stephanie's house. Her heart felt as if it might burst. An odd giddiness came over her. There was a tingle in her hands. Stepping out of the car, she felt as if her legs were jelly.

Fear.

Adrenaline.

Fear.

Minute by minute, she coped with the panic, meeting it head-on, vowing to come out on top.

The Glock was heavy in her hand, its magazine loaded. T-Ball's shooting lesson was snare drum-tight in her memory.

She stopped in her tracks. A little voice was telling her not to walk through the door. The intensity of the moment increased. Suggestions of defeat played like a broken record. She tried to float past the doubt, to use the swimming approach Tyson had taught her.

A black nothingness swept over her.

One look was all she needed. Only then would she know beyond all certainty that Peter Hart was the man who raped her.

Her fears flashed fiercely, and she began to wilt before them. Insanity was so near. Continuing on would mean never coming back. She turned away, running from the house, hating herself for giving up.

All she could do for Stephanie was call the police. She prayed it wasn't too late.

"What are you saying?"

"Jimmy Scott was my brother. I'm his fraternal twin. And you're going to get exactly what you deserve."

The words reverberated in Stephanie's head like a seismic tremor. She stared, fascinated. There was nothing familiar about him anymore. The man she'd loved for five years had transformed into pure evil.

"Your misery is my joy. It's been me all along. The driver who killed Kevin Stone wasn't drunk." He laughed, so pleased with himself. "I should know. I was sober that night."

Steel bands encircled her stomach. She almost doubled over.

"I called Bruce and told him exactly where to find Ginger."

She tried to keep him in focus, but everything began to sway.

"Lisa was the most fun. I would've killed her, too, but I figured her living with the memory of rape was better punishment. . . ."

His voice trailed. The knife gleamed. This was prolonged agony. She wanted him to finish her off. Right here. Right now.

"Matt never saw it coming." He raised his hand to his temple in the shape of a gun. "Bang!" He chuckled.

Stephanie froze. The room was spinning round and round.

"You know, it's hard to get good help these days. Those skinheads were supposed to shoot holes in Monty and let Joey survive. But I guess I shouldn't complain. For two hundred bucks, you get what you pay for."

She shut her eyes, feeling herself going down. It was just too horrible. All her strength had eroded. Nothing mattered anymore.

"Tuesday's going to find your body." He winked. "Don't worry. I'll see to it that she gets a decent foster home."

Her legs collapsed. She crumpled to the floor of the garage. It felt hard and cold. She was still conscious.

"Remember September . . ."

The solid wall of obscene truth smacked into her. It pierced her soul, danced in her mind, and cavorted in her heart. She was dimly aware of Tony Scott standing over her, of him raising the knife for the first plunge . . . of the shadowy female figure lurking in the doorway.

"This is for Jimmy." The blade started down.

"I didn't kill him!" she blurted.

He stopped suddenly.

"It wasn't me!" She was cowering on the grimy floor, pleading for her life with the truth she'd never uttered out loud. Sneaking a glance past him, she saw the woman move into the light.

It was Lisa Randall. She carried a gun that looked too big for her to handle.

"You're a liar," Tony Scott was saying.

"Maybe so, but you're a dead one!" Lisa shouted. Her arm was extended, her elbow locked, her free hand supporting the grip.

Tony Scott turned to face the complication he hadn't counted on.

Stephanie convulsed with anguish. All the sick things he'd done to everyone in her life. All the years of deception, betrayal, and plotting.

"It was you," Lisa said simply, finally.

Stephanie's feelings were buried five fathoms deep. She couldn't get rid of them in a matter of minutes. It was strange, but despite everything, she loved him. He was still Peter Hart.

Lisa's eyes were polished jewels. They gleamed with liberation. She'd broken through the carcinoma of fear.

"No!" Stephanie cried.

The shocking line of fire slashed through Tony Scott's head and chest, and a shower of blood and pulpy matter sprayed from his body.

Stephanie started to crawl away. The warm liquid was all over her. So was the vile brain spillage.

"Give me the gun, Lisa," a calm, male voice said.

Stephanie stopped and turned.

Kirk Mulroney stood there, regret all over his face.

Stoically, Lisa handed over the illegal firearm.

For the third time in twenty years, Stephanie had watched a man die. She covered her ears with her hands. The abuse screamed inside her head.

Thirty-one

New York—September, 1998

Sunday brunch at the Park Avenue Café had become a weekly ritual. As was their custom, Stephanie and Tuesday arrived there first to secure the table for six.

When Lisa Randall and Tyson Moore hit the door of the East Side eatery, there was a low rumble of recognition from the stylish but casual crowd. Tyson had landed an anchor slot with a local NBC affiliate, and Lisa had been scooped up by advertising giant Saatchi & Saatchi for a copywriting position.

Tuesday catapulted from her seat to embrace them, breathlessly announcing her role as Frenchy in a fifth grade stage production of *Grease*.

"You go, girl!" Lisa praised. "Honey, before long I'll be seeing your name up in lights on Broadway."

Tyson laughed and smoothed Tuesday's hair affectionately. "You gonna dye your hair pink, beauty school dropout?"

Tuesday pondered the suggestion a moment and nodded, her mouth set in a determined line. "It has to be authentic," she remarked gravely, as if the fate of a small country depended on it.

A grinning Tyson looked at Stephanie.

She sent back a glare, playfully promising retribution.

"Where are the guys?" Lisa wondered.

"Late as usual. Monty mentioned something about going by Barney's first. They're having a big sale." She rolled her eyes. "I hope he doesn't dawdle. I'm starving."

They ordered mimosas to start. Tuesday negotiated a sip of Tyson's drink and pulled a face, deciding her Coke was the better choice. Conversation took off and didn't stop. Weekdays were always so hectic, and Saturdays often booked with errands, so Sunday remained the only day that nothing stood in the way of getting together. With its folk art motif and awesome desserts, this spot on 63rd Street between Lexington and Park Avenues had become a favorite.

Tuesday, who possessed the vision of Supergirl when it came to her uncle, saw Monty first. She flew from her seat, greeting him at the cafe's entrance to announce her thrill at nabbing the coveted Frenchy role.

Monty beamed, hugging her tightly. He thrust an imaginary microphone in front of her mouth. "I'm here at the premiere of *Grease*, starring new stage sensation Tuesday Stone. What does this mean for your career, Ms. Stone?"

Tuesday played along, piling on major diva attitude, a Norma Desmond in training. "Ask my agent, darling. I have to save my voice."

Stephanie, Lisa, and Tyson roared with laughter.

Bringing up the rear, Kirk Mulroney was smiling at the not ready for prime time players. "I don't know these people," he said, then kissed all the women before taking a seat.

Stephanie adored him. She couldn't imagine a better significant other for Monty, and the two of them were deliriously happy together. Kirk had moved east to head up the city's hate crime unit. Monty had followed soon after and secured a hosting gig on *Wake Up, New York* a local morning show that had gained a reputation for nabbing big names from stage and screen. Ratings were taking off, and viewer response to the affable, easy-on-the-eyes Montgomery Cain was turning heads. Major networks had already put out feelers.

After a fantastic meal they lingered over coffee, chatting. Reluctantly, they broke up the easy gathering. Life was calling. Everybody put in for the check and went their separate ways—Lisa and Tyson to their SoHo digs; Monty and Kirk to work out at their gym in Chelsea; Stephanie and Tuesday to their roomy apartment in Kew Gardens.

As Tuesday was engrossed in her play script on the train ride to Queens, Stephanie mapped out the start of the week. There was so much to do. Josie and Jason Dean were arriving mid-week for a brief visit, and Tuesday couldn't wait to play the little hostess. Stephanie pulled out her Filofax and flipped to the days ahead.

The usual client meetings, depositions, and court dates awaited her. She'd expected the divorces in New York to be uglier than those in Houston. That wasn't necessarily so. There were just more of them, hence an immediate thriving practice. Stephanie had set up shop with a young man just out of Stanford, Robin Walsh, who reminded her so much of Matt.

Together, they quickly earned a reputation for being affordable, trustworthy champions for women going through the system, and when the situation called for it, as tenacious as a pit bull with an old sock. Robin had recently been dogged by the feeling that a client's soon-to-be-ex was hiding assets. After some deep digging, he'd discovered that the louse was using four different Social Security numbers in court documents. To say Robin Walsh was merely hyper-vigilant would be a gross understatement. He was a perfect partner for Stephanie.

The red circle around tomorrow's nine o'clock line caught her eye. She had another session with Dr. Sharon Cameron, the tough-as-nails Manhattan-based psychiatrist who was helping her get through the aftershocks. Dr. Cameron's caustic medicine didn't always go down easy.

On Stephanie's first visit request for medication to fight the tundra of depression: "The lines at the pharmacy are long enough. Here's my cure for the blues—find out what pleases you, and do a lot of it."

On Stephanie's vow to never marry again: "You're only thirty-four, love. If you swear off the dumber sex now, you'll be filling up a room at Betty Ford by the time you're forty. There's no such thing as a perfect man, but unless you want to become a lesbian you have to hold out the hope that you might meet one."

On Stephanie's prolonged grief and anger over Marilyn Cain's death: "So you had a lousy mother. Sometimes the cookie crumbles that way. But I'm looking at you, and I see a smart, successful woman who gives her own daughter all the love and support she needs. Your mother was a slut, and for years she held a grudge against you that you didn't deserve. But she was a good teacher. She was so fucking bad that you learned to do the opposite."

Stephanie smiled, hearing the throaty voice of the unorthodox shrink in her head. Dr. Joyce Brothers she wasn't, but effective she was. It was Sharon Cameron who'd made Stephanie comfortable enough to speak for the first time about the events that led up to Jimmy Scott's death. Now, she recalled parts of that landmark session clearly, as if she were reading a transcript. . . .

"You had the knife in your hand, and you went into the bedroom. What happened next?" Dr. Cameron asked quietly, prodding ever so gently.

Stephanie spoke in a faraway voice. "Mother wasn't there. She was locked in the bathroom, crying. Jimmy wrenched the knife out of my hand and tossed it to the floor. Then he pushed me onto the bed. He said he was tired of doing it with old women. He wanted a young, tender girl like me. I was scared. He started to kiss me and rub his hands on my breasts. I was begging him to stop. I didn't want Mother to come out and see us."

"But she did."

Stephanie nodded. "Mother told Jimmy that he was sick, and started beating him. He punched her in the face so hard that it knocked her down. She was unconscious for a few minutes. That's when it happened."

There was a long, pregnant silence. It seemed to last for minutes.

Stephanie swallowed hard.

"Go on, Stephanie," Dr. Cameron whispered.

She hesitated.

"Tell me what happened next."

"My brother Monty picked up the knife and killed Jimmy Scott."

Dr. Cameron gasped.

"He was only six years old." A tear rolled down Stephanie's cheek, and she wiped it away. "I . . . didn't want him to go to jail, so when Mother woke up . . . I . . . took the blame."

Dr. Cameron reached for Stephanie's hand. "You were a brave girl who loved her brother very much."

Stephanie's lips curved slightly into a wry smile. "She never knew. Mother always thought I killed him, not Monty. That's why she shut me out. I never dared to tell her the truth because I always thought that Monty needed her more than I did, but . . . I needed her, too."

Then the tears came in full force. . . .

When the subway careened to a stop, Stephanie closed her appointment book, tossed it into her bag, and reached for Tuesday's hand. They stopped at the corner market for fresh fruit, then ambled toward the apartment at a relaxed pace. As Tuesday prattled on about her part in the school play, Stephanie zoned in and out, suddenly finding herself thinking about Francisco Juarez, who had relocated to the city for a position at *New York* magazine. He had asked her out to dinner on several occasions. It just never seemed to be the right time, but now . . .

"I want you, Uncle Monty, Uncle Kirk, Lisa, and Tyson all on the front row," Tuesday demanded. "Okay, Mommy?"

"Reserve one more seat," Stephanie heard herself say.

Tuesday froze on the sidewalk. "Who for?"

She hesitated, making a mental note to cancel the session with Dr. Cameron. No more emotional energy wasted on the past, she vowed. Only future speak from this moment on. Finally, Stephanie said, "Mommy might want to invite a friend."

Her ten-year-old angel beamed, then crinkled up her nose mischievously. "Is he cute?"

Stephanie grinned. "Yes, sweetheart, he's *cute.*"

Tuesday started up again, this time with a distinct bop in her step. "You go, girl!" she sang.